MOLLY KENT IS TH
SUNDAY TIMES BES
MARY WOOD

G000022084

Mary Wood writes gripping sagas and is published by
Pan Macmillan.
Her Molly Kent books are Thriller Novels

BOOKS BY MOLLY KENT

THE SWEET TASTE OF REVENGE
COMING SOON
VILE RETRIBUTION

BOOKS BY MARY WOOD
THE BRECKTON TRILOGY

TO CATCH A DREAM
AN UNBREAKABLE BOND
Coming MAY 2017
TOMORROW BRINGS SORROW
*

WARTIME SAGAS
TIME PASSES TIME
A spin-off of The Breckton Trilogy
*

PROUD OF YOU
*

ALL I HAVE TO GIVE
*

AND RELEASED DECEMBER 2016
IN THEIR MOTHER'S FOOTSTEPS
A sequel to All I Have To Give

DEDICATION

To my beloved husband and children and grandchildren
You are my strength and my support
You help me to climb my mountain
I love you
xx

Acknowledgements

Always my heartfelt thanks go to my wonderful husband, Roy and to my children, Christine Martin, Rachel Gradwell, Julie Bowling and James Wood for the help and support, love and encouragement they give me. Without you all I couldn't reach my dream, I love you.

Special thanks to my son James, for reading and advising on the manuscript and producing the wonderful cover, and then editing the final draft. Not to mention the encouragement in the first place to digress from my usual genre and write a thriller. Your faith in my ability to do so, and along with your cousin Chris, cajoling me into taking a chance, has led to me achieving the completion of this novel and opened up a new avenue to my career that I never dreamed I was capable of.
Thank you from the bottom of my heart.

And my grateful thanks to Julie Hitchin, who along with James, carried out a thorough edit of my work. Together you swept the manuscript of errors, pointed out mistakes that marred the flow, corrected wrong use of words and placed pesky commas where they should be. You did a wonderful job, thank you so much.
A writer is nothing without her editors.

And neither is she whole without her readers. I have the most special gang an author could wish for. We meet on Facebook www.Facebook.com/historicalnovels and on my webpage www.authormarywood.com
Always you are there for me, and even though for many of you this wasn't your genre, you still bought the book and gave it a go, just to support me. So far you have all enjoyed it, and I'm glad to have introduced you to a 'different' reading experience.

You have all enriched my life

THANK YOU
X

1

Endless tree trunks danced in the light of the full moon as it dodged in and out of the clouds. A menacing eeriness settled around Gina as she walked along the uneven track that sliced through Epping forest. Something ahead moved. Gina stood still. Her heart thumped a fast rhythm. Her chest felt as though it was clamped in a vice.

A short distance away, the shadow of a man with a big stomach splashed onto the ground, before disappearing. Panic gripped Gina. Swivelling around to look back to where she'd come from, her fear deepened. She could no longer see Joe's car, but the thought that she hadn't heard the engine start up, comforted her. Joe must still be nearby.

What was it with him? He regularly brought her out to Epping Forest to fuck her, but always took her back to the station where she caught the last underground to London. Tonight he'd kicked her out of the car and told her to walk as he'd things to do.

Swallowing hard to try to relieve the tightness of her throat, Gina stumbled towards the trees, and hid behind one. An owl hooted. The sound compounded the feeling of terror that gripped her.

Leaning forward to try to get an idea of where the man was, she gasped in a silent breath as she saw the outline of him within feet of her!

The rough bark chaffed her back as she tried to shrink out of sight. Her stupid four inch heels dug into the soft earth. Sweat bathed her body.

A child's cry cracked the silence around her. The man's agitated, sharp, 'Bloody shut up, will you?' echoed in the stillness, disturbing a flock of birds. The air filled with annoyed squawking and flapping of wings. Realisation that the bulge of the shadow hadn't been the man's paunch, but a child, filled Gina with horror. Not moving a muscle, she listened as the snapping twigs and the crunching of fallen fir cones, trodden underfoot, slowly faded until she felt safe enough to take another peek. The man was no longer in sight.

Inch by inch, Gina eased herself away from the tree and stepped back towards the track. She'd go back to Joe. He'd know what to do. That kid was in danger; she was sure of it.

The sight of Joe's huge, black four by four Merc gave Gina a sense of relief. But as she came up to it and found it empty, despair quashed her hope. *Christ, where is that bastard?*

Tendrils of her long, dark hair caught in the breeze and fluttered around her face, giving her the feeling of a dozen fingers clasping her. Frantic, she fumbled in her bag for her mobile phone. Cops weren't her friends, but they had their uses, and right now she needed them. Lippie, fags, lighter, purse and fucking packets and packets of condoms. *Christ, where's me fucking phone?* Tapping the pockets of her jacket told her it wasn't in any of them. *Damn!* Instinct had her checking down her bra. The notes were still there. Joe had pushed them between her cleavage and told her in his slimy way that there was a bit extra for her trouble. Trouble? No money could compensate for the fear she felt at being in a forest alone and with a stranger lurking nearby. Peering around as if searching for an answer as to what to do next, every part of her trembled. She felt sick. *Oh*

God, why didn't I take the longer route that Joe told me to?

Walking back the way that Joe had driven into the forest would have taken her to the lane, which would eventually have hit the main road. But she'd chosen to carry on along the track because it was a shorter route to Epping and the station.

Well, she could walk the long way now, couldn't she? Just go, and forget what she'd seen. But even before this thought died, Gina knew she couldn't do that. She'd have to try to help the kid. She'd have to try to catch up with the man and challenge him.

Afraid of every noise – the persistent owl, and the debris crackling under her feet; Gina made her way back. Passing the place where she'd hidden, she walked on towards the bend where he had disappeared from her view. Clambering out of sight, into the trees once more, the silence crowded her. *Which way to go?*

A click had her turning her head. A tiny flame flickered in the distance. Not daring to move, Gina watched as the light died and then a smaller light glowed, and went duller, and then glowed again.

The drifting cloud uncovered the moon, its hazy beam, broken by many branches, outlined the tall, lean figure ahead. Something about him was familiar, and now she realised his voice had been too. A thought came to her who it was, but she dismissed this as impossible. If only she could see him properly. *And, where was the kid, now?*

Dropping his fag, the man ground it with his foot and moved off. His walk precise. A man on a mission. Gina jumped back behind the tree. The steps came nearer, the trodden dried foliage, sounding louder and louder. She held her breath. But his tread veered to the left. *He was making for Joe's car!*

9

Within seconds the throaty, diesel engine roared into life. Headlights glared into every space around Gina. Clinging to the trunk she watched as the car sped the way she had been walking.

Unsure of what to do, Gina stood a moment. Questions pounded her head. *What had he done with the kid? Where was Joe?* The idea came to her to call out, but if Joe was in on whatever was happening, he wouldn't like to know that she had witnessed anything. You didn't mess with the Joe Parrondski's of this world. Better she went on her way and played innocent of knowing anything. If he asked, she'd say she'd done as he'd said and walked down the lane to the main road.

*

The blackness of the walls of the underground enclosed Gina as the train sped her towards home. How she'd made it to the station, she didn't know. The lane had gone on for ever. She had blisters on top of blisters, and tiredness consumed her, but at least she felt safe.

Leaning her head back she tried to ignore her throbbing feet and relax, but her mind knew no peace. The child's pitiful whimper came back to her.

Why didn't I call out there and then? I should have stopped the man and challenged him.

She knew why. Fear. She'd put her fear for her own safety above that of a child's.

Feeling like the shit she thought herself to be, she gave her mind to Amy. Her own beautiful child. How distraught she would be if that had been Amy in that man's arms! But then, trying to deny the horrors that pecked away at her, she allowed herself some comfort with the speculation that maybe the man was the child's father. Maybe there was an innocent explanation?

None of this helped. The dread of hearing tomorrow that a child had been abducted weighed heavily on Gina. A tear ran down her cheek. Unchecked it traced a path through her thick make-up and plopped on to her breast.

Her life was a nightmare and it had just got worse.

Joe Parrondski, to all intense and purposes, was a respectable man. A business man who owned a string of jewellery shops. High class places that demanded you made an appointment to view. Joe was looked up to, but he'd dragged her down further than she'd wanted to go. Not that her life had been a bed of roses when she'd met him, but at least then she'd earned her living in an honest way. Granted, her nine to five in a cake shop hadn't paid for much, but tax credits and housing benefit had helped her to get by.

A legacy of rape, Amy was the only good thing to ever come into Gina's life. She'd thought she'd hate her, and had planned an abortion, but at the time, she'd been told there were many more couples wanting to adopt, than there were available babies. This had stopped her getting rid, and given her the notion that her child could go to a good home and have all the chances she herself hadn't had. One look at the tiny form had put paid to any idea of giving her away. She'd taken her baby back to her one room in a hostel in Soho.

Memories of her own childhood in and out of care homes and foster placements, had given Gina a determination to do whatever it took to keep Amy, and had led to her accepting all the help offered by the do-gooders. Eventually, they'd found her a flat in a tenement block in Stamford Street, owned by the Southwark Housing Association.

A rare night out in Soho, with her friend and neighbour, single mum of three, Zoe Feldon, had changed Gina's life. Zoe, always flush with money, had treated Gina to a meal.

On a pub crawl afterwards, they'd bumped into Joe Parrondski. He'd stepped out of a restaurant in front of them. Zoe had introduced him. When Gina heard his name she was shocked that Zoe knew him. Not a handsome man, but one with presence, Joe's bulk had barred their way. His piercing grey eyes had flicked from Zoe and swept over Gina in a way that had stripped her naked. Apprehension had gripped her, but had left her as his eyes had met hers. At that moment it was as if he'd possessed her. And yet, nothing about his physical appearance attracted her. Slightly overweight, and not much taller than herself, Joe's features were square. His swarthy skin tone contrasted with his floppy, fair hair. His voice had a hint of an accent. He'd spoken to Zoe, but kept his eyes on Gina, 'Something to make your evening more pleasant, Zoe.' Without a murmur Zoe had taken the package, no bigger that a wrapped sweet.

'And one for your friend.'

'She don't–'

'Then introduce her to its delights. And bring her to the walk-up, later.'

Without another word Joe had turned from them and walked away.

Gina told Zoe: 'No way. I'm not taking that stuff, and I'm not going to no fucking walk-up!' She did both.

That night Gina learnt that Zoe was always flush with money because she worked in the walk-up in Brewer Street, prostituting herself.

That night Gina learnt that Joe Parrondski was 'The Boss Man' who came and went through a door connected to the property at the rear that housed a newsagent's.

That night Gina learnt what real sex was. Joe Parrondski taught her.

That night, Joe Parrondski got her hooked on cocaine. Waking up in her own bed the next day, Gina had no idea how she'd got there. All she knew was that she needed more of the same – the sex and the powder. Weed would never do it for her again.

Wrapped around the wad of twenty pound notes on her dresser she'd found a message. *Take the underground to Epping tonight. I will meet you at the station at seven thirty.* Inside the wad had been a small paper wrap.

In those heady days of big bundles of cash and all the coke she needed, Gina had thought she was Joe's girl. But she soon found that to continue to earn her money and her fix, she had to work in the walk-up as well as be at Joe's beck and call. Joe had a fetish for sex in his car. *Well, if he's going to treat me like this, I'll think twice about pandering to his whim!* But even as she thought this, she knew there was no way that she could refuse him.

To accommodate their working hours, she and Zoe had fallen into a pattern of working alternate shifts so that there was always one of them taking care of the kids. Hers was a shit life.

Yes, she had money now, and nice clothes for herself and Amy. And, Amy had everything she needed, but . . . Another tear trickled the same path as those that had gone before as Gina thought: *If only I could go back in time.*

Fifty-four minutes later, after changing from the Central Line at Bank, to the Waterloo and City Line, Gina arrived at Waterloo. Feeling weary beyond anything she'd felt before, she made her way home.

Headline news on the local radio bulletin the next day announced: 'There is a mystery surrounding the whereabouts of local business man, Mr Joseph Parrondski. In the early hours of this morning his car was found outside the family's Mayfair jewellery shop. The door was wide open and there were signs of a struggle having taken place. The police are appealing for witnesses. We will broadcast more details as and when we receive them.'

Gina waited. No mention was made of a missing child.

2

Layla Parrondski stepped out of her Holland Park home in Kensington, London, and faced the waiting paparazzi. Cameras flashed and question followed question. *'Any news of your husband?'* *'Has he contacted?'* *'How do you feel?'* *'What do you think could have happened to him?'* *'Has there been a ransom note?'* And one that embarrassed her, *'Do you think your family is involved?'* She had no chance to answer any of them, but smiled inwardly at what she might have said if she did.

Outwardly, she maintained a pensive look, putting on an act of being in shock, but doing so with dignity. To this end, she'd chosen her outfit with care, mixing her favourite designers to achieve the effect she wanted – a business woman, showing courage in the face of adversity.

A black, Fendi 3Baguette leather shoulder bag, Gucci 'Ursula' ankle strap pumps, and Gucci oversized chain link sunglasses, complimented her Armani Collezioni blazer and dress. A beautifully textured outfit with a blue, snakeskin-like pattern on a black background. It fitted her size eight like a sheath.

Her impeccably styled dark hair, parted in the centre. The back tapered into her neck, the sides sleeked back behind her ears. Golden highlights gave a deep gloss. Layla knew she was beautiful. And her socialite lifestyle made her no stranger to attention from the media. But, she was also known for her business acumen. She liked that it was her that the success of the Parrondski Empire was put down to.

15

Today, she chose not to wear any jewellery. Flashing her usual expensive pieces could be construed as a cheap advertising gesture knowing that her husband's disappearance would be front page news and that a photo of her would accompany articles world-wide. Steering her through the crowd, her driver settled her into the back of her sleek, gold, Rolls Royce, shoved a few eager photographers out of his way and got into the driving seat.

As they glided away, Layla smiled bravely through the windows, her green/grey eyes held tears. They were put there by the humiliation she'd suffered at the random question, but they served her well and were a guise to her real feelings concerning her husband's disappearance.

'Who was that bitch who asked about my family, Nick?'

'A newbie. She's just joined The Mirror from one of the locals, but not full time, mostly she freelances. She used to stream news to them. I think she's called Nina, but already she has the nickname, Rottweiler.'

'And well deserved. It's taken me a long time to shed the image of being Gerry Loyson's daughter.'

Nick looked at her through the mirror. 'He's there for you.'

'I know. And we're in touch. Always have been, but it was useful to us both to break public ties.'

She could talk like this to Nick. Nick Radcliffe's grandfather had been her late grandfather's driver, in the days when her grandfather's notorious gang rivalled the Krays back in the sixties. Nick knew everything about her and was trusted and loyal.

Her father, who was never as good at being a gangster as his father was, but was still feared in some quarters, was currently doing twenty years for armed robbery.

With ten under his belt, he'd be out in five. She'd never visited him, but he knew her needs and had sent Nick to her a few years ago.

'Everyone's at your disposal. Gerry's alerted them all.' She nodded. 'Everyone', meant the members of her dad's crowd who weren't banged up. They numbered safe-breakers, heavies, forgers, bent cops and private detectives who would go the extra mile, and who could get hold of any other skilled con she might need the services of.

Crossing her legs, she suppressed the anger that was the only emotion she could feel at what that bastard Joe had done. Oh, she knew his game alright. Had known for a long time. She'd found out when he'd had a bout of flu last year, and she'd managed to dispatch his sour faced, so called, PA on a holiday that the bitch didn't want to take. Once she was out of the way, Layla had taken the chance to delve deep into her husband's secrets.

It had taken the skills of one of her dad's safe-breakers to get her what she'd wanted to see – a portfolio Joe had never shared with her. In it she'd found bank accounts in the name of Count Roman Rolleski. The amounts were huge, and all seeming to come from a subsidiary company, which handled the affairs of this so-called Count. With nothing on paper to help her to find the reason behind it all and with the jewellery business mysteriously losing money every week, she decided to find out what this company did, and what her husband was up to.

More revelations had been revealed. Another file contained stock holdings and business interests in a second name – Count Rommoski.

Once more she'd dug into her dad's resources and through his recommendation, had hired a Private Detective.

There wasn't anything now that she didn't know about what her husband's *other interests,* were. She knew that he'd bought a huge derelict house in Epping. That he was pimping prostitutes, drug dealing, having cars stolen to order, and producing porn films. And, even more disgusting, her D had discovered Joe's recent activity of making online child porn films for paedophiles, all under the name of Count Rolleski. His alter ego, Count Rommoski, however, was everything that was legit. The Epping house was in this name, and all accounts and holdings were traceable and above board. These were his cover.

It had all shocked her at first. Not that she cared about Joe. Any feelings she'd had for him had died a long time ago. The only affection they'd shown to each other over the last twelve years or so, had been for their public image. But she had realised that one day he planned to disappear and leave her and their two sons. And worse than that it was obvious he intended to do so leaving them with nothing but debts.

Joe had never cared for either Richard aged fifteen, or David aged twelve. As soon as they were old enough he'd placed them into boarding school and hadn't even wanted them home in the holidays. She'd resorted to picking them up and taking them away to a cottage she'd bought in the Kent countryside. From there she would commute on at least three days a week, leaving them with a nanny whom they loved. Somehow, they had grown up well-adjusted and they adored her, and she them. They were now both doing well at Eton. *God! If their school mates read anything about my family, the boys' lives will be hell! Damn you, Joe Parrondski! And damn that bloody Rottweiler of a newspaper woman for delving into my past!*

Some comfort came to her with the thought that Joe didn't hold all the cards. Six months ago everything had changed. Her dying mother, estranged from her father and living in Walton on Thames, had given her a letter her grandfather had left in her care. In it was a key to a safe box held in Layla's name by Lloyds bank. Retrieving the box Layla had found it full of keys. Each one had a numbered label attached to it. Each label gave her the bank that held a box in her name. There were fifteen keys altogether. On opening the first box she'd found cash, share certificates and accounts held in Swiss banks. All certified to her and together, worth over one million. There was also a letter stating that each box held similar contents. The letter also told her to go to Michael Flavendon's descendant, and that she would find him running, Flavendon's Financial Brokers. He should have a letter handed down to him from his grandfather and would advise her on what to do with the certificates, and how to access the Swiss banks.

'He' had turned out to be a 'She'. Marcelle Flavendon. Marcelle was ready to give her advice. A frump of a woman of around thirty, but looking much older, Marcelle had proved to be a help with all manner of financial wheeling and dealing. But, more than that, Layla had detected something in Marcelle. A sense that the transactions – near the knuckle of lawful, had sparked a flame in her. A satisfaction at being ahead of the game. Marcelle was good at her job. Marcelle had made Layla a very rich woman. Marcelle would have her uses.

Layla had formed a plan for when her husband made his move. He'd done that now, and she needed to put everything into place. Her goal was to facilitate his downfall. But more than that, what he'd built up, excited her. She wanted it. Wanted it all. Not the child porn. That was abhorrent to her. She would smash that operation. But everything else and more. But, before she could do anything she needed her own people. A loyal bunch that she could rely on.

Yes, she needed men at the top of their game – she had those, courtesy of her dad. But this operation was going to be run by women. Women would be the top dogs. And the first person she would visit, once the furore had died down and she was sure that her boys were okay, would be Gina Walters.

The phone in her car rang persistently. 'Switch if off, Nick.' She instructed. 'It'll be the cops wanting to talk to me. Well, they can fucking wait.'

Some hours later, with Richard and David reassured that she was okay – neither of them cared what happened to their dad, she dropped them at the cottage. A bolt-hole she shared with no one, but her kids. 'I'll ring every night as usual, but I don't want to lead the press here. This is our private place.'

Richard hugged her. 'You'll be alright won't you, Mummy?' She kissed his cheek. 'Mummy has never been better, darling. We're free of that monster, once and for all.'

'Have you never loved our father?' This from David shocked her.

'There was a time, David. Both of you were born of that love. But when he rejected you, he was nothing to me.'

David now had his arms around her waist. 'Boys, you're crushing me. Look. We've always been a team, yeah? Nothing is going to change that. But our lives are going to get better. Mummy will see to that. Once I've got things sorted, you needn't board if you don't want

20

to. I will have you brought home every evening. I'll convert two of the spare rooms into a study each for you. There'll be everything you need in there. We can be a proper family, at last.'

'That's spiffing, Mummy,' Richard smiled at her, 'But no can do. Daddy chose Eton because there is no choice. All pupils have to board.'

Detecting a slight inference in Richard's tone that she was a silly empty-head, hurt her. There was a streak of Joe in this son of hers that she would have to curtail, but not today.

David remained quiet and thoughtful. His next question floored her, 'Will we see our dad when we're older? I had hoped to make him like me.'

Gathering him to her, Layla didn't know how to answer. 'We'll see. If that's what you hope for, and still want when you're older, then we'll try to make it happen. In the meantime, always talk to Mummy about how you feel. I will always be here for you both with enough love for all your needs.'

David smiled. Hugged her again, then, although the youngest, took charge. 'Come on Dickie, let's go and find Nanny.'

'Hey, say goodbye to Mummy first!'

Wallowing in their hugs, she held on as long as she could. Taking her leave was difficult. Not just because she always wanted to be with them, but because she knew that danger lay ahead for her. And though the thought thrilled her, and she was ready, she worried that if it all went wrong, she may never see her boys again.

*

'Shit!' The array of paparazzi had now been joined by two policemen. Her home was under siege!

21

Managing to side-step them all, once inside, Layla took off her jacket and put a call in to her lawyer – another recommendation of her father's. 'Get the bloody cops off my back, Adrian.'

'They're there for your protection. You need to make a statement.'

'I know. I had things to do first.'

'Come to my office.'

'But I've only just got in! I'm exhausted. I need to shower and rest, God, I feel as though I'm a bloody criminal!'

'Welcome to my world.'

'But –'

The police think all lawyers are criminals, or at least, in league with them. Look, it's six o'clock now. Get here for seven. I'll take you to dinner. Don't answer the phone if it rings, and don't ring anyone but your kids. But even then, keep everything normal, as in reassuring and comforting them, no discussions about their father.'

The phone went dead.

'Fuck you!' But something in Adrian's tone compelled her to do as he said.

3

Gina's day had begun earlier than she'd wanted it to. She'd done the morning school run. Zoe wasn't capable. Zoe took too many drugs. She promised she'd be okay to do the teatime pick-up as Gina had to be at the walk-up. Gina knew that with the state Zoe was in, she'd know nothing about Joe having disappeared, but she hadn't felt like telling her and getting into a lot of speculation. She had to sort out her thoughts first, and how she was going to play her part in the situation. Amy had gone willingly to school, along with Tammy, Zoe's youngest. They had, skipped along in front of her, counting the paving slabs and trying not to step on the cracks. Two seven year olds without a care in the world. But Zoe's boys, Freddie and Jack hadn't spoken much. Heads down kicking at stones, she'd left them at the corner of Mina Road and they'd headed for Walworth Upper. She doubted they even got on the bus to take them there. They were always bunking off. After waving the girls off at the school gate, Gina had hesitated before turning away. She had to pick up some bits and bobs from the shops on her way back, but her heart wasn't into grocery shopping. She needed to do something to take her mind off everything. She needed a fix. Joe hadn't given her a wrap last night. She doubted that Zoe would have any left, and besides, she didn't want to be in her company at the moment. She'd have to go to the walk-up to get some. She'd have to face their questions.

The doormen knew she'd gone to meet Joe last night.

Her dependence – she wouldn't call it an addiction, was a part of her that she hated the most. She tried to fight it and took it less than she wanted to. But today, she didn't think she could fight the urge.

As she came up to the Rag Café, she made herself go in. Maybe she could talk herself out of having a hit. Three Americanos later, she knew she couldn't.

Outside, the sun blinded her. Donning her Prada, Heritage sunglasses, she pressed the button on the crossing.

With the beeping of the 'cross now' sign ringing in her ears, she stepped off the pavement. A car screeched to a halt inches from her. 'Christ! You want to fucking watch where you're going, mate!'

The tinted glass obscured the driver. The blackened rear windows, gave no view of the interior. There was none of the usual retort to such a confrontation. This, and the driver's window slowly gliding down had Gina swallowing hard as a feeling of apprehension came over her. A man's arm extended through the now fully open window. In his hand he held her mobile phone.

Terror snaked through her.

The car door opened. Detective Sergeant Gosling stepped out. A regular at the walk-up, Gina feared him more than any other man she knew. A masochist, he pleasured himself by inflicting pain. Sometimes leaving her so badly hurt that she couldn't work for a week. Only the brutal threats of Parrondski's men got her back to the walk-up. Always she begged not to be chosen by Gosling again. They never listened.

Gosling walked towards her. The sun danced off his bald head, his eyes, naked of eyebrows and lashes, held evil. She thought of his body – often he stripped naked before beating her. The sight of him repulsed her. His hairless silk-like skin, and the lack of a fuzz around his genitals made him appear child-like, even though his dick was huge.

Though she knew alopecia was a condition he couldn't help having, it added to the menacing effect of him.

The sun moved behind a cloud, throwing a shadow over Gosling. Her fear deepened. Realisation hit her. *It had been him in the forest last night!*

Turning, she ran for all she was worth. She'd take short cuts to her home and lock herself in. One way streets would delay him. It wasn't as if she was resisting arrest. Instinct told her that whatever he wanted, was nothing to do with lawful enquiries.

Looking both ways she willed the traffic to clear enough for her to dodge over the road to Waterloo Station. An idea had come to her. She'd take the underground. She could go to Piccadilly, or Oxford Circus on the brown line. She knew she'd only be buying time, but once away from here and Gosling couldn't catch her, she could go into the nearest cop station. She'd tell them her story. They'd have to help her.

A number 26 bus obscured her view of the entrance to the station, as it passed by, her heart dropped. Gosling's car was just behind it. Swerving across the road, he pulled up next to her and was out of the car before she could react.

Her arm burned as he twisted it behind her. An onlooker stopped, but only managed to get out the word, 'Hey!' before Gosling flashed his badge with his free hand. The man moved off.

Grabbing her other arm, Gosling snapped handcuffs onto her and frog marched her to his car. 'Get in!' Shoving her head down, he pushed her into the back seat. His fist dug into her stomach. Crunching forward and gasping for breath, her head stung as Gosling jerked her upright by her hair. His fist smashed into her face.

*

Blood, and stinking dried vomit, stained the dirty wooden floor next to Gina's face as awareness crept back into her. Nothing moved. She could detect no other presence in the room. Staying still, Gina tried to gather her senses. *Where was she? How long had she been here?*

The cold dampness of her pants and the smell of urine, told her that she'd wet herself. Shame prickled her. Lifting her head caused her pain. She managed to hold it up long enough to look around her. The room was bare, save for a broken, wooden chair, and a sink.

Using every ounce of her strength, she got up and made it to the sink. A broken piece of mirror lay on the windowsill above it. The window gave very little light. Only a shaft came through the space between the boards that covered it. Other light beamed in from ceiling windows, far too high for her to reach.

Her reflection shocked her. Red streaks smeared from her twisted nose across her cheek, and caked her split, swollen lips. Her eyes looked like slit black plums.

The water chilled her, but she kept her head under the tap and let some of it into her mouth. After a moment she peeled off her wet knickers, rinsed them and used them as a flannel to clean her vagina and inner thighs. If it was possible to, she felt better for these ablutions. She hoped her pants wouldn't take long to dry as she hung them over the tap.

Resisting the urge to sit and sob her heart out, Gina scrutinised her surroundings. A soulless room. Wallpaper peeled from the walls, damp patches darkened cracks in the plaster and completely took over

26

in parts where the plaster had lost its grip altogether. Cobwebs decorated every corner and stretched across the windows above her. The stench of the place, repulsed her.

A pile of rotting rags in one corner added to the smell. Flies buzzed around a dead rat in another. Tentatively making her way to the only door, Gina knew before she tried it that it would be locked. But having it confirmed filled her with despair.

She sank to the floor. Willpower deserted her. Tears stung the cuts on her cheeks and smarted her lips. Snot dripped from her nose.

Trying to support herself she put her hand down. Something sharp sliced her skin. A thick sliver of glass. Gina saw it as a weapon, and hid it behind her.

When she next woke she was still sat next to the door. Shadows thrown by the moon danced around her. Something scuttled across in front of her. She pulled her legs up in disgust at the feel of its fur brushing against them.

Horror at this encounter trembled her body.

Voices drifted to her. *Joe?*

Gina was certain she'd heard Joe. But then her thoughts froze at the sound of echoing footsteps coming towards her. She cringed against the wall. A lock clicked. The door flung open. Light streamed in. Gosling stood there towering over her. In his hand he held a whip. The one tool of his sick obsession that she feared the most. In his other hand he held a lamp which he placed on the floor.

'You have some questions to answer.' The whip snapped through the air.

'I – I don't know anything . . . I – I left Joe in his car!'

'I fucking know that. But, you didn't go straight to the station did you? What did you see, you sneaky, slimy, dirt bag?'

'I – I didn't . . .' The whip snapped again, narrowly missing her legs. Scrunching herself away from it, she felt the glass dig into her. Putting her hand behind her, she grabbed it, biting her lip at the pain it caused.

Gosling bent over her. His arm held above him. The whip curled, snake-like, ready to lash her with its bite. As it lowered, her movement was swift. Ignoring the pain caused to her as she rolled over and got to her feet and thrust the glass towards him. It embedded in his arm.

Taking advantage of the moment of his shock and his bending over in agony, Gina made it through the door. Keys dangled from the other side. The lock made a satisfying snap.

She was free.

In the pitch black darkness, she groped her way along a rough-stone wall until she came to a door. Turning the knob and pulling the door open gave her the feel of the fresh night air, but what little strength she'd found, ebbed away from her and she sank to the ground.

Gravel scraped her knees as she crawled away from the building. A dog barked. Then growled and snarled as if restricted by a leash. Gina ignored it, she was beyond feeling fear.

Not knowing how far from the house she was, a dizziness took her. The damp grass she'd reached offered her a soft bed. She sank into it. Everything swirled around her, taking her into a deep blackness she didn't want to resist.

4

Through the back window of her car Layla saw the Rottweiler reporter following her. Well, she'll be disappointed. There's nothing newsworthy in a wife whose husband has gone missing, having dinner with her lawyer. What else would she do?

Arriving at Adrian's office, the door opened and he stepped out. She was surprised when he opened the door of her car, and said, 'We'll go in mine, it's less conspicuous.' His smile held appreciation as he looked her up and down. Keeping the same accessories, she'd changed her Armani outfit, choosing a black asymmetric ruffle skirt dress by Alexander McQueen. It gave the same effect she'd nurtured earlier.

*

10 Greek Street's, no booking policy didn't seem to apply to Adrian. They were shown past the waiting queue to a table under the window, slightly apart from the rows of tables each side of the restaurant.

'Why here?'

'It's busy, and noisy and that will give us privacy. This is the best eating house in Soho. Food beyond excellent. Besides, it's only a stone's throw from Charring Cross Police Station, which is where we have to be after we've eaten.'

Layla could see the logic of the location, and knew the place had a great reputation, but she wasn't so sure it was her style. The surroundings were understated, plain beige walls met a light grey ceiling. Long black leather bench-seats were fixed against each wall and were fronted by tables that stood only inches apart. The parquet flooring was beautiful, but added to the noise as heels echoed on its surface. A chalk board declared today's menu.

Choosing for them both, Adrian ordered a chilled cucumber and mint soup, followed by a whole sea bass, fried new potatoes, cherry tomatoes and olive platter. Layla was happy with his choice. Adrian knew her well for the short time they'd been acquainted. The Chilean Chardonnay he ordered, confirmed this.

After a few sips of her first glass, she began to relax. Letting the atmosphere overtake her she realised she felt safer here than she would have done in a sedate, upmarket, chandelier and thick carpet, restaurant.

'You look as beautiful as ever, darling.'

Layla tensed. Though, well aware from their first meeting of Adrian's need for their professional relationship to deepen, she wasn't ready for such an endearment.

Tall and impeccably groomed in his Saville Row, soft-grey, tailored suit, Layla knew a deep and long-unsatisfied feeling to stir inside her as she looked at him. A feeling she judged as a weakness and had suppressed since Joe had stopped visiting her bed after she became pregnant with David.

Adrian's dark eyes, framed with the longest lashes she'd seen on a man, smouldered as he swirled the wine in the bottom of his glass. She, could at this moment, have paid the exact compliment to him that he'd paid to her. His features were beautiful. But right now he was being unprofessional, and she needed to bring him back in line.

'What's my next move? And why so clandestine on the phone?'

'You need to talk to the police. It was a bad move to refuse.'

'I had stuff to do. Important stuff.'

'More important than a woman would normally do, whose devoted husband has gone missing?'

'I think so. And the nation will think so. I settled my kids.'

'Never-the-less, we will go to the police station after this. I've arranged it. And, I'll speak to the press. They'll no doubt be waiting outside. I'll make them see where your concern lay, and that Joe would want that of you. Besides that, I'll convince them that there's nothing you can tell the police that would help them, you are as much in the dark as they are, and you are distraught. A few tears, wouldn't go amiss.'

Ignoring this, Layla asked, 'and why did you need to bring me out? This doesn't exactly give a picture of a distraught wife.'

'I'll say you hadn't eaten and as your lawyer I needed to talk to you. Doing so whilst we dined killed two birds with one stone. Try not to look as if you are relishing every mouthful.'

'I am, it's the most delicious meal I've ever had. But, your answer doesn't cut it.'

'Your house could be bugged.'

This shocked her. 'By whom?'

'Joe – The police.'

'I can accept Joe, but why the police?'

'Gosling.'

Another shock. Gosling had been instrumental in putting her father away.

'What's Gosling's interest?'

'I thought you would know. It's obviously not conducive with police work, though would have been done under that guise.'

'You mean; he's bent? Why didn't I know? What's Graven been up to?'

31

Graven had let her down. This information was vital to her. She'd thought Graven the best Private D going.
'He's been trying to get hold of you, but couldn't. He found out late last night. Gosling's good. Very good. But we're on to him now.' Layla listened with mounting fury how Gosling was involved in the fake disappearance of Joe.
'Graven is checking your house as we speak. But he won't touch anything, he'll just confirm or deny whether it's bugged or not. If we debug it, whoever did the deed will know that we know about them.'
'Graven has a key!'
'I gave him mine.'
Not sure whether to thank him for this invasion of her privacy or not, Layla was silent for a moment. She didn't want this. She needed to be in charge. No male in her life would ever make decisions for her again.
'You've overstepped your remit.' Reining in her fury to a level she could cope with, her voice held just the right level of steel, 'Get the bill. Let's get out of here.'
A part of her was sorry to have to make this decision. She'd looked forward to the lemon posset and summer berries sweet that Adrian had ordered. Her hunger taking precedence over business, until this moment. She'd also enjoyed the unacknowledged flirting. Adrian's apology was noticeable by its absence. The arrogance of the man!

Outside the rehearsed scenario took place. After listening to what Adrian had to say, some reporters shouted their sympathy. The Rottweiler wasn't one of them. She worried Layla. Not consulting Adrian, Layla approached her. Slight, good looking and with a figure that complimented her long blonde hair, the Rottweiler held her ground. Layla handed her a card. 'Call me. We need to talk.'

'Not up for messing with the truth.'

'Not wanting you to. I like your style. I'll give you the story.'

Amazement registered on the girl's face. 'Thanks.' was all she managed. Recovering, she adopted a sarcastic tone, 'wanting money for your story, then?'

'Not that either.'

'Good. I'm not in that league, yet. Though your story could put me there.'

Layla nodded and moved off.

Adrian's car was waiting. His driver opened the door. Sliding into the maroon Audi A6, not her usual class, but an acceptable alternative, Adrian growled, 'What the hell?'

'I have my reasons. She could be trouble. I want her on my side. Don't question my judgement, Adrian. Not ever. And never make a move that hasn't been approved by me.'

His silence told of a sulk, but she didn't care. She had to be in control. 'Graven will have to go.'

'What . . .! And what about me?'

'You are back on probation.'

'Graven's the best. He only acted on my order.'

'Exactly. I pay him. I give the orders. I should have been the first person to be informed, whether or not he could get hold of me when he wanted to. He should have waited.'

'You need a second line of communication.'

'It's on order. A mobile, pay as you go, with a number that only those I trust will have, and only to be used for business.'

'Just what business are you planning, Layla?'

'You will be told when I want to tell you. In the meantime, take care of me in all legal matters. Don't let me put a foot wrong in this business of Joe's disappearance. Don't issue orders on my behalf. Then, you may or may not come on board.'

'You're sexy when you're in this bossy mode.'

Adrian would never learn, but did she want him to? The twitch in her groin that his words had provoked, told her she didn't.

*

Gosling wasn't there when they arrived at Charring Cross Police Station.

Layla's irritation with Adrian returned. 'I thought you'd arranged this interview?'

'I did. It will be part of his strategy to keep you waiting. He'll want you as nervous as possible.'

'I thought I was the victim helping with enquiries, not the bloody suspect.'

'Everyone's a suspect to Gosling.'

They sat in a small room. Bare, but for a table, four chairs and a machine that she assumed would record the interview. The atmosphere seeped an intimidation into her. She hadn't dreamt the setting for the questioning of her would be so formal.

Some fifteen minutes later, the door opened as if Gosling wanted to barge in and take them by surprise. But, the surprise was hers. In front of her stood a man who bore little resemblance to the one she remembered. Ten years had etched on to him as if thirty had passed. Leading a double life wasn't good for keeping ones looks.

Gosling's face had a grey pallor, his skin looked clammy. Bags she could have got her shopping into, hung in layers under his eyes. His bald head shone. His physique remained the same; tall, muscly, though there was something wrong with his right arm. She could see through his immaculate white shirt that it was bandaged.

The formalities over with, a silence fell. Hate permeated the room until it was almost tangible. It came from Gosling, and was returned by Layla. She wanted so much to expose him. Tell him what she knew of his part in the so called disappearance of her husband, but instead, knowing she wasn't fooling him, she played the suffering wife. 'Please find Joe, Sergeant. I can't bear this not knowing.'

His face held disgust, but his words were those she expected him to use. 'We are doing all we can, Mrs Parrondski. But so far, it is a mystery. Have you any idea if anyone had a grudge against, Mr Parrondski?'

'I can't think of anyone who would want to hurt my Joe. It must have been a chancer. Someone after the keys to the shops . . . Oh, I don't know.' She dabbed at her eyes.

'You should have all the locks changed.'

'I've seen to that.' Adrian again. A good decision, but it rankled that he'd made it, and once more without consulting her. It rankled even more that she hadn't thought of doing it herself. Instinct had made her do the mother thing. When instead she should have kept in constant touch with Graven and seen to business. She'd have to hone her skills if she was to succeed. The mistakes had been hers, others had acted for her how she should have acted. That had to change. She'd keep Graven on, but leave him and Adrian in no doubt that they could advise, but not act without her say so.

Gosling's nod was curt, his answer of, 'Good.' clipped. It was obvious he and Adrian had locked horns previously.

'Can I ask, has anything come from the examination of the car? Fingerprints? Any scraps of evidence?'

Layla wanted to laugh at Adrian's questions. They all knew the truth. It was like a cat and mouse game. Adrian had told her that Graven had reported that Gosling had taken a kid, God knows from where, to deliver it to Joe. He'd gone to Epping in a hire car. Gosling had then driven Joe's car back to London and had left it parked outside their main shop, unlocked and as if a struggle had taken place in it. The hire car hadn't been seen again, but she guessed it would be reported stolen and have had its identity changed and been on its way to Ireland by now.

Joe had nearly mucked things up. Graven had heard an exchange of angry words between Joe and Gosling. It appeared Joe had been delayed by having his whore meet him prior to the assignment. The excitement of it all must have made him horny.

At this thought, Layla pulled herself up. She still didn't like to think of that side of Joe, denied to her for so long. And she had to stop thinking of Gina as a whore. No doubt the girl didn't want to have sex with Joe in his car, or work at his sleazy walk-up. Gina was a victim, as she herself had been until her windfall had released those shackles. Besides which, the girl was now in danger. Graven reported, that Gina had seen more than she should. That he'd followed her to make sure she'd be safe, but that he feared what Gosling would do if he found out she'd been out there with Joe.

This had incensed Layla. If she'd have had this report earlier, she would have protected Gina. Layla knew she had mucked up. She'd put sentiment before business. That would never happen again.

The one thing Layla hoped was that Gina wanted revenge as much as she did.

Bringing her attention back, Gosling was outlining what had been done so far . . . 'Every line of enquiry has drawn a blank, but it is very early days. There are fingerprints, forensics are working on them now. We will need to take yours, Mrs Parrondski, forensics will need to eliminate them.'

This was something she didn't want. 'I have never been in that car, Detective. Joe only bought it a few weeks ago, it was his and his alone. I always travel in my Rolls.'

'I'm sorry, but I have to do this. Did he not show you it, ask your opinion? That would be the natural thing to do.'

The Bastard was taunting her!

'Mrs Parrondski isn't refusing, Detective, she is merely stating a fact. She has never been near the car.'

'At this moment in time, that car is all we have. We have to thoroughly investigate it. As we will your house and your offices. I have to insist that you allow us to fingerprint you. If not in the car, your prints will be all over the house and office.'

Shit! Shit! Shit!

Though, inside panic gripped her, Layla kept a calm exterior. How, she didn't know as her mind worked frantically during the pause that followed, listing the precautions she'd taken to cover her plans:

Adrian took charge of papers and payments concerning her need to know what Joe was up to. Graven was paid from an account Adrian held in his name. His reports were by phone or on paper. Paper reports were destroyed after she'd read them. No texting or electronic reporting of any kind had taken place. There was nothing she could think of that they would find in the house or the office that would give away her plans, or link her grandfather's ill-gotten gains to her.

Her portfolios were with Flavendons. Marcelle could be trusted to keep them safe from prying eyes. She had prepared others to mask what was really going on if ever she was called upon to share financial information pertaining to Layla's affairs. She was also working on buying property in Layla's new company name.

Layla's cash had been left in the secure boxes. She and Marcelle communicated, person to person, again, no emails, no texting and only messengers had relayed a need to meet.

Certain that no trace could be found of what she was personally up to, or how her fortunes had changed, Layla relaxed.

Gosling broke the silence. It was as if he knew she'd been unnerved and had deliberately let the pause linger for a while.

'One last question. Did Mr Parrondski tell you anything at all, or hint at any future plans he might have, Mrs Parrondski?'

'What could he possibly, plan? Joe wouldn't plan anything that I wasn't involved in. We did everything together.'

'Not everything. Mr Parrondski has been seen dining with some unsavoury characters of late. What do you know about these people?'

The question threw her. She'd thought they would all keep to safe ground. But then, Gosling had no idea what she knew. Though, it seemed that he suspected it was more than she was portraying. He was fishing.

Faking a sob, she spoke into her handkerchief, 'I – I have worried about how many nights he came home late recently. Or not at all at times. I – I thought he had another woman. But, Joe told me he was fixing up a surprise for me, and I believed him.'

'I think that's enough. You can see that Mrs Parrondski is distraught. I'm going to take her home now. If you need to ask anything else, then she will be available.'

Gosling agreed. 'But, I must insist that you return as early as possible tomorrow to have the fingerprinting carried out. We need to move into the house and office very soon.'

'We will.' Adrian helped Layla up as he said this. Gosling's 'thank you for your cooperation,' snarled through almost gritted teeth. He was a man that was uncertain. He needed to know what she knew. Well, he wasn't about to find out and would have to content himself with believing she was innocent of it all and in the dark about what Joe was up to.

When they turned into Holland Park, the sight of the paparazzi outside her house was like an injection of weariness. 'I can't face going in.' Drive me somewhere. Lose them.'

The car did a U-turn in the wide road and sped away. Layla looked back and saw a scramble taking place. Equipment hastily packed, bodies running for cars. She smiled as they turned the corner at the end of the street. 'Go somewhere, they'd never guess.'

The driver took a left and headed deeper into the East End. Adrian leant over to her. His breath fanned her face. I know a decent hotel.'

'I've nothing to change into.'

'You won't need anything.'

His tone had the effect of drying her throat.

Swallowing, she tried to deny the ache that throbbed in her groin. It had been so long. So long . . . The ache

persisted. Weakening her. Could she keep control?
Satisfy and banish this ache in her usual way that didn't
involve a man? Just her fingers, her toys, and her
imagination. Tonight, she didn't think she could. Her,
'okay' came out in a husky tone.
Adrian's hand squeezed her thigh. She was lost. The
longing in her consumed her.
'Head for Batty Langley's, Redman.'
The driver nodded at Adrian's instruction.
'A regular there are you?' she asked.
'No. But some of my clients are and tell me it's good.'
She said no more.
'Drop us at that all night shop, please, Redman, We'll
get a taxi from there.'
Layla was puzzled, 'Shopping?'
'You can at least get some underwear there – cheap and
nasty, but will be better than nothing.'
She giggled. Cheap and nasty appealed.

A shyness, accompanied by a little fear, came over her
when she entered the bedroom.
Beautifully furnished with dark mahogany, antique
furniture set against charcoal grey walls, and with
sumptuous gold fabrics draping the windows and the
four poster, the décor had a calming effect, and yet,
brought home to her what she was about to do.
A clink of glasses was a welcome sound. Adrian had
stopped at the honesty bar and held aloft a bottle of
Champagne. 'A shower first?'
She nodded as she gathered her shop-bought toiletries
and pack of black lace pants.
The water of the huge shower soothed her. Losing
herself to its bliss, she jumped when hands crept around
her waist and pulled her into a hard, lean, naked body,

then found her nipples, pinching and caressing them till they stood proud.

The feelings rippling through her, banished her inhibitions. She gave herself totally to Adrian's prompting, knowing a completeness of herself when finally, he lifted her and positioned her so that he could enter her. At that moment, twelve baron years erupted and burst like a bubble, giving her feelings, she'd almost forgotten. Water cascaded over them as Adrian rested her against the wall and thrust himself into her. An exquisite feeling built within her. Stiffening her body against its onslaught, she hollered the almost painful sensation out of her, before relaxing on to Adrian, sated beyond anything she'd ever known. Slipping out of her, he lifted her and carried her out of the shower, grabbing a towel, he dried her, gently patting and stroking with the luxurious towel, renewing her urge for him till she almost begged him to take her again. When he lifted her onto the bed and sank deeply into her. She was lost. She was his.

5

Joe Parrondski thumped his fist on his desk. 'Damn
Gosling! Bloody cops! You find Gina for me, Bragdon!
Get her back here, no matter what it takes. Where's my
bloody mobile? Where's Gosling, now?'

Joe watched a sardonic smile curl Bragdon's lips. 'He
had to go and see The Doc. He needed stitches, Boss.
Gina cut him bad. He didn't want to have to report the
injury in the accident book at the cop station. Not an
easy one to explain. He went straight to the nick after,
he had to question your wife. She's been busy all day,
seeing to your kids.'

'The Doc' was the nick name they gave to Ian Hasdon,
another member of Joe's elite.

In a previous life Hasdon had been a nurse. He'd been
sacked from his post in a Sussex hospital for stealing
drugs. After doing six of a twelve-month sentence, he'd
moved up to London and had frequented the gay Soho
nightclub that Joe owned.

Hasdon had needed a job. Joe had needed a bar person.
It hadn't been long before Ian Hasdon had shown a
talent for keeping customers happy. Nor was it long
before he showed that his talents were more than were
required of someone working behind a bar.

Sneaking around was one of them. Reporting his fellow
workers for theft, and giving the nod on any dealers
doing business in the joint. Joe liked him. Trusted him,
despite his past record. And his medical skills had come
in handy more than once when it was necessary to keep
an injury hush, hush, or one of the girls had taken a kid

on board that had to be aborted. He kept the girls clean, too.

Joe smiled inwardly. For a gay man, The Doc enjoyed swabbing pussies. Liked to do it a bit rough, he was disrespectful of women. The Doc had told him once that he imagined all women to be like his mother. He hated his mother.

The Doc's boyfriend worked in the lab in Sussex. He analysed the samples to detect disease. Then Joe wouldn't let them work until they'd visited the clinic and The Doc had declared them clean. He didn't want any complaints from regulars.

When it was Gina's turn to be swabbed, Joe had watched. It had given him the biggest stiffy of his life, and sore or not, she'd had to take him. The memory twanged his groin. He needed some privacy.

'Get Gosling back here.'

'Yes, Boss.'

Bragdon, the heavy of the gang, had little up top, but the size of him perturbed rivals from making a move on Joe. With him by his side, and with his bullet proof on, Joe felt reasonably safe. Not as safe as he would in a few weeks' time. His operation was set for tomorrow. Harley street surgeon, Gavin Theogood, the best, and most crooked in the business, would be making changes to Joe's face to make him unrecognisable.

The door shut on Bragdon. Joe got up; walked over to it; locked it, and sat back down at his desk. The ache in his groin persisted, pressing his dick against his trousers. He needed Gina. What she gave him, he didn't intend to let go of. Rekindling the memory of Hasdon messing with her pussy, he unzipped his trousers.

*

44

Gosling, looking haggard and unshaven, didn't offer excuses when he arrived fifty minutes later. 'I'm sorry, Boss, Gina took me by surprise. I should have anticipated her actions.'

'I want her here. I don't want you messing with her. Whether she saw anything, or not, she didn't grass. I might keep her as a permanent fixture, I'm not sure. But if I don't, you're to keep the fuck away from her, you vicious bastard.'

Gosling shrugged. Whores, were all the same to him. Fodder to pulp. He'd never stick his dick in one of them. He had that with his wife, and loved it. But the whores were good for the other side of him that demanded satisfying. He could never inflict that on his darling, Sara.

Gina was the best of all the whores he messed with. She begged the most. She was beautiful to look at. She was a whore, he wanted to, no; needed to, reduce to nothing. He had to beat her out of his system, she gave him no peace. It was as if she owned his soul. She made him feel shame when he looked at his lovely, pure Sara. A disappointment settled in him at Joe's instruction. He didn't think he could obey.

'You left scars on her last time. I don't like that. Even though she's had a kid, she has skin like porcelain. Tight, and lovely to look at. You'll spoil that. If you've hurt her again –'

'I have my job to do. This was work. I don't interfere with yours, you don't interfere with mine. You want this disappearance to go smoothly, right? Well, I have to be seen to be drawing blanks, whilst making it look as though I am doing all I can. Gina could have seen more than she's telling. Besides, getting her hooked wasn't a good idea. That will ruin her looks quicker than anything I can do.'

The truth of this angered Joe. He channelled his rage into a sarcastic remark. So, you beat up all of your witnesses, eh? Did you smack Layla around, then? No, I bet you didn't.'

'I didn't, but wanted to, but a fat-cat lawyer is quite a deterrent. Look, Joe, take my advice and be wary of Layla. Have her watched 24/7 and never trust her. Lawyers like Prindell don't come cheap. Ask yourself, how is she affording him? Besides. I know her lot from old. She's from bad stock. When her old man gets out he would kill you soon as look at you.'

'She's nothing. Nor is her father. She cut ties with him years ago. It never suited Layla to be associated with the likes of Gerry Loyson. Neither can Gerry hurt me, if I don't exist. Joe Parrondski is dead. All my operations are now in Count Roman Rolleski's name, and that is who I am. Layla knows nothing about it, or about my businesses in my cover name, Count Rommonski. She will be penniless within two months. She doesn't know it yet, but I've set up deals that will bankrupt the Parrondski business and a crooked one that will have her up for fraud. She'll do time. Her princess image is about to crumble.'

'Christ! Just what has Layla done, Joe? She hasn't cheated on you. You've always had her watched. I don't understand your vindictiveness towards her.'

'Not that it's any of your business, but as you ask . . . I come from a proud Russian family. Our traditions go back for generations, as does the family whose name I am taking. Layla didn't tell me about her family when I met her. She said that they were all dead. By the time I found out the truth, we were married. I had given her half of my business, and she was pregnant.'

'And now you do exactly what the Loyson family did, barring the armed robbery.'

'It wasn't what her family did. Mine were not above the odd crooked deal in the old days before Russia changed. It was the deceit. I felt that she'd trapped me with lies. I would have married her no matter what. In those days I was besotted with her. But her lies eroded that.'

'And your kids?'

'They are hers. Always were. She kept me from them. I've cut them from my life a long time ago. I have plans, big plans. Stick with me and you will have a retirement you can only dream of.' *If death is your dream that is.* This thought sat nicely in Joe's mind as he shook hands with Gosling. Sealing a deal, or so the prick thought. But he would out do his usefulness, and when that happened . . .

'I'm with you, Count.'

'That is good, I like that and you won't regret it. Now. You have something to make up for. One, I want Gina back, and two, I need two more little girls. Only, fair headed this time, and fair skinned. And with no Hoo-hah. I've never asked you, but, how did you manage to get Popsicle and the little dark girl you brought to me last night?'

'I put a few threats about that I would crack a dealer's operation open if he didn't get me a kid. She was payment for leaving him alone. He faced a thirty stretch with what I have on him, but it suits me to keep him on my patch at the moment.'

'Is he the father?'

'Yes. He's an Asian, nicknamed, red cap, as that's what he wears. Never without it. His wife has to obey him, so she won't be reporting the kid missing. Too scared to. She's white and an addict. Completely under his control. How, and where he got Popsicle from, I didn't ask, but she's never been reported missing.'

'Good. And the mixed parentage of this new child explains her lovely colouring. Right, bring me two more, and quick. The filming needs to begin next week. We're shooting episodes. It may take more time to get the kids happy and pliable. Oh, and better that they don't have a father figure. The one we provide is a model daddy. He does nice things to them and makes them giggle, if you get my gist.'

'I do. I'd like to see the results. I'd enjoy that as long as you keep your promise and no other kid gets hurt.'

'We're into tantalizing, which is what most paedophiles want. There's a lot more out there than the force knows of. Men who are not averse to bishop bashing while watching a daddy 'play' with his child. We're aiming to reach the men who wouldn't physically do anything to a child themselves and wouldn't watch a child being fully sexually assaulted. We know from research that there's a vast market of these types and we want to pamper to them – the undercover perverts in America and Russia. Not here. Too risky. The first film we put out of Popsicle and Daddy, has gone wild. Pity we won't be making a second. The daddy we used for that one wanted more and visited Popsicle later. He ended up suffocating her. He had the same done to him, and is history.

Gosling felt his stomach lurch. This was news to him. He'd thought Popsicle had died by accident. Anger rose like a newly lit furnace taking hold and roaring up a chimney. His hands clenched into fists. His nails dug into his palms. But he contained himself. Whatever it took . . . Whatever, he had to keep cool to win his ultimate prize.

'We're already thinking of making a pilot episode tomorrow of the kid you brought to me last night, we've called her Princess Chocolate. She's a real

48

daddy-deprived kid. She took to the new daddy we have straight-away. He started to play with her to settle her and within half an hour had her relaxed and happy in his company. And, something else to have on your kid-supplier; she's no stranger to seeing, or touching, or being touched, so he, or someone had been doing things to her. We're expecting to put out a video ten times better than our first one with Popsicle. Princess Chocolate had a whale of a time. In the subsequent episodes I want her friends to come to tea and to play with daddy too. The new actor who plays daddy, is a special guy. He's very gentle. The kid loves him. I think you'll enjoy it. I'm not into kids, but it got to me.' Gosling knew a moment of sheer pleasure as his sadistic nature triumphed over his anger. The idea that had come to him would mean the ultimate punishment for Gina, and a similar blow to her mate, Zoe. 'I have two kids in mind that could fit the bill and serve a double purpose. With these kids in residence, once we get Gina back here, she won't want to leave.'
'Even better.'

*

A bad night turned into a good one. Being the Count is good. The Count is very happy. Joe felt full of anticipation and promise. Everything was falling into place. His disappearance had gone well, Count Rolleski, also known as Count Rommoski, was soon to come to life. And so was the palace he planned for himself. The builders would work on making the rest of this ramshackle building into a home fit for royalty. Already, this basement office oozed luxury. Decorated in Black and white. Thick white carpet, black furniture and De Gourney hand painted, Abstract Pines wallpaper

49

– a touch that brought the forest indoors to him as he would have to remain inside for many weeks after his op.

To his left a glass door showed the shimmering swimming pool, beyond that was his gym. This is where Hasdon would come into his own as it would be his job to change Joe's forty-year-old, gone to fat, body, into a lean healthy one, fit for a Count.

To his right, a bedroom. Here he'd chosen grey and white, with De Gourney's Windswept Blossom on lead grey silk adorning the wall behind his bed. His bathroom was a beautiful oasis, with a tarnished silver gilded paper, painted with a plum blossom in delicate lavender, on one wall, and solid marble on the other three. The effect was stunning.

He'd have a swim, then laze in the sunken bath with a glass of champagne.

Joe Parrondski had all but gone from this world. With this thought it came to him that they needed a body. Someone who wouldn't be missed. Someone whose physique was the same, or similar to himself.

Murdered, and burnt would be the thing. Yes. He'd get Gosling on to it. It could be done after the operation. Joe would arrange with Gavin Theogood to supply samples for Gosling to have analysed to prove the body was Joe Parrondski's. Hair, teeth, skin. Convince the world that he was well and truly dead. Gosling must know a bent forensic scientist, or could tempt one with a few thousand pounds.

Yes, that's what he'd do. His sigh was a happy one. Life was good. After his bath, he'd get 'daddy' to play some more with Princess Chocolate and he would watch from his two-way mirror.

6

The key turned from the inside. Gosling waited. It was 9am and he thought Pixie's Place, at least the upstairs, would be trading for breakfast. All good front operations needed to be seen to be doing the normal thing. When the door opened, the young woman made a sound that told him she wasn't pleased to see him. Leaning into her face, he asked, 'Massage parlour going well, is it? So well, you don't have to open the café up?'

Jade Palmer shrugged and stepped back inside. Gosling followed her. 'I have a little something I need you to do for me. Change into a business suit, you're going to be a social worker.'

'What the Hell?'

'I have some kids I want to remove from their parents. You're going to help me.'

'I don't exactly have that type of wardrobe here, Gosling. And, I'm not into abducting kids, so find yourself someone else to do the work.'

'Into police raids when your richest clients are in town, are you?'

'You, Bastard!'

'My middle name. My last one is Prick.'

'You'll have to follow me to my flat. I can get changed there.'

'Not happening. Here, take this phone. It only has one number on it and that is the one I have. Facetime me from it the minute you are ready to leave your flat. By the way, have you got a hooded jacket?'

'Yes, a raincoat type, why. Wear it when you are outside and keep your head down.'

'For fuck's sake!'

'Unless you call yourself Fuck, this is for *your* sake. It's to keep you from being identified on the CCTV. So, just do it!'

Looking scared now, Jade's voice shook, 'Look, just give me a minute to see that my manager is good to run with today's business, and then I'll get a cab.'

'Don't take too long. And remember, any foul ups and this place will be history.'

Gosling looked around the plush surroundings as he said this. Pixie's Place, a rambling café, housing a private, *members only* club in the basement, looked innocent enough, but Gosling knew it wasn't.

Around him, stark red and black décor complimented squashy, white leather sofas. This was the innocent part, where coffee was drunk and snacks were eaten. Downstairs was where it got interesting.

Over-the-top swanky, with its all white, deep tread carpets, heavy chandeliers, and plush golden leather booths, the downstairs bar was somewhere to relax before choosing which door to go through. Or, who to go through it with. Behind the doors were rooms that fronted the real business. These rooms were massage parlours around a Turkish bath. But each had a secret door which led through the padded walls. Through these could be found hashish dens, rooms for live porn shows, and fetish rooms. Down another flight of stairs were the bedrooms. Or, perhaps *boudoirs* was a better name for them, with their beds decked out like Arabian tents. Their plush bathrooms, and hash pipes stood on marble side-tables.

The girls working here were high-class. Well educated, convent-girl types. The men enjoyed teaching them how to sin.

Pixie's Place had caught Parrondski's eye. Gosling had a remit to facilitate a take-over when he thought the time was right. That time would be just before the Arab Season. The long summer weeks of August, when London filled with dripping-rich Arabs. The takeover had to be done discreetly. The Arabs liked secrecy, and wouldn't frequent a place where there'd been a hint of trouble.

It had to be done soon. Gosling knew he was on schedule for that.

From what he could see on his screen of Jade when she came out of her flat, she looked the part. That's if you weren't in the know about designer clothes. Zoe Feldon might be. 'Christ, is that the worse you can come up with? Haven't you an M&S or a Next suit, and an old hoodie? Not, that I can name the label of what you're wearing, but the prostitute we're about to visit is earning good money and she likes her designer stuff. She'll know at a glance.'

If you knew me as well as you think you do, you wouldn't ask if I had those kind of clothes in my wardrobe. It's this, which for your information is an Akris, and I wear for business meetings, or I go and buy something.'

'We haven't time, it will have to do.'

'I take it this pro is one of Parrondski's lot? His places in the red-light area are sleazy, but I'll say one thing for him, he pays those girls well. Though, I can assure you - not well enough for them to buy clothes at this end of the market.'

Damn, a fucking blunder! I'm getting tired. I shouldn't have led her into making that connection!

'No, actually, this one is free-lancing. She leaves her number in telephone boxes, that kind of thing. Offers personal massages, but we know her game. And that's all the info you're getting, so stop prying and do exactly as I say. Walk to the end of your road. There you will find a hire car, an Audi. It's black. I've text you the reg. Switch on the mobile sat nav, not the on-board one. It will take you to Stamford Street. The full address is in it. Park on the resident parking space around the corner, the fourth space along. I've arranged it with the owner. I'll be a few spaces back from there. As I get out of my car, don't acknowledge me, wait until I text you. Then walk straight to the block of flats. Ring the bell for number nine flat. Have you got that so far?'

'Yep.'

'When we are in the flat I will get the subject into the kitchen, I need to question her and as there are kids in the place I have to have a social worker with me. At that point you will offer to take the kids for a walk. Tell them you have a shiny car they will love, and you will take them for ice cream while mummy is busy. Now. There should only be two girls, and there's booster seats for the girls already in the car. The subject has two boys as well, but hopefully, they will be out. They go to a holiday school club each day, or at least that's where the subject thinks they go. In the event that they are in the flat, tell them that you have arranged for them to go with a friend of yours to see Tottenham Football ground – they're both fans. If you are seen with the boys a car will drive up to yours, call the driver, Rick. And keep it light hearted. By-the-way, you're called Rita, Rita Drewery. Got that?'

She nodded.

'Right, last instruction. In the glove compartment of the Audi, you'll find two bottles of coke, encourage the girls to drink them. Then, you'll have no trouble from them on the journey. Follow the second instructions in the Sat Nav. It will take you to an address in Epping. I'll meet you there.

'You're a pig of the first order. A Bastard Pig!'

'Correct. And, I know just where to get my pig swill from if this doesn't go to plan. Like to lose your lifestyle, would you? Your Akris and Prada, eh? They don't wear that stuff, nor do they serve caviar in a women's prison.'

She still looked defiant.

'Listen. If you go through with this, your life will carry on the same as before and no way will you be implicated. Muck it up, or squeal to any fucker, and it won't be prison walls – that was a joke. Your real fate will be the inside of a coffin. And you will be able to see the lining, as you won't be dead when we bury you! Now, get going.'

Just before she disappeared, Gosling had the satisfaction of seeing tears running down Jade's face.'

For once Zoe wasn't out of her face on drugs. The usual hate and fear showed in her eyes when she opened the door to him. He liked that.

'What do you want, Gosling?'

'A little more respect won't go amiss. Detective Sergeant Gosling to you.'

She let him in. He liked her back view, slender, tall, dark hair immaculately cut short and spiky, hips rounded, and swaying from side to side. Black mini skirt hugging them. He'd already appreciated her low-cut grey, silk top that gave a view of her bulging breasts. Zoe Feldon was once beautiful, but now,

55

though still attractive, the cocaine had taken its toll on her looks.

'I have a social worker on the way. Rita Drewery. I'll just text to see where she is.'

The hate lost out to the fear in Zoe's widening eyes as she swivelled around to face him. Social Workers meant just as much trouble as cops in these quarters.

Inside, the surroundings surprised him. Instead of the usual dive he expected these dirt bags to live in, the flat presented as pristine, and beautifully decorated and furnished. *Parrondski paid these shits too much.*

Enjoying seeing the shakes taking hold of Zoe, and knowing they weren't down to withdrawals, he asked, 'where's the kids?'

'They're playing in the bedroom. W – why? They're alright, I ain't been neglecting them.'

'This ain't about that. It's policy now to have someone with us when we carry out investigations where there might be kids present. Today there were no WPC's available, not that that lot think family liaison should be down to them. Jumped up little arseholes.'

'What is it about, then? I ain't done nothing.'

'Ha, that'll be the day. You're up to your neck in doing stuff that ain't legal, so don't give me that. But, this ain't about you either. Get the kids in here, the social worker's on her way. Then you and I will go into the kitchen and talk while she takes care of them.'

Shaking even more now, Zoe went to the door of the lounge and yelled the kids. Two little girls came running. Good, the boys were out. Disposing of them was one job less to do.

'Hello, you're two nice little girls, aren't you? I've got a really nice lady to look after you for a while as mummy's going to be busy.' The intercom buzzed. 'That'll be her now. Let her in, Zoe.'

Zoe went to obey, but the kid who looked like her, started to cry and cling to her mother's leg. She had to drag her with her.

Shit, I don't need this!

Having no kids himself, he hadn't thought about this scenario.

Jade glared at him as she came through the door. Taking charge, she took hold of the now screaming child's hand. 'Come and sit with me, darling. Mummy has to talk to this nice man. I'm Rita, and I'm going to play with you while mummy is busy.'

The blonder of the two kids went immediately to Jade's side, and looked up at her eagerly. Seeing this the screaming one quietened her screams to sobs and went to Jade too. Gosling imagined they were used to being palmed off to a woman, but feared men. Neither had one in their lives that he knew of. He hoped what Parrondski had said was true about his acting daddy being good.

Once in the kitchen he wasted no time. 'Right, Zoe, this is about Gina Walters. That little blonde child is hers, isn't she? So I take it Gina hasn't turned up yet?'

Zoe didn't answer.

'She should've turned in for work last night and she didn't. We want to talk to her, but she's disappeared off the face of the earth. We think she's connected to the disappearance of Joe Parrondski. We know she was his whore. Has she been in touch?'

'No, I'm sick with worry. I've no idea where she is, or what I'm to do with the kids when I go to work. She looks after them for me. If she's with him, she didn't go willingly. She wouldn't leave her Amy. She'd give her life for that kid.'

'Tell me exactly what you do know. When and where you last saw her, when and where you last saw

Parrondski. Anything, it doesn't matter how small and insignificant it may seem, it could be important.'

God, I hate this shit. Fucking questioning these low-life scum. Even if it was all a pretence. I want out. Gosling cheered as he thought this as his part in the disappearance of Parrondski was his ticket to do just that. He could almost taste the Caribbean air, and feel the sun. He and Sara would do nicely there with a few bob in their pockets. Maybe he'd get over his fetish. With his frustrations gone, he wouldn't need to beat the crap out of these filthy dregs of the earth. Though he wouldn't mind doing that right now to this heap of shit. Make her squirm in pain and beg for mercy.

These thoughts, and his view of her breasts rising and falling had him swallowing hard.

Zoe talked ten to the dozen. He wrote some of it down. Mostly though, it was scared rambling, nothing useful. She was useless. His urge to beat the crap out of her increased. His dick was hardening. Stopping her in full flow, he said, 'Hold on a moment. I need to piss . . . No, you stay here. I don't want the kids to see you, it might unsettle them. I can find the bog. I've been in a few of these flats, know them like the back of my hand.' He also knew that Gina lived next door and as she wasn't there, and the neighbours around were at work, there was little chance of being overheard. Not that this lot of flat dwellers would do or say anything if they heard a woman screaming. It was part and parcel.

On checking he found that Jade and the kids had gone. Gosling looked around the room. The curtains caught his eye. Coiled tie backs would serve as bonds. His belt as a whip.

Before collecting the ties, he dug his hands into his trouser pocket. The rubber of the gloves that he always carried, in case of a call out to an incident scene, weren't all he felt. His dick was throbbing against his trouser. He ran his handover it. He was ready, more than ready. It wouldn't take long. He struggled to get the gloves onto his sweaty hands.

Back in the kitchen Zoe was turned away from him. Over her shoulder she asked if he wanted tea. The lash across her back had her gasping in her breath. He moved swiftly, knocking her to the floor and trussing her before she could protest, though he took a kick on his shin that angered him.

Holding her legs rigid, he opened them and got between them. No pants. His urge increased. The sight of her stockings and suspender belt increased it more.

Smashing her across the face, he worked fast while she was stunned.

Flexing the stockings, he'd peeled off her, he rolled one up. Prising her mouth open he stuffed one of them into it. The other he wrapped around her neck. She stirred. Her eyes opened in terror.

Oh God, he was going to cum!

The ecstatic agony of pumping into his trousers had him holding the stocking tighter and tighter. His moan reverberated around the room.

Gasping for breath, he relaxed back. Sweat blurred his vision. Zoe didn't move. Zoe would never move again.

7

Gina opened her eyes, but instantly closed them against the bright light that increased the pain in her head. A pain that gnawed away at the fog that had held her in a nothing sort of place, where nightmares penetrated to almost suffocate her with fear.

Trying to get her thoughts straight, she concentrated on remembering the events that had taken place. Most of it was worse than the nightmares and no matter how she tried, her memory wouldn't let her get past the moment when she opened that huge wooden door. *What happened after that?*

Something touched her lips. Words were spoken in a coaxing voice, but they weren't English words. Gina forced her eyes open again. A young girl in a nurse's outfit came into her vision. Gina opened her mouth to speak. It filled with something sloppy, a porridge-like substance. Her throat retched.

'Nu, trebuie sa mananci'

Confused, Gina tried to speak, but no words would come. As the nurse was offering another spoonful of the food, she assumed she'd told her she must eat. She kept her lips pressed firmly together.

Where am I? Looking around told her this wasn't a hospital ward, nor was it a place owned by the likes of her kind. It was plush, if a little old fashioned, with huge mahogany wardrobes, a kidney shaped dressing table, and chintz curtains falling the full length of the wall and meeting an Axminster, patterned carpet. Above her hung a huge chandelier. She wouldn't call this bedroom, tastefully decorated, but it had been put

61

together by a large budget. A door at the far end stood open and through it, Gina could see a bathroom.

Was she in Joe's house? Fear clutched her breast at this thought. She had no idea where Joe lived, or what his taste in décor was, but no alternative would come to her. If Gosling had caught up with her, where else would he take her? It wasn't as if he could take her to the nick with the beating he'd given her. Besides, he hadn't been on police business when he picked her up.

The nurse gave up and walked out of the room.

Gina tried to sit up. Managed to lift her head. Her eyes rested on the phone next to her. It sat on top of a bedside table which had an embroidered cloth draped over it. This, and her surroundings gave her the idea that the room belonged to someone of advancing years. Though her arm was stiff she managed to reach out for the receiver. She'd call Zoe. Zoe would know what to do.

'Don't bother with that, it's dead.'

Pain racked Gina's neck as she swivelled her head around. The owner of the voice was a beautiful woman. Gina registered the kind smile on the woman's face, but not much else as she slumped back on the pillow.

'I'm Layla Parrondski.'

Christ, Joe's wife! The terror of the revenge this woman might want to take, trembled through Gina.

'Don't be afraid, you're safe from my husband and his cronies.'

Confused, Gina waited.

'You probably heard that my husband was reported missing yesterday morning, but you and I know that he isn't. He's gone underground and is planning a new life. I'm planning one too, and, if you agree my terms, you will be part of it.'

'I – I don't understand. W –where am I, and how did I get here?'

'You were taken by Gosling to a derelict property in Epping, which is owned by my husband. I have had a Private Detective watching everything that goes on there. He saw you come out of a door of the basement, make it to the lawn and collapse. He contacted me, and I had him bring you here. This house is in Walton on Thames, it belonged to my mother. She died recently. No one who matters, knows of its existence, not even Joe. He stopped having anything to do with my family years ago, and my mother moved here long after that. Joe doesn't even know that she is dead.' For a moment, Gina thought she detected a sadness at this, but maybe Layla was just feeling the pain of her mother's loss. She didn't like to ask about Layla's father, but in the next breath Layla told her and the information shocked Gina. This woman seemed too well-bred to have a lag for a father! Gina said nothing, waited once more. Leaving the talking to Layla.

Layla changed the subject, 'The nurse in attendance looked after my mother in her last months. She is nursing you back to health, but she is Romanian and will not speak English to you. If she does, she stands to lose a great deal of cash, which she will benefit from when she goes back to her country once she has got you well. I don't want her knowing anything, so don't try to speak to her. I have cameras on you, and they are monitored 24/7.'

The fear Gina had felt earlier returned. None of this made sense. She found her voice, 'So, I'm your prisoner now?' her fear turned to anger, 'Look, I don't know what you're planning, or want me to be part of, but I've got a kid and I fucking need to go back home

63

to her . . . I'm not involved in all of this, I just happened to be in the wrong place at the wrong time!'

'Shagging my husband.' The silence that followed this, held a threat. 'I know all about you, Gina. I know what you have been to my husband.'

Sweat stood out on Gina's forehead.

'But, I'm not wanting to harm you, I need your help. Are you feeling up to hearing me out?'

Gina nodded. She had no choice.

Listening to Layla outlining her plans, Gina felt more and more incredulous. 'Look. I don't blame you for wanting revenge, Joe Parrondski is a bastard, but I don't want anything to do with it. I told you, I've got a kid. I've got to get the hell out of London and try to find another life for her and me. Somewhere no one will find us.'

'It's too late for that!'

Horror clung to every fibre of Gina's insides. There was something final about the statement. Anger crept in banishing the horror and giving Gina an edge. 'Too fucking late for what? You're going to let me out of here, Layla fucking Parrondski. I'm not doing anything for you. If you've hurt my kid, I'll fucking kill you!'

'I haven't, but Gosling has –'

'Gosling! No! No. No-o-o!'

The nod of Layla's head had Gina retching. *Amy, Amy, oh God, no!*

'An associate of my Private Detective – who I always refer to a 'D', has been following Gosling ever since I heard of his involvement yesterday. A couple of nights ago I was at the station being interviewed by that slimy, hairless geezer. The moment the interview was over, he went to Epping, no doubt in trouble for having lost you. You did well to get away. You have the right qualities that I need.'

'Fuck that, tell me what has happened to my Amy.' Out of the bed now – the strength of knowing she was needed by Amy lifting her and conquering her pain, Gina faced Layla.

Layla told her.

'Christ! So that bitch of a woman has taken them to Epping. What about Zoe? Didn't she stop them? She wouldn't just hand them over.' Pacing the room, Gina couldn't get her thoughts in order and dare not ask why Joe wanted Tammy, and her Amy, her precious little Amy.

'I don't think for one moment that Jade Palmer did this willingly. She owns Pixie's Place, and was probably threatened with its closure, you know Gosling.'

Gina's nausea returned, her mind frantically searching for a way to get her Amy back, but nothing presented. In despair she vented her anger again, 'The rotten cow, putting her business above what might happen to my Amy and to little Tammy. They're just kids for Christ sake.'

'You can't judge Jade, Gina, fear is a powerful thing, after all you did nothing when you saw one being abducted.'

Defeated, Gina slumped into a gold coloured, velvet, high-backed chair, positioned near the window and listened to what Layla had to say.

'My D is of the opinion that something went wrong. Jade sat outside the Epping house for a while with your child and Zoe Feldon's child, as if waiting for someone. But then one of my husband's heavies came out of the building and took her and the kids inside – Jade put up a fight, but was clobbered. My D doesn't think that was what she was expecting. His guess is that Gosling was meant to meet her there. Gosling didn't turn up until a good three and three quarter hours after Jade and the kids were taken inside.'

After a moment, it dawned on Gina. 'Zoe. Oh God, you don't think . . . Christ! It's a nightmare, a fucking nightmare.'

'It's one that we have to pull together on. We can beat them at their own game. We can get those kids out safely. From what I know they are there for filming –'

'I'll kill him! I'll kill every one of them if they harm my Amy. Oh God, I can't bear it, I can't.'

'I'm offering you a chance to get your kid back, and to get revenge. There won't be any killing – at least, not yet, but if you come in this with me, we'll not only get those kids safe, but we'll be running the biggest operation in London.'

'No. I'm going to the cops. We have to. I just want Amy safe then I'm quitting London – England, even. The police will get her back and bring that lot to justice.'

'That's not an option.'

Gina's blood chilled. Layla's beautiful face snarled into an ugly, determined look. 'You're in, or, you're dead. Those are the options.'

Gina tried to absorb this. The truth of it wrung dry – she knew too much. She was a liability. If Layla was thinking of running the sleazy side of London, she must have a hard core. She'd said no killing, but did add, *not yet*. Gina knew she could end up being the first if she didn't comply.

A feeling of being beaten worse than anything Gosling had done to her, took her, but then Amy's smiling little face came to her and empowered her. Layla exuded power. With her as boss, they could do it. They could save the kids. Save Amy. And, they could take over the operations. One thing she would do if it all happened –

she would make sure the girls that worked for the operation were well taken care of. There'd be no clients like Gosling.

An excitement zinged through her. She looked up. 'I'm in.'

8

Gosling pleaded with Joe, but Joe was having none of it. *The jumped up shit would be nowhere without me.* Deciding to play his trump he went nearer to Joe. 'There's something you need to know. There's a dossier on you, written by me and kept by a certain person, who has instructions that if I should meet an untimely end, or not check in with him each week, then the information contained will be released to the police. There's enough in it to put you away for three lifetimes and all backed by evidence.'

'You, Prick!'

'Ha, you just found my last name. Look, I've let you call the shots, but on this, I'm going to be obeyed, otherwise I'm in deep cow dung and so are you. You're not going to kill Jade Palmer. We can't afford another missing person at this time. We will get her to do the deal, then she is to leave the country with the riches you will give her. I'll tighten the screws on the lid she'll have to keep on everything, so she won't dare squeal. But, she stays alive and leaves legit. Everyone must think that the deal is what she wants.'

Joe chewed on his thumb nail. Gosling knew there wasn't much time. He knew that in just over two hours, Joe was to have his op. everything was ready in a room behind his gym that had been prepared for the plastic surgery. Almost one million pounds had been spent on turning it into an operating theatre and Gavin Theogood, was to be paid another million, once he'd completed the surgery. By tonight, Joe Parrondski would be no more. But he'd be laid up for a while. Gosling had to get him to agree to this now. As it was he was shitting bricks.

If Jade went missing, they would know back at the station that he'd visited her that morning. He'd be on the CCTV. They'd see her leave just after – everything would be put together like a child's jigsaw. The kids going missing . . . The murder.

Had he done enough to cover his tracks? DNA checks could find the minutest thing. Christ, the orgasm he'd had as Zoe died had rocked his foundations, he'd hollered like a stuck pig, he could have sprayed spit everywhere.

Trying to calm the rising panic in him he went over all his actions after realising Zoe was dead. A feeling of trepidation washed over him. He had to get back to the station, and soon. He should never have left that fucking dog's bollocks, Cleaston – The jumped up cock sucker hasn't been in the force five minutes, and already he's up for a Detective Sergeant badge. *He'll make a meal of the fact that I had been in the building!* He'll not leave a stone unturned. He'd already called the Chief in. *I should have stayed there. Making an excuse that I had something important to do only added to it all looking iffy.*

His mind went over how he'd put someone in the frame for the murder of Zoe and some peace of mind came to him. Patrick Finney. The perfect choice. A pervert. A known peeping Tom. Patrick Finney had done time for rape, he fitted the bill.

Joe brought Gosling out of his thoughts; 'Okay. Jade Palmer lives, but you cover everything, right? If this goes tits up, you'd better have a way of getting us out of it.'

It had already gone tits up! But, he wasn't about to tell Joe that. He had to minimize the damage first. Joe's next statement threw him.

'I have something for you to do, and quick. I want a body to be found.'

'A body? For fuck's sake, what body. Why?'

'My body, I have to be seen to be dead.'

Gosling listened in amazement to what Joe told him. Gavin Theogood was going to supply the DNA to match Joe's! But first, someone of similar build had to be found. And Joe was expecting Gosling to do the deed!

'I need the man bringing here. Theogood will check him over and make a few alterations to him. His teeth, will be mine, etc. Then he will be killed and his body burned. A few days later, you – the brilliant detective that you are, will have him found. It will be taken that I have been murdered.'

Gosling couldn't speak. The plan was brilliant, but flawed, and to his mind, almost impossible to pull off. And another thing, it would leave Layla free to claim everything. 'You do realise, you will be giving everything to Layla on a plate and you'll never get it back. She can cash in insurance policies –'

'Lapsed. And, that is just what I want. I want everything in her name. I want her downfall. I told you, I set up deals – crooked gold deals, in her name. I will give you details and you can nick her and put her away with her fucking father. Let's see if she can keep that a secret. The lying bitch.'

This was a logic that Gosling couldn't understand. What girl wouldn't keep a background like Layla's secret when she'd fallen in love with a multi-millionaire who had as much pride as Joe had? His lack of forgiveness and bitterness over this issue was difficult to comprehend. Though Gosling had to admit to feeling a deep satisfaction at getting at Loyson again.

71

The dread he'd always had at the thought of Layla's father, made the prospect of hurting him even more enjoyable. That lot didn't give up on grudges and Loyson's time for being released was getting nearer and nearer. Gosling would make sure he was far away from these shores when it came about.

'Right. I'll leave you to see to things with Jade. I have to go and have my pre-med.'

This was music to his ears. Gosling wanted to see Jade safely off these premises.

Within five, everything was in place and Bragdon brought Jade into the office. She walked up to Gosling. Before he could react, spittle sprayed over his face. Joe's sidekick chuckled. For two pennies, Gosling could have kicked Bragdon's balls in and smashed Jade's smirk off her face. Christ, he'd saved her from death, the shitfaced, whore!

Wiping his face, Gosling spelled out just what Jade had to do to gain her freedom. She was to sign Pixie's Place over to a Count Rolleski. She would receive a million – a fraction of what the place was worth. And, she had to leave Britain. 'You squeal about anything, and that kid you keep hidden away, will end up here having fun before she goes to her maker – buried alive, in your arms.'

Jade's jaw dropped.

'Thought no one knew about your petal, your precious secret? Never underestimate me, it will be your downfall '

There was a long silence. Jade's body trembled.

Gosling liked that. He liked it even better when a tear plopped on her cheek.

'Ready to sign?'

Jade nodded.

'Right. I assume you have the papers all ready?' The suited, deadpan-faced, man who hadn't spoken yet, nodded at Gosling's question. A weasel-type, he'd been struck off as a lawyer for fraudulent dealings, but worked for a company of solicitors who weren't above doing deals that were dodgy, as long as they didn't have to do the dirty work.

Jade didn't read anything. She just signed away the gold mine she'd built up over ten years. Her dignity was almost touching. If Gosling hadn't been feeling euphoric at finally nailing her, and in a far better way than he could have anticipated, he would have felt pity for her. As it was, he almost wanted to hug Joe Parrondski.

He leant back, feeling his body sink into the plush leather office chair. Swivelling this way and that a feeling came over him, that he could get used to this.

An idea pinged in his head. Yes, and he could take over the whole fucking lot if he thought it all through. He hadn't much money in the scheme of things, but he did have what could buy more than money – information that will bring them all to their knees.

An excitement clutched him. He looked around at the geeks in Joe Parrondski's employ. They were nothing. None of them held the power he held.

Just look at today's work – he'd abducted two kids, murdered a whore, set up a scumbag to take the rap, and overseen a take-over worth millions. And he was going to add more knowledge to his dossier – Hasdon, The Doc, would see to that. Hasdon was in attendance, helping with the operation that was about to start. Hasdon was wired and had a secret video camera on him. Not everyone was loyal to Joe Parrondski, or Count Bollocks, as Gosling and Hasdon referred to him.

An urge came over Gosling to laugh out loud. But he pulled himself together. Dismissing the lawyer, he asked Bragdon what had happened to Jade's stuff.

'She has it. She only had a bag with her. I just gave it back to her.'

Turning to Jade, Gosling demanded, 'Give me the mobile I gave you, Bitch. You're all done here for now. Bragdon will take you to the tube station. You will go back to Pixie's Place, call a staff meeting, and tell them that you've been mulling over an offer you received for the place for some time. That today you decided to accept it. That as of this evening they are all redundant, anything due to them will be paid. Then tell them that they will be contacted within a week to reapply for their jobs and that you have given them all a good reference. I take it you can do that?'

Jade nodded.

'Right. You will close at 6pm this evening. At that point you will contact all of your cleaning and maintenance staff. Tell them what has happened. Then, tell them that they are to come in as usual. That you will be there to meet them tonight, and will introduce them to the person who will be in attendance on other evenings. Put a notice on the door which says 'Closed for one week – Reopening under new management.' You will be working late tonight. Maybe, all night. The lawyer you just met and his assistant will be arriving dead on six. You will work with them until they feel satisfied that everything is in order and they know the ins and outs of every part of the business.'

'But, I need to be with my child, I – I –'

'Make arrangements. And, Jade, you have been told will happen if anything goes wrong. They were not idle threats. Be off these shores in one week.'

Her reaction to lift her head in that almost regal way she had, infuriated him, but he kept it in check. No matter how she played this, he'd just wiped her clean of everything she had, and it felt good.

Gosling walked to the car with Jade and Bragdon.

'Hold on while I check everything has been left in the hire car as it should be.'

It was all there. Sat nav. Coke bottles. Booster seats. Taking them out, he put them in a pile on the floor. He called Bragdon over, 'When you get back, incinerate this lot then, do the necessary with the car.' Bragdon nodded.

The hire of these vehicles, was not traceable to anyone, false papers had seen to that. Always from a different firm. They were an easy steal.

More than satisfied with a good day's work, Gosling stood and watched Jade being driven away. He couldn't wait to get home to his Sara. But first there was the business at the station to see to.

He didn't hear the whir of the camera trained on him. Nor did he know that it was recording his every move when, hours later, he arrested a door-sleeper. A man who had the same build as Parrondski. A man who couldn't speak English. A man whose body he delivered to Epping.

9

'Gina, in this emotional state, you're no good to anybody. Least of all Amy. We have to be strong. Nurse tells me you were crying most of the night. I need you to regain your health and to channel the hate you have in you for Gosling into a positive, where you want with all your might to defeat him. We can do that. That is, unless he proves useful.'

'I hear what you're saying, but the pain is so terrible. And the guilt –'

'Stop right there. Guilt is a destroyer. It wasn't your fault that you were used by Joe that night. That was a blunder on Joe's part. He should never have met you when he had an assignment ahead of him. And now, with taking your kid, they'll be crapping themselves in case you talk. They will be hunting you down.'

'Christ. It just gets worse! And, what do you mean, useful?'

'Think about it. If we could get Gosling on our side, we would be home and dry. He knows everything about Joe's operation. He'd protect you, instead of hunt you and he'd help in getting them kids out.'

'I'm not working with him. I'd sooner kill the Bastard.' This was going to be harder than Layla had thought it would be. She had to get Gina thinking like a gangster, or she would be useless. Her hand-picked women, were all she had. Zoe, another she'd intended approaching, was now gone - though her addiction would more than likely have ruled her out. However, there was another possibility now. Jade. Given her business sense, and the anger that must be seething in her at having lost

everything, she would be an ideal, and more than likely
– a willing candidate to help bring Joe down.

There were a lot of operations to take over. Maybe her
D could find out who the mothers of the first two kids
were? Surely they'd want to come on board? They must
have enough reason for wanting revenge on more than
Joe, as how come they haven't posted the kids as
missing? Fuck. This was all taking longer than she
thought. And, she hadn't cracked Gina properly yet!

'You're going to feel like killing Gosling even more
when I tell you the news. I'm sorry, but, what we
thought might have happened has. Zoe's dead.
Murdered. Her identity was given out this morning.'

'Christ, Gosling's a monster!'

'Yes, but a careless one. It's now out that Zoe's kid,
Tammy is missing. That's the last thing Joe will want.
The other two kids Joe had, weren't reported. Without
this death, Gosling might have been able to keep you
and Zoe from reporting yours missing. Now he's in the
shit. The whereabouts of you and your child is
unknown as well as Zoe's little girl. There's a huge
investigation.'

'And Amy and Tammy? W – What will happen?'

'It seems the cops have a suspect for the murder, but are
looking for a woman regarding the abduction of two
girls, one they have said they suspect is yours. *We* know
the woman was Jade, but from news reports, the police
have no idea who it was. But we can't be sure. Anyway,
I have to go. I need to contact Jade, get her on board.'

'For fuck's sake! How can you expect me to work with
those who took my kid? I can't do it. I can't.'

'Don't turn into a liability, Gina, Jade was used just like
you have been used, both of you powerless to say no,
Get the perspective of who is to blame before I return

or . . . Well, let's just say, you're on board, or you're dead. You know too much.

*

Getting into the taxi that would take her to Kent, Layla smoothed the skirt of her Roland Mouret crépe dress as she settled herself in the back seat and stretched out her legs. The thought of being so near to her boys and yet not being able to see them rankled. But she had business to see to and the detour was to cover her tracks. Her driver would be waiting for her about a mile away from her cottage. If information of where she'd been was needed, they would only be able to pick up her journey from London to and from her cottage. The taxi driver was on the payroll. He'd picked her up in a country lane in Kent and brought her to Walton on Thames the day before. Her driver had gone on to the cottage and parked the car outside her cottage.

She should feel satisfied at the subterfuge and of having Gina in place, but anger nestled in her. Gina had to step up! If not, Layla would put a call into Frankie Droile. Frankie was her father's hitman, and even though in his sixties now, he was still willing to work. The stretch he'd done for fraud had lessened his stash – most of it had gone on a so-called, hotshot lawyer, who failed to get him off. The lawyer came to an untimely end. Frankie was up for hire the moment he stepped through the prison gates to freedom.

It would be tough having Gina taken out. But, the world Layla wanted in on was more than tough. She couldn't afford any weak links. And, she couldn't afford to leave loose ends to go their own way, either. Feeling empowered and in control, Layla relaxed back and put a call into her D on her new pay-as-you-go antique mobile.

His first question: 'Where are you?'

'On my way to Kent. Just set off.'

'Get back to Gina, now.'

'What the fuck?'

'Tell your driver to turn back then I'll explain.'

'He's doing a U-turn.'

'Right. Listen to this. Joe wants Gina. I'd advise that you let that happen. Gina could be our second insider, but one with a lot more access than the bit part I have at the moment.

'Christ. Why does that hurt?'

'Pride. You'll get over it. We need Gina back in circulation. She needs to go to the cop station in a distraught state and wearing the clothes she had on when she was brought to you. Even make her injuries raw again. It has to happen, now! She needs to tell the cops that she's only just heard. That she had a client who drugged her and she woke up in some sleazy flat. That she'd been hurt by him, and that she escaped, then walked and walked, eventually getting a taxi to the police station. Brief your cab driver to take her there, and if asked he is to say he picked her up. Say, around Clapham somewhere and took her to the cop station.'

'She's been missing for two nights.'

'I doubt they'll probe. She's much smaller in height than Jade, so they won't think she's the one with the kids on the CCTV. Give Gina some stuff so she has it in her system.'

'That's if she'll play ball. She's being a pain in the ass.'

'Tell her Gosling has been warned not to hurt her again. It's more than his life's worth to not deliver on this one. Though it is all much more complicated now that her kid's missing. The cops will be like flies around her. Joe doesn't know yet. He had his op last night and is not so well today. Too much done at once if you ask me. Gosling's mucked up by killing Zoe. He will want to appease Joe by having Gina there for when he wakes up.

'I'll sort Gina, but what about Jade?'

'It's all fixed up. I had a note passed to Jade on the train last night. She contacted this morning. She'll meet you. I didn't expect to see her again after she was dragged inside the building, but I think we know why she was let free. Gosling didn't want her taken out. She had to be seen to leave her business and her London life of her own accord. If she'd become another missing person, he would have had to explain why he visited her that day. And the link could have been made to the kid's disappearance. Ha, bet he curses the wonder of CCTV now. Problem is, he won't want Jade alive. So she is in grave danger.'

'Fuck! Everyone I need is becoming a liability. Gosling will have to come on board, or be taken care of.'

'Not necessary. We have all the trump cards. Jade is being watched, but guess who by? One of mine. Gosling rang me the moment Jade left the premises. I was only feet from him, but had my phone on silent. I had to knock the call and ring him later. He wanted a tail on Jade. Naturally, I obliged. My man will keep her safe and doctor the reports he sends to Gosling.'

'That's the first bit of good news I've had. But, surely we can't keep Gosling alive without reigning him in?'

'Leave it a while. My instinct is that he is up to something. Playing a double game. I told you, I have an insider. He's not party to much, but he did hear a heated exchange between Gosling and Joe. Gosling is keeping a dossier on Joe. If Gina plays ball, I think it best to keep Gosling as he is for now. Out of all those you have to deal with, he is the least trustworthy. Carry on with your plan. Knowing about him is enough for now. I have him under surveillance at all times, he can't even take a shit that I don't know about. At this moment, he's at the nick tied up with questioning that poor sod he put in the frame. He has paperwork up to his neck, and there's the added complication of the missing kids. I don't think he will be mobile for the next twenty-four. You have to meet with Jade before then. And, she has to go abroad for a few days, just so that I can report to Gosling that she's complied with his orders. Leave it with me. I'll work it all out.'

*

Jade wasn't what Layla expected. Hard-faced, with bright red hair, cut short and spikey, she had an air about her that intimidated. Layla liked that. Her appearance was immaculate. From her strappy, grey, five inch, Gucci shoes, to her straight cut, grey dress that Layla would guess was by Prada, and was accessorised with an unmistakable, Prada classic vintage leather jacket in cream. Her St Laurent tote was the perfect colour match to her shoes, all blended perfectly with the décor of the Savoy's Gold and grey Beaufort Bar.

Layla had the sense that she was looking at the perfect package for her needs. Though another surprise was in store when Jade stood up. She was tall. Model like skinny, which, with her high cut cheekbones, and cat-like green eyes, had given the first impression, but now that she smiled, her face softened and a striking beauty was revealed.

'You should smile more often. I'm Layla Parrondski.'
'I know. And as for smiling. I have little reason to.
Especially since your bastard of a husband, who I
believe now goes under the name of *Count Rolleski,*
stripped me of millions.'
'How did you know it was him?'
'It was done by all his cronies.'
'You're well informed.'
'Have to be.'
'I take it you want revenge then?'
'That and to get my place back.'
'Let's talk. . . Coffee?'
'Brandy, large.'
Layla stuck with coffee, ordering a Remy Martin for
Jade and a cappuccino for herself from the waiter who
was in immediate attention to them.
The bar was busy. Soft music muted the conversations.
They both attracted glances, but didn't stand out. Layla
wondered which one of the three men sitting on their
own was Jade's shadow.
'What exactly are you offering?'
The directness of the question further pleased Layla. A
relief after her problems with Gina, and getting her
fully on board. 'A chance to get even. And, on top of
that, to become part of an organisation that will run big
time operations. Jaunts like yours, only larger.
Everything my husband has his finger in, in fact.'
'Not the kid thing.'
'No, not that. And a lot of the obvious sleaze will go.
The walk-ups for instance.'
'They're needed and have a part to play. They're also
lucrative and not seasonal. I would keep them. Besides,
a lot of contacts are made through them.'
'Petty ones. I want what my grandfather had back in the
sixties and seventies.'

'Your grandfather was a thug, like the Krays. We've moved on in the last fifty years. Today, you have to be clever. Control in a business-like way. Have a front that's an empire. Like your jewellery business. Expand that. It's been perfect for your husband. It will be so for you.'

Surprised Jade knew of her grandfather, Layla had a prickly feeling that Jade would be hard to handle. She had to get this conversation back in line. Jade was taking the lead. She liked what she said, but needed her to know who was boss. 'That won't be happening. Joe Parrondski, has almost ruined it. I have something else in the pipeline that will be our front. I see you know what there is to know about fashion. I'm building an online empire selling the top designers. I need a buyer. I have acquired a number of disused warehouses along the river in dockland. They came at a price as property developers were my rivals, but they will be our empire. What I can salvage from the jewellery firm will be part of it. The warehouses are being prepared as we speak. My architect is factoring in space for shipments that are not to do with the front business. Lock ups that won't be discovered. Drugs will come in with the shipments of clothes and jewels. I have a source of supply already for that. The web page is being built by the best. You need to go abroad. I want you to source my garments, shoes and accessories, while you seem to be complying with Gosling's orders. Travel to Paris, Italy, Switzerland. I'll give you a budget. Plus, expenses and a salary that won't shame you.'

'Sounds good, but where does the revenge come in? That's the important bit along with getting my place back.'

'If you're in, I'd prefer you as my legit executive for now, you have the right qualities. I plan a much bigger den than what you've lost, with facilities that are out of this world. The Arabs will clamber at the door and even come over out of season to take advantage of what it will offer. It will swallow your old place up. You will head that when it is up and running. That will be your revenge. Take from Joe's set up – not what you've lost, but more.'

'I like the sound of it, but I don't want to be an employee.'

'Partner, then?'

'Partner.'

Layla sat back and sipped her coffee. It gave her a moment to think. This was moving at a much faster pace than she wanted. But, she wanted Jade in. Jade had as many useful contacts as she had. Jade had already run an operation. She offered her hand to Jade. 'Partner it is, but can you match funding? I'm putting ten million in.'

'That's some revenge. I thought you said that the business was going down.'

'I don't talk source of funding. Can you match it?'

'If you think that's what it will take, why don't I take on half of that? Then the budget remains the same.'

Christ! I need to sharpen my thinking. This bitch is a clever business woman. I'm noted for that. I need my edge back. Recent happenings have shaken me. 'Total funding may need to be more. I was starting with ten. I'll agree to your five, but if more is needed, can you get it?'

'To a max of eight. I've a good bit stashed, but I'm not parting with it all. Most is tied up in shares. And, remember, I've just lost millions in property and ongoing business. Just as it was coming up to my busy season.'

'Eight it is. Any more, I put in as a loan to the company. You will bear half of that liability.'

'Done.'

Jade took a large swig of her brandy. 'As regards the Massage Parlour you're planning. I want most say in that. And fifty-fifty ownership. I also don't want that to start to even get into the planning stage until I can come back here.'

A slight annoyance entered Layla, but she had to admit, she liked Jade's style. And, she was coming to the conclusion she needed someone like Jade. 'Agreed in principle, but I have the property and work has begun. I'll get the plans to you and you can have the say on all the interior, but that's all I can offer.'

'So, you were planning to rival me, eh?'

'Something like that, though it was in my source of info that your place would be taken over.'

'Thanks for the warning! Where's your new place?'

'I bought several buildings in the clean part of Soho. They're all Victorian and adjoining. They will make one huge night club, and casino, which will be a front for you know what.'

'I like it.'

'Good. I have a mobile here for you. This is solely for conversations between us. It isn't registered to you, and can be used anywhere that I intend for you to visit. It has my number in it. And, it has my lawyer's number in it. Though, he isn't up to speed yet with everything. So tell him nothing, just take instructions from him. I have someone else sorting my financial dealings. Her name is Marcelle; she is in your phone as Mark. She will be in touch. You will only use this phone to speak to the three of us. We all have a phone that we will only use to speak to you. I would make similar arrangements with anyone you need to contact. Cover your tracks at all times. You are booked on to a plane to Paris, leaving Heathrow on Friday. Have you arranged to shut down your apartment?'

'Yes, it's up for sale and the furniture is going into storage. I have someone taking care of that. By-the-way, I need three seats.'

'Three?'

'I have a kid, and she has a nanny. If you've booked a hotel, then unbook and make sure everywhere we go, I have a suite with a room for them.'

This shocked, Layla. Why wasn't she made aware of this? 'That has to be the world's best kept secret.'

'It is. Her father's an Arab. He must never find out.'

'Tell me about it sometime. In the meantime, everything will be seen to. Any other requests, contact me or my lawyer, Adrian Prindell, or my financier Marcelle Flavendon. There is also a code you need. If this is text to you, don't answer any calls or make any, and don't send any text. The code is simply, 'stop'. On receiving it, destroy the sim and await further instructions. Oh, and never save anything to the phone. If you have to, save it to the sim only. Right, here are the business cards of both Adrian and Marcelle. Memorise the details and destroy the cards. And remember, they don't communicate, or even know of each other, so don't mix them up. Don't give any information about the clothing business to Adrian, or the operation we are planning concerning revenge, to Marcelle. Now, I have to go. Your remit as a Buyer is to stock me with the best. Marcelle will set up bank accounts, and will give you the account number to pay your share into. Credit and debit cards will be ready for you at a bank to be communicated.'

'What's our business called?'

'At the moment everything is being done under a registered company. Belle et Belle.'

'Like it. Let's stick with it. But I want full partnership status. Get the papers drawn up, and we'll meet and sign together. You say where and when. I have a château in the South of France. Could be a good place. No one knows of it.'

'Great. I could do with a break. And as nothing yet is up and running properly, I could take one. I'll arrange it.'

'I like you, Layla.'

Layla smiled and nodded. She wanted the meeting over. 'First impressions of you bode well. This has to work. We have to leave Joe with nothing but his bare feet.'

'You'll get them kids out soon, won't you?'

'On to it. Now, I must go. I'll be in touch.'

The talk of Adrian had put an urgency into her. She had more than Jade's involvement in the planned revenge to discuss with him. Though how she'd say she was to use her, she hadn't worked out yet. Her reluctance to give him the full lowdown of her plans remained.

As she waved goodbye to Jade, and walked towards her car, the urge to have Adrian make love to her increased. The power of the meeting had fuelled the feeling. She pulled out her mobile and dialled Adrian's office. 'Meet me at the hotel.' He didn't object.

10

'What the fuck's going on, Gosling?'
Gosling stared at the blue veins visible in the puffed up neck of his superior. The Chief didn't take lightly to messes like this on his patch.
'A top business man missing. A prostitute fucking murdered, and her mate has vanished. And, on top of that, there's two kids missing without trace. Christ the press is all over this one and we haven't one lead as to the whereabouts of the two adults, no lead on the kids, and a not too tight, suspect for the murder! How the fucking hell did it come about that you were in the bloody same building at the bloody same time as the kids were taken, and the killing took place, and you bloody saw fuck all?'
'It's a big building. Coincidences happen. I was investigating the disappearance of Gina Walters, because I saw a possible link to Parrondski.'
'Coincidences my arse! If you're up to something, tell me now. Christ, this stinks and so do you!'
'I haven't been home for days.'
'There's a fucking shower downstairs . . . What link?
'Parrondski was known to frequent the walk-up she worked in.'
'Aye, and so are you, so what does that tell us, eh?'
'Me and a few others not so far from me.'
The Chief sat down. Gosling had a moment's satisfaction. He had a lot on his, meant-to-be, clean as a whistle, Chief. They'd gone to the same training school many years before. But, Mike Bealver had licked arses and risen quickly up the ranks. There wasn't anything

about him that Gosling didn't know. And he wasn't above using it.

'Look, Gosling. Sort this. Get it out of the way. And bloody quick. I've had that Cleaston snapping at my ankles. He's after rising and quick, and he sees your downfall as his route. He's already up for Sergeant in a couple of weeks. Watch him. Clean this lot up.'

'I've already started. Our suspect for the murder is no longer a suspect. He's confessed.'

'He what? But –'

'He did it. I left him nowhere to go. His DNA is all over the scene.'

Bealver dropped his head into his hands. When he looked up he had a threatening look on his face. 'This had better look kosher, Gosling. I don't want any smart-arsed lawyer tearing your evidence up in court.'

'Patrick Finney has confessed.'

'So you said. But has he given details about how she died.'

'He'll have them. I just need time alone with him. He's in a bad state. Withdrawals. He's saying he did it, but can't remember how.'

'Was everything done to the letter?'

'Everything. You have nothing to worry over. We've got our man. He confessed on tape and in front of his brief.'

'I won't ask how you managed that. But make sure you get all the details soon. If heads roll over this, yours will be going down the hill faster than mine.'

Gosling could have told him it was easy. He had many favours to call in from many diverse people – briefs included. This had been one of them.

Finney had seen there was no way out. And, with a bit of prompting had seemed to come to realise that a nice twenty stretch was better for him than being on the outside where he was lonely and picked on and had urges he couldn't control. In prison, he was amongst his own. Especially with a murder rap. He'd be respected. His drugs, or an equivalent would be supplied. He was a million times better off taking this rap than fighting it. Gosling felt sure that all was sorted and tried to convince the Chief of the same, 'Relax, Chief. Everything concerning the murder is watertight. I'm working on the kid's disappearance, now. I'll find them and bring the bastard responsible to justice. And, Parrondski going missing? Well, I think that will come to light in due course. I –'

A knock on the door interrupted them. 'Come in, and it had better be urgent!'

Cleaston walked in. His look of contempt angered Gosling. 'What do you want you jumped up arse creeper?'

Cleaston ignored him. 'Chief, Gina Walters has just walked into the station. She's with a WPC at the moment. She's distraught. It seems she has been with a punter. She's saying that he drugged her and knocked her about. She's only just heard what's happened to hers and her mate's kid and that her mate's dead.'

Gosling had to stop his jaw from dropping. *Christ, what was Gina up to?'*

'She wants to see you, Sarg.'

How anyone could put so much contempt into saying six words Gosling didn't know.

'Well, thank Satan for that. One of the baddies has turned up. Go carefully with her, Gosling, she could be telling the truth. I mean, why should she suddenly turn up after being missing for three days? You can't plan that.'

Huh! Why indeed? What the fuck was going on?
Pushing past Cleaston, Gosling moved faster than he
had in a long time.
'Gosling, have someone in the room with you. That's
an order!'
'I'll go with him, Sir.'
Gosling could have smashed the Chief and Cleaston in
the face. Rage had him almost to the point where he
thought he would. But on the walk down two flights of
stairs he managed to calm himself.
'Gina. Gina Walters. Well, well. Been letting somebody
straddle you while your kid gets taken and your friend
is murdered, have you?'
'Piss off, Gosling.'
'Oh, very nice. But that's for the likes of you, leaving
your kid for two days. Out of your face, and then
suddenly caring where she is and what's happened to
her.'
The look in Gina's eyes took him aback for a moment.
He gave her a warning one back. But, he still didn't
have an inkling why she was here and what this was all
about. He looked over at Cleaston.
Cleaston took the soft approach. 'We understand what a
shock all of this has been to you.' He turned to the
WPC, a cute little thing – whatever happened to the rule
of having to be over five foot six – anti discrimination
gone mad in his book. What could this dainty, sex in a
uniform, do against the thugs they came across? Give
them a stiffy and that's about all.
'Would you please get a cup of tea and some tissues for
Gina?'
The WPC glared at Cleaston as he said this. Her face
reddened. Gosling was surprised she didn't tell
Cleaston to fuck off and get it himself. Didn't he know

these little girls were really tyrants and as feminist as they came?

The stand-off lasted a few seconds and ended satisfactorily with the WPC asking if Cleaston would step outside a moment. A brilliant opportunity. Leaning forward, Gosling growled, 'what's your game, Gina? What're you up to?'

'I'm up to nothing. I didn't want to come in here and bawl you out or make accusations, but neither did I want to be hunted down. I want me kid back and I want to get back to normal. Well, as normal as I can now Zoe's gone. I figure if I help you, you will help me.'

'And how can I help you?'

'Get me kid back, how else?'

'I actually can do more than that. I can get you a new life with your kid. A life of luxury.'

The door opened. Cleaston walked in with the tea and tissues. 'The feminist kicked you into to touch did she?' Cleaston reddened, but didn't retaliate. Gosling could tell he was rankled. But he still had his kid gloves in place where Gina was concerned. 'There, get that down you. Now, can you tell us anything helpful? Has one of your punters made approaches to you about your kid?'

'No! And if he had done, I'd have kicked his balls in. Look, just find me kid. Ple-ease!'

Gosling admired Gina. Thought he'd put her up for an Oscar.

'We are doing all we can, but we need help. Anything at all, no matter how insignificant.'

'I know nothing. I've not been approached about me kid, and neither to my knowledge had Zoe. Yes, we're working girls – at least, Zoe, was. But, I still am. I know that's against the law, but I don't deserve this. I want me kid! I want her . . .'

'Try to keep calm. I can assure you that we're doing our best. The CCTV has shown a woman taking the children. We would like you to look at it. See if you can recognize her.'

Gosling nodded at Gina. Conveying to her that she should agree to Cleaston's suggestion. She went with it, 'Anything. Anything at all, if I can help.'

The disc clicked into place. An image flickered across the laptop screen. Gina went into a fit of sobbing, calling out, 'Amy, my baby. Amy.' Her body collapsed into a heap on the table, sobs heaved her chest.

'I'm sorry, I had to show you.'

Gosling cut in. 'Who is that, Gina. You know, don't you? Stop this play acting and tell us.'

Gina lifted her head. Her eyes bore into his. 'I could say things but I won't. I could say that I hate you, but I won't. I need you. I need your help.'

Gosling coughed. Cleaston looked triumphant. 'You can say anything you want. Don't be afraid, no individual here has the power to intimidate you.'

During the silence that followed this, a trickle of cold sweat found its way down Gosling's back.

Gina sat staring at him as if she was trying to make up her mind. He cursed himself. *Christ, if she utters one word!*

'I don't have anything more to add. I have told you all I know. The woman is a stranger to me. All of this is a mystery. Why would anyone take two little girls? Was it to do with the man you're holding for questioning?'

'No. That is a completely different angle to this whole thing, and though happened simultaneously, the two are not connected. I'm sorry, Gina.'

Gosling cut in: 'I think she's had enough. I'll get you driven home, Gina. If there's anything else we find out, or need you for, we will contact you.'

'There's just one more question I would like to ask.'
Cleaston paused, looked over at Gosling. Another
droplet of sweat traced the same path down Gosling's
back. Cleaston asked, 'What do you know of Patrick
Finney?'

'That pervert! I don't trust him. He was always leering
at me and Zoe. He's a creep. You don't think it was
him, do you? Oh God, please don't say it was him.'
Gosling relaxed. He couldn't have wished for a better
answer if he'd rehearsed Gina.

Cleaston leaned back. 'I don't suppose it will hurt to
tell you, but Finney has been charged with Zoe
Feldon's murder.'

'The Bastard. The slimy creep. We were always afraid
of him. He'd lurk in the stairwell, and once we caught
him taking pictures of us. Christ, you should have
thrown away the key when he went down for them
rapes.'

Cleaston closed his notebook. 'Thank you, Gina. No
doubt if this goes to trial, you will be called as a
witness. Can you let us know at all times if you change
your address?'

'I'd gladly testify. That creep wants stringing up by his
balls.'

'We'll get you a cab. Will you be alright going to your
home?'

Gina nodded.

'I'll take her. I'm off duty now and it's not out of my
way. Come on Gina. Let's get you safely home.'
Though she rose willingly enough, she shrugged
Goslings arm off her when he went to assist her. He had
an inkling she knew exactly what had taken place and
this made her dangerous to him. He needed to deliver
her to Parrondski, or Rolleski, whatever his bloody
name was now, but for two pins, he could snuff her out.

95

Once in his car he told her exactly what he thought. 'No more games. You know don't you? And what I want to know is, how you know. I'm to take you to Parrondski, or, as you will find out, Count Rolleski, as he is now, but I can just as soon dump your body in the Thames. Who helped you get away from Epping?'

'No one. I crawled into the forest. Spent the night there, then made it to the main road the next day where I got a lift.'

'In the state you were in? You're lying. I want the truth. Someone found you who is working against me. Who was it and who are they working with?'

'I don't know what you're talking about. It is as I said. Only, the bloke I got a lift with, wanted something for his trouble. He lived Clapham way. He took me to his flat, and as if I weren't in enough of a state, he drugged me. Every time I came round he raped me and drugged me again. I got away in the early hours of this morning when he was out for the count. I walked the streets, then managed to find a cabby who took pity on me. He brought me to the cop station. And that's the truth.'

Gosling thought it through, but couldn't shift the idea that she knew exactly what was going on, where her kid was, and for some reason wanted to go to Joe. 'We'll have the cabby on our cameras, he'll be easy to trace. If he ever existed.'

'He did. And, I hope you do find him, you ungrateful, sod. I could have squealed in there, but I didn't.'

'Why didn't you? What hidden agenda have you got?'

'None. Look. I reckon you know more about me kid than you're saying. So I thought, if I help you, you will help me. Where is she, where's my Amy?'

'You will see her sooner than you think. Like I say, Joe wants you. I have to take you to him. Only he's not

96

well. And I find it strange that you're not questioning going to him.'

'I'm not in a position to question anything. You know, that I know that Joe isn't missing. I heard him when you shoved me in that room, you bastard! Anyroad, I saw you drive off in his car, so you must have planted it outside that shop of his.'

The bitch didn't know it, but she was digging her own grave – literally. She knew too much. For now, though, he'd have to take her to Joe.

'Am I to go missing again, then?'

'No. You can report into the station. Tell them that you're going to stay with an uncle, but don't want to give your address. Tell them that you'll ring again and give them a way of contacting you. Tell them you're scared shitless, and don't want to be found by the heavies at the walk-up. Our lot will be able to trace you, but won't bother. You're not a suspect, just a possible witness if that scumbag pleads not guilty.'

'I thought you said he'd confessed?'

'Just shut your mouth and listen.' He told her about Joe's operation. Still convinced he didn't have to. *Christ, I could knock the fucking whore to kingdom come.* The thought gave him a stiffy. He ignored it. He had to. Parrondski was a force to be reckoned with. One day he wouldn't be, then he'd take all he wanted from Gina. He might even fuck her. Though the thought repulsed him, it had it's merits. That way there'd be no marks on her, and yet, he would have dominated her. This increased his stiffy. It now uncomfortably pushed against the restrictions of his trousers. But no. He wouldn't be able to do it in the state she was in.

'We'll go to your flat first. You can get some stuff. Clean yourself up.'

Gina didn't reply.

Stamford Street was minutes away. Nothing would be amiss with him taking her there. He was expected to take her home.

Once inside he grabbed her and marched her to the bathroom. Ripping her clothes off her, he shoved her under the shower and turned on the tap.

Gina didn't utter a word.

'I can't hurt you, but I'm going to fuck you.'

'What, *you*? Put your precious dick in a whore? Ha. Never thought you would do that.'

'Shut up and douse yourself, go on, clean it. I haven't got much time.'

'Ha, that's well known. And a blessing. The one thing we all say about you is that you're a premature ejaculator. We reckon that's the truth of you never fucking us. You come before you can.'

Gosling raised his hand, but hesitated. *Christ, if I do that, I'll come.* He didn't want to prove her right, but neither could he explain why. He wanted more than anything to stick himself up Gina. Maybe having the last laugh over Parrondski was part of it. But he had to do it.

Watching her writhe about under the water and then soap herself, he could contain himself no longer. Removing his trousers, he grabbed her, and dragged her to her bedroom and flung her on the bed.

She lifted her knee, but he was ready for her. Grabbing it, he forced it down. In one movement, he was between her legs. She spat in his face. He left the wet slime to run down his cheek. He had one intent now. It would be like a victory over Parrondski, he had to achieve it. The urge to cum was getting too strong. Mounting her he sank deep into her. His orgasm shook his body.

Slumping down, he was incensed to hear her giggling. But his shame was too much to cope with and stopped him punishing her how he'd like to. A picture of his Sara came into his mind. He'd betrayed her. *Sara, oh, Sara, I'm sorry.* A tear found its way down his cheek. Gina rolled away from him. 'You disgust me!' The disdain in her voice angered him even more. But still he resisted hitting her.

He'd made it inside her, hadn't he? Parrondski fucking Rolleski, wouldn't like that would he?

'Get dressed, dirt bag. I'm going to leave now. You leave ten minutes after me. Catch the underground to Piccadilly, then get the blue line to Southgate. Turn right out of the station and walk along the High Street. Just keep walking. When you get out to the tree-lined area, you'll be picked up and taken to Joe.

As he went down the steps, he took a deep breath. If he could do it once, he could do it again. Sara need never find out. It would take nothing from her. This was different. Feeling his conscience ease, his mood lifted. From now on, he wouldn't be hurting Gina Walters, he'd be fucking her. What it was about her that had got to him, he didn't know. But Rolleski wasn't going to have her to himself. No way.

11

Gina was shocked to see the state that Joe was in.
Bandages covered his face and hands, and a drip hung
above him feeding blood into his arm. His eyes were
closed.

'Joe, it's me. Joe?'

His eyes flickered then opened. 'Joe, I'm here. Where's
me kid, Joe? What have you done with me kid?'

The eyes she'd always thought of as pools of evil filled
with tears touching the soft part of her that she had for
this man. He'd ruined her life, used her as and when
he'd wanted to, and now he'd done the ultimate in
taking her child for his own foul intent, but there was a
part of her that loved him. Seeing him like this had
given her that truth.

'Let me see her, Joe. Please, let me see her and
Tammy.'

Joe nodded. A hand gripped her arm. 'This way.'

Bragdon, the man she feared even more than Gosling
and Joe, was indicating that she should follow him.
Blowing a kiss to Joe, she went with Bragdon.

Everywhere he took her, upstairs and along corridors,
showed dilapidation, or was under reconstruction. Dust
clung to her. Hammer drills that she hadn't been able to
hear in the basement rattled her teeth.

'Through here.'

He unlocked a padded door. Going through it was like
going from a hell hole to heaven. The peaceful room
beyond was all decorated in pink. A row of beds neatly
made, were draped with pink lace canopies and
bedspreads. Each had a teddy bear sitting on them.
Standing on the pink bedside tables was a heart-shaped

picture frame with a photo of a good looking man with a floppy haircut and a boyish grin on his face. Gina's heart pounded. Her stomach churned.

At the other end of room, they passed a bathroom. Through the open door she could see a row of sinks. Above these a shelf holding Boots' luxury range of baby care products by Tiddly Tom.

The bile reached Gina's throat. It was all so beautiful and yet, held sick connotations. Too afraid to say anything she held her breath as another padded door was opened and children's laughter came to her.

'She's in there.' The indication was towards a door with a mirror set into it. 'You can see them, and hear them, but they can't see or hear you.'

Trembling now, Gina stepped forward. Her breath caught painfully in her lungs as the scene inside, what looked like a playroom, revealed itself to her.

'Christ. Open this fucking door!'

'No can do. Filming is in progress. You watch or you don't, but nothing is to interrupt it.'

Gina's world closed in on her. A feeling of utter hopelessness descended on her. She couldn't help her darling Amy, or Tammy or the other little girl. She couldn't stop the depravity that was happening. And yet, she couldn't stop watching the so-called 'play' going on.

Sobbing out her pain, Gina knew only one small thanks, that the man wasn't trying to penetrate any of the children and though what he did was wrong and depraved, the children hadn't been distressed. It had all been a game to their innocent little minds. Watching had been the worst thing she'd ever experienced.

She turned from the door and vomited.

'You, dirty bitch. There's a mop and bucket in a cupboard in the kid's bedroom. Clean it up.'

Wiping her mouth with her hand, Gina attacked him. 'Dirty bitch! You dare to call me a dirty bitch. You depraved monster! How can you allow this?'

'It ain't down to me. And if it's worth anything, I don't like it. But, I'm not paid to like what goes on, am I?'

Seizing on this revelation Gina told him, 'I know someone who'd pay you double what you get in one year, to help me get these kids out.'

'Ha! That'll be the day. You're a scumbag prossie, How're you going to find that kind of money?'

'I can. And, not only that. I could see to it that you disappear. You could live the good life where no one could trace you.'

Knowing she was putting her life on the line, Gina prayed he'd listen to her and not report her. His face went through many expressions, the last one made her heart sink. It told of his disbelief and contempt. 'Clean that up, it stinks, just like you do, you lying bitch. We'll see what Gosling has to say about this, shall we?'

'No. Please. Don't tell anyone, please! Think about it. It's true. I'm telling you. Besides, you don't know Gosling, not really know him. He'll shop you as soon as look at you. You can't trust him. I *can* do as I've said, but you have to keep it to yourself, or we'll both be dead meat.'

Again Bragdon hesitated. After a moment he said. 'I won't tell, if you can give me proof. One thousand smackers by the end of the week. If that amount is in the shed by next Friday – the one painted green that stands on the edge of the estate, I'm in. But it won't stop the operation. The Count likes it, and he likes the money it's bringing in, so more kids will replace these. Gosling will see to that.'

'It'll be there. And as for other kids, we'll deal with that when it happens.'

103

'So, how do yer reckon you can get this lot out? I ain't taking any chances even if I agree to help.'
'I don't know. Someone who can handle this sort of thing will. You'll get your instruction of what to do and when.'
Looking up towards the mirror, Bragdon yelled.
'They're packing up in there. Get that fucking bucket will yer!'
Gina did as he said and was just drying the patch on the wooden floor with paper hand towels that she'd brought through from the bathroom, when the door opened. The kids came dancing through shouting, 'bye, daddy.'
"Daddy" laughed as he called out, 'bye, my precious ones, see you tomorrow. Be good girls for nanny.'
'Yes, daddy,' was the chorused answer. Then a squeal of what sounded half delight and half disappointment came from Amy as she saw Gina. 'Mummy?'
'Oh, my darling.' Dropping the soggy paper, Gina scooped Amy up into her arms. Tammy clung to her leg, 'Aunty Gina, Aunty Gina, where's my mummy?'
Scooping Tammy up too, Gina held them close.
'Don't cry, Mummy. We've been happy. That lady brought us here and we've got this nice daddy who takes care of us and plays with us. He does funny things with us.'
Gina held them as if she would never let them go. Her sobs uncontrollably shaking her body. Her thoughts screamed their innocence to her. Guilt entered her as she knew, that deprived of a daddy figure, her little Amy had accepted as 'normal' what this man, under the guise of being the daddy she'd longed for, had done to her.

'What's going on?'
The voice of the "daddy".

104

Through gritted teeth Gina snarled, 'You bastard.'

'No, daddy's nice, Mummy. Daddy –'

'He's not nice, Amy. No, nice daddy would do what he's done to you. He's not nice.'

Amy wailed at her. 'He is, Mummy, he is!' Tammy's wail matched Amy's and was joined by the other little girl. All three were screaming now.

As the door started to close on the man his sarcastic comment of, 'I think it's mummy who isn't nice.' Grated on her. But what he said as he finally closed the door 'I hope you kept those cameras rolling. That was a great closing scene.' shook Gina to the core.

'Come on, my darlings, come on. Rocking them back and forth, Gina managed to quieten them.'

As she looked at Bragdon she felt heartened. The look on his face was one that told of the scene having sickened him. As he turned away he muttered, 'get that grand.'

Unsure what to do, Gina held on to the two girls while trying to soothe the third. 'Mummy's here now, everything will be okay.'

'Who are you?'

The words were demanded in a heavily accented voice. A stern faced, square-looking woman stood in front of Gina. Her jowls hung each side of her mouth, her beady eyes seemed barely open as they glared out of fleshy sockets. Her dumpy body was clad in a kind of old-fashioned nurse's uniform.

'She's my mummy, Nanny.'

The woman's mouth dropped open. A glint of fear showed in her eyes. Gina could have clawed her to death, but as Amy spoke fondly to the woman she allowed common sense to keep her in check. These kids had been through enough.

'I've come to help with the children. I'll bath them. Then we can talk.'

'How did you get here? I don't think you should do anything with the children. I'll have to see the boss.'

'I found my own way here. That minder bloke came across me and was trying to get me away when the door opened. Anyway, if by the boss, you mean the Count, you know he isn't well. I am his mistress, and he has brought me here, so you can do as I tell you. Now, what is the children's routine?'

All of this belied how Gina was feeling, but Layla had told her that she must stay in control of her emotions at all times. She hadn't managed that so far, and had probably made the biggest mistake in her life in trying to get Bragdon on her side, but from now on she would play this how Layla had told her to. She had to play her part. Layla would get this sorted.

12

Layla cursed when her front door swung open. 'For
fuck's sake!'

'This is why I insisted on coming with you. You should
have let me get a cleaning firm in.'

'Oh, Adrian. Look at it. Oh, God.' The hallway doors
of her lovely Holland Park home were covered in black
dust, as was the wrought iron balustrade, and the
beautiful, deep pile, gold, pure wool carpet looked
filthy as footprints marked where the cops had trodden
all over it.

'It gets worse.'

'I can't bear it. I'm going to complain. What were they
looking for?'

'Look, Gosling's lot had a field day. He's a bastard,
but, don't let him have the last laugh. Keep your
dignity. Let's close the door on it and I'll arrange for it
to be all put back as it was.'

'No. It all has to go. This was my life. I have a new one
now. All I want are my photographs and papers. You
have most of my stuff at your office. But I have letters
and mementos here. Burn anything that relates to Joe,
except papers relating to the business and any
memorabilia a doting wife might keep. Burn all my
clothes. Sell my jewellery. I'll go shopping for new
outfits and shoes etc. I'll have this placed stripped and
redecorated and refurnished. Get James Wood, the
designer, to ring me. He's up and coming, he designed
one of my friend's homes and it is beautiful. I'll start
from scratch.'

'You will have to go through these things yourself, no
one can make those decisions for you. Besides, you're

acting on a knee jerk reaction. The stuff is worth a fortune, your jewels, your clothes; the furniture.'
'Okay. Let's get all the papers now, and my jewellery. I'll ring my housekeeper, she'll pack my clothes up and send them to charity shops. Then we'll get a firm of cleaning contractors in. After that, contact an auctioneer.'
Will you stay at mine while all this is being done?'
'No. book me a suite at The Ritz.'
'Layla. . . Layla.'
There was something in his voice that had her turning towards him. His chocolate eyes smouldered. An instant reaction set up in the pit of her stomach.
'There's something about you when you take command.' His body was close to hers. Her longing increased. This man was like a drug to her.
Her, 'Not here.' Hardly made it past her dry throat.
'Mine then?'
The thought of his beautiful penthouse overlooking the Thames excited her for a moment, but then came the feeling that she'd had when she was last there – the thought of the many females that had been there before her, and she hadn't liked that. Back in control, she refused.
'I have to get things sorted. I only have a couple of outfits that haven't been tainted by this intrusion. I need to book an appointment with a personal shopper at Harrods and a couple more shops in Mayfair. And, I need to check into my office and catch up on a couple of things. The managers of two of the outlets have been leaving messages. Just get me booked into that suite.'
'I'm not your personal assistant, I'm your lawyer. And, lover. I'll do this for you this time, but we need to sort you out a PA.'

'No. I don't know who I can trust. Just help me till I find my feet, please.'

'Okay, but dinner tonight and I'm staying in your suite with you. No arguments.'

Layla nodded. Taking a deep breath, she went towards her, once loved office, come den. 'Let's do this.'

Adrian put in a call to the Ritz. *Fully booked. Shit.*

'I know of a penthouse that is let on short term. I think it will suit you.'

'I haven't time to cook meals etc.'

'It comes with a full complement of staff. You've nothing to worry over.'

'Staff have ears. Phones in private buildings can be monitored. I want privacy.'

'It's the beginning of the Arab season. It will be impossible to get you a suite in any hotel within miles of London. Take the penthouse, or stay with me. Two choices.'

'The Penthouse.'

With sealed boxes of papers and photographs in a taxi on their way to Adrian's office, and the jewellery taken from her safe and sent on its way to her deposit box at her bank, Layla put a couple of calls in. She sighed with relief when she managed to book a personal shopper at Harrods for around three pm.

She'd shut down her emotions as she'd worked. Not allowing Adrian's closeness, or the terrible destruction of her beloved home to distract her. There was so much that she had to see to.

A text message pinged into the mobile that was exclusive to Gina. *We have to get moving on the operation we are shutting down. I have inside help. Need a grand planting as down payment. Will let your D know where. Gina x*

A wave of nerves clutched her. Who was this bloody insider? God! Gina was like a loose cannon. If this went tits up!

Her fingers clicked a quick reply: *Contact D to check him/her out first. Money will be with him tomorrow.*

In her office, Layla called one of the managers who had been braying for attention. Nothing amiss, other than a congratulations needed for the best sales this year!

Other calls revealed the same. It seemed even the rich liked a scandal.

Her last call was to her own personal baby in the chain. Her Mayfair outlet. The manager there was one of the braying managers wanting attention. 'Hi, Hal, what's to do?'

'A shipment of gold is awaiting collection from the dock. We have no idea where the assignment has come from. We had a communication from the Lesley, Forrage and Dyston Warehouse, saying they have the shipment and when can it be collected or delivered. It's only insured their end for another two days.'

Layla's back straightened. Hal managed the only outlet that housed a Jewellery Designer and Goldsmith. Jewellery was made to order there to a client's own specification. This was the one shop she planned on keeping, though it was draining the business. Mayfair leases and taxes were crippling. Mostly, she was the only one who did the ordering. Sourcing the best she could price-wise from Quarter Bullion. She hadn't ordered this. 'Is there no indication where it's from?'

'Well, I didn't ask, but they didn't say, either.'

'Right. Leave it with me. I'll check with my agent; he should know who ordered this. Have you checked that Roland hasn't?' Roland was her designer and very much a closed book. He wasn't allowed to order the precious metal, or stones he needed, but with her out of action for a few days he may have needed an urgent order.

'Yes. He is adamant that he hasn't. He says we have enough in stock and he would rather run out than do something like that without your permission.'

The stock they had was kept by Quarter Bullion in their secure vaults until needed. The last time she checked there was plenty for the orders in hand. Saying goodbye to Hal and batting off his attempts to give her sympathy on Joe's disappearance, she immediately put a call through to her agent. No orders had gone through him. Sinking down in her chair she swivelled back and forth. Almost without registering, her fingers dialled a number.

'Adrian Prindell speaking.'

'Adrian, I'm worried. I can't talk over the phone. Come to my office.'

'Oh, and drop everything? Layla, you are not my sole client!'

'How much would it take to make it that way?'

'More than you can afford.'

'I haven't been straight with you. I've fifteen times the amount you think I have.'

'Christ. Exclusivity is yours. But, it will take some arranging. I'll see you tonight.'

'No. Now. It has to be now. I think Joe might have left me a goodbye present. One that could put me behind bars.'

'Shit! I'll be there in fifteen.'

A call to the warehouse revealed the shipment had come in by van. It had no company name on the box. The delivery man said it was precious metals and needed putting in a vault. There was a paper that had to be signed for it. Looking at the copy of this the manager of the warehouse told her it was from a Mr Harris. The order was in the name of Layla Parrondski.

Layla instructed him to open and check the assignment. 'It's thirty ounces according to the paperwork.'

'Thank you. Store it in your vault, I'll be in touch.'

The phone dropped out of Layla's hand. That was a whole gold bar, worth around a hundred grand! Harris was a code name for someone who Joe dealt with. She'd seen it in the portfolio from which she'd first discovered Joe's *other* dealings. Fear tightened her chest. Her D had told her that Harris was also the code name for the head of a gang that had perpetrated the gold bullion robbery from Heathrow airport. He was never apprehended. And neither was most of the bullion.

'D' had said Harris now lived in Brazil. *How the hell did Joe manage this*? How the hell was she going to get out of it?

*

Adrian paced up and down. 'The order must have a return address. Tell the warehouse to return it as not needed.'

'There is no return address. Everything, the copy of the order and the invoice, which is marked as paid, is in my name.'

'Right. We'll collect it and dump it. It's the only answer.'

The phone rang.

'Detective Sergeant Gosling here. We've had a phone call from the owner of Lesley, Forrage and Dyston warehouse. His manager has reported what looks like a dodgy shipment ordered by you. I'm about to get my officers to look further into this. I might need you to come to the station to explain.'

The word, 'Gosling' would hardly come from her lips as she passed the phone to Adrian.

'Prindell here, what's this about, Gosling.'

'It's about one million, or ten years. Meet me down at the docks. There's a bar just around the corner from Lesley, Forrage and Dyston warehouse.'

'We'll be there.'

Adrian called at his office on the way. Layla didn't go in. She couldn't face anyone. It was all she could do to keep from being sick.

Her mind was made up. They needed Gosling on board, but could they trust him? Adrian thought not.

It surprised her when Adrian said a taxi would be picking them up. Within seconds of Adrian helping her out of his car, their regular pulled up. Layla greeted the driver, and for the first time in over an hour began to feel safe.

Adrian dialled a number. His words were short. 'All set?' Whether he got an answer, Layla didn't know. He shut his phone off almost immediately.

*

Gosling sat in the corner of the scruffy bar. The stench of stale beer mixed with that of urine coming from the open door of the toilets, wrinkled Layla's nose.

'You shouldn't have brought her. She stands out like a cock in a whore house.'

'I don't do deals without my client. What's going on?'

One of a group sitting in the opposite corner, from where a distinct smell of stale fish came, gave a low whistle.

'Let's get out of here.'

Gosling nodded at this from Adrian.

The taxi was waiting. 'Just drive us around,' Adrian instructed before turning to Gosling, 'Well?'

'This is a set up. That shipment is stolen gold.'

'We know. Who else knows?'

'No one. It was a ploy of mine to get you here by telling you the lie that the warehouse manager had reported it. I happen to know that he has been paid to do so the moment the assignment was delivered and accepted.'

'You've done well to get that far in your investigation! But where do you think my client can get her hands on a million?

'Don't give me that. I know and you know that the million won't pose a problem. Oh, and on top of that I need a hundred grand for the manager. Then the gold gets taken into your stock. Its worth will compensate for the manager's silence money. After that, nothing more will happen. I'll tell the boss, and I know that you know full well who that is, that the manager welched on the deal and disappeared. The gold was delivered to his wife, but there's nothing we could do without it being reported. He won't be about to report it missing, so you're home and dry.'

'I have to make a call.'

Layla waited. Saw the anxious look on Gosling's face. Adrian spoke into his phone. 'Call it off. Speak soon.' To Gosling he said, 'This is Layla's shout, but my advice is take it.'

'I'll take it. Once the gold is delivered and a week with no hassle has passed, Adrian will contact you and arrange the deal. In the meantime, Adrian will deliver enough funds to pay the manager off. I will ring and ask for him in a couple of days and I expect to be told that he left suddenly.'

They'd come back round to the pub. Gosling got out.

'You don't fool me Prindell. And, I would advise you not to mess with me.'

'Ditto.'

Gosling slipped in the back way of the pub.

'What did he mean? And, what was all the phoning about?'

Squeezing her hand, Adrian leant towards her. 'I can't wait for tonight. I'll drop you at Harrods, you're late. Ring me when you're ready. I'll take you to your new home.'

A cold shiver went down Layla's spine. There was a power about Adrian that she liked, but she didn't like not being in the know, or the way that he took decisions without consulting her. 'Adrian, I asked you a question. I want to know the answer. If this is going to work with me and you, there has to be no secrets.'

'My phone calls were to Frankie Droile. He was waiting around the corner. If Gosling hadn't made the right noises he was history. Still might be, we'll have to see how this pans out. His aside to me was letting me know that he knew my game. I'll have to be more careful.'

Annoyed she turned on him.

He stopped her before she could speak. 'If this is going to work with you and me, you have to let me take decisions. I was ready, you weren't. You need me.'

She swallowed her anger. Adrian was full of surprises. His little black book was full of her dad's contacts. She was glad he could be that ruthless. He was right. She needed him.

13

Gosling smiled when he heard that the call had come in for an incident code and that he'd been left off the list of detectives called together to form a major incident investigation. A charred body had been found by a man out walking his dog. The body was in a sack dumped near the edge of the river Thames and only just inside their patch.

After only being newly appointed for one day, Detective Sergeant Cleaston had been on duty when the call had come in. Gosling knew it would be all systems go. The paperwork would mount, and there'd be sod-all at the end of it, except an ID of Parrondski.

No murderer would ever be found, no motive, and Layla would have to wait months, maybe years, before she could have a funeral as the remains languished in the morgue. *Ha! You'll be cold there you scumbag door-sleeper!*

His mind went to Layla, and he wondered what type of merry widow she would make. Already having a field day, fucking Adrian Prindell, it would just get better for her.

Or, so she thought. But, there was no chance to play the merry widow behind bars! Ha, life was good. All I have to do is figure out a way of taking over operations set up by Count Bollocks and life will be very rosy indeed.

Five days later the million was delivered. Deposited in a safe box in a bank in Gosling's chosen name. One that couldn't be traced to him. The necessary forged papers to allow him to access it, were delivered soon after. Once he'd visited it, he phoned the ex-manager of Lesley, Forrage and Dyston. A few threats had the

117

outcome he wanted. A call was put into the police station.

On the same day the charred body was identified as being that of Joe Parrondski.

Layla looked at the cocky, ginger-haired, pimply-faced detective as if he'd gone mad. He'd introduced himself as Detective Cleaston, and had then asked her to confirm who she was. At her nodding to his stating her name, he'd told her that her husband was dead, and that she was under investigation for dealing in stolen gold! 'What are you talking about? M – my husband, DEAD! No . . . no! When . . . How?' The shock prevented her mind from sorting out what had happened.

'I'm very sorry, but a body was found a few days ago. It was badly burned. Identification has only just been possible through his teeth and some hair that had survived.'

'Is – is that how he died, by fire?'

'No. We think he was killed and then burned to try to disguise who it was. We are waiting on the how. Now, about this other matter –'

'You, Callous Pig! I want my lawyer. I want him NOW!' Panic took all reasoning from her. How was this happening? Joe dead! The gold reported! It can't be . . . *Shit! Shit, shit, shit!*

'We will ring your lawyer for you. We'll get him to meet us at the station. I'm sorry, but I have to ask you to accompany me and to answer some questions. We have already cordoned off all of your premises and searches are in progress for the gold. Your office is being searched as we speak, and there's a team waiting to start in here, and in your Holland Park house. Have you any other residences?'

118

With her head reeling, and nothing making sense, Layla told him of her country cottage. They knew about it anyway and had searched it before. Though this green-behind-the-ears, didn't seem to have heard of it. She left out any information about her mother's house, which had, on paper only, been sold to a French Family and couldn't be traced to her.

'If you fuck any of my places up like you did my house, I'll sue you to Kingdom come!'

'Look, I'm not Gosling. I have no history with you. Now, you can do this screaming and ranting, or you can come with us with your dignity intact. The press is already on to the identity of the body, and are waiting outside the cop station for a statement. Don't give them cause for speculation when we arrive.'

'A cop with a heart, eh? It doesn't wash. You're all the same, you're all bent bastards.'

'I take exception to that. Very few of us are bent. I certainly am not.'

The prick looks as though he's only been two minutes out of school. Gathering her jacket from where she'd slung it across the back of the sofa, she still couldn't get her head around Joe being dead. She never thought that his demise would affect her in any way, but it was doing. Her whole body was trembling with the shock of it. But she had to calm herself and deal with the terrifying situation of the cops knowing of the gold!

A sudden thought came to her. *Christ, my mobiles!* She had deleted all messages, as and when they'd come in from Jade and Gina, and the phones were basic and old, but would they be able to get the data anyway? She doubted that they could get locations, there was no GPS on them as internet hadn't been invented for such devices when these had been made. She relaxed a little. 'I need my bag from my room.'

119

'I'll come with you.'

'Got a fetish about women's bedrooms, have you?'

'Cut the crap. You're in deep shit. You don't need to antagonize the investigation officer. And, I'm sure, with a family like yours, you know the procedure.'

'Hit me in the gut when I'm down, why don't you? I left my family in my past a long time ago. Anyway, where's Gosling? I thought he was the one that was investigating anything to do with my husband's disappearance?'

'The body was found on my watch, so you've got me. I have access to everything that has been done before.'

By the time they reached the station, fear had mixed with her shock and the reality of her situation had her in tears. The press stepped back a little, showing a respect they'd never shown her before. The tears had worked. The Rottweiler was there. Layla could see she wasn't taken in, but she gave some space as she whispered, 'My story getting bigger, Layla?'

Layla nodded at her.

In the same room where she'd been questioned by Gosling, Layla paced up and down. Adrian seemed to take an age to arrive. When he did he looked composed and calm. 'Can I have a few moments with my client, Sergeant? You must understand that she has suffered a tremendous shock and may not be in a fit state to answer your questions.'

'Two minutes.'

'Cold Bastard!'

'That won't help, Layla. Right. As I understand it –'

Listening to Adrian spell it all out again, Layla felt as though she would be sick. With his voice low, he told her. 'One – We know Parrondski isn't dead. I don't know how he has managed this, but that is a lie. That body probably belongs to some drop-out who won't be missed and whose DNA has been tampered with. And, two – they can't be certain the gold is stolen. Though they would have checked legit outlets and found that there isn't an assignment that big that is registered as coming to you. Anyway, they will have to find the gold first. And, that won't happen.'

'Are you sure?'

'Certain. I deposited it into various bank vaults, using different names. It will take a hell of a lot of tracking down. Now, continue to act upset, and keep saying that you did get a parcel, but it didn't contain gold. It only had bits of brick in it, which you threw away. You tried to ring the manager – that can be verified as you put a call in to check he'd left. When you found he was no longer there, you just let it go. You hadn't ordered it. It hadn't been delivered. There was no payment to make as the shipment said it had been paid for, so you didn't do anything else about it.'

'What about the searches, and my mobiles?'

'They won't find anything. Christ, those mobiles must have come from the Victoria and Albert Museum, where did you get them?'

'From Ebay.'

'Right, tell them you have an interest in old phones and are beginning a collection. Tell them you liked to use them, but that you hadn't yet, and if they ask about the numbers in them, tell them that they must have already been there. And, don't worry. I've already text the code to Gina and Jade. They won't answer their phones, and should destroy them before they can be rung. As per instructions.'

'Thanks, Adrian . . . Adrian a, Marcelle Flavendon, of Flavendon Finance Brokers has one. She knows who you are. Contact her, just say: 'The flavour of the month is Flavendon's.'

'What? This isn't a Bond film and you're not 007! What the fuck's going on . . . Is this to do with Jade being in Paris? Christ, Layla. You'd better come clean with me. How can I protect you when –'

'Right, I think that is time enough. I need to begin the questioning.' The pimply face said, as he came back into the room. His voice arrogant and cocksure, 'I have to warn you that we have the right to lock your client up for 24 while we carry out investigations, therefore you might be wise to advise her to come clean. We can get her in court tomorrow to face charges, and you can apply for bail then.'

'My client will answer your questions, but you had better have more than a suspicion to hold her on. However, before the interview, I want a doctor to see her. She is shaking with shock. I'll go and ring her private practitioner and get him here.'

'She will see the usual GP. I'll contact him. Would a cup of sweet tea help, Layla?'

'Mrs Parrondski, to you.'

His sigh told volumes. 'Right. Mrs Parrondski. The doctor will be called. In the meantime, we will give you bed and board.' He turned to the constable standing by the door. 'Take her down, Larkacre.'

'I object to that!'

'Objection overruled! Ha, I've always wanted to say that, thanks for the opportunity, Prindell.'

'Prick.'

'Two promotions in one week! Look, Prindell, Gosling didn't see me coming, and neither did you. I'm a new entity to you. You will find me unshakable. I have plenty on your client. I was willing to deal with her as painlessly as possible. You have spoiled that. She will see a doctor as you request, but then, she will be questioned at my convenience. I need to tie a couple of ends up.' This time in his telling the constable, his voice held a command sternly delivered. 'Take her down, Larkacre.'

Layla's terror deepened at this. And the seemingly hopeless position of Adrian to intervene, compounded it.

The dark foreboding corridor the officer took her down echoed the sound of her heels. But that didn't match the clanging of the keys on the officer's chain, or the creaking of the thick wooden and iron door as it was opened to reveal a room Layla had only seen the likes of on telly. She couldn't believe that it was now a reality for her.

A WPO stood waiting. She scribbled on a piece of paper. Then looked up. Her pretty face and dainty figure sat well in uniform. Her voice belied her five foot nothing height, 'Hand me your bag!' Looking at Larkacre the WPO tutted. 'What's Cleaston doing letting her bring that with her? Has she been searched?'

'Her lawyer rattled him, Sergeant. Delaying tactics. Probably got things to put in place. You know Prindell! To my knowledge, she's not been searched, nor booked in for custody. I think Cleaston made a knee-jerk decision to send her down here.'

'Christ. I'm fed up with babysitting that lot. They need to follow procedure. Right, have you got all of her details?'

'Cleaston hadn't even got that far.'

'This'll cost him. Bring her to my desk.'

Leaving the cell that she dreaded staying in, Layla followed the pint-sized Hitler. Her nerves jangled with every step and desolation filled her.

An hour later she re-entered the cell, with the aid of a shove from pint-size. Now though, she was minus her jewellery, bra, stockings, suspender belt, shoes, and jacket. Not to mention, her dignity. She had two new things – A pair of handcuffs and a sore arse from the, not-too-gentle prodding around up there that the doctor had done before he'd declared her orifices clean of drugs. A procedure, she suspected had been ordered out of spite.

Thankfully, pint-size released her from the cuffs before slamming the door shut and turning the key.

Hearing pint-size say in a loud voice, 'Think we should throw these away and let the bitch rot,' incensed Layla. 'Fucking. Pussy licker!' This shout echoed back at Layla as another door clanged shut leaving her in darkness.

Tears followed tears until, drained at last of emotion, Layla found the bed and lay down exhausted. The thought that this would be her future, weakened her. But then an image of her despised husband came to her. If it was true that he was still alive, she'd get through any stretch she had to do. Her focus would be his *real* death, and at her hands. As would Gosling's demise. She'd make sure they both suffered before taking their last breath.

14

Adrian Prindell stood still, shocked to the core at what he saw in front of him. 'Those bastards! Darling, I'm sorry. I was powerless. They had enough on you to hold you. Oh, my baby.'

Layla didn't respond. The look in her eye told of hate and mistrust. Adrian was at a loss as to how to comfort her. Stripped of everything that made her his Layla, she looked vulnerable and lost.

'Have they allowed you to wash? Brought you food?'

Still Layla didn't speak. Sixteen hours she'd been locked up. Her lips looked dry, but for a bruised split in the corner of her mouth, which oozed blood. This matched one on her cheek and the eye on the same side, was swollen.

'Who did this? Speak to me, Darling. How can I help you if you don't?'

'A pint-sized, twat of – a woman officer, no bigger than a twelve-year-old.'

'Why, How? Did you fight back?'

'She paid me a visit just before she went off duty. She cuffed me. I thought she was taking me out of this cell, but then she kicked me in the stomach and said that she would show me what a pussy licker was like when angry.'

'You called her that?'

'And a lot more since. That cow is dead.'

'Layla?'

Her hair felt like wire as he stroked it. The usual silky sheen of it was gone and strands of it matted to her head.

'I'm going to have a word with Cleaston. I'll be back.
I'll get you out of here. They've gone too far!'
Leaving her sitting on the bench in her cell, his soul
hurt as he heard the door slam behind him. The police
officer accompanying him made no apologies for his
action, nor did he open and close the door at the end of
the corridor with any less ferocity. *What was the reason
for all this antagonism towards Layla?*

'You tell, Sergeant Cleaston, that I want to see him
now! If he doesn't see me then I am going to the
Chief!'
As he finished saying this to the desk sergeant a door
opened behind him. Turning, he saw Gosling come out,
then step back and close the door. 'Right. Take me to
see the Chief. And, I'm not going anywhere until I've
seen him – Though, I will make a phone call to a
certain press officer waiting to hear from me, and show
the photo's I've just taken, if I'm not seen
immediately.'
'Just a moment, Sir.' A phone was picked up, spoken
into and then put back down. 'Come this way.'
Mike Bealver, one of the youngest Chiefs Adrian knew,
stood up to greet him. His age would have surprised
anyone who didn't know him, because his forty-odd
years were worn like sixty.
'What's going on, Mike? This all stinks. Why is a
bereaved woman being treated like a hardened
criminal? Christ, you stand to lose your job on how this
case is being handled. You do know that she's been
beaten up, don't you?'
'Adrian. Come in and calm down. Mrs Parrondski was
a little worse for wear when she was brought in. She
fell several times and had to be assisted. The doctor
took samples of her blood and she was well loaded with

126

alcohol. She took exception to my police sergeant trying to help her and started to lash out. She had to be restrained, hence the bruising. She's also a self-harmer. It's on her school records. She spent time in a mental hospital ward because of it. That and anorexia. It's all very sad.'

For a moment the impact of this left Adrian speechless, something that had never happened to him before – they were building a case against Layla before she'd even answered a question!

'I came in with her and she wasn't drunk. This case is being trumped up. Look, let me tell you this, Bealver. I've seen the allegations against her, and I have proof that none of it is true. She didn't order that gold from that dealer. Her husband must have done it in her name.'

'Why would he do that?'

'Because he was mixed up in something bigger than he could handle. He must have been, or why has he been murdered? There was no ransom demand, nothing. He went missing and turns up dead, doesn't that tell you something about him. He was covering his tracks. How could his wife arrange a shipment of this nature from a known robber living abroad?'

'Her father.'

Adrian sank down into a chair that stood by the wall. A sense of defeat was seeping into him – another feeling he'd never experienced before in his life.

'Look, Adrian. We all know you are personally involved with your client. That was your first mistake. Your second was underestimating Sergeant Gosling. This case was taken out of his hands when a stiff was reported on Cleaston's watch. Gosling lost interest after that and I decided to let Cleaston run with it, not dreaming the case was as big as it is now. However,

Gosling has been to see me with some historical information. Roderick Harrison, known as Harris, to the underworld, and the mastermind behind a bullion robbery at Heathrow, was one of Layla's father's cronies. He never got pulled in because he is a slippery eel of a man, but he owes big time favours to Gerry Loyson. Gerry finds his daughter has been left with a failing business, and so he calls in the favours – the gold is payment.'

'And, you can prove all of this, and who says that my client's business is failing?'

'Company records and accounts are easy for us to look at. And, we're getting there on the evidence. It is also on the cards that Frankie Droile – a hit man of Loyson's lot, took Parrondski out. An innocent man who happened to get tied up with the wrong woman.'

'Innocent!'

'We have nothing on him. If you know something you should give us the information.'

Adrian would love to do just that, but was sure that letting the cops know what Parrondski did under the guise of being Count Rolleski wouldn't be in Layla's plan, so he held back. 'I'm sure Gosling could fill you in, but then, you probably don't care who owns the walk-up on Brewer Street, do you, Mike? You wouldn't like it to disappear. You and Gosling wouldn't know where to go to get your kicks, would you?'

Bealver paled and did what most would do when under threat – attack. 'Think you're a regular mind of information, don't you, Prindell? Well, if you haven't proof to back up that statement, then shut the fuck up! And, don't come in here threatening a Chief Inspector!'

'Oh, I have proof. Discs and discs of proof. It is amazing what a grand can buy these days.'

The sixty-year tag Adrian had put on this forty-something, increased to seventy as the blood drained from Bealver's face.

'If it's any consolation, you won't walk the aisle of shame alone. Gosling will walk with you.'

'You're lying, Prindell, you fucking prick! Gosling picks up the discs on a regular basis so don't try that one.'

'And you trust him to destroy them? Ha. You're not that naive are you? Besides, these are not the ones recording you in and out of the place. Gosling knows nothing about these discs. Ever seen the camera in the room where you perform? No, I didn't think you had. Hidden in a gargoyle in the corner of the ceiling they were. But, not to worry, you and Gosling can use them to secure jobs in the porn industry.'

His, 'What do you want?' came out in a measured, evil tone.

'Layla's release. Charges dropped. And an apology. Oh, and all the properties belonging to her, or rented by her that have been searched, have to be professionally cleaned. And, while you're arranging all that, I want her to stop being treated like an animal, and for me to be allowed to get her own doctor here. For that, you will get a copy of each of the discs I have. Her insurance policy will be the copy that I keep locked away.'

'It's not possible. Cleaston is as straight as they come, he'll block it. He'll sniff and sniff till he gets what he wants. If anyone steps in his way, he'll take it to the Police Investigation Board.'

'Not that straight. He's allowed a prisoner to be beaten, and he has gone along with the cover up.'

'He believes our story.'

'Bullshit. He knows that Layla wasn't under the influence when he brought her in, and so do I. How did your doctor get that sample? This stinks. Cleaston is going along with your story because he's shagging the perpetrator. How would that bit of information go down with his investigation lot?'

If it was possible, Bealver went a paler shade of white.

'You come up with something, and fast. In the meantime, order better treatment of Layla Parrondski, and set the ball rolling on widening the investigation, and release her on insufficient evidence to hold her. Pull in that ex-manager. Look into his bank balance. And, keep your eye on Gosling.'

'Are you trying to tell me something?'

'What would be the use? Just remember what I've got stashed away. Now, pick up the phone and start acting like a Chief of Police!'

15

Layla came out of the bathroom. The stitch her, *ask-no-questions, private doctor* had put in her mouth was uncomfortable and her eye had blackened. 'Those Shits! How could you let them get away with this, Adrian?'

'I haven't.' He told her what he had put into place. She noticed his eyes skimming her from head to crutch. Her robe draped too much. She pulled it around her. She was in no mood to have him aroused. Turning away from him she went towards her bedroom. 'Give me a mo. I need to dress.'

There was disappointment in his asking, 'Are you sure?'

'I'm in no state.' She wasn't about to become his whenever he got the urge. He worked for her. He fucked her when she wanted him to. He still had a lot to learn.

Having dressed, she returned to the lounge of the Penthouse she was renting, feeling less exposed in a blue check, Armani, Fan Print Jumpsuit. She loved the comfort it offered, and the style. Her bare feet sunk into the deep red carpet. The soft, smoky grey, leather armchair gave relief to her aching limbs as she sank into it. She savoured the cool feel on the exposed parts of her back.

'So, you think you can get me out of this shit?' she asked.

Adrian's answer didn't sound confident, even though his tactics so far had been brilliant and had put them in a bargaining position. 'I will do my best, but I don't know their motive, and that is a problem. Why are they gunning for you? It has to be Gosling, and it is most likely Joe is pulling his strings on this. But what reason would Joe have for wanting you put away? Does he have a need to punish you?'

'He thinks he has. He has some twisted thing about honour. He didn't find out who I really was until I was pregnant with my second son, David. He changed after that. But can Gosling bring influence to bear on the Chief?'

'Possibly. That whole show is corrupt, from the Chief down. In fact, he is the main problem. His behaviour has compromised him. Gosling has enough on him to hang him, and, I imagine, uses it to give him power. If Joe is pulling Gosling's strings, then. . .'

'He is. That's certain. I tried for years to win back the love Joe had for me before he found out I had a father in the nick and an ancestry that rivals the one he's now giving to his kids. But from that moment, he hated me, and would do anything to punish me. It was a shock to learn what he was up to. I have no idea how he got into it all. Or, how he can still justify wanting to punish me for keeping my background a secret from him, when he's up to his eyes in the same thing as my lot were. Anyway, what can you do to get me off? And what about all this?' she indicated her face. 'That pint-sized pig can't get away with it.'

'I'm ready to file a police brutality complaint, I took photos of you while you were in the cell. We will have our day.'

'Send it to the Rottweiler.'

'Hold on. If she has this, she'll want to know why you were being questioned. We still have a big problem. Your position isn't good, yet. You're out because I had the forethought to get evidence that I could blackmail Bealver and Gosling with, but don't underestimate them, they are powerful men. And that Cleaston, is an unknown quantity. Straight, but with curves. They are the worst kind as you can't get under their skin.'

'If he's straight, why has he allowed this?'

'The curve in him is the WPO who did this to you. She's the only kink in his armour. Even the Chief can't believe that he's gone along with the report that says you were drunk. But she has a hold on him. He's shagging her. Can't get enough of her apparently. She has sadistic traits and keeps him in his place like a puppy on a lead.'

'Christ! I don't want to go down. I don't even want the hullabaloo of a fucking trial. I'll have to disappear.'

'It hasn't come to that yet. We still have our blackmail and as I said, I've planted other suspects. But, I have to admit that it doesn't look good that Harris was an associate of your father.'

'Christ, I can feel the walls closing in on me. I can't go to the jail, I can't! I have to contact my D, get him to dig further on what you've achieved. We have to stop Cleaston. Get so much on him that he drops the case against me.'

'I doubt there will be much. Anyway, I have a message from your D. He's establishing contact between you and Gina, but feels all messages ought to come through him, not by phone direct to you. He's worked out a way she can leave him notes. He told her of the procedure she'd need to follow, when he informed her that the grand was in place.'

'I agree. What else has he said?'

'Well, on Gina, he wants you to act fast to get her kid safe. He fears that Gina has deeper feelings for Joe than she realises. He's afraid they may cloud her judgement. His insider has reported that Gina is tending to Joe, and in a manner that a loving wife might do to a sick husband.'

'Shit. I've worried about her.' Getting out of the chair, Layla walked to the window. The view over the Thames did nothing to calm her. She wished she could be in one of the boats she could see, and that it would whisk her away.

'No need to worry yet. At the moment, Gina has a bitter streak over what Joe is making her child go through. They shot another episode. Gina insisted on watching again. Her insider helped her. Your D is willing to trust this bloke as he has been informed that the man goes mad every time the kids are used. Apparently it sickens him. Your D's insider has witnessed him ranting with Gina. D has told Gina to be careful and to tell her insider to be careful. If it is discovered that he's expressing an adverse opinion on one of the operations in progress, he could be in danger.'

'How do we achieve getting the kids out, though? I've promised, and I want to, but I can't come up with any ideas of how to do it.' *And, what to do with the kids? Will Gina stay put if her kid is taken out? Will she be in danger?*

'I'd put it out to contract, and soon. Use one of your father's lot. Jackie Noble, would be a good start, he's ex SAS. He was part of the armed robbery, though your father kept his involvement secret and he was never implicated. He was involved in setting up the plan.'

'Contact him and set up a meeting for me. Though, we need to mull over Gina staying there. Anything else?' Adrian opened his briefcase. 'Your ex.'

Layla walked over to where Adrian still sat on the grey and red tapestry covered sofa. A beautiful piece of furniture. She loved the carved wood that framed its high back, and the arms that were padded and covered

134

with tapestry, but had carved wooden claws to match those of the legs. Sitting beside him she stared at the photo he'd handed her.

The man in the photo, sleeping in a chair, was unrecognisable to her. The face, still very bruised, was long and thin. Joe's had been square and chubby, tending to drooping jowls. The nose on this stranger was wide and short. Joe's had been long with a flat bridge, the body was slimmer, Joe's had been chunky. 'Count fucking Rolleski! Ha! Uglier than ever!' An anger welled up in her. Joe had really gone. A bit of what her son, David had said entered her. Yes, she'd harboured that same sentiment. To make him like her again, or even, love her, one day. Had he hated her that much? That much that he wasn't content with leaving her and feigning his own death, but wanted to ruin her? Well, goodbye, Joe – watch out, Count's Rolleski and Rommoski, whichever guise you are under when I make my move, your number will be up.

'Don't let it affect you.'

Adrian's comforting hand on her thigh sent an electric-like shock through her. She rose quickly and crossed back over to the leather chair. 'Affect me, it's giving me the creeps and strengthening my resolve to get even with the bastard. Anything from D about Gosling? Has he been seen to meet up with the manager of the warehouse?'

Adrian once again showed his disappointment. He had it bad. But he kept to the point, her gesture of moving had been enough of a hint to him. 'No. It must have all been done by phone. He does have pictures of us meeting Gosling.'

'What the hell for – he won't double cross us, will he?'

'Relax. They are from his tail on Gosling, but they're insurance for us. I'd say that was a good man you have there.'

'Another one of my dad's.'

'He also told me to tell you that Gosling has visited the bank and looked happy when he came out.'

'So, the bastard made sure he'd been paid first.'

'He hasn't.'

'What?'

'I have a client that deals in counterfeit. I used some of the million to buy some of that. The top layer of each bundle in Gosling's box is kosher. The rest, well, let's just say, Gosling is in for a big surprise.'

'You're one step ahead again!' Layla couldn't keep the annoyance from her voice even though this pleased her. She thought a moment about this new twist. 'We should let him know. Tell him the rest is owed, but was our insurance. Tell him he gets me off this rap, and he begins to work for me, not against me, or we expose him with the evidence you have of his dealings at the walk-up. We'll give it to the Rottweiler.

'He's not going to be a happy bunny.'

'He'll be a dead one soon, but I need to make him hop a bit first.'

'You can't trust him, Layla. I strongly advise that you don't let him know about the revenge you want. Which, by-the-way, I'm still not party to the details of. I need to be. I can't keep staying one step ahead for you, if I don't know what I'm protecting.'

Layla knew this had to come, but she was still not sure she wanted to trust Adrian with everything. He was a powerful ally. Too powerful at times. Powerful enough to take over her plans. She didn't know how to control him. 'You are in the dark about my plan for my future, because my plan is to have only women in the key positions. Women who have a need to get revenge on the former Joe Parrondski. To that end, ask D to find out who the mothers of the first two kids are. I'm banking on them joining me, they must want revenge. Especially the first one when she finds out her kid is dead. But, I need to know they are of the right calibre, and won't just go snivelling to the cops.'

'For God sake, Layla, tell me what you're planning. I can then vet anyone you need vetting. You've asked me to work exclusively for you, and yet, I don't even know what you are working on. I can't even say if I'll want a key role. I do know I want to protect you, and I can't without knowing what from.'

'I asked you to protect me in everything legal. Keep me from putting a foot wrong in the aftermath of Joe going missing, and then this gold scam surfaced. I don't think you have done a good job so far.'

'That's hardly fair. I couldn't possibly act on the gold scam before it happened, I had no way of knowing of it. And, you have your freedom back. I did that. You haven't been charged, and I've manoeuvred a good hand to go into the next round with.'

'It's all still hanging over me.'

'We have to take each step as it occurs. I've planted stuff in the Chief's mind about the manager and Gosling. I have material to blackmail the Chief and Gosling with. The wheels are in motion. You need me, Layla. You need me in more ways than one. Why don't you trust me?'

'You're always ahead of me. It frightens me.'

'It should please you. Isn't Marcelle ahead of you in her role? Doesn't she think for you? If she doesn't then get rid of her.'

'Well, yes, she is - does, but . . .'

'But she's a woman and acceptable. What is this with you and women? You're surrounded by men from your father's day, including me. And most of us are doing the dirty work for you. Could any of your women have done half of what we have done? Change your mind, Layla. Wake up and see that you need both men and women to help you. Whatever it is you're planning, you need me. I have a criminal mind because I have to beat the law away from criminals. I cover people's backs. I have to be in the know as to what the police are thinking and doing. They have to tell me. That's what gives me the edge. You have to do the same.'

She knew he was right. But when she set out to get her revenge, she'd vowed there would be no men involved, other than those paid to do a specific job. Men always took over. They didn't seem capable of taking orders from a woman. They would crush her desire to be number one and never have to be beholden to a man again. But part of all that was to use men to her own end, and Adrian was right to a point, so far they had been more useful.

'Get me off this rap and you're in. It's big.'

'I don't do bargaining with my own clients. I do loyalty and trust.' He rose. Headed for the door. Still in her view, she saw him turn, put his briefcase on the hall table, open it, and look back at her. 'Oh, I forgot. A new – old phone. Not registered to you. It has Marcelle and Jade's new numbers in it. It won't work without a password. I've used, Cell Block H.' His face twisted in a sardonic grin. Her stomach muscles clenched.

'I have several sims for it. Each time you make a call or text from it, destroy the sim. Then contact me and I will put a new one in. They have the same arrangement. I suggest you put this in your antique collection.'

A draught caught her bare feet as he opened the outer door. His body silhouetted against the light of the sun, and the power of him awoke in her a desire, she couldn't deny herself. She hadn't given into him at his whim. This was her whim. 'Adrian!'

'Yes?'

'You're in. Come back.'

The door closed. The desire threatened to choke her as he walked towards her.

16

'What're you staring at?'

'I'm trying to come to terms with the new you.'

'I'm not new inside. Come here.'

Gina went closer to Joe. His bandages were now off and she could see, despite the swelling and bruising, how different he looked. She was surprised how deeply this affected her. She'd liked the way he'd looked, and had got used to his squishy body. This Joe looked cruel and was getting scrawny.

'So, do you think I am handsome, then?'

'Why did you do it, Joe? Why?'

'Are you on about my operation? Or are you still banging on about those kids? And cut the Joe crap and call me Count.'

'Both, but mostly the kids. It's broken my heart, Jo – Count. I never would have believed it of you. You seemed to have a normal sexual appetite – well normal if you were a rabbit.'

'Ha. I like that. And you'll be pleased to know that it's returning. Let's go and have a swim together, I fancy it in the pool.'

'No. I don't want sex with you until you stop this thing with the kids. That's my baby you're corrupting. You bastard!'

'Corrupting? I think you'll find if you watch the films that she loves her *daddy*, and likes *playing* with him. She takes after you.'

'You're a prick, Joe – Count, whatever your fucking name is. I'll never go with you again while you put my Amy, or any other kid through this, you're sick!'

'I think you will.'

His tone frightened her.

'What you want, Gina, isn't going to happen anytime soon. Those films are already bringing in a good stash and have the potential to earn me a mint once they get known by every ear with a fetish for them. No harm is being done to the kids. They love it. And, I'm told that since you arrived they're very happy all round. They're all doing well at their school lessons. Nanny is very pleased with them. So forget trying to persuade me and go and get into one of the bikinis I had delivered for you. The leopard-skin one. And join me in the pool in ten.'

Walking through the door that took Gina from the office and into a long corridor, she headed for the stairs at the end and went towards the room she'd been staying in. One of the foreign girls, an East European, who said she didn't speak English, was going through Gina's drawers lifting out piles of the undergarments and other folded clothes and placing them in boxes that were stood on the bed. 'What the fuck?'

The girl shrugged. Gina picked up the internal phone. Joe's voice – nothing had changed about that, spoke into her ear before she had time to ask the question, 'You're moving to my quarters. I want you on hand whenever I need you, I've liked having you around me. I'm ready for more and on a regular basis. We might even go out in the car occasionally. You'd like that, wouldn't you?'

Gina slammed the phone down.

'Where's my bikinis?'

The girl shrugged. Gina felt like hitting her. 'My Bi – ki - -nis.' She acted out putting one on and swimming. The girl pointed to one of the boxes. Scrambling amongst the contents Gina found the garment. For now, she had to do what Joe wanted of her. She'd play her part. But, not for long. The plan was in place. Layla had agreed to her trying to persuade Joe from carrying on the child porn operation, but if that failed, as it had, then all she had to do was to leave a message for Layla's Private D.

Changing in the bathroom and liking what she saw as she passed her mirror, Gina made her way back downstairs. She planned to turn this situation to her advantage by giving Joe the fucking of his life. Exhaust him. Then she'd slip out and leave the note.

Reaching the bottom of the stairs she stopped and stood still. A noise coming from the shadowy area under the stairs had her listening. Gosling stepped out and faced her. 'Looking good, Gina.'

Gina pulled at the towel she'd draped around her neck and tried to wrap it around herself. Gosling snatched it from her. 'Very nice. Like the bikini. You've got taste. I think I'll let my seed swim in it before you go to the Count.'

'No. He'll kill us, you idiot! Besides, you've only had it up once, how do you know you can manage it again?' His hand raised. She didn't flinch. Knew he wouldn't dare. 'Ha, thinking about being violent is affecting your dick. Poor thing looks as though it'll burst out of your trousers.' Tossing her hair back and walking past him she asked, 'What's a premature ejaculator doing with such a big fine tool anyway? Crying shame. No use to you, is it?'

His hand gripped her arm, pulling her back towards him. She cried out with the pain. His breath, tinged with recently smoked tobacco, fanned her face as he released a gasp of painful rhapsody.

Pulling free, Gina laughed. Gosling's body trembled. Sweat stood out on his forehead. 'You've got a big problem, man. You'd better find a bathroom and clean up the sticky mess in your pants while I go and fuck with a real bloke.'

As he slumped against the banister, Gina had a moment of feeling sorry for him. But, it didn't last. Instead she gave reign to the loathing she had for him and left him with the sound of her laughter, hoping to increase his humiliation.

The water was just the right temperature. Swimming away from Joe and not letting him catch her was the first part of her plan, though she was careful to give him a few feels of her between gliding away. She didn't want him to lose the urge. To this end she dived under water, released him from his trunks and took him into her mouth. For as long as she could hold her breath she sucked him. When she came up he grabbed her. Not in the plan, but he was too strong for her.

Allowing him to manoeuvre her and helping him, she straddled him and took him into her. It felt good. Different. 'Have you had something done down there, Joe?'

'Count. And, no, no need. I like it how it is. Pleasing you, is it?'

'Very pleasing.' She kissed him and savoured the feel of him deep inside her. Maybe it was because she wasn't restricted for room as she was when in his car, but this felt like the first time when he'd showed her what real sex was. She clung to him resisting the pull of the water as it tried to float her upwards.

Joe complimented her, caressed her, and drove her wild with his movements. Her groans of pleasure echoed around the pool room. His words of: 'Baby, I think I'm in love with you.' Thrilled her. And yet, shocked her. Joe had never spoken to her like this. Something stirred in her. Something she had felt before. She was falling deeply in love with Joe – Count Rolleski, and that was dangerous.

Easing off him she swam a few yards before turning towards him. Treading water, she asked, 'Do you know what you're saying, Joe?'

'Count! And yes, I do. I felt it when I came here. I missed you. That's why I had you brought to me. I love you, Gina.'

'Christ, Joe . . .'

'For fuck's sake, it's Count!'

'To me you will always be, Joe.'

'Look Gina, I want to be, but I can't be. You call me Count, or you'll suffer the consequences of disobeying me.'

'Ha, love me one minute, threatening me the next, nothing has really changed has it, fucking bollocks, Count!'

His laughter echoed back at her. He swam towards her. His arms enclosed her.

It felt good.

They tightened around her. And tightened . . . and tightened!

'Joe . . . J – o –e, stop it. St-o-p!' Her breath left her body as his powerful grip crushed her. Excruciating pain stung her lungs. She couldn't take a breath back into her body. The lights dotting the ceiling came down towards her, then went out as she went into the blessed relief of a faint.

'Come on Gina, come on, darling. I didn't mean to hurt you. You made me angry. Gina . . . Gina . . .'

He must have lifted her onto the tiles surrounding the pool as she could feel the coldness of them beneath her. He was leaning over her. His face, the face that didn't yet fit with the voice came close to her. Taking a breath hurt. She still couldn't fill her lungs properly. Closing

145

her eyes, she had the sensation of her legs being opened, and a feeling of being crushed again. Joe's dick slid up her. *The bastard!* She tried to pummel him with her fists, but was too weak.

Each deep thrust of him caused her back to scrape along the floor, ripping her raw. Hoarse cries came from her. Cold tears thread a path down her cheeks. On and on it went. Till at last his cries of ecstasy joined hers of agony and he slumped down on her.

Once more the blackness descended and took her into its peaceful depth.

*

'Christ, I've heard of fucking someone to death, but never thought I'd see it.'

'Tell me she ain't dead, Doc.'

'Very near. You idiot. Well, I hope you enjoyed it, darling, because this little whore isn't going to be serviceable for some time to come. If ever.'

'Why, what's the matter with her? Doc, do something. For Christ's sake, do something!'

'We need to get her on oxygen. Get someone to carry her down to the operating room, we've got some there. Ha, Count, you're a fucking genius fucker, you've taken a whore out with your dick!'

'Shut the fuck up and get her seen to. And, stop calling her a whore. I'm intending on her being my wife, so you get her well, or else.'

'Ooh, get you. Threatening your little boy who's been nothing but a good servant. You know, I could give you a better time than any of these women can, darling. Even better than you get from watching those kids with daddy.'

'Just shut up, Doc. I'm tired. Just save her. Do all you can for her; I can't lose her.'

'Got it that bad, darling?'

The Count didn't answer as at that moment, Bragdon's voice came over the walkie-talkie system he'd called him over. 'Yes, Boss?'

'Get to the poolside as quick as you can. Gina's hurt.' It seemed that he and Gosling had been standing outside the doors, they both came in almost instantaneously. 'What the fuck are you doing here, Gosling?'

'There's been developments, I'll tell you of them. I was waiting for you to become free. Come on Bragdon, you get her shoulders.' Grabbing Gina's legs, he asked, 'where to, Doc?'

After being told where to take Gina, Gosling backed towards the door. The deadweight of Gina making him pant. 'What's wrong with her, Doc, has she collapsed?'

'I'd say that a rib has pierced her lung. Shift yourselves, there may not me much time.'

'She's going to die!'

'Don't sound so shocked, honey. I'd have thought you cops were used to this kind of thing.'

Gosling cursed inwardly, he hadn't meant to show his feelings like that. 'I was just surprised; she only looks as though she's fainted. I didn't think she was in danger of dying.'

'That or have brain damage, unless I'm in time. Hurry, darling, run as if you have a big black man after you with a huge cock he wants to stick up your arse.'

How The Doc could make jokes at a time like this, Gosling didn't know. But then, he had no respect for any women, not even his own mother. He'd heard him call her everything from a prick to a dog.

As the doors swung closed behind them, Gosling felt as though he'd entered a hospital theatre. Everything was exactly as the real thing.

147

Bragdon took the burden of Gina's weight as they reached the operating table. His actions gentle and caring. Gosling frowned. A massive complication if this ape of a body and mind was falling in love with Gina. It could mean he'd jump to her tune. *That could be dangerous. Something to keep my eye on.*

He wasn't averse to feeling sorry himself at seeing Gina in this state, barely clinging on to life, and felt relieved when the oxygen was in place and some colour began to come back into her face. There was something about her. His eyes travelled her beautiful naked body. Not missing the bruising that was forming on her arm. Bruising, he'd caused, but would be lost among the others that threatened to blacken her limbs.

Looking at the Count he was shocked to see tears running down his face. 'She'll be alright, won't she, Doc?' The words sobbed from the Count.

'One can never tell. She needs an op. I think I'm right, about the puncture, though an X-ray would confirm it better.'

'Get Gavin Theogood here, and quick!'

'That will take too long, Count. I'm going to have to do it. Instruct that nanny you have up there to come and help me. She told me she started her career as a nurse. And all of you, get the fuck out of here, I have to scrub this place. You've all tainted it with your sweaty bodies. Especially, you, Count.'

Gosling smiled as the doc pursed his lips and looked the naked Count up and down. Hung like a donkey, his dick even rivalled what Gosling had got. Though now, it looked in a sorry state, limp and still dripping. Covering it with his hands, the Count's face went red with embarrassment, though it came out as rage, 'Fuck off the lot of you! You fucking pricks. Get out! Get out!'

Gosling contained the laughter that bubbled up in him as he told the Count, 'Meet me in your office in twenty minutes, you're going to want to hear my news.'

17

The Count's face when he entered his office had Gosling worried. 'What's happening?'

'He's done the op. He's a fucking genius. Wasted he is. Should have been a surgeon. Says, she had fluid on her lung and one had collapsed. He's drained the fluid and reflated the lung. Her ribs weren't broken, just bruised. So Gina, though not well at the moment will soon be right. I've told him I'll show my appreciation to him for saving her life. He'll be in for a big pay day.'

Gosling took this news with pleasure. The Doc would need funds if he was to be the equal partner he hoped he would be. He was also glad to hear that he was doing all he could to save Gina. He'd worried that there had been no intention in The Doc to help her, and had given him a warning look as he'd left the theatre.

'Talking of money, how did the gold scam go? I trust my plan was put into action?'

Gosling's attention was brought back to the Count. 'It was, but there has been a complication. The fat-cat lawyer!'

'Take him out. He's getting to be a nuisance.'

'He's more than that. I think you should know that he's fucking Layla.'

'Didn't think she was fuckable anymore, thought it had dried up.' The Count laughed at his own joke. 'Ha, maybe trying to crack that cold bitch is punishment enough for him.'

'How can you hate her so much? It doesn't make sense, and has led to a sticky situation. I told you it was too risky to set her up like this. We're in all sorts of a mess with it.'

'How come? It was straight forward. What's happened? Gosling had his story ready, knowing the truth would send the Count into a rage: 'She paid the manager off when he informed her of the delivery. He took the bigger pay packet and didn't report her. She has the gold, and time to sort something out.'

'Pay him more! He can still report her, tell them his conscience pricked him.'

'I did, and he agreed, but by that time she'd got her cover story and the gold has disappeared. Her Fat-Cat is trying to lay it at the manager's door, saying that he took the gold and left bricks in its place. When the cops went to check him out, he was gone. Vanished without a trace, but they did find that he'd deposited a large amount of cash in his bank account. Tosser! What a fucking idiot. I told him to put it in a safe deposit until he was in the clear.'

This last was the truth, it was a mystery as to where the manager was, and his bank account had shown too healthy a balance – Over two hundred thousand.

Continuing with his charade of a story, Gosling told the Count, 'The Fat-Cat must have arranged it all. He's either had the manager taken out – which I wouldn't put past him, or he's whisked him away somewhere with another bundle of money that he can access.'

'Has the manager any family?'

'No. A loner. A geek.'

'Shit, Gosling. A right fucking cock-up. Not only has she got my gold, she's going to walk. I wanted her banged up.'

'This vendetta will be the undoing of you. But all isn't lost. The theory is that it is all something to do with Layla's old man.'

'Will it wash? I tell you I want that bitch behind bars. I want her to suffer.'

Gosling's phone pinged. Checking the screen, he noted a missed call and a message. Both were from his Chief. He read the message, but didn't return the call: *Where the fuck are you? I have a CD here that you should take a look at. Not to mention Cleaston lifting too many stones and checking under them. Get back here. NOW!*

'Are you listening to me?'

'Sorry, Count, police business. Yes, I'm listening.'

'If you stick it on her father, how will the manager's part come into it?'

'I'll have to make it. If it really *had* all happened through her father, then he and Layla would want the manager in on it so that he didn't query the delivery. I need to find that fucking prick of a manager so that I can make him confess to this as being the truth. I need to make him say that Layla tried to buy him off. That she gave him the money to deposit and then sent him packing with more. But, it's a long shot.'

Gosling eased himself out of the deep comfortable armchair. The Count's expression worried him. He shivered. The Count swivelled back and forward on the luxurious leather chair behind his desk, his eyes scrutinized and dug deep into Gosling's, almost as if he'd entered his soul.

'Don't shit with me, Gosling. Don't shit with me.'

'Have I done up to now?'

'Yes. I've seen the news. Zoe's now a fucking dead whore and there's a nationwide hunt for her kid and Gina's. – That's shitting with me.'

'That's sorted.'

'It's a long way from sorted. Gina's and Zoe's kids will have to be found dead. It will happen tonight while Gina's still out of it. You see to getting me two more like them, but with no cock ups this time. I want no police investigation into missing kids. You'll get your

153

usual pay-check if you do this.' After a pause, not long enough for Gosling to answer, the Count's voice lowered to a menacing whisper, 'You'll get a bed for ever and ever, lined with silk, and six feet under, if you don't.'

A trickle of fear clenched Gosling's chest. 'I'm on to it. I can get more kids, but killing, or even hurting them, wasn't in the plan. They were to be found alive and returned to their parents when you'd done with them. There has to be another way to what you plan. Give me a few hours to come up with something. Besides Gina's going to be devastated. She'll hate you.'

The Count was silent. His eyes never left Gosling and Gosling's skin crawled with fear under the steely gaze. 'Any other way would mean Gina leaving here and I'm not letting that happen. She'll get used to it. But, put her in deep shit, just to make sure. Compromise her. Put her in the frame for the kid's murder, not so as the cops come gunning for her, but just so that she thinks she's under suspicion. That way she'll be scared and want to keep quiet . . . And, Gosling. Don't try a double cross. I've every angle of you covered. I've even got your dossier.'

'What? How?'

'A client of your solicitor is a friend of mine. He pulled strings. You should keep your back covered.'

'For your information there's more than one copy filed with more than one solicitor. It makes good reading doesn't it? I assume you've read it? If not, take it to bed with you and enjoy. Let it be a reminder that I'm no push over.'

'Prick!'

'Thank you. I have to be, working with the likes of you. I ain't after a double cross, I'm after one way tickets to retirement for me and me missus. That was our bargain, and once this mess is cleared, you keep your half of it, and you'll never see me again.'

'Get out!'

Gosling couldn't settle the sick feeling in his belly as he made his way out to his car. Things were getting hairy. *I should open a few off-shore accounts, go to the safe box, get the money and deposit it, then get the hell out of here with Sara.* But, the thought of the fortune he could make heading the Count's operations, stopped him. Yes, a million was a good start, but it didn't come near to giving him what he wanted. Riches untold.

His mobile pinged again. *'What the fuck are you doing in Epping?'*

Christ, the Chief's becoming a fucking liability. He's even tracking my movements now. What's so damned important about a fucking CD?

Pressing the call button gave him the Chief's angry voice. 'Get back here now, Gosling! And just what are you doing in Epping? Why fucking Epping?'

'I came out to have a picnic and to think. I'm off duty. I spend my own time how I want to and I don't expect to have work tracking me in my free time.'

'Bollocks. Get your arse back here. We're in deep trouble.'

'Why? And what's this CD?'

'Me and you in the walk-up. Me, I'm doing what comes natural, though being married and a Chief of Police it won't go down well. You, you vicious bastard, are beating some poor girl to within an inch of her life. Prindell sent them over. He has copies, which he will take to the press if we don't clean up this mess surrounding Layla Parrondski. Only Cleaston won't let go, he's got his teeth into this as if it's fucking personal. He wants to bring the Parrondski bitch in again. *Now* do

155

you think you can get back here, or do you want to finish your butties?'

'Christ. Cleaston's shagging piece will be his motivation, the bitch has it in for Layla Parrondski. She must have pissed her off big time! I'm on my way.' Grabbing the money and running, seemed the best option at this moment, Gosling thought as he put his foot on the throttle, spraying clumps of earth in a wheel spin that would rival any joy-rider, and sped towards London.

By the time he arrived Mike Bealver was in even more of a state. 'Shut the fucking door. Christ, this is getting out of hand! How I ever let you talk me into going to that fucking walk-up I'll never know!'

'You fancied a bit of young. You got it and wanted more. It's what we do.'

'I don't do what you do, you cruel bastard. If your Sara saw that!'

This crumbled Gosling's insides. He sat down. After a moment, he composed himself. 'Whatever. Each to his own. What we have to do now is get out of this mess. Get Cleaston in here, Chief, and let's see what he has. If it doesn't hold water, then order him off the case and put me back on it. Parrondski's disappearance was mine in the first place.'

'You wanted off it, remember? Once the body came in that was that as far as you were concerned. If I'm to give the case back to you, I want to know what your angle on it is. And, by God, you'd better have one and it'd better be good.'

'I have.' Gosling hoped that the possible scenario he'd been thinking through and planning on the journey here, would sound plausible. He also hoped that despite all that hung over him, he was still a good liar as he fed

the biggest load of shit he'd ever fed, to his boss: 'I think Joe Parrondski was got at by his father-in-law, Gerry Loyson. Gerry's time for release is getting near.'
'I wouldn't call five years getting near.'

Too near for my comfort. Keeping the fear this thought gave Gosling from his voice he continued. 'Nor would I, but in terms of turning assets into cash as huge as we know Loyson has, it's no time. Especially when those assets are gold bullion.'

'I buy that. So, go on. Convince me of the rest of your theory.'

This was said in a tone that told Gosling, his boss wasn't going to believe a word he said, but as long as it was all believable, that was all that mattered.

'Although we've never been able to prove it, or to track it down, we know that Harris has the gold Loyson's gang stole. We know that Joe Parrondski's business was failing. I believe that Loyson offered him a way out. And though an upstanding member of the community, Parrondski took it. But then; say he got cold feet? Well, now he knows too much and would have started to receive threats. So, he figures he'll go through with the deal, but have it delivered in his wife's name. Then, if it goes tits up, it is she who is in the frame for it. With her background no one would believe her if she played innocent of it. So, if all of this is what happened, then Loyson would be angry that his daughter's husband stooped so low. Loyson probably blamed Parrondski for his daughter breaking contact with him anyway and this would prove to be a step to far. He orders that Parrondski is taken out. I would say that Layla Parrondski, is completely innocent of any dealings in the stolen gold, or the murder. She was dealing with her husband's disappearance, and with the intrusion into her life caused by the investigation. It is

157

likely that she didn't give a second thought to the consignment that had come into the warehouse for her. To her it was just a delivery. She accepted it, but when it came to light that is was stolen she panicked, and turned to that shit of a lawyer we all know she's shagging. He comes up with the plan to implicate the manager of the warehouse by paying him to disappear then coming up with the bricks story. This fits in with how the manager of the warehouse has done one, and his account has money in it, don't you think? However, my investigation will take the lines that he stole the gold – he would have contacts in the business as that warehouse takes in a lot of bullion. But I really think that Layla Parrondski did pay him off and it rankles that she's still got the gold.'

'I buy all of that. And, I like the theory that she bought him off, and think it the most likely scenario. However, I think we should go with the manager being the thief. Just to keep me and you out of the shit. As for the murder, if you're right about it being Loyson who ordered it, we'll need evidence, and that won't be easy to get. Or, to plant, if you're not right.'

A satisfaction entered Gosling. He'd done what many had tried to do and failed, committed the perfect murder, and not one single trace of suspicion rested on him. Resisting the urge to smile he continued to summarise his web of plausible lies:

'We'll have to list the murder as an unsolved case. I'll dig, but I can't see what I can come up with. Our suspect is in prison. He wouldn't get messages out using the conventional method. He's too clever for that. Besides, the body was burned beyond recognition, with only identifying DNA available, there was nothing to tie a perpetrator to it. We have to build a case against that manager and mark him as a wanted man, because I reckon he's gone to where the sun shines and he ain't coming back.'

'Right. But build it all on solid ground. Cleaston is a little shit and won't stop digging away.'

'Order him to. And if he doesn't use the threat of an internal inquiry as to Layla's injuries.'

The Chief picked up his phone, dialled a desk number. 'Get in my office NOW!'

Gosling liked that. Cleaston would be shaking in his shoe.

When the door opened nothing was further from the truth. The jumped up prick walked in with all the confidence in the world. 'Anything wrong, Chief?'

'A whole bloody lot. What's happening in the Parrondski murder and stolen gold case? I want to know every little detail of what you're working on, thinking, and planning to do regarding this case, and all of it had better be backed up by solid police work and rock solid leads.'

Cleaston sighed before indicating that he would like to take a seat. The Chief nodded.

'I'm working on the theory that Layla Parrondski did take delivery of the gold, and that she still has it. I believe her father is involved and that he was also involved in some way in the death of Joe Parrondski . . .'

Cleaston's voice droned on. What he was saying was so far from what Gosling knew to be the truth he almost laughed, but it was all clever stuff and could hold water. As the real truth could never be told, and Gosling's own theory on the case had been made up, he could only hope he'd put it over with as much, or more conviction than Cleaston was doing. Cleaston's undoing was having Layla Parrondski firmly in the frame. The last thing the Chief needed. And this showed in his face, which looked as if it was about to explode.

'So, you've got fuck all, on the murder, or the gold delivery. Yes, what you say, could have happened, but that's not good enough. I want something solid. What were you hoping to achieve by having the Parrondski woman brought in again? A fucking confession? Well, if that's the only evidence you're chasing, you can forget it. I'm taking the case off you. From now on Gosling will take the reins.'

A shocked expression crossed Cleaston's face. Gosling couldn't resist a snide remark: 'Don't take it to heart, Newbie, you've a lot to learn. You'll get there. Watch and see how the real cops work. I'll have this case tied up in a couple of days and I'll have my notes sent over to you. Be good homework for you.'

Cleaston stood, made a semi bow to the Chief and walked out, slamming the door so hard behind him the walls almost shook.

The laugh Gosling released must have followed him along the corridor.

The Chief's next remark sobered him: 'Before you get too complacent, have you anymore on those missing kids? I suppose you've forgotten that the mother of Zoe Feldon, the dead pro, is on TV tonight? We wanted Gina to appear for her child too, but we can't contact her. Get on to that. She has to be on the radar at all times.'

'You mean Cleaston has let her slip. Tut tut.'

'This isn't the time to score points. Zoe's mother is having the two lads on with her. They are all going to make an appeal as to the whereabouts of Tammy Feldon and Amy Walters. I have to make a statement. I'd like something reassuring to say.'

'Sorry, Chief, nothing new. Still drawing blanks. Not a sighting, or a lead of any kind. We filmed a re-enactment which is to go out on Crime Watch next week, I've seen it and it's good. Whether anything will come of it or not, I don't know. There's just nothing. They and the woman have vanished into thin air. The car was a hired one and that's never turned up. We followed the lead of the person who hired it, but it turned out to be a bogus company. The re-enactment is our only hope now.'

'Christ, the fucking crims are getting ahead of us. How can that be? What kind of idiots are they making of us? It all stinks. All of it.'

Gosling knew what the Chief meant. Knew too that the Chief had his suspicions regarding his own involvement in Zoe's murder and the kids being taken. But he also knew he would keep them to himself.

He had to if he wanted to keep his job and his marriage.

18

Layla stretched her lithe body. 7am. Thirty minutes of exercise behind her, she strolled over to her bathroom, switching on the TV as she passed it, she would hear the news while soaking, she didn't have to see it. Nothing much was going on outside her own world that she needed to know about and she had a busy day ahead.

Today, was her first official day back. Meetings were set with the Company Secretary, then the Branch Managers, and finally, the bank that held the Parrondski jewellery business account. All of them she dreaded. There was no way forward for the business. All except the Mayfair branch were to close in three months' time, unless she could find a buyer. It was a sad time. She'd put so much of herself into it. But, there was the excitement and compensation of the online business soon to be activated and everything was coming along amazingly well with that. Of course, she could rescue Parrondski's, but it wasn't in her plan. Too much history had gone before.

About to turn on the taps, she stopped. The reporter's words dragged her back to the screen:

*'We'll go now to our reporter who is at the scene –
John, has it been confirmed that these are the bodies of
the missing girls, Tammy Feldon and Amy Walters?'*

Layla swallowed hard, trying to keep from being sick.

*'No, Mark, there is no confirmation, as of yet, but we
have been promised a statement in about an hour by
Chief Inspector Bealver.'*

'What can you tell us so far?'

'The bodies of two girls were found an hour ago, here in that skip you can see outside the only cottage in this sleepy countryside lane in Kent. There aren't any neighbours for at least five miles. They were found by a man walking his dog. The dog became very agitated when they neared the skip, and the man admits that what he saw poking out from the top really interested him, it was an old-fashioned coal-fuelled cooking range. We haven't been allowed to speak to him, but it seems that when he looked closer, he found the bodies. We don't know who the owner of the house is, but hope to find out once the statement has been issued.
We can only say, that our hearts go out to the families of the dead children whoever they are, and if it does turn out to be the missing girls then we send our condolences to Tammy Feldon's grandmother who, as you know, only last night, gave out an appeal on our channel, as to their whereabouts.'

The voices droned on. Speculating about this and that. Behind the reporter a man walked away from the scene and towards the police cordon. Gosling.

A bevy of reporters and cameras surrounded him. Layla's legs gave way. She sank onto the end of her bed. Thank God the boys were back at school - the skip was outside her house! The renovations she had wanted to do for a long time were underway. Those going on in her Holland Park home had spurred her on. A kind of *clean sweep.* In the cottage she'd wanted a wall taken down between the kitchen and dining room. Wanting to make it lighter and more spacious, now Joe had tainted her haven forever. *God, will he never let up?* The voice of Gosling came over the TV, answering a question as to the ownership of the house:

'Yes, we know who owns the house, but they are in no way implicated. It seems that a random place was

164

*chosen. Nothing my officers have given me so far
indicates anything other than that. Now, no more
questions. We are investigating a double child murder.
We will give you something once we know it ourselves.
Thank you.'* This was said as Gosling got into his car.
He slammed the door and sped away, beeping his horn
to rid the lane of bystanders and more reporters. A man
in a hurry.

The words: *Not Implicated?* Screamed at Layla. Christ,
this will stink when the house is linked to the wife of a
supposedly, murdered man! Layla's heart beat wildly as
she reached for her bag, but the phone linked to Adrian
rang before she could get to it.

'Have you seen the news, Layla?'

'Yes. I'm devastated. Things have to happen and
happen fast! Christ, a fucking gold scam, and now a
murder of two kids, and all implicating me. What if it
does turn out to be Tammy and Amy –?'

'It will.'

'Gina will be devastated. Oh, Adrian . . . Adrian –'

'Keep it together, darling. I'll ring the Chief. I'll tell
him that you've seen your house on the television, but
that you don't even know the two children that went
missing. No one knows that you are in touch with Gina.
We have to keep it that way, or this is going to look
bloody bad. I have a message from D. He tells me that
Gina isn't well. Joe hurt her and that the ex-male nurse
there had to do an emergency procedure on her last
night. D's last report was that she should recover quite
quickly.'

'The day I kill that bastard husband of mine will be the
best day of my life!'

'That day will come. In the meantime, we need to limit
this as much as we can. Leave it to me. You cancel all
you had going on today. It would look very callous if

165

you carried on. Stay indoors. I'll come to see you later today. Destroy the sim of the phone we are speaking on. I will too. Put one of the new ones in, then text my code name so I know you are on it. The code for me in this one is Hector. The others have the same codes as before. And Layla. I know I haven't said this before, but I love you. Together, we will win. Joe Parrondski will be history.'

Layla clicked the red phone symbol and cut him off. She didn't need this right now. What they had was enough for her, a fantastic sexual and business-based relationship. Talk of love didn't come into it, it complicated things.

Taking out the sim, she cut it into small pieces then wrapped them in toilet paper and flushed them down the loo. It took two flushes to get them to go completely. Another sound came from her bag. Jade's phone.

'Jade, everything okay?'

'Yes. I've secured another order. We now have access to the new Christian Dior collection. I have a link that will click straight to their designs. We don't have to stock the items, just relay the orders. The commission is handsome.'

'Well done. Jade . . . any chance of that holiday soon?'

'You sound down, what's happened?'

'Can you get the British news?'

'Yes, watched it an hour ago.'

'Those kids are on it. Didn't you see it?'

'What . . . No! Gina's and her mates? Christ, what's happened?'

'They've been murdered. At least, every indication is that it is them. That bastard has dumped their bodies in a skip outside my country home. It's in Kent, and –'

'No . . .no . . .no!'

'I'm sorry, Jade. I'm distraught myself, but can't imagine how you feel having been forced to take them to him, I –'

'I shouldn't have – Oh God, why did I? Why did I?'

'Stay strong, Jade. We can get him and we will. Don't even think of contacting the police. If you do, you will go down for a long stretch too.'

Sobs resounded down the line.

'Jade? Jade? Look, I promise you, we will move soon. We'll get rid of that bastard good and proper. He's trying to get me, and at the moment has more power than I do. But that will change. You know he's staged his own death? Well, he was trying to frame me and my dad for that, as well as a rap of buying stolen gold, but Adrian has got me off that hook.' She wouldn't tell Jade that she still had the gold. That was a private venture.

'Now it seems Joe is trying to get me into the frame for kidnap and murder of the girls. I need you to stay strong. I need Gina to as well. Together, we can be just as ruthless as he is. We can run all the operations he has set up, barring the child porn. We will be powerful and strong and feared. Isn't that preferable to slopping out and taking abuse from other inmates? *Think* about it Jade. Any lag with an attachment to child crime will be hated in prison.'

The sobs had died down and a determined voice came down the line. 'I want to personally kill Joe Parrondski!'

'I have that tab. You can enjoy his downfall before I call it in.'

'How long now before Belle et Belle is launched?'

'Hopefully next week. That will give us our front operation, and we can then make our move.'

'And the nightclub, 'Tête à Tête'?'

167

'Love that name. Everything is going to plan. The building work is done and work on putting in the fittings you chose online is well underway. The decorating is following each stage, so once a room is fitted out with its furnishings and electrical goods, or plumbing, in the case of the Turkish bath area, the decorators, tile fitters, or carpet fitters move in and do their work to your specifications. After that, the contract cleaners take the room over and it is then sealed so that no one can muck it up. It is all shaping up beautifully. You will love it. It has been a rushed job, but a quality one. Once the bars and cellars were completed the stock was delivered and pumps, cooling systems and refrigerators all put in. The cellar man comes in daily to check temperatures and is making sure everything is spot on. He has organised the displays on the bars too. The lighting also is wonderful as are the music systems. Different levels of sound in different bars. And piped, gentle music in the 'special areas'. The bedrooms are to die for. You are a clever girl where decorating and fitments are concerned. Now, I think you need to start to concentrate on contacting entertainers, then we could advertise an opening in two weeks' time. But, there's the matter of the contract first. Have you transferred funds?'

'Yes, they should be in the account by now.'

'I'll get Marcelle to check all of that. And I'll fly over in a few days.'

'Okay, let me know your arrival time and I will meet you.'

'I can only stay two to three days, then it will be time for you to return. We only have a few weeks of the Arab season left. Your old place is doing a bomb. We need to take some of that.'

'I have the main girls and members of staff on board. They are already putting the word in a few ears. Some of the Sheik's are itching for us to open. And the staff are ready to walk out at a minute's notice.'

'Tell them to put their notice in now. I know you like the idea of the disruption it would cause if they walk, but we don't want them in any danger. Joe is capable of putting the frighteners on them and others. The girls are a little trickier. I thought you might be able to get new ones – fresh blood and all that. Have you an agency that you work with? I could do some interviews for you?'

'Yes there is, but it needs me. Look, let's think about opening in a month. Yes, I know we will miss a lot of the Arab trade, but better that than disappointing them by not being up to standard. Besides, if the place is right in what it offers and the word spreads, they will fly in in their private jets for the odd weekend, a lot used to do that to get the delights of Pixie's.'

'Okay, I said I would be guided by you. I'm just impatient to get everything up and running and to fuck Joe, like he needs fucking. Going back to the prostitutes, what about the male element? You didn't have that at Pixie's, but what do you think to some male prostitutes being installed in Tête à Tête?'

'Gays and straights?'

'If you think it would work.'

'It would. I've often had a whisper of a few Arabs wanting male company, but I didn't have big enough premises. And, there's an element of forty-something women exec types who would pay good money to be helped to relax.'

'And lesbian sex?'

'I like the way you're thinking.'

'Thought you would.'

Layla smiled as Jade's surprisingly girlish laughter came down the phone.

'Glad we're on the same wave-length, but let's get the one section going full tilt first. I want the Arab trade from Pixie's, then we'll branch out.'

'Agreed, and no problem seen in that quarter. What about Gina. Can you contact her? You have to get her out of that house. God knows how she's feeling.'

'Leave it with me. I'll be on to it. Don't forget to destroy your sim, I've moved on to sim number two. Take care. And remember, stay strong.'

Somehow she knew she needn't have said that to Jade. Although Jade's initial shock had seen her break, she had soon recovered. This pleased, Layla. *And, I guessed right about her sexual leanings.* It had occurred to Layla a while ago that nanny was with Jade for more reasons than to look after her child.

A few phone calls later and all of Layla's meetings had been cancelled.

Still shaking from the shock and wishing she'd insisted that Adrian come around immediately, Layla sank into a hot bath, but didn't dawdle too long, it was already nine and she couldn't settle her mind. There must be something she could do to help Gina.

After dressing and feeling in need of a breath of air, she opened the glass doors and stepped out on to the balcony. Normal life buzzed far below her. Boats trundled along the Thames, as if gliding on a diamond studded sheet of ice such was the effect of the sun dappling the water's surface. She loved the view, but longed to be back in her own home.

Looking down to the street level, she saw a group of people jostling. *Fuck! The bloody press. Bloody wolf pack!* There must have been some sort of leak, they must know the cottage was hers, but how did they know

170

she was here? Fucking Gosling! There was no other answer.

The doorbell shrilled. Going to the phone she picked it up. 'Let me in, Layla. No fuss, just press the release and let me in.'

Fear streaked through her. Why was he here? *Christ, he must have come like a bat out of hell, it wasn't two hours, well a little more, since she'd seen him on the TV in Kent. Surely he hasn't come to arrest me!*

Her fear compounded as he walked through the door, but she determined not to show it. 'I presume you're here about those children being found in my skip?'

Gosling lashed out at her. The blow missed as Layla stepped back in time to avoid it. 'Not your best idea, you prick! Look good wouldn't it, me with a black eye again? There's already a police brutality suit in the offing.'

Putting space between them as she said this, Layla stepped behind the sofa. Gosling still hadn't spoken. His face held a rage she'd only seen the like of on his colleague who'd she'd called a pussy licker. Bad error of judgement that had turned out to be.

'What's this about? Though I think I can guess. You've found out about my insurance policy?'

'Fucking insurance policy? You would have been rid of me by now if you'd kept your half of the deal! I'd decided to quit. The death of them kids was the last straw for me. I went to get the million to off shore it, and eight hundred thousand of it is fucking counterfeit. Did you think I wouldn't know? You stupid cock-sucker!'

'I didn't trust you and I was right.'

He stepped forward. His fist raised. The doorbell stayed his progress.

'I'll just let my lawyer in, shall I?'

'How do you know it's him?'

'I have my ways.'

'You cow! You're going nowhere!'

'Don't come near me! Start thinking like the fucking cop you're meant to be. My lawyer's at the door, and there's a pack of press hanging like blood hounds for a snippet. I only have to scream and it will carry through the open windows and be recorded by the press of the world, who, by the way, saw you enter! You can turn this visit around. You came here to inform me that those kids have been found at my property and that's all, right?'

Thank God, he took this on board.

'You only have yourself to blame, Gosling. You welched on the deal. And so, you got your comeuppance. If you hadn't got that manager to inform on me after promising not to, I would have made good the counterfeit.' The bell rang again. Banking on her theory that the tail they had on Gosling had informed Adrian that Gosling had come here, was correct, Layla said, 'I think I should let Adrian in or he will have your colleagues swarming this place in seconds.'

Gosling nodded. A look of something dawning on him crossed his face, this soon changed to an air of defeat as his body sagged. Layla smiled to herself as she pressed the intercom. 'Come up calmly. Everything's, okay. Don't alert the pack hounds.' Turning back to Gosling, she experienced a feeling of power. The feeling that had deserted her since the gold first came to light.

'Look. I don't need this. None of this is my usual life. Yes, I'm the daughter of a lag, but I broke ties with him years ago. I had to take steps to save myself from what Joe did with that gold assignment, but that was forced on me.'

'And you came out of it smelling like roses. I helped you with that.'

'Ha! If you call double crossing me, helping me? I don't. Well, you've got what you deserved.'

His eyes screwed up as if weighing something up. What he said next, frightened her, 'Little Miss Goody Two, Fucking Designer Shoes, isn't so squeaky clean is she? I smell a rat. And, I know one when I see one. What are you up to, eh? You're planning something. I can feel it in your fear. I'd say you were your father's daughter, through and through. Well, who'd have guessed that?'

Adrian came through from the hallway. 'Guessed what?'

'Gosling thinks I truly am my father's daughter. Well, if he'd wanted to insult me, he couldn't have done it better. I don't know what he's talking about. Unless he is referring to me being involve in those kids' murders. Christ, how did they come to be in my skip?' Feigning a sob, she sat down. A fear had gone through her at how Gosling had nearly guessed the truth. 'I – I almost think it must have been Joe . . .'

'He's dead, so how could it have been?' This came out a little too quickly from Gosling, but also held a note of surprise.

'She's talking hypothetically, as he was behind the gold scam, and now this has come up. You have to admit it is a coincidence, almost as if someone has it in for my client. You wouldn't know anything about that, would you, Gosling? And, what are you doing here anyway, threatening my client?'

'Counterfeit notes.'

'I've explained to him that it was my insurance policy.'

'And a good one. You're not to be trusted, Gosling. You proved that. Well, that might teach you not to mess with us. You have Two hundred thousand of kosher

173

cash, you should be grateful for that. You did nothing for it.'

'We've been through that. And now, I think he should leave. I've persuaded him that if asked by the press, he should say that he came to inform me of what is happening. I think it best, Adrian, if you see him off the premises. Shake his dirty hand in front of the press to make it look good. They'll be in a frenzy by now seeing him and then you arrive.'

'Watch yourself, Layla fucking Parrondski! I'm on to you.'

A shiver travelled down her spine but she held her head up high. 'I have nothing to hide, you can watch me all you want to.'

*

'Layla, what did you do, why is he suspicious of you? He's a snake. He'll eat you alive. How much did you tell him?'

'I don't know. I only treated him with the contempt he deserves. It felt good telling him we put that insurance of the counterfeit notes in place and why.'

'ONLY! That immediately alerted him that you were up to something. Showing contempt shows that you think you are ahead of the game. He will want to know why you have such confidence. I told you, always, always act the wronged wife in his presence.'

'I don't see what he can find out. The nightclub, is being set up under the name of the French company we registered. None of it is traceable to me. The story will go that Jade went to France and met this entrepreneur. She was given the job of managing the Tête à Tête. He won't like her being back, but there's nothing he can do, and she hasn't broken her half of the bargain. She could have told the police about what happened and why, but she hasn't.

Then there is, Belle et Belle. That is mine, but it would be extremely difficult to crack that it is just a front. And there is nothing wrong with me, a widowed business woman, starting a new business. Forget Gosling, damage limitation is well in place with him. I want you to get me tickets on a plane to Nice. Make it before the end of the week. Oh, and I rescheduled the meetings I had for today. All you have to do now is undress.'

His laughter relaxed her, but didn't hide his immediate reaction as her words lit a spark of desire in him. Watching him loosen his tie and unbutton his shirt clenched the muscles in her groin.

Power was an aphrodisiac to her. 'I want you to fuck me till I cry for mercy and then some.'

In his arms she drank in the smell of the Clive Christian No 1 cologne he wore. And savoured the feel of his designer stubble brushing her cheeks as he brought his lips to hers. She wanted to cry out his name as his hands travelled her body, but she was in charge. She had to be. Drawing away from him, she grasped his hand and pulled him to her bedroom. 'First you undress me. Then I will tell you what to do next. You are my slave.'

It thrilled her to see his veiled eyes almost begging her. Well, he would have her, but it would be on her terms. Always on her terms. Layla Parrondski was back. The gold scam had rocked her for a time, but she was now well and truly in the driving seat once more.

19

'It stinks! There's something going on. Look Chief, I'll
be truthful with you, I don't trust Gosling.'
Cleaston stamped up and down the Chief's office.
'Sit down for Christ's sake, man!'
'Look at the facts. Parrondski goes missing. On the
same night Gina Walter's goes missing. Then her friend
Zoe Feldon is murdered, and Gina's and Zoe's kids are
kidnapped. All while Gosling is in the fucking building!
Gina turns up with a cock and bull story – and I can tell
you, Gosling was shitting himself at that point. Then we
get a body – one that could be anybody, it's that
charred. Next we get some of the Heathrow gold hoard
showing up and Parrondski's wife is implicated, and
now those kid's bodies are dumped right outside her
house! On top of that, no one can contact Gina. How far
can you take coincidences, eh? How bloody far? Surely
you've got your suspicions?'
'I may have, but no proof, and that's where you're
falling down.'
'You took me off the case.'
'Yes, and for good reason. You're a rookie. Have you
thought that it could be Gina Walters who's behind it
all? No. Thought not. Look, this is too big for you.
Gosling can handle it. Leave it to him. Apart from the
link that you're trying to make with having him
involved, I'm sure he is sifting through the rest of the
coincidences and will come up with something. Police
work takes time. You should know that.'
'I believe Gosling is involved in some way. There, I've
said it. And I truly think it. So, if you won't reinstate
me, at least put someone other than him in charge.'

'Don't be ridiculous! You're talking about an old-school cop here. Straight as a die. Now take that allegation back or you may find yourself in big trouble.'
Cleaston stood up. 'I'll take the trouble first.'
As the door shut after him, Bealver mopped his brow. He knew Cleaston was right. Gosling was in on something, but he could do nothing about it. Gosling held cards and his whole hand were aces.

*

Cleaston stormed down to the booking-in desk. The clerks seeing him dropped their heads. Sergeant Helen Tring looked up and smiled. *Christ I could rip her knickers off here and now!* But then, he knew that sex, like everything else, had to be on her terms, and he had to be a good boy to taste the delights of her.
Speaking formally to him, she asked, 'What can I do for you, Detective Sergeant? I didn't know we housed anyone you were interested in?'
His whispered, 'you are housed here, aren't you?' had her swivelling her head to look at the small band of her staff, before looking back at him. Anger tainted her own whisper, 'Not in work!'
'I need to ask you a few questions concerning someone we held overnight, I have a form to fill in, when can you spare the time?' As he said this in a normal voice he looked at her with his best pleading, I need you, look.
'We're quiet for the moment, I can come now if you like, have you a room for the interview?'
He nodded and asked her to bring her personal notes on Layla Parrondski. Her eyes shot up and held fear. He liked that. He needed to be master of her sometimes, even if it meant he would be in trouble later. But then, he liked some of the trouble he got into with her too. Trouble that made her slap him about. Not so that she

178

marked any visible part of him, but places he could cover up were often bruised. He felt a twitch in his trousers at the thought of her domineering him in this way, and the little whip she kept to punish him with. He couldn't resist brushing against her as she came from behind her desk. Her eyes flashed at him. Her beautiful green eyes that complimented her glorious red hair. No one knew how glorious it was but him, as always she had it pinned up in a tight coil at the back of her head. When it fell loose . . . Another twinge in his groin had him pull in a sharp breath.

'Don't play games with me, Cleaston!' She always called him this when angry with him. 'What do you want, and why have you brought me here?' She looked around the, barely bigger than a cupboard sized room housed in the basement that was used for nothing more than a storeroom. Pulling her petite frame up to its full height she snapped, 'you'd better have a good reason!'
'I wanted to talk to you and to hold you.'
'Fuck off. Not in work. I've warned you. I have ambitions, and you don't see sexual relations in a broom cupboard on the fucking application forms.'
'No one saw us come here.'
'I don't fucking care. . . What the hell are you doing?'
'Locking the door.'
'Christ, have you gone mad. I'll kill you for this. Come near me and I'll scream the place down!'
'I love you when you're mad.'
'Oh, you do, do you? Well, you're loving me days are over after this, mate!'
The pain from her kick had him buckled over. His legs gave way. Vomit stung his throat. She bent down beside him and gave him a dazzling smile as she picked up the key he'd dropped. Her eyes held the sexual

179

desire he'd been trying to cultivate, 'You're a naughty boy. Mummy's cross with you. Come around to mine at eight. Mummy is going to give Cleaston a good thrashing. Your balls will be recovered by then!' Slamming the door behind her she left. *Fucking vixen.* But despite the pain he was in he had to admire her. He knew the rules. He should have played by them. All he'd wanted to do was to talk to her about his theory on Gosling. Get her input. He should have stuck to that. Now he was in agony and somehow had to recover. God, he loved that woman!

After fifteen minutes, Cleaston felt able to leave the room and head back along the corridors to his desk. On his way he called into the bog. Winced as the pee he forced out stung him, then washed his hands and swilled his face. Someone entered the room. Peeping through eyes that had taken in water, he made out Gosling.

The two men stared at each other. Gosling spoke first, 'Drop it, Cleaston. No one likes theories, or blatant accusations. You're treading on nails and one is going to pierce you big time.'

'I don't frighten easily.'

'No? Well, I'll just have to use heavy tactics then, won't I? I saw you go into the store with Sergeant Tring. I was in the basement. I'd gone down to look for a file. I'd just got to the door of the file room when I heard footsteps and then Tring's voice asking why you were taking her down there, and you replying that you wanted somewhere really private. I slipped inside the darkened room until you'd passed. I then trained the camera so that it was focussed on the window and would record you walking back. After that I made my way along the corridor and heard you in the store room.

180

I listened outside. She didn't like your advances, did she?'

'You fucking bent bastard, you!'

'Humm, more allegations. Haven't I just warned you? Sackable offence the pair of you have committed. Sexual relations on the premises is a no no.'

'We didn't . . .'

'But that's not the tale I will tell. And you both getting the push wouldn't go down well with your pint-sized vixen, now would it?'

Cleaston's body shrunk in on him. Gosling moved closer to him. He was so near that he could feel his breath on his cheek. 'Drop the witch hunt, or I go to the Chief with this.' Gosling flashed a tape in front of his eyes. A deep fear cut into the very soul of Cleaston as he realised the implications. The strength of the feeling had him clenching his teeth.

'If I was you, I'd be a good little boy. But then, Tring won't pleasure you if you are, she likes naughty boys. If you don't keep your nose out of my business, she'll never pleasure you again. The ambitious little tyke will kill you for causing her to lose her job.'

Gosling turned and left the room. Cleaston wiped the stupid tears that had gathered in his eyes and thumped the wall. Now his fist as well as his balls stung. He just wanted to curl up and cry. Instead, he swilled his face again, squared his shoulders and left the bog with as much dignity as he could muster.

It sickened him that he would have to let Gosling off the hook. But he knew he had no choice in the matter.

20

Gina stared at the ceiling. Every movement caused her pain. Not just physical pain, gut wrenching heartache pain. *Why, why? My baby, my baby.* A scream formed in her mind and released itself in a bloodcurdling holler that bounced off the walls of the bedroom. The Nanny came running over to her. Her hand trembled as she tried to take Gina's in hers. 'Don't, don't, it won't help.'
'Nothing will help. Only killing that bastard. I HATE HIM!'
'Hush. Look, all this shouting is putting a strain on you. You could undo all the good work the Doc has done.'
'I don't care, I want to die. I want to die.'
With nothing left to say, the nanny sat down. Gina lifted herself into a sitting position ignoring the pain this caused her. 'How did they die? Did you see anything, Nanny?'
'No. I saw nothing. I only heard about it on the news this morning, then he called me and told me that I was to inform you. I had nothing to do with it, nor would I. They were fine when I left them. I tucked them up in bed as usual and switched out the lights. When I checked on them two hours later before retiring to bed myself, they were gone. I went to the boss and he told me not to worry, they had been taken somewhere where they would be found. I knew then what their fate would be. I knew he wouldn't let them free in case they talked.'
'Oh God, I can't bear it. Take the pain away, Nanny.'
Although it seemed childish to her own ears to call this woman Nanny, Gina had no other name for her.

'Look, my dear. Bragdon is asking to see you. Quieten down or I daren't let him for fear of the boss coming along to quieten you himself.'

'Yes, fetch Bragdon. Please fetch Bragdon.'

*

Bragdon looked as though he'd been crying. A strange thing to see on a man of his ilk. A bulk of a man and a vicious bully, he'd genuinely loved the kids.

'Oh, Bragdon, we didn't get them out. Oh, God, we didn't . . .'

'Look, I ain't got long, I only came because I have a note for yer. It were in me shed. If I'm caught I'll be skinned, so take it and shut the fuck up!'

This brought Gina out of herself. She took the note. Part of her was afraid. How far could she trust, Bragdon?

'How the hell did a note for me get into your shed?'

Christ, that private dick had been just that – a dick – in daring to leave a note! What if Bragdon told of him!

'I don't care how. I just don't want it associating with me. I just wanted to help in some way. I'll go now, and you're not to say as I've been. I know nanny won't, she always does what I tell her.'

Gina nodded, she knew that Bragdon ruled the staff with fear. She stuffed the note under the pillow as nanny came back into the room.

'He's going soft. He'd better watch himself. He had tears running down his face.'

'It ain't soft to feel something when kids have suffered, Nanny.'

'You mustn't think that I don't feel anything. I have them kids on my conscience and will for ever more.'

Gina doubted that. This vile woman had got the children ready every day for their photo shoot, and had bathed the filth off them when it was done. She'd

184

looked after them and cared for them, only to give them confidence to do what they had to. For two pins Gina could scratch the old bag's eyes out. But she knew better than to do it.

'I'm alright now. You can leave me. I need some time alone. I just want to go to sleep.'

'Yes, sleep's the best thing. Just call out if you need me.'

Ripping the note open, Gina read: *Come into the garden as soon as it gets dark.*

A hope entered her. They were going to get her away. *Thank God.* She didn't think she could bear to stay here another moment.

Watching the note swirl down the toilet pan an idea came to her. This was her chance to get the other little girl out. At least that would be something. It would be dangerous, but she could do it.

'Are you there, my dear?'

His hated voice came to her. She couldn't face him. Silently she turned the lock on the bathroom door.

'Now, don't be silly. I need you to come and play with me.'

A sick feeling lay in the pit of her stomach. Yesterday he'd near killed her, and now he expected to play! 'I'm not well enough. Go away, you bastard. I'd sooner run a knife through you than play with you.'

'Ha, I was only joking. I've come to see how you are.'

'How do you expect me to be, you murdering bastard!'

A thump on the door made her jump. Terror streaked through her. She slumped down on to the toilet.

'Come out here, now!'

'No. Go away. Leave me alone, Joe. I never want to be with you again. You're a monster. How could you? H – How could y – you?' The words caught in her throat.

185

Her body heaved with sobs that racked pain through her.

'I have some nice powder for you. Come on, babe, you know it will make you feel better.'

The thought of a line of the good stuff had her lifting her head.

'Come on, we'll sniff it together, you know it makes you feel good.'

The temptation was too much. Gina clicked the lock open.

'There's a good girl. Come on. Let's go to our bedroom, there's no fun in this sick room. Doc said that with pain killers you'll be fine to perform. I thought that with the coke, you'll be even better than fine.'

'Just give me a line and leave me alone, Joe.'

'COUNT! And, no. there'll be no line without payback, then you can have as many as you want. Look, I have it here.' From his smoking jacket pocket of bright blue silk, Joe took a small bag and shook it at her.

Her hand shot out to grab it.

'No, no, naughty, naughty. Gina will have to pay for that. I will have to smack her arse.'

'No more violence, Count. Please. What's happened to you? You're not Gosling, for Christ's sake. You never used to use violence.'

'Well my pretty Gina became a naughty girl and I like to make her into a good one.'

'I'll be good. I promise. Once I've filled my nostrils, I'll be your old Gina.'

'You'd better be. Come along then. I have hot water in the jacuzzi ready for us, and we'll put two good lines out. How will that be?'

Knowing she was beaten, Gina smiled, 'That'll be lovely. Thank you, Count.' But inside she seethed with hate and malice towards this heinous man. How could she have thought herself in love with him?

She'd had a plan before he hurt her to exhaust him with sex. Well, no matter what it cost her physically, or emotionally, she would do the same again, then she would go to the children's bedroom, get the other little girl and go out into the garden. From there she would leave her fate to others.

The line had tickled her nostrils, then eased her pain before taking her into a floating world where nothing mattered. In the jacuzzi Joe had been his old self, stroking her, saying nice things to her until she was more than ready. Then he'd helped her out and had dried her on a soft luxurious towel before carrying her to his bed. A huge round affair covered in soft, slippery silk. There he'd taken her to heights she'd almost forgotten she could reach and had hollered out of her with all the crudest swearwords her mind would give her. This had increased Joe's ardour, and he'd had the fuck of his life, or so he kept telling her before he'd drifted off to sleep.

Now Gina's hazy brain was nagging her. There was something she had to do. What was it? Sleep beckoned her. God that line had been good. She closed her eyes. But the persistent feeling that she had to do something wouldn't leave her.

Getting off the bed, her legs felt like logs of wood. She was so tired. What should she do first?

Seeing her robe, she grabbed it. She needed to get out of this room that was certain. A snore from Joe made her cringe in fright. The room spun. *How much was in that fucking line?* She couldn't function. Making an effort she lunged at the door. The noise she made stilled her when she reached it. Joe snored again, an

187

aggravated snore as if she had disturbed him, when he didn't want disturbing.

Gina waited. No sense of what she was doing would come to her. She liked that feeling, but knew she had to follow the urge in her.

Through the door, two strong arms grabbed her. Fear made her let go and allowed her to take the safety the haziness in her brain had beckoned her to do so.

In the blackness she found a lovely swirling peace where she didn't care who had hold of her, or what he would do to her. She didn't even care that her baby was dead. Such was the bliss the line had given her.

21

Gosling saw the great bulky figure of Bragdon cross the lawn and noted who he had in his arms. The business he had with Joe could wait. He needed to follow to see where Gina was being taken. She was obviously unconscious.

From the shadow of the tree he'd managed to get to without being seen he, watched.

Another figure came forward. *Interesting.*

This figure took Gina from Bragdon and carried her into the forest. Gosling waited. Bragdon went back inside the house. Crossing the lawn, Gosling peered after the shadowy figures. They were headed for the lane. Getting back to his car he eased the handbrake off and let his car freewheel backwards down the sloping drive. Once near to the gate he engaged the gear and did a u-turn, then drove like a madman along the lane to where he saw a car parked. Stopping, he reversed back and into a gateway dousing his lights. Again he waited. Ten minutes or so later the figures emerged. Gosling waited until the engine of the other car started up and its lights became a spot in the distance before pulling out and then putting his foot down. He hoped to be near enough when the car reached the main road to see which way it turned. He followed it as it went in the direction away from London. *Got you!*

In the forest, the man dressed all in black held Gina in his arms. He made his way towards the trail where he had an associate waiting in a Range Rover.

The cop had fallen for his subterfuge and followed the gardener. It had cost him a packet to get the chap to take a sack of twigs to his car and drive them to Harlow, where he was to make a great show of putting them in a skip that was parked outside The Chequers. He chuckled to himself as he imagined Gosling's face. For a cop he was something of an idiot and easy to predict. Graven, the Private D had guessed Gosling would visit tonight as he would need to update Parrondski on what had happened regarding the dead kids. In the likelihood that the visit might coincide with his plans to get Gina away, Graven made arrangements with the gardener. It had only taken a phone call to activate the plan and meet the chap in the woods. The rest had gone smoothly. The Chequers was his local, he knew they were closed for renovations, and had a skip outside. It had all gone like clockwork.

He stood a moment as the Range Rover pulled away. Gina hadn't come round. She must have had a good dose of coke. Layla would look after her. He had to get back to the house and try to save Bragdon's skin.

As he approached it, the sound of a single gunshot told him he was too late. That bastard Gosling must have phoned Parrondski as soon as he was on the trail. Poor Bragdon. But then Graven chuckled, *Ha! It will be more like, poor Gosling when he has to report to the Count that he's lost Gina!* That was one clash he wanted to hang around for.

In the meantime, his immediate problem was to try to get another insider. He needed that or his information would dry up, and that would serve no one.

22

Gosling approached the skip. Growing horror knotted his stomach till he thought he'd throw his guts up. He hadn't thought they'd kill Gina. God! He couldn't take that! He'd planned that she would eventually be his, at least, his mistress. No one would replace his Sara.

The jagged, rusty metal chaffed his hands as he jumped up and grasped the side of the skip. Heaving his bulk over it he reached out towards the sack he'd seen thrown into it. His mind didn't question when Gina had been put into a sack, he was just convinced she had been.

Reaching out and grabbing the bag he was surprised how easily it came towards him. Realisation began to dawn on him. *Fuck! Fuck! Fuck!*

Jumping down he stood looking at the skip as if it had somehow let him down and he would beat the guts out of it. *Christ, they've fucking had me for a fucking idiot!*

The sound of the kick he lashed out boomed off the metal. A light came on in a nearby house. Getting back into his car he throttled it and sped away heading for London, putting in a phone call to the Count on the way.

The one-way conversation bellowed around him.

'You're a fucking crap cop, you. How could you let them trick you like that? Get Gina back, or you're dead! And I'll personally pull the trigger. You fucking turd!'

There was a pause, then in a cold calm voice,

'Bragdon's dead! I need him disposing of and I need another heavy. Sort it!'

Tapping the 'end call' symbol, Gosling sighed. It'd been a long day. And far from the Count killing *him*, he could strangle the heinous child-killer with his own

bare hands. Just in case, he'd not return there tonight.
He put in another call. Bugsy Brown had been
unemployed since coming out of jail. He'd done a
stretch for violent assault. He should have done a
thousand stretches for a thousand violent assaults but
he'd got lucky as he'd been useful. 'Bugsy, I've got a
job for you. It's a live-in job out in the country with
plenty of action. Pack a case and get a taxi to The Black
Bull in Epping. I'll meet you there. The money's good
and there's kids involved, as well as shooters. . . Yeah, I
thought you'd like that. Right, I want you there in less
than an hour and a half, so get moving.'

As he pulled up outside The Black Bull, Gosling put
another call into the Count. 'Right, I have someone on
his way. He's called Bugsy Brown, real name, Brendan
Brown. He's big, he has form and if treated right will
give good service. He likes to feel in the hub of things,
and will do anything if it bigs him up. He won't take
much training, knows all the same people Bragdon
knew. The only thing is, he has a sight more
intelligence than Bragdon, so watch that. His first job
will be to dispose of Bragdon and clean up the mess.
He'll do that with the minimum of fuss. Treat him right
and he'll be a good body guard and a whole lot more.
You can trust him to check out your premises and keep
order in them. He's well known and feared.'

'Good. Now, get on to getting Gina back. I need her.
And, don't forget to get me two more kids!'

The whine in the Count's voice sickened him. But at
the same time increased the sick fear inside him.

Dropping Bugsy off, Gosling steered for London. A
tiredness ached his bones. He put another call into HQ.
Left a message that he was working on a job where he
might need back-up. Telling them that he had a lead to

192

the Asian. The Chief had gone home, but they would contact him.

Another call to the Asian was needed. Put the frighteners on him, and get him to source a couple of little blonde heads that Gosling could pick up now and deliver to the Count. Hopefully, that would sweeten him.

Punching a number into his phone he adjusted his ear peace. The Asian answered. 'Gosling here. Another job for you.'

'Oh, man, not another? I've got me missus going nuts over her kid. . .' Gosling noted that the Asian didn't claim the kid as his.

'And the mother of the dead one has slashed her wrists. She ain't gonna make it, man. It's too much, init?'

'Just do it, and do it now or, shall I put in a request for a raid?'

'I'll take me chances, man. I ain't into this sex with kids, man. I ain't supplying you no more.'

Gosling couldn't believe he was hearing this. His rage made him lose his rationality. 'Fucking do it, or I'll fucking make sure you're shot dead during the raid. This will be big. I'll tie you to them dead kids in the skip and come with armed cops, and that's a promise!'

There was a silence at the end of the line, then a slow drawl that sent a shiver down Gosling's spine. 'Do it, man, and you'll be one banged up, ex-cop. I've had to cover me back, init? I've got picture evidence, man. It's with me brief, man. He will receive a key to a certain box if anything happens to me . . . It has to be done, init?'

The cold that had taken him now encased Gosling as if someone had shoved him inside a refrigerator. He ended the call. *That Bastard! He was my only source for the kids, what the fuck, now?*

193

He needed some normality. He'd go home to his Sara. She wouldn't be expecting him. When he'd left early this morning in response to the phone call that had ripped at his guts, he'd said he didn't know when he'd be home. She hadn't questioned him. Still seeing him as he used to be, a dedicated cop, who wouldn't rest until he'd solved a case, she'd given him her support. Told him that she'd be at the end of the phone if he needed her. Then she'd held him in that special way she had, as if he was her little boy, before giving him a sweet tasting kiss and seeing him off. Sara was the only good thing in his life. He needed her right now.

His fingers went to speed dial her number, but he changed his mind. He'd surprise her. She'd love that. The house was in darkness, save for a small light glowing through the bedroom curtains. It gave him a nice feeling to think of his Sara tucked up in bed reading one of her favourite books. She liked those sloppy romance sagas. Cried tears over them, and let the downtrodden lives of the characters really affect her. Bless her, she was all that was soft, loving and kind. God he needed her at this moment. Needed to wrap himself around her. Enter her, and love her in the gentle way that was a million miles from anything he had sexually with anyone else. His need heightened as he imagined her soft yielding body beneath him. With Sara, things were different, he didn't know why, but with her he could last and last. Making love was a different experience than gratifying himself sexually.

His key clicked in the lock and the door gave easily, gliding over the wooden floor. Stepping inside, Gosling stood stock still as if someone had tasered him. The space around him filled with the sound of sexual moans.

The scream started in the pit of his stomach and yelled out the horror of his shocked emotions. 'No . . . No-o-o-o-o!'

It died into a silence that saw him flooded in light and looking up into the face of the Chief as he appeared at the top of the stairs, a shocked, frightened expression on his face. Casting his eyes down the man's magnificent body, gleaming with sweat and rippling with muscle, he saw the Chief straighten and stand strong and defiant.

Taking off as if shot from a gun, Gosling clambered up the stairs and flung his full body weight into Bealver. They crashed into the wall. A winded Bealver gasped for air. Gosling grabbed his balls and twisted them, eliciting a scream that he shouted over, 'You bastard! You fucking bastard!' Tears and snot mingled as they squeezed from his very soul ripping his broken heart into shreds.

Bealver's eyes bulged and almost bled. His gasps of, 'let go, for Christ's sake, let go,' were hoarse and desperate. Finding strength from somewhere, Bealver took in a deep breath and pushed Gosling off him sending him tumbling down the stairs.

Lying at the bottom, disorientated, but not hurt, Gosling heard the sobs of his Sara. But, she wasn't his anymore. The only good thing in his life was tainted. He was finished. Rolling over he got up. Walking through the door, the night air shocked reality into him. He needed to get away. He needed to end it all.

23

'Detective Sergeant Gosling, the officer in charge of the 'children in the skip' murder has been reported as missing.'

For the second time in two days, Layla stared at the TV, only this time it was the evening news. *God! Gosling, missing?*

'The detective's last known movements, as tracked by his mobile phone, placed him in Bristol, where his car has been found abandoned. His police badge and mobile phone, along with a wallet-sized picture of his wife were found on the seat of his car. Our reporter, John Starin is at the Police station now. . . John, what can you tell us about this mysterious disappearance?'

'Mark, Chief Inspector Bealver has issued a statement saying that Sergeant Gosling has been under a lot of strain recently and they are very concerned for his welfare. Here is a picture that they gave out of the Sergeant.'

Gosling's hated face flashed into Layla's lounge.

'The Chief has asked that everyone keeps an eye out for the Sergeant as he may have suffered a breakdown and be in need of help.'

'Could he throw any light on why Sergeant Gosling had left a photo of his wife in the car?'

'No. As far as they all know, his wife is his life and his prop outside of work. It appears that she is in a very bad way.'

'Yes, as can only be imagined. . . Let's go over now to Sergeant Gosling's home, where our reporter, Mary Fish is waiting to hear any news. . . Mary, what can you tell us? Is Mrs Gosling still inside her home?'

'Yes, she hasn't left, though a car pulled up not long ago and we believe the couple who got out and went into the house were her parents. As you can see, there is a policeman on guard outside her door. He stepped aside for the couple as if he had been expecting them. It is believed they live in Cornwall, so would have taken this long to get here.'

'Have you been able to glean anything from the neighbours? Were the Goslings really the happy couple we have been led to believe?'

'Yes. Extremely so, according to one source, though because of the nature of his work, Sergeant Gosling was rarely at home, at least, not in normal hours. Their immediate neighbours are not saying anything, though. It is as if they have some sort of loyalty pact, which is leading to speculation amongst my fellow reporters.'

'But, as we have it at the moment, the couple were happy and there was no marital reason for Sergeant Gosling's disappearance?'

'Yes, that's correct.'

Touching his earpiece, the newscaster looked disorientated for a split second, then was back in command, and said, *'Thank you, Mary, we are now going back to John who appears to have some breaking news.'*

'Yes, Mark, it has just been announced that the two bodies in the skip were in fact those of the missing children, Tammy Feldon, daughter of the murdered, Zoe Feldon, who was a known prostitute, and Amy Walters, daughter of Gina Walters, also a prostitute and the friend and neighbour of Zoe Feldon. It has also been announced that Detective Sergeant Cleaston, a recently promoted sergeant is to be assigned to the case. He will be supervised and under the direction of Bill Riley, a Detective Sergeant from Scotland Yard.'

'That seems to indicate that this is a much bigger case than we all first thought, are there any other indications that this is so?'

'Yes, it is obviously bigger than we imagined. Let's look at the facts that we have. The murder of Zoe Feldon. There has been a suspect charged with this, but it hasn't yet come to court. Now, is that really unconnected with the abduction of the two children by an unknown woman? The children were missing for weeks, before the awful discovery of their bodies. Now we have the disappearance of the main police officer dealing with the case. And, he isn't the only one that can't be located. There was a picture given out of Amy Walters' mother, Gina Walters. She is wanted urgently to come forward. It's not known if she actually knows about her daughter's death as of yet, or indeed, if she is involved in any way.'

Gina's picture filled the screen.

Shit. Fucking Gosling! Christ, what now? My plane leaves in just over three hours! Layla clicked the remote button to switch the TV off. Her eyes went to the ceiling. In the bed upstairs, Gina lay in a semi-unconscious state. She'd overdosed on something or other. Layla had brought her to her mother's old house, and the Polish nurse was looking after her once more. Layla had paid the nurse half the money promised and she'd sent that back home, but, just in case, Layla had kept her on a little while longer, promising her that she would be home for Christmas.

Now, she wondered how far she could trust the girl not to expose Gina. From the moment those bodies had been found, she'd known it was a mistake to get Gina out. But her gut feeling of looking after her own had made her go through with it. Now she wasn't sure. Gina could lead the cops to her, then they would have the link they needed to pin the whole lot on her!

These thoughts led her to do what she knew she shouldn't, she put in a call to her Private D.

'Do we know where Gosling is?'

'No. Did he have money? I can't contact the agent who was tailing him. He'd done a great job up to now.'

'Yes, two hundred thou, in kosher and eight hundred thou in almost undetectable counterfeit, which, if he was clever, he could launder easily enough.'

'He could have bought my man off with that. That's if he sussed him out, which he must have done, but God knows, how.'

Layla remembered how Gosling had been when he'd last been at the Penthouse. There had been a moment of something dawning on him when she'd known that the next caller would be, and was, Adrian. *Shit, that was careless. He must have guessed she had someone watching him and that that someone would contact Adrian!*

Not mentioning this, Layla continued with the reason she'd rung her D, 'We have a problem – Gina. The cops are looking for her. I have a nurse caring for her, but I'm not sure that I can trust her not to report Gina to the police if she sees any pictures on the TV.'

'I'll take care of it. It won't be pretty, but necessary. Leave it with me.'

Layla felt her spine tremble and her skin crawl as the truth of what he'd said dawned on her. *Christ, if Gina is found here, I'm finished!*

'Layla? Layla?'

'Yes, I'm here.'

'Go to the airport and get on the plane. Just do it. Everything will be sorted. Gina is expendable. She is a liability to you. With Gosling in charge we had a chance. He could have been seen to locate her and to eliminate her. We had enough on him to force that from him, but now. Christ. Scotland Yard are involved. I'll contact Adrian. He'll sort that hit man. This has to be done, Layla, you know that, don't you?'

'Can't she just disappear, never to be found again? There must be another way.'

'If you are to succeed in taking over, you have to be hard, Layla. You can't have one ounce of softness in you, or allow yourself to become attached to others so that it clouds your judgement. Go to France. The mess will be cleaned up once you've gone.'

Layla knew he was right. She straightened her shoulders. 'Okay, I'm out of here in five. I'll take the nurse to the airport with me and put her on the first flight to Poland. Adrian has a key to this house.'

Shaking as if she was stood in an ice hotel with no clothes on, Layla tapped another number into her phone and summoned her driver. Nick wouldn't bring her usual Rolls to pick her up, as that had long been under wraps in her garage in Holland Park. Afraid that with its personalised number it was too distinctive and could be picked up anywhere, on any CCTV, so she regularly hired a car now. This week it was an Audi.

Checking she had her documents, and her cases were stacked ready, Layla went to her safe, then ran upstairs. Reaching the top, she saw the nurse just about to go into Gina. 'Come. Come quickly. Now, get a bag. Put in it what you need to take home. Get your passport. Hurry, we leave in five minutes. You are going home. Here's a thousand pounds. I know I owe you more. I will transfer it to your bank account in the next couple of days, and our arrangement will stand, there will be a regular payment. But if you utter a word to a soul about anything, or anyone that you have seen here, then it will stop. Do you understand?'

The girl nodded, her expression flitting from incredulous to happiness. 'Yes. I understand. Thank you.'

'Now, hurry. I will take you to Gatwick. You will have to go on standby until you get a seat on a plane.'

'Yes. I understand, I did this before. Thank you. Thank you.'

Layla hadn't realised just how much the girl wanted to go home, but now as she scurried away she felt a slight pang of guilt at having welched on their earlier deal. Opening the door to Gina's room, she put her head around and peeped at the sleeping form. Tears stung her eyes. Going in, she quickly searched around, there was no mobile in sight. She hadn't thought there would be and was very glad that messaging had taken the form of notes between her and D. There was still the house phones though. She'd have to cut those off, just in case Gina woke before they came . . . God, what if that happened? No, she wouldn't think about it.

Going out of the room and closing the door was the biggest test she'd had to face so far. But, she did it. Leaving the house locked and with Gina having no access to keys, broke her heart. Though part of her knew, that the action showed she was ready. Ready to become a Top Dog, in the underworld of London.

24

Gina stirred. Her head hurt and her throat felt like sandpaper. Memory evaded her. She looked around the room. Recognised it as the one she'd been in before in Layla's house, and a sense of feeling safe came over her.

As more of her senses came to life she had an eerie feeling that she was all alone in the world.

Struggling to work out how she got here, and why, made her head throb even harder. Inside her chest there was a heavy, sad feeling, as if something really bad had happened, but she didn't know what it was.

Closing her eyes, she didn't resist as the mist that clogged her brain and took her once more into oblivion. Into this swirling nothingness came Amy. Her blonde curls tumbling over her face, her grin wide and her tinkling laughter echoing as if Amy was in an empty room. Gina smiled and reached out for her. 'Mummy's here, baba, come to mummy, Amy.' Amy came towards her, but when close she disappeared into a floating cloud. 'Amy, Amy . . . 'A-M-E-E-E-Y. . .' As the last syllable of this cry died, Gina shot to a sitting position. The full horror of what had happened slapped her hard in the face. She gasped to get air into her lungs. The pain that ripped through her tore her heart in two. 'No, no, no . . . Don't let it be true, I can't bear it. I want my Amy.' Tears clogged every part of her till it felt as though they dripped from her fingers and her toes as her whole body wept.

Nobody came. Lifting her head from her hands she looked through the blur towards the door. Someone must have heard her distress. Why was it all so quiet?

Fear trickled in to her despair. Throwing the covers back she swung her legs out of the bed. Her feet sunk into the deep pile carpet. She steadied herself for a second or two as the old fashioned, but beautiful furniture seemed to wobble on its carved clawed feet. After a moment she lifted her body to a standing position, but the room spun around her and she sat back down again. *Christ, that was some shit that bastard gave me!*

This thought filled her with hate for the vile man that had taken the essence of her life away from her. From the moment she'd met him she'd lost everything. He'd possessed her. Sucked her dry, and then moulded her into something different to what she had been. Now, he'd taken the last of her reason for existence away from her. All gone. Everything that she was – gone.

A seething, burning hatred entered her. Well, she'd do for him. She wouldn't wait for Layla's plan to bring him down, she'd go to the police and tell them everything - everything about everyone in, her stinking life. The fucking Count, and Gosling, that so-called, daddy, and even Layla and Jade. They were all rotten. How they made their money and what they did to other people's lives was rotten.

With this determination, she stood up again. This time she didn't experience the disorientation.

Walking unsteadily towards the wardrobe, she stopped as the sound of a door being opened took her attention. Listening over her rapidly beating heart was difficult, but now she could make out footsteps treading the stairs, coming closer.

Fear gripped her. Why she felt like this she couldn't think. She was safe here, wasn't she? It would just be Layla or that nurse. But nothing she tried to calm herself with, would reassure her.

Sweat dampened her body. Her breathing laboured. The door handle turned. Her eyes stung as she unblinkingly stared towards it. Little by little the door opened, until she was looking into the evil eyes of Frankie Droile!
'What . . . Why?'
Unable to move she watched mesmerised as he crossed the room towards her. His hands shot out and grabbed her. 'No . . . NO! Frankie, don't . . .'
His fingers held her neck in a grip that felt like a vice. She tried to pull his arms away from her. Felt her breath leaving her lungs, in a stinging rush. Her eyes bulged out of their sockets.
Powerless to stop what was happening, her legs gave way. But even though they buckled beneath her, Frankie Droile held her upright. All her weight was now on her neck. She couldn't breathe. The space around her went into a zinging high pitched noise that brought with it a darkness. Not resisting, Gina went into the black hole that had opened up beneath her.

When she came around, Gina could feel something close to every part of her body and a sensation that told her they were on the move. But she couldn't move. She couldn't move a limb. She was trussed up, and the horror of the knowledge that she was inside some sort of crate, struck a terror into her. She tried to call out, but her mouth was bound tightly. The drumming of an engine told her that she was being transported somewhere.
A small hope entered her. Maybe they were taking her back to Joe. It wasn't what she wanted, but it was better than dying, which is what she'd thought would happened to her.
She tried to relax. Tried to talk herself into thinking that everything would be alright. Yes, Joe would

punish her, but he loved her, didn't he? He'd told her that he loved her and wanted her. And what Joe wanted, Joe got.

As her mind relaxed she began to make plans. She'd be good to Joe. She wouldn't make him angry with her ever again. She never wanted to be frightened again, or to feel alone. If she gave Joe what he wanted, then she needn't be.

Her fear dissipated. But with the release of that emotion another entered her. The horror of facing years and years with the man who had killed her baby. Hate once more swathed her. She would make him pay, she had to. She would revenge her darling Amy's life one way or another.

On and on the journey went. Her limbs cramped, her throat dried. Surely they would reach Epping soon? Closing her eyes, Gina tried to allow the constant moving and drumming of the engine to lull her to sleep, but then the pace of the rocking of her changed, and with it, the agony of her screaming joints burned deeper, as she was being bumped about and violently thrown from side to side bruising every part of her. Maybe they had reached the lane that led to Joe's? Trepidation began to seep into her as they came to a halt. How had she fooled herself into thinking everything was going to be alright? This was Frankie Droile she was dealing with. A notorious hit man. Everyone in the East End knew of him. Frankie Droile, the killer!

Panic had her pulling short, sharp, snorting breaths through her nose. Her body dampened instantly as a cold sweat broke out all over her.

The sound of a vehicle door creaking open and then slamming and footsteps crunching on twigs and dried foliage, struck a terror into her.

Another door opened, she guessed it was the back doors of what must be a van that she was in. A voice came to her. 'Are we going to knock a round off her first, Frankie? She's known for being good to shag.'

'Shut your dirty mouth and have some respect.'

Respect . . . Respect, Christ, did Frankie Droile think it respectful to someone to kill them!

She didn't want to die. *Oh, God, please don't let me die!*

The rasping, tearing sound of a knife hacking through cardboard released the stuffy atmosphere and brought her light and air.

As the hole got bigger, hands grabbed the sides of the box that encased her and ripped it open. Those same hands grabbed her. She tried to resist, but when the second pair got hold of her other arm and dragged her, there was nothing she could do.

Sounds of woodlands met her. Rustling trees, birds twittering, and the warmth of the dappling sun kissed her skin.

Her limbs resisted standing as they screamed the pain of being cramped up for hours. But overriding the pain was the despair of facing her own death.

Unable to utter a word she pleaded with her eyes. The bloke who held her up was a stranger to her. He grinned a yellow and black-toothed grin at her. Behind him she could see Frankie's outline. Heard the distinctive click of a gun being taken off its safety catch.

Her terror burned into her brain. Her head shook. Tears sprayed from her eyes onto her cheeks. Frankie stepped in front of her. His gun pointed at her head. A violent tremble shuddered through her, then a noise clapped around her and a searing pain exploded all that she was and took her into an impenetrable blackness.

As this cleared, Amy came dancing towards her. 'Mummy, Mummy . . .'

25

Joe hadn't slept much. Last night's news had shaken him. He stomped up and down.

His agitation interfered with his usual morning's work of checking the figures coming in from his various outlets, all linked by computerised tills to his own computer. Nor had he taken calls from the main source of his drug dealing operation.

There was a shipment due in very soon on a cargo ship from Brazil. It was to be off-loaded at sea onto a yacht, whose owner would bring it into a bay between Port Patrick and Stranraer.

Ewan Denvy made the trip regularly from Ireland to Port Patrick and was very well known and respected there. Staying overnight and making merry, then making the trip home in the morning. Always generous to the locals, he was rarely turned over by the coastguard. The odd times he had been, he'd been clean. To all intense and purposes, he was just a rich Paddy, with time on his hands.

Joe needed to arrange for his courier to take half a million quid up to Ewan and collect the drugs.

Ricky Houndill, did a brilliant job as the Count's main courier. A self-employed, white van man, he took consignments up to Stranraer on a regular basis for shipment to Ireland. Parcels that were not big enough, or plentiful enough, for the sender to have delivered by the big firms, but too expensive to send by Royal Mail. And, he did collections from the port too. Another well-known character, he hadn't yet been subjected to a customs search or a random police search.

His van had a false bottom that wasn't discernible, and was so thickly encased that a sniffer dog would be hard pressed to detect anything emitting from it.

The assignment, worth over three million on the streets, had been arranged through The Brazilian, a mysterious character, much feared by everyone. Joe's cutters and packers were ready waiting at his warehouse in Coventry from where the dope would be distributed to the dealers of Coventry and Birmingham. All Asians. All good payers and all reliable. If everything went as smoothly as normal, a fat wad of two million would be going into Joe's safe, and eventually into his off shore accounts under the name of Count Roman Rolleski. A nice, smoothly run operation.

But one that could all go to pot, if he didn't get his arse into gear. He just couldn't settle to anything since Gina had gone. Where the hell was she, and where was Gosling? He'd had Gosling down as someone waiting in the wings, plotting and scheming to take the fucking lot from him, not doing one, without a minute's warning. *Christ, the whole thing was worrying. They were getting one over on him, Gina and Gosling.* Were they together? They hadn't gone together, but . . .

The theory wouldn't leave him. *With what I gave to Gina, she would have been out of it for days. Someone had to have helped her. It had to have been planned! Fucking Gosling, the bastard . . .! God, I miss Gina.* This thought came with regrets of what he'd put her through.

The euphoria of disappearing, and reinventing himself had gone to his head. It had made him make rash decisions. Treating Gina badly was one of them. Killing Bragdon another. Gosling could have set Bragdon up to take the rap for Gina's disappearance. Bragdon had been a good man.

Joe shook his aching head as he continued to see everything in a different light. Now he was saddled with this Bugsy Brown, who knew nothing of how he worked, or of his past. The latter was a good thing, but having a stranger around to do your bidding, wasn't. Pulling himself together, Joe made the call to Ricky Houndill. 'Pick the parcel up here tomorrow, 2pm. You must deliver it to Stranraer by 10pm tomorrow. Usual place, usual signal from the boat.' He didn't hear the low-pitched sound as he put the phone down.

*

Layla's Private D, put his listening device down and smiled. The tap on the Count's phone was working well. That must have been the arrangement for the pick-up of the drug assignment his insider had overheard about and passed on the information to him.

The Romanian cleaner was proving very useful. He made out to everyone that he could only speak a little English, but in truth he understood everything very well. D had thought of him as a bit-part, but he was proving to be a real asset and a good investment. Not even Gina had known about this deal, at least, she'd not indicated anything about it in her notes before she'd taken that beating. And it had been in the planning stages for a few weeks now.

Putting a call into Adrian, he waited. The ringing tone went on and on. At last Adrian answered.

'How did it go, Adrian?'

'Everything was sorted. Watch the news bulletins. We'll know when Gina's found. Nothing will look suspicious about her removal from the house. She was removed by what, to all intense and purposes looked like TV repair men. They called at the house in Walton on Thames and left with a box that looked like it contained one of those huge televisions. Sadly, Gina is

211

history, and even I don't know the method used, or where it took place, or where she will be found. I only know that they were to render her unconscious and take her away from the house alive. Layla's only wish was that she didn't die in the house. It's a waiting game now. Oh, by-the-way, there's just been a report of a man's body found washed up in Bristol. Gosling has been eliminated as the possible candidate. Your tail, maybe?'

'Christ, I hope not. But, it seems likely. How the hell did Gosling spot him?'

'He's nothing if not good at his job. He used to be a straight cop and excellent at his job. Even I had a job to get the lags off when he'd wrapped up a case. My father failed with Layla's dad. Gosling dotted all the 'I's' and crossed all the 'T's'. Now, he's using those same skills to feather his retirement nest. But why go missing? Have you any ideas?'

'None. My agent didn't report in. Gosling must have made a sudden decision to go, and my chap must have just stuck with him. I can't contact him. Though after the first time I tried, I destroyed the sim. Had to, in case Gosling had the phone, in which case my chap would find it difficult to reach me. If this stiff is him, we'll be left wondering, I'm afraid.'

'Worrying more like. I rather like to know where Gosling is and what he's doing. This is creepy.'

'Yes. Anyway, the deal is on. My insider found out that it's to take place at 10pm in Stranraer. The same place we trailed the white van man to last time. It's likely to be big as these pick-ups are getting less frequent, indicating that the Count is buying bigger loads at a time.'

'Right. Are we ready?'

'Did you run it by Layla, Adrian?'

'Yes. She left it with me, but she wants this big time.'
'Did you get the unit in Danes Road, Romford?
'Yes, all set up with all the cutting gear that will be needed to access the drugs, and everything needed to cut, weigh and bag them for distribution. I only have to make a phone call and the right people will be there waiting. And another call will have the dealers pop up ready with their cash. They know its source and that its good stuff. Johnny Griggs, the once, well-known dealer and friend of Layla's father, is fronting this operation for us. His is a name they all know and trust and are glad to see out of retirement. I am too, as I know of a few ops he's been involved in and he rarely needed my father's legal assistance.'
'Good. This is fast turning into a predominantly male organisation.'
'Layla knows that has to be. There are no women that we know of who have the right skills. She is even running out of women to front her outlets, but I think she accepts that now. As long as everyone knows that she is boss, she doesn't care anymore.'
'I'll take your word for that, but it was something she was passionate about. Anyway, we'll need Frankie Droile and his mate for this one, and an untraceable hire car.'
'No problem. Bertie Bestrun, another of Layla's father's contacts will see to that. What's the plan?'
'Get Frankie and his mate to get up to that café on the A75, The Tarff Truck Stop. It's this side of Dumfries, make sure they know the one. I sent you photos of it and map references for the sat nav.'
'Got them.'
'Well, Ricky Houndill – the white van man and courier, always stops there at around midnight. He never misses. It's a strange phenomenon, but in his regularity he finds

213

immunity. There was a picture of him and his van in the information I've sent over. The truck stop is a bit remote and the ideal place to hijack him. It's up to them what they do with him. His van has a false bottom, so will have legit parcels inside. It's also well-known on CCTV cameras, and by and large is left untouched. So tell them to drive normally. Tell them to pull into the Moto service area between junction thirty-three and thirty-two in Lancashire. Park in the lorry park and wait. A breakdown truck will come to them and take the van from them. They can continue the journey in their hire car. The breakdown truck will bring the van down to the industrial estate. Instruct Frankie not to tail the breakdown truck. Just get on their way. Their involvement ends at the service area.'

'Sounds good. I'll let you know when everything is set.'

The phone went dead. D rested back in his van. His surveillance cameras were on and gave him a view of the grounds and the inside of the Count's office. The Romanian had done a good job in placing the cameras, and the taps on the phones. The cameras were tiny and fitted just above the curtain rail, none had been detected, and God knows how he'd done that without being detected himself. But he had.

The Count still paced up and down. He made several phone calls. One concerned a huge shipment of drugs. He'd get the Romanian to sniff out more about that. This operation was going very well. Except of course for the loss of the agent following Gosling. In some ways he'd prefer it if the body did turn out to be his, otherwise that would mean he'd taken a bribe and would have to be disposed of at some time.

It would be a good thing if that job had been done for him.

But, now to find Gosling. He knew just the man for the job.

26

Cleaston stared at the incident board – a map of events so far. An old fashioned concept in his eyes, but the Chief had insisted on it so that Bill Riley of Scotland Yard could see at a glance how things were progressing. He had to admit, it did give the bigger picture. He took a moment to add those he thought should be on the map.

Cleaston watched Bill Riley study the board. Knew he would pick holes in it. He could see himself they were gaping.

'Why the mystery man murdered in Bristol? I fail to see where he comes into the picture.'

'He was found in the same city, on the same night that Gosling's car was found abandoned.'

'Is there some logic in that, Sergeant?'

Cleaston sighed. *Is there only me that can smell a rat where Gosling's concerned?*

He watched Riley surveying every aspect of the board.

'It seems to me, Cleaston that you have two main focuses. Layla Parrondski and Matt Gosling. Here you have connections to them both, and yet it is all very circumstantial.'

'I'll get the evidence. I just need a break. I mean coincidental, or what? Those arrows pointing to Layla Parrondski all happened. She was involved in a shipment of stolen gold that can be traced back to her father –'

'Yes, I see you have a picture of him in the background. Are you sure it isn't his record that is prejudicing you against his daughter?'

'No, Sir. Look at the other coincidences: Her husband's disappearance and death.'

'Yes, but I like the theory that Gosling was working on, that Layla Parrondski's husband was up to no good, and so was taken out. That could be connected to Layla's father, Gerry Loyson. It makes more sense to me.'

'What about those two kids being found in a skip outside Layla Parrondski's country home, then?'

'Inside information, perhaps? Someone who knows of your obsession with her thinking they will deepen the scent.'

'Gosling!'

'Well . . . Look. Concentrate on hard facts. Get the ground work done. We need some evidence, not theories and, so far, you have Sweet Fanny Adams!'

'We have Gosling in the building when the kids were abducted.'

'But not the woman who abducted them.'

'Maybe the reconstruction will bring us something. It's going ahead tonight.'

'Umm, I don't like this. I don't like it at all. It needs some fresh thinking. I know you have a gut instinct and that's good. But what makes you suspect Gosling? Convince me.'

Cleaston shrugged. He didn't have anything more to give Bill at this moment. Only Gosling being in the building, and his gut instinct. No matter how hard he tried, and God, he'd tried to uncover something, he drew a blank. Gosling's bank accounts were in order. He had a good home life. There was nothing sinister on him, no rumours, *fucking nothing!* Well, there was the threat in the toilet, but he couldn't bring that up. If he did he'd have to admit to trying to molest Helen!

Christ, it was a mess. Gosling's making a right prat out of me!

218

'Well?'

'Sorry, Sir, I wished I did have more.'

'Then drop it, it's clouding your thinking. Closing your mind to other possibilities. Maybe none of these things are linked. You're making a case out of hypotheticals. Come up with something fresh, or I'll have to request someone else is put on the job.'

Frustration stung Cleaston. He *knew* he was right. Something had to happen soon to break this deadlock! His phone rang. 'Yes, Chief?'

'My office, and bring Bill Riley with you.'

'The Chief wants to see us. Sounds agitated.'

'There's another body. Found in Epping Forest. A Forrest Commission worker found it. The Chief over there rang me. He is at the scene and recognised her from the case notes of the kids in the skip murder. Take a look at the picture on the sharing of information screen.'

'Christ, it's Gina Walters!'

Cleaston knew a sick feeling of excitement grab him. Another link to Gosling! Another body to chalk up to a case Gosling was working on. *They have to believe me now!*

Bill Riley stepped forward. 'The mother of Amy Walters?'

'Yes, that's her. Initial thoughts are that this is a contract killing. A single shot to the head, and the body trussed up. There's pressure marks on her neck and some old bruising.'

'Frankie Droile? That's how he worked. I've been looking up all of Loyson's old cronies. This could be the breakthrough we have been waiting for. Another link that goes back to Gerry Loyson.'

'Oh? And you know for sure it was him, Cleaston? No police work, just assume and accuse because it fits your bloody theory! Chief, I've about had it with this rookie! I'd like –'

'I'm sorry, Sir. I shouldn't have said that. I'll not jump to any more conclusions, I promise.'

'Too fucking late! Chief, give me someone who is meticulous about doing ground work, will you? This moron is wasting my bloody time!'

Cleaston watched the Chief shrug, hoped he would come out in his defence, but no. It appeared he'd really blotted his copy book this time.

'I'll assign Detective Sergeant George Fromer to you, Bill. He's old school, ready for the knackers' yard, but though slow, George does the work you're looking for.'

'Give me old school any day, rather than a wet behind the ears, know it all. Because that's what you are, Cleaston. A fucking know-it-all. You'll go far, no doubt. But not off the back of my case, you won't. Sod off out of it!'

Humiliated, Cleaston left the office. Why had he opened his big mouth? But something told him he was right about this case. Layla Parrondski, Matt Gosling, and Gerry Loyson were up to their fucking necks in the shit of it. *I am right. I fucking am! Fucking old school. The only thing that they've got that I haven't is contacts. Snouts. Well, maybe it was time to get one.*

Getting back to his desk, Cleaston logged in and began trawling through the cases he'd been involved in. He needed someone that he had something on. Someone who'd got away with something that was evident he'd done.

There weren't many cases, him being newly appointed, but he'd worked on a few on his training, and with George Fromer, too. He even knew who George's snouts were. Hadn't liked the system himself, so hadn't cultivated it, but he had to admit that someone with their nose to the ground would be very useful right now.

'The Girl in the Flat' murder! Perfect. A name sprung up to mind. Reardon. He'd been implicated in this case, but he'd come up with a witness that had placed him elsewhere.

The girl had been hit from behind, a single blow from a blunt instrument that had never been found. The indications were that she'd answered the door of her flat to someone she knew, turned to walk back into the property, and been hit on the head. It was found that she owed money to her drug dealer. The case had gone cold now. Reardon wasn't a known contract killer, but had been put in the frame by several snouts who said that he was now working with Frankie Droile and had to prove himself.

An excitement clutched at Cleaston's stomach. *The more I think about it, the more convinced I am that he's my man! The perfect snout. If he is working with Droile, he'll know whether it was Droile who carried out Gina's killing – and, more importantly. Who ordered it and why!*

It was a long shot, but if he turned up out of the blue to arrest Reardon, telling him that he now had concrete evidence of him being the perpetrator of The Girl in the Flat murder, he could then judge if the prospect of going to jail for a long stretch scared him enough to make him turn into a grass. *It has to work. I have to get at him.*

Picking up his phone he buzzed through to the Chief.

'What now?'

'I need to have a word.'

'Fuck off, Cleaston, I've had as much as I can take –
are you looking for demotion and further training, or
what?'

'I need a break, Sir. I admit, I've gone at things with
too much enthusiasm –'

'Like a ram at a ewe, you mean? I agree. Take a few
days. Go sick. That will give me something to tell the
media boys and girls as to why you're off the case.
Three days, right? That should give the experienced lot
time to cobble something together, then you're back
here and will be involved in straight forward cases until
I'm satisfied you can do the job as it's meant to be
done.'

'Thanks, Chief. And sor . . .'

The Chief's phone banged down.

*

Drawing deeply on his fag, Cleaston looked down from
the cradle used by the window cleaners of the
Arkwright building. A twelve storey high complex of
offices and shops that was a new development in an
otherwise rundown road with a rundown pub which was
frequented by the low-lifes, and those who thought they
ran the show.

Using his ID card, he got by the night-watchman with
ease. He'd even given him a hand to get onto the cradle.
The cold seeped through his coat. People had come and
gone, and now the pub was emptying without a sight of
Reardon, but, he'd stay put. The area was well known
and well used by the criminal sector, and the cops. He'd
watched as a couple of patrol cars had driven slowly
through.

It was three o'clock in the morning when he got his
reward. A car pulled up. Cleaston set his night vision
camera rolling making sure he trained it on the number
of the car as well as the occupants.

Rearden got out of the car. 'A good day's work, Droile, goodnight, mate.'

The driver's door opened. Droile stepped out. 'Shut the fuck up, and don't ever mention my name where others might hear it. Never, or you're one dead fucker!'

This said in a semi-whisper floated up to Cleaston. He smiled. He'd caught the Holy Grail on video.

Tomorrow, he'd have something to frighten Reardon with.

As the car drew off, Cleaston's phone vibrated against his leg. Reaching for it he read 'Pussy Doll calling' Swiping the accept call, Helen's tones came down the line. 'Are you still out in the cold, bad boy?'

'Just coming in, and with something good!'

'Get your backside outside the station at six in the morning. I've had a hell of a night on duty. Pick me up and take me back to yours, I need to give you a good spanking for bunking off work, then you can tell me all about it.'

His dick twitched.

'Don't be late, or you will get the whip across your arse.'

The phone went dead. His erection fought to get out of his trousers. He considered pulling one off it, but thought that would spoil what his Pussy Doll had in mind for him. Better to wait in anticipation. He laughed at this thought as he put his phone away, slung his camera over his shoulders and tucked his coat around the bulge in his trousers. Inside the guard was in his office. Cleaston didn't see him put his own mobile in the drawer of his desk.

As he left the left the building, Cleaston began to hum. Checking his watch, he had just over an hour before his Pussy Doll was free. The thought of what she'd promised made him hornier than he'd ever been and the thought crossed his mind that everything about his life was about to take a turn for the better.

A screech of skidding tyres, and Frankie Droile had seen to it that his life didn't get better. It ended. Sergeant Cleaston went into eternity with the best chance he'd ever had of bringing Gosling and Layla Parrondski down, and with the biggest stiffy he'd ever experienced.

27

'For Christ's sake, Layla, tell me that you didn't have anything to do with Gina's death.'

'I didn't. I'm as shocked as you. My God. Gina? Dead! I can't take it in. Why? Why would anyone want her dead?'

Jade switched the British news channel off, 'Poor Cow. She didn't get a very good hand dealt to her. We could have made her life better.'

'It must have been Joe. I mean, look where she was found, Epping Forrest!'

A stroke of bloody genius. I wonder whose idea that was? Must have been Adrian's. Christ, I miss him.

Layla had kept it from Jade that they'd managed to get Gina out, and she would see to it that no one told her for as long as it suited her to keep Jade in the dark about the truth. If Jade ever stepped out of line, then was the time for her to find out just how ruthless Layla could be.

'We've got to get Joe, and soon. I hate the very soul of him.'

'You can't match what I feel, Jade. But don't worry, his downfall has begun. I'm just waiting for Adrian to call then, if he confirms what I want to hear, I think the news will cheer you up a bit.'

The way Jade looked at her had Layla concerned. What she said had her on the attack.

'It hasn't touched you has it? What kind of a hard nut are you, Layla? Gina is taken out, and you carry on planning your revenge. You beggar belief, do you know that?'

'I'm the kind that will lead us to riches and see the downfall of that bastard Joe. That's who I am, and you'd better get used to it. I had you down as being like me. That's what I want in a partner. Now, am I to tear up those papers we've signed and refund your money, or are we in this together – two tough females who are not knocked sideways by every poor cow, or fucking disposable fella that we come across murdered. I need to know, Jade. You're either in this up to the tip of your head, or you're out, which is it to be?'

'I'm in. I don't see me living long if I take a rain check.'

'Too right. The deal's sealed then. No more accusations, or histrionics, what happens, happens. We instigate, or we shrug our shoulders and deal with it. It's the only way. Now, I'll have that gin and tonic please, and bring it out onto the balcony. I need to enjoy this sunshine before I return home.'

On the balcony, Layla chose the better of the two loungers and relaxed back. As she willed her phone to ring. It did.

'Adrian. Everything going okay?'

'Great, and with bonuses. I take it you've seen the news?'

'Some of it. We switched it off after the report about Gina. I like the twist you put on that.'

'Epping Forest you mean? I didn't. Frankie sorted everything. No one tells him how to do his job, you just order him to do it.'

'How the Hell . . .?'

'He said he'd heard word on the street that that's where Parrondski had gone to and thought he'd leave him a present. Don't ask. Who knows where they get their information, but while he's on our side, he'll use what he has to our advantage. It's upset D though. He had to move out and sharpish, there's cops everywhere.'

'Shit! That's bad news.'

'He's not happy. He's having to rely on his insider for a few days. Anyway, as you haven't mentioned a certain something, I take it you missed the breaking news?'

Layla sat up. 'What's happened?'

'Look, am I allowed to tell you that I love you and am missing you like hell?'

A warm trickle wet Layla's vagina. The muscles deep inside her contracted making her draw in her breath.

'Keep it business like, if you don't mind. Tell me what's happened?'

'I heard your reaction, and that's good enough for me. I'm horny now.'

Layla swallowed hard. 'Stop pissing about and get on with it. WHAT'S HAPPENED?'

'Now, now, don't shout. Droile took three out, yesterday. Gina, the white van man and . . . Cleaston!'

Shock held Layla silent for a moment. Then happiness flooded her, 'Cleaston, gone? Wow, how, why? Oh, Adrian, that's the best news . . . though I take it the white van man's demise means we got the dope?'

'Yes, we got it. Ha! I'd love to see Joe's face, well his new *Count Rolleski* face. His girlfriend gone *and* his two million dope, *and* his courier. Not to mention his bent cop missing. I wonder which one of these incidents will hurt him the most?'

'The dope. There's plenty more women and bent cops to take his fancy. But, fuck him, we did it! Our first couple of stings and we did it! Brilliant.'

'I want you. I want to fuck you like I did before you left. Hurry back.'

Layla ended the call.

Jade stood over her. 'Here, I imagine you need this. I made it a stiff one.'

'Sit down, Jade. It's begun.' By the time she'd finished telling Jade everything except for her involvement in Gina's death, Jade was smiling.

Clinking her glass with Jade, gave Layla the feeling that she and Jade were singing from the same hymn sheet. She had an idea that Jade still suspected her involvement in Gina's death, but if she did, she'd dealt with it. That bode well. Releasing a deep sigh, she relaxed back in the lounger.

If only another call would come through about Gosling having been found. He was a loose cannon with too much information. Not about her, she hoped, though he did hint that he would find out and she dared say that he had his sources, but about Joe, too. She wanted no one but herself to be the instigator of bringing Joe, fucking Count Rolleski, tumbling so low that he'd be begging to be taken out.

The nice two million she had stolen from him was a start. A great start.

The view she had over the San Tropez port soothed her. 'Do you know? We should get a yacht. What a good place that would be for meetings. No one could tap our phones, or listen in. I think we'll look into spending the money we'll make on Joe's drugs on one. That would be a nice touch. Look at that one there. The one with the blue stripe and sails flapping in the breeze, I like that one. I wonder how much a rig like that would cost?'

'That one belongs to a friend of mine. I'll ring him and ask him to take us out to dinner on it. He can sort that easily. Would you like that?'

'I would, very much. Thanks, Jade. Would I seem rude if I asked him the price of such a boat?'

'Probably. But I have a feeling you will do it anyway.'
'Ha. You're beginning to get my measure. I like that.
We'll work well together, you and I Jade. Are you sure
you wouldn't be happier as my buyer instead of running
the Tête à Tête?'
'Have you someone in mind for that job, then?'
'No, but, you're good at this one and you and your little
one are out of harm's way here.'
'We're no more safe here than we would be in London
and you know it. While your bastard husband and
Gosling draw breath, none of us are safe. You'll do well
to remember that, Layla. No, the Tête à Tête, is my
baby. I'll be running the show.'
'And your child?'
'My nanny is going to look after her. I've bought
another property in France. They will live there. I have
sourced schools for her and will visit her as often as I
can, but never at her home.'
'Won't you miss her nanny as much as you will your
child?'
'That's not your territory. Okay, I know you have my
measure, as you say I have yours, but don't come too
close to my personal life.'
'Is that a threat?'
'No, a request. But one I want you to take seriously.'
'Right. Just testing the waters to see if I was correct. I
see I am. Pity. I had hoped that your sexual
involvement was with someone who wasn't here. I
rather fancy you, and wanted to taste what you have to
offer.'
Jade looked astonished, before her eyes travelled the
length of Layla's body. A shiver went through Layla.
The earlier wetness that Adrian had evoked, now
soaked her. Their eyes met. Jade's hand reached out to

her. Taking it sent a tingle through her. She could never remember holding another woman's hand before.

For a long moment they were suspended in time. Then Jade shook her head. 'You're a beautiful woman, Layla, and I want you, but I don't think it's a good idea, and neither will you when you come down from this urge that you have.'

Hardly able to speak, Layla whispered. 'I agree. Christ, I could do with something happening down there though, have you any toys that I could take to my room?'

They both laughed at this. Jade got up. Once more she offered Layla her hand. Come on. It's the effect of the sun and the gin and tonic. Go and shower – and keep the temp of the water down. And, if you're still horny later, I'm sure my friend will oblige. He's a male prostitute. He charges a mint, but I have it on the grapevine that every penny is worth it.'

'Interesting. And if I still feel like this, I'll engage him for the night. Never had it off on a boat before.'

They linked arms as they went inside. The last hour had sealed not only the deal, but a special bond between them. Layla felt less lonely than she had in her whole life.

28

Red-faced with rage and grief the Count wiped a tear from his eyes. *What the fuck was happening? Who is doing me over? Gosling? No, he wouldn't, would he?* Though he had to admit, Gosling would have the contacts to pull a job like that, and with the sort of money that dope would fetch, he'd have the wherewithal to do even more damage in the future.

 Why had he trusted him? *Christ, the prick has so much information on me! If he hasn't done this, but is thinking of turning good cop after a break, he could put me down forever!*

The tears he hadn't acknowledged were running down his face and came even faster on a sob as part of him gave way to the shocking truth of what had happened to Gina. Who would want to take her out and why? Again, Gosling fitted the frame. If he'd disappeared in order to take the operation over, she would be a threat with the knowledge she had of him. God, it was a mess!

His head dropped into his hands. For a moment he felt defeated. Who did he have as an ally now? Bragdon and Gosling gone, and his Gina . . . His beautiful Gina. After a moment he straightened his body and wiped his eyes.

If it was in fact Gosling that was behind all of this, then he couldn't do it alone. He'd have had to use lowlife's that he had contact with through his work. *Well, I have a few contacts in that world too and it's about time I started to call in a few favours and put a few threats around.* Though none of them had actually known who Count Rolleski was, they knew to be afraid of him. They knew he was a boss man.

He pressed a buzzer. Bugsy Brown entered the room almost immediately. There was something about the man that irritated the Count, but right now, he needed him.

'I need to get a message to Gerry Loyson. He's in Leicester Prison.'

'Aye, I know where he is. And, I can get a message to him.'

'Good, make sure he gets it. Tell him that a lot of people he might know seem to be working against Count Rolleski. He would have heard of me. Tell him to get the word around that they stop working for whoever's got it in for me. Tell him that if he doesn't do this, his daughter dies. And her demise will be very slow and very painful.'

Bugsy nodded. He looked like a man caught in a trap. The Count knew that he and everyone in the underworld was afraid of Gerry Loyson. 'Do it, man, or you're dead too. And bring me his answer.'

As Bugsy left the room, the Count picked up the phone. Having tried to contact Gosling a million times on the special number that he had, he tried once more. The number rang and rang. Slamming the phone down in frustration he sat back and thought about his next action.

It was a call to The Brazilian. 'The assignment went tits up. Fix another for me, but find out who is giving information out, oh, and I'll need a new courier.'

'No one gives me orders. I set up the deals, the logistics of it are yours. I'll set up one for you, but the price just went up because you insulted me. The next time you do that, you will die.'

The phone went dead. 'Shit!'

Time to call in all his heavies. Send them around to put frighteners on a few lowlifes.

'Kenny boy, how are you? It's the Count here. Gather the troops and find out some info for me. One: who took Gina out. Two: who took my shipment. And three, where the hell is Gosling. Then put a few threats out. Kill some dispensable geezers. Hangers on who are no more use to us. Just to set the fear spreading. There's a hundred G's in this for you, if you do a good clean-up operation.'

'You've got it boss.'

Slamming the phone down, the Count picked it up again, and dialled a number as if in great urgency.

'Boss?'

'Ronnie, take out Kenny Boy, and quick. He's a weak link. Then have a clean-up, put frighteners on anyone you think has been slacking. Find out who took Gina out, and who fucking stole my shipment. And where that dickhead Gosling is. Do in a few hangers-on, to spread some fear, put it around that they weren't towing the line.'

'You lost a shipment?'

'I like that question. Kenny didn't ask it, and yet there was no way, unless he was involved, or in the know, that he could have known about it. On second thoughts. Bring him back to the house. You can put him through some of our best torture gadgets and get out of him what he knew and why he didn't alert me. Then take him out.'

'Right, Boss.'

'And, Ronnie, if you do a good job, you take his place as my top man on that side of things. There's fifty G's in this one operation alone for you. Prove yourself to me and that will be doubled.'

'I'm on to it. And, Boss, if there's other things you need, run them by me. While I've been waiting in the wings, I've made myself useful and have a few good contacts.'

'A courier amongst them?'

'There is. My son. He'll go anywhere, fetch anything, and discreetly. He can handle himself, and has a clean record, that goes for driving offences as well. I've been getting him ready, keeping his nose clean for the big time.'

The Count felt cheered at this news. 'Good man. You just earned the one hundred. Collect it later today, when you have news to bring me. I might have another hit job for you.'

You just might be taking my cow of a wife on her last journey any day soon. The Count liked this idea. And as it took root he warmed to it more and more.

The phone clicked louder than usual when the Count replaced the receiver. Looking at it, he was surprised to hear a small buzz come from it. *Shit, it could be fucking bugged.*

There was no time to react to this as The Doc came mincing into the room, not even stopping to knock on the door. His body trembling from head to foot.

'What? And it'd better be good. You've forgotten your manners.'

'The cops. They're at the door. Ooh, Count, what shall we do-o-o?'

'Stop twitching like a big girl's blouse to start with you, stupid ponce. Pull yourself together. You'll look suspicious and be in the nick with this place turned over before they even ask you a question! I've been expecting them. It will be part of their enquiries. A body's been found near to here; in case you haven't noticed. Who answered the door, and where are the cops now?'

'The Romanian, what's his name, oh, I don't know. He didn't speak English to them.'

'That's because he can't, you dickhead. Christ, I hope his papers are in order. Though, I'd think so, he came from an agency, and they'd make sure. What's he done with the cops?'

'He's shown them into the library. How can you be so calm? The operating theatre, the film studios, glory me, we're right up the shit.'

Grabbing The Doc burst the top button of the far too tight shirt The Doc wore. 'Fucking calm yourself. They'll want to speak to everyone. Just answer their questions and don't embroider your answers. And go and tell nanny to say that she is the housekeeper, and daddy to say that he is an office worker. And you, just say that you are my designer, or something. And, tell everyone to remember that I'm Count Rommoski, not Rolleski, or they're dead.'

Shoving The Doc backwards, Joe took no heed of sending him sprawling, but stormed out of the room.

'Officers. I can guess why you are here. A very unfortunate business. And right on my doorstep.'

'Yes, Sir. And you are?'

Using his cover name under which he had business interests and stock shares in his legit world, where he rarely ventured, Joe answered, 'Count Rommoski. I'm from Russia. I'm a businessman who has to be in London frequently. I hate hotels and so I recently bought this house as a country retreat and am in the middle of renovations as you can see. Please sit down. Would you like tea?'

'No thank you, Sir, we shouldn't take up much of your time.' It was the older bobby who said this. The two of them, a young, just out of school, looking lad, and this older, fat and long in the tooth spokesman, looked as though they were more used to walking the beat than doing house-to-house.

'And, yes, we are here about the body that was found near to here as I guess you were referring to. Can we have your full name, nationality, age and occupation, please, Sir, oh, and we will need to see documentation to support the information you give.'

That done, the officer seemed satisfied that Joe was who he'd said he was. This pleased him as he felt he'd passed his first, real test, to being other than Joe Parrondski.

'Now, we need to know if you saw anything unusual, a vehicle, or something you normally wouldn't see, or someone, doing what looked odd at any time yesterday?'

'Nothing at all, Officer. I'm sorry. I have an office in the basement of the house and I spent the day down there. There are no windows to the outside world and I didn't come up for dinner until after dark.'

'Thank you, Sir. How many are there in the household? Staff, family? We checked the electoral list and no one is registered as living here. Do your staff live out?'

'There has been no time to organize all of that, I'm sorry. I have been using mostly agency staff, and still am. They only live in when they are on duty, a few days at a time. I don't have records of their addresses or anything.'

Going over to his bureau he clicked it open and produced a file. This is the name of the agency. They will have all the details you need of the staff they have sent me recently.'

'Are there any here who were here yesterday?'

Knowing they could easily find this out, the Count nodded. Yes, four that I know of. And, they are all here

236

today. They are regulars. The others, you will have to ask, though none of them seem to speak English so you may have to question them through the agency, they have an interpreter there.'

Shuffling the other papers in his bureau he produced several other files. These are the builders I have on site. Their contact details are all there. I have no idea how many were here yesterday, but it sounded like a lot, I seem to have a constant headache. A bad mistake living with a build.'

'Yes, I can imagine, sir. Right, we'll see the four that you have on board, then we'll get out of your way and seek contact with the others through the agency, as you suggest. Thank you for your co-operation.'

'I only wished that I could be of some help. Sorry Officer. It's a really bad business. Poor girl.'

As he left the room, the Count mopped his brow. Picking up the internal phone in the hall, he spoke to each of those who would need to be questioned. They all came rushing from various places looking as nervous as kittens. He glared at them. Did a swift slice across his throat with his finger, and was relieved to see them take this on board and were now acting normally. For good measure he made the teenage sign of pointing at his own eyes and then at theirs, to indicate that he was watching them as he walked away and left them awaiting their turn to be called through into the library. More furious than he'd ever been, at whoever took Gina out on his doorstep, he vowed to find them and hang them out to dry by their fucking balls!

29

Layla sat on the tapestry sofa in the penthouse and watched the news clip of Cleaston's funeral. Killed in the line of duty, the commentator said. The collection for his family had reached a massive hundred grand. *Huh, killed when snooping more like!*

But, why? What had alerted him to Frankie's activities? Her phone buzzed. Adrian, as always dispensing with the niceties of 'hello', 'I've been talking to Frankie. He can think of no reason why Cleaston was watching him. He wants to know if you approved of him taking him out?'

'Yes, I do. But, I'm worried.'

'So is he. Though he's seen no sign of any other surveillance on him, which he can't understand. If Cleaston was on legit business, then surely that means Frankie is somewhere on the radar of the investigation team.'

'We need someone on the inside. Is there anyone down at the nick that's known for taking a bung?'

'I only knew of Gosling, though the Chief was easily blackmailed once. But you know, thinking about it, your husband must be looking for a replacement for Gosling, so it could be dodgy for us to go putting feelers out as well.'

'I think I'll try the Rottweiler. I've seen her pushing herself forward in every news scuffle on the telly, she might know something.'

'I'm not sure, I don't like your association with her.'

'I haven't had an association with her. She's left me alone since the so-called body of Joe was discovered.'

'Leave it that way.'

'Don't tell me what to do, Adrian!'

The line went quiet. 'Adrian?'

'I'm still here. Look, I'm sorry, it was advice not an order.'

'I'll get back to you.'

Picking up her house phone Layla dialled the Rottweiler.

'Layla Parrondski here.'

'Oh, I thought you'd gone cold on me.'

'Well, it was a shock to hear of my husband's death.'

'Yes, I'm sorry. I thought I would leave you alone for a while. Though it was hot at the time, you being pulled and kept overnight. I guess you'll be suing?'

'Not made my mind up yet. It seems the nearest and dearest are always suspects.'

'But not usually beaten up. I tell you there's still a few murmuring about that.'

'I'll have to sue then to put the record straight.'

'Any sign of a funeral yet?'

'No chance, they won't release the body, it is part of a murder enquiry. Who the hell would do such a thing?'

'They don't seem any nearer to finding out. Look, how can I help you?'

'I'm worried. This cop killing, and Gosling going missing, they were both working on the case, now they've found another body, and they are saying it may be linked to my husband's murder. It's frightening. I just wondered if you knew anything.'

'Yes. I know something. I hear a lot that never gets to press, but could be useful.'

Was that a vague hint for a bribe? Nina's next words confirmed this, 'What I know could help certain people.'

Layla played the innocent, 'I'm not used to all of this. Do you mean you could let me know things that will keep me safe?'

'What game are you playing, Layla? I'm not fooled, so don't come it with me.'

This call was a massive mistake, but she'd come this far. 'No game. I need certain info and you have your nose to the ground.'

'And you have yours in a lot of places. We could be useful to each other. Shall we meet?'

'I'm not trusting of newspaper types. I'm sorry I rang. My fear made me irrational.'

'No, don't hang up. Look. I'll get someone to vouch for me. You'll hear soon, okay?'

'Okay.'

Intrigued, Layla replaced the receiver. Not many minutes later, the shrill ring made her jump.

'Layla?'

'Who's this?'

'Frankie.'

'Christ, Frankie what are you doing ringing me here?'

'Just to say, Nina, the reporter, she's my granddaughter.'

Experience had taught Layla to dot the 'I's' and cross the 'T's'

'Make sure my lawyer has this info in the usual way. Along with an outline of what she wants and how far she will go.'

Putting the phone down, Layla tried to grasp this information. If it was right and that was truly Frankie, and not a trickster that the Rottweiler had employed, then this could work out well. And, might lead to another woman on the team. She needed that. She also needed to tread with care.

Pouring herself a large red wine, Layla went towards the bathroom. A long soak, a takeaway pizza, washed down with another glass of wine, was the order of her evening. Her 'Adrian mobile' rang as she crossed her bedroom.

'Frankie just phoned.'

'Right, I needed to verify it was him. Good. The Rottweiler might be coming on board.'

'For God's sake, Layla!'

'I can't fight now. Tomorrow's a big day. The rescheduled meetings, and going to look at my home to see how it is progressing. Then there is the arrival of Jade. We're going to look at the club in the evening. Hopefully, Jade will like what she sees and an opening date can be put into place. It really needs to be up and running.'

'Okay, darling. But take care. By the way, I could relax you so that you sleep well.'

'Get your arse over here.'

The combination of the hot water and smooth, rich wine enhanced the feelings Adrian had provoked. Her fingers slid down her smooth skin. Opening her legs, she sought the most sensitive spot. Gentle massaging sent shivers of pleasure through her. An urge took her to increase the pressure. Sensations built. She drew in a deep breath. Knew she was going to climax, didn't want to, and yet wanted to with all her being. *Oh God, Oh God.* Her moan filled the space around her. Clutching herself she accepted the waves of pleasure pulsating through her.

'You started without me.'

The shock of this stopped her orgasm. Opening her eyes, she looked on Adrian's beautiful naked body as he lowered himself into the water.

Curling around him, she took him into her, and screamed out as his entering her pulled the climax back and took it to heights beyond endurance.

Through the unbearable ecstasy when she seemed to leave her own body, she could hear his declarations of his love for her. At that moment, she so wanted this. Her own man to love and to cherish her, but as she came shuddering down, she knew a weakness, a wanting to give her all to him, and this frightened her.

*

'Christ, you don't let the grass grow, do you, Nina? You've picked a busy day. I have to be out of here and on my way to my office in ten minutes.'

'I have it that you've checked my credentials overnight. And, as I would have come up smelling of roses, I want in. I don't know what your operation is, yet, but I've sniffed out enough to know that you're up to something. My granddad told me you need more women, but that's all he said. He knows and trusts me and has vouched for me. He also knows that I'm bored in what our family terms 'Civy Street' I thought being a reporter would give me excitement, but it doesn't. You can trust me. I promise.'

'Adrian is counselling caution.'

'Your lawyer?'

'Yep.'

'His daddy was my grandfather's, and your dad's, lawyer, how can he not accept me? I'm one of you. I have the same credentials as he has.'

'I think so. But there was a little matter of his dad's disappearance once your grandfather came out. It was said that Frankie Droile did that as a revenge for not getting off.'

'Maybe. Who knows?'

'Anyway, enough about Adrian, I recognized your potential from the start when you were being a pain in the arse. I wondered then how you knew about my family.'

'Well then?'

'Look, if I take you on, you will have to stay as a reporter for a while. You'll be useful in that job. Like you say, you know a lot more than you can report. I need to know that much too.'

'You still don't trust me, do you?'

'I'm getting there. I like the stock you came from. Look, if your granddaddy trusts you, then I do, but I do need you where you are for now. How about a grand every time you give me something useful?'

'It's a start.'

'Yes, it's a start, and if you come up trumps it will be more than that.'

'Don't like being tested. With who I am, I should be in. Your dad won't be happy.'

'You are in.'

'Not in, so that I know what's going on.'

'That will come, no one but me really knows that. Some know bits of it, but only as much as I need them to know. Just do as I ask. I have to take these precautions. You must understand that.'

'Right, let's whet your appetite. As you probably know, Cleaston was spying on my Granddad. Granddad would only tell me that he'd done a job for you, well, two jobs. He didn't have to tell me what they were, I know his calling, and the mother of one of the murdered girls was found shot that day. Then a bloke was shot in a café carpark up in Scotland later that night. Cleaston was snooping when Granddad dropped off his associate. Granddad couldn't let Cleaston live to tell what he'd seen. Granddad wasn't taking any chances.'

'Your Granddad does trust you, girl. That's a lot of information connecting events to me. Could have moved you up the ranks in the reporter world, but you haven't used any of it, that bodes well.'

'I'm using it now. Anyway, after I had this, I dug deeper. Before them at the cop shop had time to fix a story. I spoke to Cleaston's girlfriend and she initially told me that he was on sick leave at the time. She was very bitter and gave me more than I normally get. She said he'd been thrown off the case of the children in the skip, the prostitute in the flat, and your husband's murder, but had carried on investigating his own theory. Then the official line came out before I had time to use this, and I decided to hold on to it. The statement given was that Cleaston was working under cover, which, they said, was only known to a certain few. And that because of the sensitivity of the work he was doing, they'd told his colleagues that he was on sick leave.'

'Why would they do that?'

'You do need me, girl. You can't even figure that out!'

'Don't play with me, and don't cock off with me. It won't work. Respect will.'

'Never heard the word.'

'Learn it. Now stop these games and tell me.'

'They have cottoned on that Cleaston must have been on to someone, someone who would kill rather than let him report back. They want that someone, and anyone involved with him, to think that they're on the incident board. It worked. You phoned me, didn't you?'

'So, you're thinking that the cops don't really know anything, and that they're playing a game hoping to fool someone into making a wrong move.'

'Yep. Cleaston knew who to go after, but they didn't believe him, now they do. He may have left notes, he certainly would have tried to get certain people onto the incident board, he was like me in that, never let go of a bone. My guess is he was one track minded and that led to him being pushed off the team. But he kept gnawing at that bone in his own time. What Granddad did was prove that Cleaston was right. Not that Granddad had a choice in the matter. The cops may follow the line Cleaston took, but they don't know what he found out that night.'

'Do you?'

'Only a theory. Granddad kept that information from me.'

'Look, we'll have that coffee. This call is going on too long. Where are you phoning from?'

'I'm a newspaper sleuth. I'm using a phone box.' Where can we meet?'

'The best bet is in the open, on expenses. We could make out that you are giving me a story. Opening up about your life. You're still newsworthy. I could go along the angle of your life in tatters, and how you're picking up the pieces – the loss of the business, that sort of thing.'

'You know that!'

'Yep.'

'Right, where? The when can't be today, but you're on my payroll from this moment.'

'Great. How about The Woolpack, it's a middle of the road pub, busy, a good haunt and near to my office?'

'Eleven thirty tomorrow then? And, Nina, welcome aboard.

'I prefer it when you call me The Rottweiler.'

'You knew that?'

'I know most things. See you tomorrow.'

*

Pulling on her MaxMara hooded camel coat, Layla tied the belt to pull in the waist, surveyed herself in the hall mirror. Decided today was a red-lipstick day.
Taking the Guerlain Rouge G De Guerlin, Jewel Lipstick out of her clutch bag, she smiled at the memory the shape of its case evoked, then applied it liberally. She was ready. Her hand of cards was coming up trumps. She was on her way.

30

'That fucking rookie could have been right!'

'Not a very nice address after him only being in his grave for three days.'

'Being dead don't make him less than the arsehole he was, but why is he dead, *why?* And by whose hand?' The Chief watched Riley stomp up and down his office.

'That, I think, will remain a mystery. Sergeant Tring said that when she spoke to him on the phone that he said he had something good. That can only mean a lead on all the shit we thought he was wrong about. But, the phone she spoke to him on was gone, and so was the camera she said he took with him. And, there was no CCTV coverage where the hit and run took place.'

'I know. We've been over that ground a thousand times. Even the paint from the wall that the car crushed him into hasn't helped us come up with a car. And no one has been nervous enough to wrong foot themselves. It's a fucking mystery.'

'It is. But, at least we can take the same line of enquiry that Cleaston was taking now. We can put all of those people he had on the incident board back on and start to dig in earnest.' As he said this, the Chief wiped his finger around his shirt collar. With Riley digging, he just might unearth something, something that he'd rather wasn't dug up.

'I've tasked George with putting pressure on all of his snouts. Maybe that will bring something in. If only Gosling would turn up. He probably has evidence he hasn't logged anywhere, but his continued disappearance does tie in with Cleaston's theory. Christ, a bent cop is all we need in all of this.'

Again, the Chief eased his collar from his neck. Life was pretty uncomfortable as it was without someone finding the reason why Gosling had gone off. Poor Sara. How he missed her, but he daren't contact her, other than on police business.

Their affair had started after a police ball five years ago. His own marriage to Jill was a cold affair. Gosling had left to see to something or other, and Jill had been in the company of a few other cold wives, gossiping, when he'd heard a little voice next to him say, "You're as lonely as I am, aren't you, Mike?" He'd looked down into the beautiful, watery, hazel eyes of Sara.

In that moment something had happened between them. Within a week they were meeting for a drink. Within two weeks, he'd bedded her and had experienced the most intense feeling of love and protection towards another human being that he'd ever felt in his life. Their lovemaking had taken them both to heights he'd never thought possible.

Thinking of it now as Riley's conjectures went over his head, had him longing to hold her to him.

They'd comforted one another over the phone, but both knew it would be playing too near to the coals to meet for a while. *God, I love her.*

'Why? Why?'

'Sorry, why, what?'

'You haven't been listening. What kind of a fucking place is this? Do you ever get results? I was talking about Gosling going missing. I need a reason for that. Something that takes him out of the 'bad cop' frame that Cleaston put him in, and off my incident board! No one round here likes him being on it.'

'Yes, we get results. But you're the fucking wise-boy from God's Police Place, and you're no nearer than we were to solving all of this, so don't come in here with your insults.'

'I'm sorry. I shouldn't have spoken like that Chief. I can understand you going off into your own mind, you've heard all of these theories so many times.'

'I accept. Now, if you don't like Gosling staring at you from the incident board, remove him, or put him down as a victim. Maybe that's it. Maybe he's been taken out because he knew too much. As far as I know, he was a good cop.'

'But we come down to his car and the things he left on the seat.'

'Planted to put you off the scent. Has forensics come up with anything from the car?'

'Nothing. Christ, the unsolved cases are mounting. And, though there are tenuous links that Cleaston believed in, there's nothing solid to tie them all together. Nothing. Well, except him being snuffed out. But that's it. Was he killed because he was on to something? Or are we all overreacting and his killing was just a hit and run after robbing him?'

Everyone hated dead-end cases, and this one was fraying the Chief's nerves raw. He wanted to order it closed as a combined case and put someone on solving the individual murders, but he knew in the heart of him, that they were all linked.

His fist hit the desk. 'Someone's having a laugh at us, and I don't like it!'

A knock on the door brought him some relief, the feeling inside him had him wanting to burst out of his chest with frustration.

George stepped into the office. 'I've got something. It's from one of my snouts. You're not going to like it.'

'Shut the fucking door, George, and tell us what you have.'

'It's about Gosling. Checkers, my car-thief snout, says that Gosling regularly sourced hire cars in false names, and the cars never showed back at the depots they'd come from, usually way up North. He knew who fetched them for Gosling. Bugsy Brown. He said that Bugsy has also gone underground and that he thinks that he's working somewhere over in Essex, but he doesn't know where. Apparently, Bugsy showed up a few days ago. He went to the walk-up in Brewer Street. He was flush, very flush and had himself a good time.'

'Find him and bring him in.'

As George left the office, Riley looked at the Chief.

'Gosling stays on the criminal side of my board.'

The Chief could do nothing but nod.

Left on his own, he buried his head in his hands. *Where would all this end?* Suddenly, he knew where it would end for him. Getting up, he crossed over and put the lock on his door. As he went back to his seat, he punched a number into his phone. 'Sara?'

'Yes, Mike. Oh, Mike . . .'

'I know, darling. Look, we're not going to hide forever. I love you. I'm going to seek a divorce. Until that's settled, we may not be able to see each other, unless we can find a way. But, we'll telephone. Stay strong, darling.'

'Mike, don't go. I have something to tell you. I've been willing you to ring me. A parcel was delivered. Not by post. It just appeared on my doorstep. It was a box. Inside was a small roll of barbed wire.'

'What the heck?'

'It'll be from Matt. I'm scared, Mike.'

'But why, barbed wire? What is there to be scared of?'

'It's a warning. I know exactly what he means by it. He's referring to TV drama series. It was five or six years back. We watched every episode. I think it was on in the seventies the first time around. Anyway, it often had us both in tears. It was about betrayal in a marriage. He used to say, "You'll never do that to me, will you darling? I couldn't bear it." Then, one day, he got really angry while it was on and said he'd kill me if I did. Over the years he's often referred to the programme and begged me not to leave him. Oh, Mike. I don't know what to do.'

Shit! The bastard is alive then? A lead weight seemed to drop into the pit of the Chief's stomach. 'Don't do anything, Sara. Just throw it away. We don't need it confirming that Gosling is alive. It's a blow to us, but if you report this, your house will be swarmed once more. Surveillance will be posted and we'll never get the chance to be together again. Just ignore it. I'll get another phone and ring you regularly on that. I don't want your number appearing too often on my phone bill. I can get away with it at the moment as I can say that as Chief I was checking up on you, that's all. Giving you support. I'll ring you in a few days to give you my new number. Just list it under any name, but not mine. Okay?'

'Yes, Mike. But, why doesn't Matt just get in touch with me? This seems a bit extreme. I'm afraid he might carry out his threat.'

'He won't. He's hurt, that's all. I don't think that he would harm a hair on your head. He'll contact when he's worked this through.'

'I love you, Mike, and even if Matt comes back, I won't stop loving you.'

'You would leave him, wouldn't you?'

'I – I don't know.'

The phone went dead. The Chief sat staring at it. His heart now held the lead weight. He couldn't lose his Sara, he couldn't.

The Chief stretched and let out a deep sigh. The day had been torturous with all of this on his mind. Glad when home time came, though wishing he could just go home to Sara and bury himself in her lovely soft embrace, he walked to the car park and aimed his fob at his car. The lights flashing coincided with his phone ringing. 'Chief, where are you?'

'I'm just about to get into my car and go home, Riley, please don't say that you're going to stop me.'

'Sorry, Chief, but you'll want to know this. There seems to be a gang-world war going on. Several small timers have been taken out. The word amongst the snouts is that one of the big bosses is angry at Gina's passing. No one seems to know who he is, but I suggest we look into who owns Brewer Street. walk-up where Gina and her mate Zoe worked. But, what's more interesting, and possibly unconnected, as it is a different kind of killing, is that we've just had a report that Bugsy Brown's body's been found. It's in a car behind a closed-down pub in Essex. The body of Checkers, George's snout who gave him the information on Bugsy, is with it. The local branch let us know in response to the 'Wanted' post we sent around asking to keep a look out for Bugsy. It appears that Bugsy had a CCTV CD stuck in his mouth.'

The Chief's legs sagged. His voice sounded foreign to his own ears, 'How long ago, and have they been able to watch the tape?'

'Forensics are on to it now.'

'I'll come back up to the office.'

Christ, don't let this be the tape that shows me in the walk-up!

Putting his hand on his car to steady himself, he opened the door and sat inside. Slapping the steering wheel, a vicious blow with his open hand, he leant back.

'Fucking Gosling. I'll kill him if it is!'

With his hands gripping the wheel, he leaned his head on them. *How will Sara ever forgive me? How?* He'd only gone to the walk-up out of frustration, and to keep Gosling off the scent. Yes, he'd had a couple of good fucks, but it hadn't meant anything more than a release from the tension in him. They'd been so few opportunities to be with Sara at that time, and Jill was like fucking a rice pudding. And a cold one at that. This would mean the end of his job. Put him on the fucking incident board. But most of all, it would mean . . . *God! I can't bear to think of it . . . Oh, Sara, Sara . . .*

31

Ronnie Flinch, still preening himself for suddenly being elevated by the Boss, was enjoying his first job of torturing his old adversary. He watched as the blood dripped onto the floor from Kenny Boy's nose, mouth, stomach and face.

Hung like a piece of raw meat from the beam Kenny was no longer the main man. The vicious Jed-the-Knife, as Jeffrey Cummings was known had almost cut Kenny into pieces. Not so much that he would die, but enough to have him moaning in agony.

A small time hit-man wanting in on the big time, Jed had put himself forward for a few cutting jobs, but had mostly been ignored. Tonight, he got lucky as the bigger hit-men with more of a range of methods of disposing of the unwanted than he had, were out and about taking out those unfortunates who had made it to the Count's hit list.

Kenny had been respected and thought of as The Boss's number one. Now Ronnie had that position and Kenny was destined for an unmarked grave. But not before they got from him what the Boss wanted to know.

'Lower the fucker down.'

Jed obeyed. He mounted the ladder and not too gently jerked the rope pulley, sending Kenny hurtling towards the ground with the beam still strapped to his back and crushing the breath from him.

Ronnie put his foot on the beam and with Jed's help, rolled it over eliciting a scream from Kenny as the movement stretched his body ripping his shoulders from their sockets.

'Get him back in the chair. I'm fucking losing my patience now.'

Jed motioned to the two heavies who stood by the door. They hadn't uttered a word only nodded in response to instructions, and had carried out Ronnie's bidding as if they were robots.

One fetched the chair forward, the other dragged the beam towards it. Kenny's cries of agony were quietened to a muffled groan by the dirty rag Ronnie stuffed into his bleeding mouth.

Ronnie waited as Jed cut Kenny free. He watched the heavies haul Kenny into the chair. How the man had resisted this long, insisting he knew nothing and hadn't betrayed anyone, Ronnie didn't know.

All the way from London to the Boss's huge house in Epping, Kenny had protested his innocence. He hadn't known about the drug deal going wrong. And, to Ronnie's question as to why he hadn't asked about it when The Boss commissioned him to sort it, he'd said, he never questioned The Boss, he just did as he was told.

But Ronnie was having none of it.

Ronnie knew that if it was him in Kenny's place, the moment he'd been brought into this underground shed, once an air raid shelter and the size of a garage, he'd have given in and taken the swift death. Lined with contraptions from a man-sized mouse trap with steel teeth, to knives, whips, and a bed of sharp nails, not to mention the chair. A heavy wooden and iron monster with straps for neck, wrists and ankles and studded with broken glass, it had an armour type vest that clamped the torso to it. The tighter it was screwed the deeper the glass shards penetrated the body. Ronnie shuddered at the thought of the pain it would inflict.

But, he was glad that Kenny wasn't the coward that he himself was as he was enjoying the spectacle of seeing him go through the various tortures and especially the times when he called on Jed to go to work with his knife. He knew exactly how to cut and had started by removing Kenny's nose, so that he now looked hideous. Though he'd left his nasal passages clear so that he could breathe during times like now when his mouth was restricted.

Pulling the rag out of Kenny's mouth caused the space around them to be filled with a moan, more pain-filled than any Kenny had released before. Jed's high pitched laugh intruded. The two heavies glared at him. This had the effect of sobering Jed, but his joy at being involved in this, what must be his dream job, still showed on the sick bastard's face.

Ronnie lit the torch he'd picked up and brushed it slowly by Jed's arm. Jed jumped. The expression on his face changed. Ronnie gave him a nod, glad to have him back from whatever ecstasy the torture of Kenny was giving him. Jed needed to learn to stay focused.

Holding the torch next to Kenny, Ronnie asked him again, 'Tell me, Kenny, who was behind the drug heist? Who took Gina out? Tell me!!'

Kenny shook his head. Blood sprayed with the movement. Spitting out a gob full of it, Kenny croaked, 'I don't know, I swear, I don't know, Ronnie. For pity's sake kill me. Kill me.'

'You fucking idiot. Just tell me and all of this will stop. You'll be useful to The Boss, he'll want to use you as a plant in the gang that's doing all of this to him, can't you see that?'

'Go t – to The B – Boss, tell him that I – I'm loyal. T – Tell him, I – I don't know anything. T – Tell him, I – I just took his order a –and didn't question the reason. N

259

– not because I was working for s – someone else, b – but because, I work like that. P – please go and t – tell him, Ronnie.'

Ronnie hesitated. Part of him believed Kenny, but he wanted that number one position.

'You're lying, Kenny. The moment The Boss mentioned the heist to me, I questioned it. I was shocked to hear that he'd been done over. The implications are enormous. A rival gang daring to challenge The Boss! Christ, anyone would have been shocked, unless they already knew because they'd helped the fuckers to do it.'

'No . . . no – o – o!'

Ronnie brushed the lighted torch slowly up and down Kenny's legs, scorching the skin, blistering it, exposing the raw flesh beneath it.

The smell was putrid. The smoke smarted Ronnie's eyes. Kenny passed out.

'The fucker's going to his death without giving us anything! The Boss won't like that. Get some water.'

As Jed did his bidding, a moments silence descended. Ronnie stood the still flaming torch into a bucket of sand, his mind in a turmoil. Kenny wasn't lying. He knew that now. The only reason he was standing the agony was because he truly didn't know anything.

*

A loud buzzing noise broke the silence. Jed saw Ronnie freeze, his eyes stared at the internal phone as if he would smash it to pieces rather than answer it. Jed watched him slowly walk towards the phone and unhook it from its crib on the wall. He looked like a defeated man walking towards the gallows.

'Yes, Boss?'

Jed waited. His acute hearing picked up some of the tirade that was making Ronnie hold the phone away from his ear. Jed didn't know who the Boss was, but knew he was the most powerful man on the streets of London. At this moment, the Boss wasn't happy.

It appeared that his personal bodyguard Bugsy Brown hadn't come back from a mission, and had had the audacity to visit the walk-up. Then there was something about a message to Gerry Loyson and that Ronnie had better find out if it had been delivered, before the Boss asked what information Ronnie had been able to glean from Kenny.

'Nothing yet, Boss, but we're getting there.'

'Getting there, Getting there! You've been at him for an hour now. What's taking so long? Are you treading too softly with him? I hope you've got the guts for such a job. You won't be my number one if you haven't. Get on with it!'

'He's almost a gonner, Boss, and yet he's still insisting that he knows nothing. I've never had one hang out this long. They usually give in just so they can die. Kenny keeps saying that he didn't question you as he never would. That he carried your orders out without asking why, or prying into your business, and that's why he never questioned the fact that you'd had a drug deal go down.'

There was a pause. Ronnie waited. Jed thought it'd taken a lot for Ronnie to say that. He might just be giving up his chance of taking the number one spot. Jed didn't hear what The Boss said next, but Ronnie turned and walked over to Kenny still holding the phone. Jed followed him and saw what Ronnie saw. The silence descended again. Then Ronnie said. 'It's too late. He's gone, Boss.'

The phone clicked and went dead. Ronnie hooked it back in place on the wall. Jed still held the bucket of water. Ronnie took it and bending, emptied it over his

261

own head. Shaking off the residue he said to the heavies, 'Clear up here.'

Outside Ronnie looked at him for a long moment. Jed's blood went cold. He'd seen and heard too much. A good bloke had been done over to the point of snuffing it. Jed thought that someone had to pay and that someone would be him. But then he heard the words he'd been longing to hear for most of his life, 'You did good, Jed. You'll be the one I call for any job of this nature. Put the word out that we broke Kenny, and he went to his maker for messing with The Boss.'

Jed nodded.

'Right, get yourself washed-up, and changed, there's a shower room through that door over there, and clean clothes hanging up. I'll take you to the train. You're on The Boss's payroll from now on.'

'Right, Ronnie, thanks.'

'Who do you know that can get a message to Gerry Loyson?'

'You're looking at him. Me brother's in Leicester with Gerry. They're mates.'

'Keep that quiet. Gerry is number one enemy of The Boss.'

'Okay, I can use another source. A mate's got a cousin in there. He's alright this mate. He'll do anything for a grand.'

'You've got it. The Boss wants Loyson to know that unless he's informed who took his drugs, and the gangsters working him over are called off, then Loyson's daughter, Layla Parrondski, will be taken out, and none too prettily.'

Jed nodded. He'd wanted to gasp at this knowledge. Loyson's daughter was the socialite, Layla Parrondski! She's been implicated in quite a lot of doings lately, not least the murder of her husband. Why would the Boss go to Loyson? And why threaten him with the death of his daughter? There could be no other reason than Loyson must be running things, or at least a counter operation, but how? Jed, had a mind that could work out the five-star difficulty-rated Sudoku within minutes. It was piecing together quiet a scenario with this information, and coming up with something that could be sensational. Only he didn't know if it was possible whether it could be true or not.

What he'd do with it when, or if he did, he wasn't sure, but suddenly, small time, Jed-the-Knife, could see himself at the top of the London gangland tree.

This was compounded when Ronnie finally came back to him after his meeting with the Boss. Jed was glad to see Ronnie come through the door of this palace of a house. His balls were freezing off after standing in the garden, and though he'd knocked at the door to be let in, a sour-faced housekeeper had given him short-shrift and told him to wait outside.

'Right, Jed. You're in. Bugsy's been taken care of. If you pull off this mission, and The Boss wants confirmation by way of a written, signed note from Loyson, saying that he hears what the Boss says, then you can have Bugsy's job as bodyguard to the Boss. You can start now, on trial. I'll take you to the train, you put the motions in place to have the message delivered. Then get back here and give me a call from the station. The Boss has to be protected at all costs. You stay discreet at all times. You do everything he tells you, or asks of you, without question. I'm his number one, so if anything bothers you, you contact me. Whether you survive longer than a week is up to whether you come through with this first assignment. So you need to put the frighteners on your mate to make sure that the message is delivered, right?'

'Consider it done as I'll deliver it meself. Me mate will arrange a visitor pass for me to see Loyson. He can do it through texting, as his cousin is another big-wig amongst the lags and has access to a mobile. He'll give the message on the text and say that I'll need the written and signed answer when I visit.'

'How long will that take?'

'No more than a couple of weeks, like I say, the cousin has influence, as Loyson has. Loyson will want to reply to this as soon as. He can arrange the pass in a quarter of the time it would normally take, though I'm going to need a fair sized bung.'

'You'll get it.'

Jed couldn't believe his luck. He was to be bodyguard to the Boss. Live in this magnificent house. Ha! He'd see that bitch of a housekeeper squirm if it was the last thing he did. And, he'd stand over his mate, Pigsy with a knife ready to slit his throat while he oversaw him text a message to his cousin. He had to be sure it was done to the letter.

*

Two weeks later Jed felt his brain slump with the relief felt when finally, a sought-after fact is remembered. In this case it was the mystery that had been dogging him since he'd heard the name Layla Parrondski, that was solved.

The note Loyson had given him gave him the knowledge of who the Boss really was. Although how he'd achieved looking nothing like himself, Jed didn't know. He stared at the words, trying to take it in as he read: *Parrondski you're a dead man!*

Very useful information to have.

32

Layla stared at Adrian. 'Joe wants me dead! Why, does he know what I'm up to?'

'No, he sent a message to your father threatening him with your death if your father didn't call off whoever is working him over. Which shows he doesn't know who it is. He just knows that your father would know and still has influence to act. It didn't work, instead your father sent a death threat back to him. Now your father insists you have a bodyguard at all times.'

'That's not in my plan. Having a bodyguard tells the world that you're up to something. I won't agree to it.'

'Please, darling, for once listen to those that know.'

'Only Nick, then. He is my driver anyway and is by my side or waiting for me most of the time, so it won't look like someone has a special remit. But call my dad off. Tell him that Joe will be killed, but by me and me alone. Only it won't be until I have crushed him. And tell dad that if he foils me on this, I'll never speak to him again!'

'I'll tell him. He's put you in further danger by reacting like he did. He should have handled it better, but it's only what any father would have done.'

'I get that, but just stop him before he has the deed done. Now, I have to get going, I'm meeting Jade at the club in half an hour.'

'Thought I might get an invite. I'd like to see the finished article.'

'As long as you can get my dad to call off anything he might have put in place, first. Then you can meet me there in an hour. Jade is coming about that time.'

Layla sank back into the soft cream seat of her Rolls. It felt good. She'd had enough of hired cars. The cops seemed to have gone cold on her, so she hadn't had to take so many precautions to cover her whereabouts. She breathed in the luxurious smell of the walnut and leather and felt content.

A green KA crawled away from the kerb outside a row of shops and slotted in behind the Rolls as it left the quayside.

As they pulled up outside of Tête à Tête, an as yet, unfamiliar sound of the phone Layla had assigned to the Rottweiler on their first hurried meeting rang out. She wondered what the girl wanted as all Layla had given her for now was direct contact if she found anything out that could be useful. For some reason she'd wanted to hold back until the girl proved herself.

Layla reached into her bag. She needed a new system of communication, her phones now numbered five and would be a very strange find if ever she was searched.

'Layla, you're being followed.'

'What?'

'I'm behind you, in a green KA, but your tail just got out of a taxi.'

'Are you following me?'

'Yes.'

'Why'

You're not telling me enough and I'm used to snooping.'

'I told you we would meet again.'

'I know. It's the journalist in me that is suspicious. You should be thanking me. Granddad told me your life is in danger.'

Layla shut the phone off. 'Nick, drive on. Quick. And keep your bloody eyes open. You're supposed to be taking care of me. That was the Rottweiler. Did you see a man get out of a taxi?'

'Yes, but –'

'Christ, he was a hit-man, Nick!'

'I'm sorry, Layla, but I can't suspect everyone who gets out of a taxi in our vicinity.'

'No, but you should have bloody noticed the KA following us. Thank God it was the Rottweiler; it could have been a killer.'

Layla caught Nick's expression of utter horror, through the mirror. *Perhaps Adrian is right and I need a trained bodyguard. Fuck! This is getting too hot to handle.* Turning around she saw the green KA still on their tail. Her fingers dialled the Rottweiler. 'We'll meet now. My home in Holland Park. That won't be suspect, nor will it be a likely place for anyone to think it is where I would go as the builders are still in finishing off. I'll ring the foreman and tell them all to leave early as I want to bring some friends to have a look around.' Nick did a U-turn. 'Keep the KA in your sights, Nick.' As she said this, Layla tapped out Adrian's number. 'Where are you? Don't go anywhere near Tête à Tête. Contact Jade and stop her going there. There's an unwanted visitor hanging around. Meet me at Holland Park, but not Jade. Tell her we'll make contact.' Layla told him about meeting the Rottweiler there. 'If we're seen, I want it to look like I'm granting her another interview, but with my lawyer present. I want you to listen to what she has to say and advise me. And, think of another system for communication, these phones are driving me mad. It's ridiculous that I have to carry so many around.'

'Will do, but the phones were your idea, I never did know why one wouldn't have done.'

Layla felt silly. She didn't like the feeling. 'Contact Frankie, The Rottweiler is saying that Frankie knows I have a contract on me. How does he know and who wants me dead? Or rather, I should say, which one is coming after me at the moment?'

Adrian's amused laughter maddened her even more. She cut him off, but then rang him back. 'Has the deal been done?'

'Yes, the drugs changed hands this morning. Two million will hit your French account tomorrow.'

'Good.'

Again Layla cut Adrian off. This time she sat back. A wry smile came over her face. She'd really done it. She just needed direct contact with the supplier now. She knew he was called the Brazilian, but didn't know how to contact him. She'd get D on to it. His new insider seemed to be able to get anything they wanted.

*

'How does Frankie know I have a contract out on me and who by?' Layla played this one close, she wanted as few as possible to know that Joe was still alive.

The Rottweiler held her gaze, a slight impudence in her look. 'Granddad doesn't know who ordered the kill, but he knows who has the job and that he plays dirty. Always with a knife.'

Layla shuddered. 'And, how did you know he was at the Tête à Tête getting out of a taxi?'

'I know most of the hit-men, but this one I don't know. Granddad phoned me and said he'd seen him in a pub with Ronnie Flinch. Ronnie Flinch I do know. Granddad said they left together and got in a taxi. He told me the number of the cab and in which direction they went and told me to follow them. I was in my Granddad's flat just around the corner having a cup of tea with my Gran. I figured they would go to your place

268

on the Thames, so I made for there. I caught up with them sitting in the taxi outside the shops around the corner from you. They set off before me, but they went a different way to you. As you and I were slowing to stop outside Tête à Tête, I saw the very same taxi pull in front of you.'

'Shit, this means that J – someone, knows I have that place. It's impossible. And not only that, but that I was due to go there today. But how? Unless . . . we have someone giving information from inside, Oh, God!'

Adrian looked as horrified as Layla felt, but the Rottweiler showed no emotion. 'If you don't tell me everything, I can't help you. I need to know everything that's going on and who you have as your contacts. Once I know that, I can get to work. I already know that your husband isn't dead.'

'So you're a sleuth now? You're barely out of nappies!'

'Adrian!'

I know, but I don't like it. She's not cut her front teeth yet and she purports to be able to do so much and know so much, how come? Are you a plant, little Miss Rottweiler? Is this what this is all about? You think you can infiltrate Layla's life and double cross her?'

Layla, though shocked, knew Adrian could be right. There were so many coincidences in Nina's tale. But how to play this? Nina already knew a great deal. But then, she was Frankie Droile's granddaughter.

'What I am is an ambitious granddaughter of a hit-man. I've been around gangsters all my life. My grandfather recognised my potential. He's sick of being on the side lines of those with the big money and the influence and yet, doing their dirty work. He couldn't send his daughter, my mother, to a posh school of the likes you went to Layla, or live in a big house. Yes, he's made some money, but him and my gran live in a high-rise,

269

and granddad still has to do the dirty work for those living in clover. His only holidays have been at Her Majesty's pleasure, while he's seen those he works for swan off abroad in their yachts. Well, he wanted different for me. From an early age, he has taught me how to be cunning, and to keep my ear to the ground. He encouraged me in my education, to follow a career which would help me to gather information. He tells me all he knows so that I can be one step ahead of the game. I know everything about you Layla, except what you're planning. I know whose deaths you've been involved in. And I could have been a top paid journalist by now with that information, but that's not what I want. I want to achieve what my granddad couldn't, and I want to achieve it for him. I want to be big in a big operation. I'm no grass, and no insider. I have the same ambitions as you both have, because I come from the same stock.'

Layla was smiling by the time Nina had finished speaking. She'd found her fourth woman. Herself, Jade, Marcelle and Nina, also known as The Rottweiler, were going places. And of these, Nina was going to be the most useful ally. She had more pedigree than the others. She thought the same as herself. And yes, they would need men, but they would use them, pay them well, but not elevate them to top positions, that is, except for Adrian. Adrian, too would be a partner, he'd earned that, in more ways than one.

'Okay, my plans are that I want the lot –'

'Layla, what are you doing? You can't take her on face value and let her in on everything you're doing, you have to be–'

'Careful? Careful of what, Adrian? Nina is now a partner as you are, as and from this moment. And as such you will respect each other. We will run the operation through the legit businesses of my Mayfair jewellery shop, and online designer store, as well as the nightclub, all of which we will expand. We'll set up a Corporate Company with me holding the majority share and being the overall head of all operations. Jade will hold the next highest as she has come in with capital. Then you, Adrian, and Nina and Marcelle, will be equals. Marcelle will advise on everything financial, you, Adrian, on everything legal, and Nina on strategy, and head of the drug dealing operations and anything else we may dip our fingers into, with the front of being the company's PR and Press Release Officer. Though, you are not to step on Jade's toes, Nina. Where the sleaze side of the business is concerned, she has full control. Right. I've no staff here, yet, and very little furniture, so, can we move to your office, Adrian? In your boardroom we can hold our first board meeting. We'll call Jade and Marcelle and get them to meet us there. One of our first jobs will be to set Marcelle the task of sourcing and renting our business premises and we'll decide on a name for our company. After that, Adrian, you will put everything in motion to register the company. Marcelle will see to it that the off-loading of the Parrondski holdings show a good intake to cover where the money has come from. Though I have, it, it isn't from a legit source, and the wherefore is something I am keeping to myself. Some very clever wheeling and dealing will need to be done by Marcelle. It's time for London to know that Layla Parrondski is not down and out, and that she is back, and for that bastard Joe, to know that too.'

Layla could see that Adrian was torn between being extremely pleased, and very annoyed. He expressed neither emotion when he spoke. 'I am a criminal lawyer, although I have acted on other matters for you,

Layla, in doing so, I have taken the advice of my partners in my practice whose expertise covers all fields. I will either need a legal department to be able to cope with all avenues our business will require, or continue to use my own business as our legal advisors. Is there the money for all of this?'

'There is. However, let's not discuss everything now. We will all have items we need to bring to the table. Once the meeting is underway, we will draw up a full agenda and everyone will contribute to it.'

Nina hadn't spoken, but the look of satisfaction along with excitement on her face said it all.

'Are you both happy with everything, then?'

Nina's immediate response was to nod and say, 'Yes, very happy.'

Adrian was less enthusiastic. 'Of course, it is what I have striven for, but I can see problems ahead, and the first one is, the death threat hanging over you.'

'Granddad can see to that. He wanted to, but I wouldn't let him. He knows who has been engaged, and can take him out at any time. I wanted him to wait until I could negotiate him a proper rate for his trouble. I want enough money for him to be able to set him and gran up in a bungalow in the suburbs, with a garden, and for them to be able to take a good holiday when the coast is clear. That's the price of removing the immediate threat.'

'And knowing you could take that threat away from Layla, you allowed it to remain, and put her life in danger!'

'Adrian, can't you see? Nina is my type of girl, and the exact kind of person we need. You and Jade are soft on certain things, and Marcelle is not to be involved in anything to do with our criminal element. Not the nitty, gritty, anyway. I would have taken the exact decision that Nina has taken, and for me, that bodes well for our future. Yes, Nina, have Frankie do the job and all you want for him will be his. Now, let's get to work.'

Layla smiled at them both. She could see that Nina and Adrian would be arch enemies for a long time to come, but that too could work in her favour. Yes, life looked good. Really good. And it wouldn't be long now before she claimed the ultimate prize. The death of fucking Count 'Joe' Rolleski!

33

'Calm down, Sara. Please, darling, I can't make head nor tail of what you're saying.'

'I – I've had a – a letter. It's written in blood. It says: "The day is coming!" Oh, Mike, what am I going to do. Matt's going to kill me, I know he is!'

'Get some things together and leave the house. Go to a hotel and ring me from there. I'll meet you later. I can't leave right now. Everything will be alright, I promise. Now, do as I say, Sara. Remember, I love you and will protect you.'

'Oh, Mike. I'm so afraid. Matt wouldn't normally hurt me, but we've broken his heart.'

'I know. We didn't mean to. We can't help how we feel. Hopefully, he'll come to terms with everything, but in the meantime, we have to take care. I have to go now, darling. I'll see you later.'

Christ, the fucking barbed wire, the CD and now this! What the fuck is Gosling up to? The Chief slammed his fist on his desk. Sweat stood out on his forehead. Gosling was playing with them.

At least the CD of the CCTV footage hadn't shown anything other than Gosling and himself entering the walk-up. But what about the others with more information on? Was that CD just a warning?

Thank goodness Riley believed that they'd visited the walk-up on an investigation and that although the place was an illegal brothel, they'd decided not to raid it yet. Not with so much outstanding that's connected to those premises. They were hoping one of the players would make a false move and then they could move in.

Riley had ordered 24-hour surveillance, which was more than an annoyance. He could do with some relief.

275

But then, at last, he would get that with Sara tonight. The thought gave him a twitch in his groin. At forty-seven, Sara still had a beautiful body. She was passionate, accommodating, and loving. There was no 'just having sex' with her. Every time was a beautiful experience. He felt wanted, adored and as if he was the greatest lover the world had ever known. Sara was sensuous. The smell of her drove him wild, as did how she prepared him for loving. Bathing him. Oiling his body. Serving him a delicious, chilled wine and feeding him chocolates, or grapes, which she had wiped around her nipples.

Her breasts were something else, not large, but perky and her nipples always hard. He loved the way she trembled when he caressed them . . .

Oh, God!

The Chief's head dropped into his hands. It felt to him as if a net was tightening around him and as he saw it, he had two choices, go to Sara and get the fuck away from everything – go abroad, Mexico, or somewhere similar and change their identities, or find Gosling and stop his stupid games, get him to divorce Sara, then he could do the same to his wife, and Sara and he could be together and live a normal life. He didn't know how to do either.

Pulling himself together, he tried to get his head around the meeting that was going to take place in five. There were so many threads to the original Parrondski, missing person incident that he felt he'd lost control, and no one else seemed to have a handle on what was going on either.

Rising he made his way to the main office. Someone spoke to him, but he ignored them.

Reaching the incident room, he found it empty. His watch told him there was still a few minutes before the meeting attendees would start to gather. Slamming the door behind him, he locked it, before crossing over to one of the biggest incident boards he'd seen in his career.

Parrondski headed it. Under his picture, the word: murdered, and the date – charred body unidentifiable. Forensic identification. Poss. owner of the walk-up. This warranted a line going from him to Zoe Feldon and Gina Walters.

There was also a line drawn from Parrondski to Layla Parrondski, her picture taken when she was arrested, didn't do her justice. Under her name was written – wife of Parrondski, poss. gold theft, and the discovery of two children's bodies outside her holiday cottage in Kent, prompting a line to go from her name to the pictures of the two little girls. A second line went from Layla to a picture of her father, Gerry Loyson.

From the girls a line went to Gina Walters, mother to one of the girls. Under Gina's name was written: murdered, and the date. Another line from the girls went to a blank head and shoulders, a mystery woman kidnapper, and then one to Gosling – in the block of flats at the time. And a fourth one to Zoe Feldon. Murdered. This linked back to Gosling being in the flats at the time, and a line from Zoe back to Gina, as they were friends and worked together as prostitutes.

Another line went from Zoe to the pervert being held for her murder, Patrick Finney.

On the side lines was the names of Frankie Droile. A hit man whose trademark killing was everywhere, this name was linked back to Gerry Loyson.

And Cleaston. Murdered, or accident, a question mark remained.

And lastly, Checkers, George's snout and Bugsy, the line that went from these had a picture of the CD.

To the Chief, there was no mystery about their deaths. Gosling. *As I live and breathe this is the work of that bastard, trying to put the frighteners on me and Sara.* As if to confirm this his mobile rang. No name, just 'caller unknown' flashed across his screen. Accepting the call, Gosling's voice came down the line. 'Sara isn't at no bloody hotel.' The phone went dead.

The Chief stared at it. Sweat dampened his body. *Christ!*

A knock on the door had him shaking from head to toe. 'Sir, we're ready to start the meeting.' Riley's voice. Opening the door, he snapped. 'What bloody use it will do, I don't know. We're no further forward. It's a jumble. What the bloody Hell are you doing to solve it all, Riley? I'll have a word with your superiors. Have your meeting and report back to me if anything else has come to light. I've got things to do on cases that are actually going somewhere.'

Finding a relief in his attack, he stormed back to his own office, banged the door shut and turned the key. Tapping Sara's name, he listened to her mobile ringing out. The tone went on incessantly. Where would he start his search for her? He hadn't named a hotel. He'd left it to her to choose one and then to ring him from her room. Come to think of it, Gosling's call was only minutes after his and Sara's . . . *God! Had Gosling been inside the house?*

His heart thumped as the implications of this hit him. Gosling wouldn't risk dragging Sara out of the house! Grabbing his coat, he stormed out of his office, told the desk clerk on his way out that he'd be out for an hour or two but contactable, and made his way to the underground car park. *Please let me be in time. Oh, Sara, Sara . . .*

The house looked as it normally did. Nothing disturbed. Nets hung at the windows. Winter poppies gave an array of colour from the pots each side of the dark mahogany door, but what Mike dreaded, became a truth as he stared at Sara's car still parked on the drive.

There was an eerie silence as Mike's window unwound. Not even the trees lining the street, moved. A shudder rippled through him.

Out of sight of anyone looking through the windows of the house, Mike sat a moment thinking what his next move should be. He could call for back-up. But then the truth of why he was here, and much more, was likely to come out. No, he had to go it alone.

Knowing the layout of the house and how the garden backed onto a tranquil park leading down to the Thames, Mike knew his only option was to approach from the front. The back of the house was accessed by a side entrance as a huge hedge barred any entrance from the park.

He also knew that he would be seen by Gosling and therefore give him the advantage. His mind dreaded what he would face. If Sara wasn't hurt, he knew Gosling would use her to inflict emotional torture on them both. But what would be the outcome? Would he be able to talk sense into Gosling? He doubted it.

Each step towards the front door gave him the folly of his decision not to call for help. Pressing the bell, gave him confirmation of this as it flew open and he was confronted with Gosling holding a knife to Sara's throat.

'Matt, for Christ sake!'

'Get in and shut the door. We need to talk!'

Sara moaned as Matt roughly turned her round and frogged marched her into the kitchen behind him.

'Let her go, Matt. Nothing can be served by behaving in this way. You're committing an assault.'

'Oh, and you're going to arrest me are you, you fucking wife-stealer?'

'We can talk calmly and sort this out. You can't bully your way out of the situation, and you can't change it, now let her go, and do it now! Or arrest you is just what I will do, besides call for back-up.' Deciding to lie and to put some doubt into Gosling's mind, he added, 'I've already left a note as to where I am.'

'Ha! What did you put, 'Off to fuck Gosling's missus, may need some help?'

Gosling laughed out loud at his own joke. A hysterical tone tinged the sound and worried Mike more than he already was.

Sara's eyes showed her fear as the knife dug a deeper dent into the fleshy part of her neck.

Though he wanted to reassure her, he couldn't. Using the skills of the trained negotiator that he was, he kept a calm, persuasive tone to his own voice. 'You're not thinking straight, Matt. Jealousy and hurt are eating you up, and I can understand that and am sorry, but Sara and I couldn't help the feelings that grew between us, we denied them for a long time. You neglected her. Your job always came first, amongst other things.'

This last was a step Mike hoped would bring Gosling to his senses as surely, even now he wouldn't want Sara to hear about his extra-marital sexual activities.

Mike soon realised that was a big mistake.

'You mean my fetish for beating women up? Well. I've told her all about that, and was just about to begin to show her, when you turned up. I got my timing wrong, I didn't think you would come straight after my phone call, but later, and find my darling wife after I'd

280

gratified myself. Well, no matter, this way, I'll have even greater pleasure.'

Mike didn't expect the swift movement Matt made, nor had he seen the rolling pin left on the side. His attention was taken by Sara's body being flung to the floor and going to her aid. The blow to his head blackened everything around him. The room spun as the floor came up to meet him. Sara's scream echoed around the long dark tunnel he found himself hurtling down, knowing that when he reached the bottom there would be a nothingness that he may never be able to rise from again.

*

Sara looked up in horror as her husband wielded the rolling pin above her. 'Now . . . Yes, now, I'm going to show you what that bleeding Mike was trying to tell you – how I got off when I didn't come home. The rolling pin cracked down on her legs.

'No . . . no, Matt, please, I'm sorry. I – I, aggh . . . Oh, God, help me . . .'

Sara felt her ribs crack under the second blow. The pain racked her body. Saliva dripped from her mouth and mingled with her tears. 'No more, Matt. I'll never betray you again, never.' Matt had dropped the rolling pin and now held his belt in his hand. Raising it he brought it down across Sara's stomach. Gasping with the stinging pain, caused her agony. She couldn't beg any more. Slumping down she took the onslaught, sickened to the heart of her when she realised the sexual pleasure Matt was getting. At last, as she lay in a semi-conscious state, she heard him gasp and then let out a holler of sheer ecstasy as he clung to the back of one of the kitchen chairs.

Was this really the gentle Matt she'd known all her life? This monster, who'd near killed her, and had most

probable killed her darling, Mike. As he staggered towards the hall, she called after him, her throat rasping as she told him: 'I hate you. I HATE YOU!'
No pity entered her at the sound of his sobs as he climbed the stairs.

Sara didn't know how long had passed before Mike stirred, she'd been in and out of consciousness and time had only meant the bearing of the pain. The relief at seeing Mike move and hearing his groan was overshadowed by her fear for him. 'Mike . . . Mike?' Mike groaned again before rolling over. His eyes were bloodshot and swollen. Blood trickled from his nose. His stare was of a man who didn't know where he was or why, or even who she was. 'Mike, darling, he's gone. Can you get your mobile out of your pocket? We need help. I think my legs are broken and I have broken ribs, I can't move. Help me, darling, please help me.' Still looking as if he wasn't focusing properly, Mike tried to sit up, but slumped back down again.
'Mike, Mike, stay with me, Mike. Don't go to sleep. Make yourself stay awake.
Pain racked Sara. She cried out with it, and called on God to make it go away, but as she felt herself slipping from it, she knew a contradiction of her desire for release, as she must stay alert. She had to keep Mike going and hope that he would recover enough to get help for them.
Mike had closed his eyes again. This time she tried shock tactics. 'Mike, I'm dying, please help me.' It wasn't a lie, she knew that with broken bones her blood flow could be interfered with and her organs could be starved of oxygen. 'Please, Mike.''
Mike stirred again. 'Mike, pass me your mobile! Please, darling.'

Again Mike fumbled. This time he found his phone and shoved it towards her. Reaching for it she released an animal cry of sheer agony, but knew she had to get it. They had to receive help, whatever the repercussions would be, and she knew there would be some, how could there not be with them both found together in this state, but better that than being the victims of a double murder.

Managing to open his contacts she found just one name. Adrian Prindell. She looked up at Mike. He nodded at her. Pressing the call button, she waited

'What can I do for you, Mike?'

Gasping out what had happened and where, and begging for help, Sara was surprised to hear the calm reply: 'I'll be there in five.'

*

On his way to Gosling's house, Adrian put a call through to Layla.

'What? What the hell are you getting involved for, and why did Gosling's wife call you?'

'I don't know. But I assume, given the state they are in as described by her, that The Chief must need my help to cover it all up. This is good, as it shows he trusts me, and besides that, we could do with having more than his trust. So far we have that by blackmail – the discs I have, but to have it sealed by helping him out can only be a bonus. We know little about what is going on with all the investigations. We need to know more. We also need to drop the right information into the right ear, and that ear belongs to Chief Inspector, Mike Bealver.'

'Okay, but be careful. Everything is ready for us to really move in on Joe's businesses and the time of his elimination is near, I don't want anything to muck that up.'

'All of that will be much easier having the Chief dancing to our tune. I'll ring you with what I have decided to do. None of this is going to be easy to cover up. I need the rest of my journey to think it through.'

As the line clicked and went dead, Adrian sighed. Would that woman ever give him a nice goodbye and not just cut him off when the conversation was over according to her?

He wished he could treat their relationship as lightly as she did and that he hadn't fallen in love with her. Love hurt.

34

Gosling sat in his car staring at his own house, which seemed like an alien place to him now. He wasn't sure what to do next and could hardly see through his tears. The street was still very quiet. He'd picked his time right, but soon the serial shoppers and coffee morning wives would begin to return to their homes, and may even start to call on Sara, wondering why she hadn't joined them on whatever outing they'd been on. Not that she always did. Coming from a wealthy home, Sara was used to the same life these stockbroker wives led. Her father, a financier, looked down him, disapproving of her choice of husband. He'd funded this detached home in the leafy suburbs of London, not wanting his daughter's standards to drop as far as they would have done married to a copper.

Wiping his face on his handkerchief, Gosling wondered what the outcome would be of what had just happened. Phoning Mike before he'd beaten Sara had been a big mistake. He should have been long gone before Mike arrived. But the need to punish him had been too great. Now everything would be out in the open and he would be a hunted man. Probably was already now that Cleaston had been taken out, as surely that would give credence to everything that bastard rookie had tried to make others believe, and once they did believe, they would dig and dig.

They would soon find out that he was up to his neck in what he knew they had begun to term the Parrondski mystery and he doubted that his story of why he'd been in the flats at the time the kids were taken and Zoe was murdered held any water now.

His mind went through the possibilities as he wiped his face on his sleeve. Going abroad was the favoured one, but without Sara as he'd planned? What life would he have anywhere without her?

His hope, now that he'd punished her, was that she would come to see how wrong she'd been. That he'd been right to punish her and once the dust had settled she'd come back to him. Surely all the years of happiness they'd had, counted for something? Yes, he knew he'd neglected her for his masochistic needs, but he'd even done that for her sake. He'd never wanted to do to her what he'd done to them whores. He'd been protecting her from that by getting it elsewhere and giving it to them who deserved it. Well, now she knew that side of him and had become deserving of it. Christ, it had felt good. He never thought it would, but to do it to the woman he loved had given him the biggest orgasm of his life.

Gina came to his mind. Someone had taken her out. He could guess who by the method used, but why? Why would someone put a contract out on Gina? Parrondksi? It had to be.

Whoever it was would pay. He'd had deep feelings for Gina. It was her taking his ways that had helped him not to practice them with Sara. But now he had, he knew he'd have to do it again. Not so much as to break Sara's bones again, but enough to get the pleasure he'd had today.

If she agreed to toe the line and things got back to how they were between them, he'd try not to take his pleasure in that way from her too often. But what about his future prospects, had he blown them? Yes, he still had the measly two hundred thousand that bitch Layla had parted with, but it wasn't in his plans to eek out a retirement abroad with that piddling sum.

He had to get at that fucking Layla Parrondski. She was up to something. Planning something, and he wanted in. Yes, he'd wanted it all at first, but he couldn't achieve that now. Joe Parrondski wouldn't have him back on the payroll now he wasn't a cop, not to mention him not being able to provide the kids. Parrondski, probably had a contract out on him as it was.

The tears flowed again as the hopelessness of his situation took hold. The worst thing he'd done was to have disappeared. As a cop, he'd had power. He'd have been useful to both Joe and Layla Parrondski and could have taken his pick or even played a double deal. Now he had nothing to offer.

His mind went to George, his main worry. He knew a lot, but kept everything close to his chest. He was a funny cop, George. There was many a case solved by him, but for which he didn't take credit. He'd work away in the background and then pass on what he knew when he felt the time was right. Those snouts of his were the best in the game. He could get the trust of anybody, the crims liked him. *George has probably known for a long time that I'm a bent cop.* He'd be waiting his time. But, would he? George liked him. Gave him respect. Knew he concluded cases in a tight way. Maybe he was forgiving of him trying to line his pockets. Maybe, if he contacted him . . .?

The idea took hold and hope began to trickle in where despair had been strangling him. Better that I bide my time, see what happens about today's lot, and then try to get a path back to being a cop. A few palms would need greasing. There'd have to be a good story as to my disappearance. Kidnapped, perhaps? Or had a breakdown?

Maybe, he could make them all believe he'd been framed. That he'd got too close to the truth. He'd have to give them some of what he knew. He'd have to think everything through. Yes, he rode close to the wind and did things a little unconventionally at times, but didn't he get results? They'd swallow that one. And everything else too, if he gave them quite a bit of what he knew, well, enough to convince them that those involved would need him out of the way. He'd say they were going to kill him and even though he'd escaped, he'd had to lie low, but now he wanted to come back and continue with his work. He'd be a hero.

The possibilities were fantastic. He'd have his life back again.

But it all depended on how Mike handled today. Surely, he wouldn't want the truth coming out. If that happened, he would see to it that the stuff he had on Mike also went into the mix, which would mean he would face the sack. No pension, all honour and his standing in society, gone. He'd have nothing.

Yes, Mike would find a way of sorting out today's mess. Without a doubt.

Now, all he needed was to get George on his side. He would find a way back for him. Get a few of his snouts to put truth to his story. *Yes, George is my best bet at this time. He's probably known all along what I was up to. Maybe even had a plan to move in at the last minute and get his own retirement package out of me. Ha. The more I think about it, the more I realise that could have been what he was up to, I'll have to find out.*

Gosling knew, that he had to move fast. Before George told everything, thinking he'd lost out, and may as well take some glory and his pension instead of what he could blackmail out of Gosling.

Gosling pressed his contact number. 'George, it's Gosling.'

'Where the fuck have you been?'

'Went off the rails.'

'You found out then?'

'You knew?'

'Yes, I knew. But it was one bit of information I wasn't going to give you. Christ, you'd have killed, both of them. I'm surprised you haven't.'

'I just nearly did.'

'What? God, Matt. How are you going to get out of this one? And come to think of it, why are you ringing now?'

'I want to come back in.'

There was a silence. 'I've to be honest with you, Matt. I've given them stuff. I wouldn't have done, but I thought you'd bunked off abroad and that wasn't in my plans.'

'What plans?'

'I've been playing you at your own game. You had contacts that could have made you big time, I didn't, but I wanted what you wanted – a better retirement than this shit can give me. I planned to ride on your back. I keep dossiers.'

'I figured that out, but only five minutes ago. Fair play, but can you undo what you've done? Say it was false information? What have you done anyway?'

'A lot less than I could have, but I've told them about the hire cars.'

You knew about that?'

'I know everything; I've made it my business to. Had to, if my plan was to succeed.'

'Christ. Have you any suggestions as to how you can look plausible if you backtrack?'

'Depends on what you have to offer now. My sources tell me you've blown it.'

Matt Gosling thumped his steering wheel. Frustration at his own stupidity filled him. And all because of fucking

289

Mike Bealver! And Sara of course, who wasn't worthy
of the love he had for her.

'You still there, Matt?'

'Look, I'll come back in a week, I promise. I'll have
this mess sorted and be back on top. Don't do anything
else to incriminate me. I have fifty-grand that asks that
you begin to post doubts about the information you
have given, and about my disappearance. Hint that they
should have been looking for me as a victim, not a
criminal. I'm returning to the scene of my crime. I'll be
in touch.'

'Right, I'll take that, thank you very much. But, if I
don't hear from you, and don't have the money, in cash,
by the end of the week, then I give more. And, I have
plenty.'

Gosling ended the conversation. *Fucking, George. Who
the fuck would have guessed? Fucking wanker! But a
clever one, and a useful ally. Yes, he might prove to be
very useful.*

For a few moments, Gosling sat pondering how he
could unwind the last couple of hours. Sara and Mike
needed urgent medical attention. There was only one
possibility, other than A&E, The Doc and that surgeon,
Parrondski had used. But how to get past Parrondski?'

About to telephone the Doc, Gosling stopped. A car had
pulled up. *Fucking Prindell! Shit!*

Grabbing his phone, Gosling rang The Doc. He'd been
a good ally to have. Gosling hoped he was still on his
side.

The familiar voice came down the line, a question in his
voice, 'Gosling, is that really you?'

'It is, how's Count Bollocks?'

A sob made Gosling sit up. 'What's to do, Doc?'

'Everything's been horrible. It's all going wrong. Count
Bollocks is like a sore dick.'

'Ha, that's what I like to hear. What's my situation?'

'He has a contract out on you. Ooh, Matt, I can't go on .
. .'

'Thought as much. And yes you can. We can still screw
him. I have plans.'

'Where did you go, and why? You left me, I thought we
were friends.'

'Never mind all that now. We are friends and I need
your help. I also need Gavin Theogood. And quick. Can
you get hold of him?

'Yes, but –'

'Don't question me. Just do as I say. Have you the
means of knocking Count Bollocks out for a good few
hours?'

'I do, but, Gosling, You're not going to play me, no
matter how much I fancy you. I want to know what all
this is about. I want what you always promised me.'

'You'll get it and more, but I need you to just do as I
say. Get hold of Theogood, I have some bastards with
broken limbs that need operating on, and one has a
possible fractured skull.'

'Theogood isn't the right bloke for that. He's a plastic
surgeon!'

'Christ, he's a doctor, isn't he?'

'Yes, but not a fucking brain surgeon.'

'Is that what's needed?'

'Possibly. Not always, nursing is enough as long as
there isn't fluid on the brain. And I can see to the
broken bones as long as it is a clean break. I don't like
the sound of this, what have you done?'

'Don't ask. How will I know if there's fluid on the
brain?'

'The patient will vomit, and drift in and out of
consciousness, he won't be able to move much and may
be very slow when he does. He may show signs similar

to him having dementia, not knowing who you are or where he is and why.'

'Right, I've got to go. Just be ready to act if I call again.'

Gosling got out of the car and walked towards the house. Using his key, he let himself in. The kitchen was still carnage. Mike was on his feet. Tears rolling down his face. Sara lay where he'd left her. Her eyes were closed. She wasn't moving. Prindell stopped tapping out a number on his mobile and stared at him. 'Is this a good idea? Don't all murderers return to the scene of the crime?'

'Mur . . . Sara's dead?'

'You, Bastard!' Gosling moved out of the lunging Mike's way, but still caught the blow on his shoulder. Pain ricocheted through him. *Sara, dead? She can't be.* 'No! No! She was alright, she . . . Christ! No. Sara, Sara, no!' His knees gave way. He sank to the floor. Sara's unmoving body lay beside him. He touched her skin. Still warm. She'd died in the last minute or so. How? If these bastards saw it happening, why hadn't they tried to save her? He looked up at them, there was no sign that they'd done anything. They weren't out of breath as if they'd administered to her. There was no blood on their hands as if they'd even touched her! *What's going on? Christ, they've finished her off!*

'What have you done to her? You've killed her!'

'No, you killed her, you bastard. We only let her die.'

'Why . . . Why?'

Prindell's calm voice came back to him. 'She was near to death by the time I arrived. Her breath was laboured. Probably from her ribs puncturing her lungs. Mike went to help, but I stopped him. I want Mike out of this. The only way is to have Sara disappear, and for her body never to be found. The thinking was that the conclusion would be drawn that you had come for her and taken her away. Abroad, perhaps. We planned on making it look as if she'd gone willingly. Cases missing, clothes and toiletries all gone, then maybe in a few weeks a message to her parents from abroad saying she was alright, but couldn't ever come home again as she was with you and you were a wanted man. A plan that would have filtered through to you via the news and given you the chance to disappear too. We thought you had done.'

Despite his grief, Gosling could see it was a good plan. Though flawed, as he didn't intend on disappearing. He nodded his head. 'Do the necessary, then we'll talk. You have it right, except for my involvement. I want back in. I want to be a cop again.'

Prindell lifted his phone. His eyes held steel. His words made Gosling's blood run cold. 'That's not happening. Now that you've turned up, you're a dead man.'

In a flash, Gosling stood up, taking his mobile from his pocket as he did so. Before they could react, he'd struck the camera button. With a shot of the amazed faces of Mike and Prindell, with the body at their feet, he made for the front door, shutting the kitchen door as soon as he was through it.

As he got into his car, he thought he saw the front door open slightly and then close.

His laughter rang out. Talk about saved by the bell! His neighbour had arrived home at that precise moment and had swung across the road ready to back her Jag into her drive.

Confident that the shade of the trees would obscure his face, Gosling pulled the sun blind down and his collar up, selected first and drove away from the kerb as if he had all the time in the world. Even if she looked, Jacqueline Bell, his hated, stuck up ex-neighbour, wouldn't recognise his hire car. He made a play of turning his head to look behind him, just in case. He was well past her drive, before he looked ahead.

35

'I should have stopped you getting involved! But I could see the logic of having Mike Bealver on board. But, Christ! Gosling has a picture of you at the bloody scene of a murder! You've cocked up, Adrian.'

'I know. But we have to keep calm, Layla. Gosling may only keep the photo as his own insurance. No doubt we will receive a note very soon telling us that if anything happens to him, then the police will have access to it. And a whole lot more, according to Mike.'

Adrian tried to ignore the deep-seated fear churning his stomach. Never in his life had anyone had anything on him. Now this. He needed to think things through.

Layla was getting on his nerves as she strode up and down the plush office suite, Marcelle had acquired for them in Hanover Square.

Decorated in soft blues, it was meant to give a calming atmosphere. The opposite was happening at the moment.

'But, Joe has a contract out on him! D found out about it. What if that succeeds? The photos will surface! And D's report mentioned that The Doc had received a phone call from Gosling. It's a loose end, Adrian. A fucking mess, just when things were falling into place. It suited us to have Gosling taken out at someone else's expense, now it doesn't. He's a fucking liability. We don't know what his plan is. I don't like it!'

'Well, we know he wants back on the force, and we know who has the contract to take him out. The same man who has yours, and Droile is commissioned to take care of him, so don't worry.'

'I do worry. It's been three weeks since we commissioned Droile on this. Christ, what's he doing? He's never taken this long before. I can't live my life under such close wraps for much longer.'

'I told you not to trust the Rottweiler.'

'You mean, she may have told him to leave the threat hanging over me, but why?'

'That I can only speculate on. Maybe she wants it all. Or maybe she wants more for her granddad than the promise of a better life.'

'I'll talk to her. What about the disposing of the body? Did that go smoothly, have you heard?'

'Yes. Droile has worked well on that one. A message went from Sara's phone to let anyone know, who might wonder, that she would be away for a couple of days and that while she'd gone she was having new furniture and her house would be cleaned – carpets and upholstery. The text said, she'd made a sudden decision as she'd needed something to focus on. Choosing new furniture had helped her. She also put that she was sorry she hadn't talked this over with anyone, but that she couldn't have taken all their protests and advice, though she knew it would all have been well-meant. This covered the reaction that would have come from her friends who are always involved in anything of this kind. Her body being taken out on a sofa, that was wrapped in the way removers do, and was not visible as anything other than a shape of a sofa, raised no eyebrows. Nothing could be seen. Several other items were taken out, and this fitted with what the text said. A team worked day and night cleaning the house. There won't be a trace of DNA, or any other evidence of anything taking place there once it is realised that she is missing. The men carrying out the work, will be non-traceable. Mike's story of him falling and hitting his head is holding water, too. He's off work with concussion, but he has no other injury. The X-rays at the hospital didn't show any fracture of his skull. His eyes are black and bloodshot, but other than that, he'll be okay after a couple of weeks' rest. Physically, that is. He'll need time to recover from his grief, and shock, but he knows he has to get that under control before he goes back to work. He'll have to be able to deal calmly and professionally with everything as it comes in about Sara. Our only loose cannon is Gosling.'

'His update almost makes up for everything. But, I'm on the radar, Adrian. I need to come off that incident board. I don't need my movements being noted by the cops.'

'I'm on to it, but nothing much can happen on that front until Mike returns to work. We've no one in our corner. We have to concentrate on getting the hit-man taken care of.'

Layla knew he was right. Everything was going so well. Tête à Tête was ready and opening tomorrow. Belle et Belle was up and running and orders coming in thick and fast. The television ad was really coming along and slots for it going out twice a night during the soaps was going to cost a mint, not to mention the cost of the top models, and the filming in Barbados. And, they hadn't managed to retain a new buyer, which was causing a headache.

But at least, away from business, the stress had been less. She was back in her home in Holland Park and it was now legally in her name, after the *death* of Joe. *Ha, I can never get over how his gold scam back-fired and turned into a nice little earner for me. I bet he's livid, as now I own everything he thought would go to the wall. Nice feeling.* Thinking of Joe made her realise how she hadn't heard of any activity lately where Joe was concerned. She voiced this now. 'You know, Adrian, Joe's very quiet. It's worrying me. Get onto D. Get the latest report. After all, there must be some activity, despite the death of Gina, not having a supply of children, and his loss of the drug deal. And find out who, or at least, how we contact The Brazilian. Ha, I love that name. He must be foreign to have chosen it, he'd be laughed at here. And if he turns out to have a bald head, that will crack me up.'

Adrian laughed. A picture of Layla's vagina came to him. He loved that she had a Brazilian. The thought made him feel horny, but he distracted himself. The golden rule was: no sex in the office.

Some of his tension left him. 'I'll see to everything. Are we having dinner tonight?'

'Yes. But keep focused for now. I need to talk over so much with you.'

'You were the one that led the conversation.'

'True. It just amused me. We'll talk some more about that later.'

The look she flashed him increased the heat in him. Leaving the room, he told her, 'I'll contact you later, once I've spoken to D. Then dinner at seven?'

'Yes, come to mine. I'll ring my housekeeper to arrange it with cook. Then I'll give the staff the night off.'

*

The deep meaningful look Adrian gave her, had Layla swallowing hard. It didn't matter how much they tried; keeping their feelings out of business hours wasn't proving easy. Pressing her intercom, she spoke to reception.

All admin staff were from an agency. They used five different ones and intended to take staff on for one month at time. What problems this would bring with the

298

constant training of new people, she didn't know, but
the protecting of information this would bring was
worth it. So far with the first batch, of staff, everything
had gone smoothly. They were all professional, highly
skilled, if very pricey!

'Get Nina Farrow on the line for me.'

'Nina, where are you?'

'I'm being your Rottweiler. I'm onto something that
will please you. Granddad told me about it. We have
another bent cop, only a very discreet one who has no
suspicion on him whatsoever.'

'I have one already lined up.'

'The Chief?'

'Yes. Why did you say that in that mocking tone?'

'Because, I don't believe he will commit. Not wholly
commit. I believe he will play you. He's too clever and
he doesn't have anything driving him. Not now he's
lost his mistress. His world's over. I know you have a
lot on him, but I don't think he will care that much. My
man has just lost his golden goose. There isn't going to
be another. To get what he wants he has to start doing
the dirty work himself.'

'You're talking in riddles, Nina. Give it to me straight.'

'Right. I know about this cop who's always worked his
knowledge to his favour without anyone realising it, or
having to work with the criminal world, that is apart
from his snouts who are acceptable and the best in the
rotten game of giving information. This cop's main aim
was to live off the back of Gosling. Once Gosling made
his fortune and reached his retirement, my cop was
going to be ready, having primed Gosling, but at the
same time gathered and collected information and
concrete evidence about his antics, he would then
demand a big pay-out for himself and retire in luxury.

All without getting his fingers dirty, or becoming a bent cop. But now that it has all fallen foul for Gosling, my man will be forced to earn his own nest egg. I'm about to give him a way of doing that.'

'Good work. And even better that we will have two fingers in the pie. Neither will know about the other. That way we will have two angles on everything we know.'

Three. Don't forget that the one you call The Bitch – Helen Tring, is eating out of my hand too.'

'I hadn't forgotten. A thorn in my side, but a necessary one, I hate to think of my cash going to her. Anyway, I'll leave everything to you to set up, but, Nina, work with great care. On the surface this cop sounds just what we need, but if he's worked everything in such a cunning way, as you say he has, he's not green behind the ears and can play us in much the same way. Make very sure of him. Find proof of any dirty dealings, or of his association with Gosling.'

'I will, and that's not going to be too difficult. Word is that he is back in touch with Gosling. I could do with a tail on him and getting a film on a meet-up between the two.'

'You've got it. Now, I need to meet with you and soon. There's another pressing matter we have to discuss. And I want answers, lady. I told you once before never to cock off with me, and I think you are doing. I don't show any mercy, Nina. You're one Rottweiler who has met her match, and don't you forget it.'

The silence on the end of the line pleased Layla. For once the cocky bitch didn't have an answer. But when she did, she showed no signs of dropping her, know-it-all, having all the answers, arrogance.

'You know that your lover-boy don't like me. So now he's been planting doubts again, and you've fallen for

300

it. Is that it? Well, there's a reason for the delay. Granddad told me that too. The hit-man has two contracts, you and Gosling.'

'Tell me something new. Look, whatever reason your granddad has for not carrying out the hit, tell him it has become more urgent. We don't want Gosling done in. He has something on us that will smash us wide open, and then we'll all lose out. He has to stay alive for now. He's surfaced, and is causing problems but not so much as he would if he was dead. So get the job done and get it done today.'

'Not easy. The hit-man is holed up with your ex most of the time. It seems he must have more pressing priorities at the moment that supersede taking you and Gosling out. Granddad can't get at him. You could do with having a watch on the house in Essex.'

'It's in place, but you haven't told us who the hit-man is. I know your Granddad's information is his own, and he doesn't have to share it. He's doing well feeding you with what he thinks we ought to know. I appreciate that in order to do his job he has to play his cards close to his chest. I've always respected that. But in this, we need him to tell us more. The game has moved on. We need the name. My Private D will put a tail on him and let us know the minute he leaves the Essex pad. We can feed that to your Granddad far quicker than he can get the information from his underground sources.'

'Right. I'll call in on him, then I'll come in and meet with you. But, Layla. I'm not carrying on like this. Lover-boy has to trust and respect me, or I'm out. He can plant doubts in your mind quicker than I can justify myself, and that's not comfortable. You trust me, or you don't, it's as simple as that.'

'Then keep me informed. You only have yourself to blame. Adrian protects me. You let me down. Your granddad has let me down. I've been living in fear. I don't like that.'

'You either respect my granddad to work in his own way and keep his own counsel, Layla, or lose him. That's how he is.'

'I do, but when it concerns my own safety, then I need to know about everything.'

'You need to open your eyes. My granddad worked for your father and, with him. He's loved you like a daughter from afar, and yet you never acknowledge him, other than to give him jobs. If you had been in any danger at any one point over these last weeks, Granddad would have eliminated the threat. He has his eye on the situation. You putting a tail on his subject will help him, so I think he will now agree to letting you have more.'

'I'm sorry. Nina, believe me, I'm really sorry. I have everything it takes to run this organisation, but in some things I'm still learning. What you told me about your granddad, is all new to me. I thought my father treated him properly. I had nothing to tell me otherwise, your granddad has always been loyal to my father.'

'Like a puppy promised a bone you mean? Yeah, he's been that all right, only the bone never came.'

'Things will be different, I promise. I remember your granddad rocking me on his knee. I wouldn't do him down now I know the situation, and I'll see to it that my father makes amends once he's out. In the meantime, I can't be seen to be in your granddad's company, but please tell him that I hold him dear to me and always have done. I've always thought of him as an uncle. I'll look after him. I promise. And tell him too, to prime somebody to take over from him. I'd like to see him retire someday soon.'

'Thanks, Layla. You're not all bad, are you? I'm glad.'

'Right, but remember, lady, this heart of mine isn't soft. So toe the line in future.'

'Yes, Boss.'

This was said with a mocking tone just before the line went dead. Far from being annoyed, Layla had a smile on her face. She liked Nina. Liked her spirit. And yes, she had the right nick-name. For she'd never known anyone more like a Rottweiler than Nina was. She just had to be careful that she channelled her in the right direction. There was no room for a loner in the camp and Nina had those tendencies. She worked away at putting things into place without consultation. Why hadn't she mentioned this potential bent cop before? But no. She'd promised not to doubt the girl. But she would make sure that Nina towed the line in future.

*

'Jed-the-knife, ha, the names these low-life's give themselves. They must do it to make themselves somebody. I'm not just Jeffrey Cummings, I'm Jed-the-knife and don't you forget it. Here's looking at yer.'

'Stop it, Adrian. It's no laughing matter,' but even as Layla said this she doubled over at Adrian's James Cagney, impression. Sobering she told him, 'Get 'D' on to it, then get your arse over here, and quick as I've one hot one waiting for you, and I don't mean just dinner. I've just got out of my bath and I'm needing help to get dressed.'

'I'll do that for you, but you may need another bath first. Love you, my darling.'

Layla hesitated. She wanted to tell him she loved him, but to her there was a weakness revealed in admitting such an emotion. She had enough weaknesses where Adrian was concerned, she didn't want to give away the last vestige of herself. She couldn't. She replaced the receiver.

36

'Gosling! Where the fuck are you? You're a dead man!'
'Are we forgetting the dossier I have, on a certain Joe
Parrondski, eh?'
'Joe Parrondski is no more, you killed him, remember?
Set fire to his body. I'm Count Rolleski now, and don't
you fucking forget it, you bleeding arsehole.'
'Ah, but I have more than you think and can prove who
you really are without one phial of blood, or a swab of
your spittle going to the lab for DNA testing.'
'No one has any DNA on me. I've never been in any
trouble.'
'Forgetting the teeth and hair supplied to authenticate
the body, are we?'
Parrondski swore under his breath. Sweat beads broke
through his pores and trickled a cold trail down his neck
and back. 'What do you want?'
'I want back in.'
'You're no use to me. What can you give me, that I
don't already have?'
'A bent cop, who will do my bidding for the right
money. And, kids. Foreign kids.'
'How?'
'This cop I have in mind is working on a case of people
smuggling. I could find out who's behind it and with a
bit of friendly persuasion, and the right money, get
them to smuggle in some kids. It's less risky to you
than taking kids off the streets of London. They bring
girls in for prostitution, but some of them are young
enough to suit your needs. They can bring younger to
order.'
'I know about such gangs of course, and their wares
were the next on my list. Yes, a contact with these men

would be useful. You could be my go-between. Get over here as soon as you can.'

'Not happening. All communication between us will be done on the phone – me, to you, that is, I'll be using phone booths, as I am now. As it is, I'm a wanted man, but also on the missing list. I want things to stay that way, but not to be made permanent by the likes of you. You already know about my insurance. Well another one who is on my list is your ex's Fat Cat lawyer, which means I'll be able to get information from him about what she is up to. I told you once not to dismiss her. I think she's behind the loss of that drug deal.'

'Ha, don't give me that. She's an empty-headed shopaholic. She couldn't plan how to get a lollypop out of a paper bag.'

'Don't underestimate her, or her sidekick, and lover, the Fat Cat. Besides, they have Loyson, and his gang to back them. I'm telling you, Layla's behind the whole bloody headache.'

'She's already a marked woman, but not for the reason you think she should be. I had a showdown with her father, and her demise is his punishment. Besides, I have information that Jade Palmer is back and has set up in competition to me. Tête à Tête. Ever heard of it? No? Of course, you're behind times, I forgot. I told you we should have taken her out. She's the one to get. It's my guess she is running the whole show that's causing me problems. This new place she's opened took more money to set up than she was left with. Where did that come from, I ask? And two and two make five as the answer. A little matter of getting her own back and taking my drug deal!! You cocked up leaving her alive.'

'I'll take her out. That will prove something to you.'

'Not on its own it won't. Deliver me her place, first. I want ownership of it. It's going to crush Pixie's Place into oblivion. We lost a lot of money when she opened over a week ago, and none of its coming back as the delights of Tête à Tête, far outweigh those of Pixie's Place.'

'You're wrong on her. If she has what you say she has, then she's working for someone, but she hasn't the knowledge, or contacts, to pull off the robbing of that deal. Layla has. The killing of your driver was a typical Droile trademark. Droile is Layla's father's man. And how do you think she got away with the gold scam, eh? Open your fucking eyes, will you? You're letting pride take first place. You can't bear to think of Layla pulling one over on you. Well, in thinking like that, you are giving her all the room she needs to play her game.'

Joe couldn't take this in. Was it true? Had Layla that much power? That much money, even? And if she did have the money it took to pull off all that Gosling is putting at her door, then where did she get if from?'

'Who's sourcing her?'

'That I don't know. I can dig. It could be historical. Gerry Loyson's family go way back in the criminal line. I could research if his father, or any of his uncles were in the frame for anything really big. If so, Layla could have benefitted from a nice legacy.'

'Do it. Get me all you can on the bitch, and on that Jade too. I want whatever assets they have. Can you do that?'

'I can. I told you, I have something big on Layla's boyfriend, the Fat Cat. And, on my ex-Chief of police. Besides that, I have my soon-to-be very bent cop and his snouts, who are the best in the business. Though I had to take one of them out recently to show them I shouldn't be forgotten. Pity about that, but I rid you of Bugsy at the same time.'

'After bringing him into my home, you turd.'

307

'Ha, you haven't used my real second name yet. Haven't made you mad enough have I?'

'Prick.'

'That's better.'

'Don't play games with me, Gosling. I may have lost a few tricks lately, but I have a powerful ring, and one that you don't know the half of, they could make your dossiers into tissue paper. Now get these jobs done, and quick. Let's get a hold on everything again.'

As Joe, alias Count Rolleski slammed down the phone, he missed the tell-tale click.

*

Graven sat back in his seat in his van, parked discreetly amongst the trees. A satisfied smile played around his lips. 'Yes! Bingo! His hand went to his phone.

'Layla?'

'Who is this?'

'Graven.'

'What the hell are you doing calling me?'

'I have some information, and it's big. I've told Prindell that I want more money. I've lost one of my men, and a good one at that. Now, you need another to tail Jed-the-knife. Prindell doesn't seem to get the message. No more information, without me seeing a much better return. And, Layla, you really need what I have at this moment.'

'What! Christ, what the fuck is Adrian playing at? Of course you can have more. But I'll want a yearly contract drawing up with no more rises until it is up for renewal. What are you talking? How much more?'

'Two hundred grand on top of my present fifty, and I want it up front. The wife wants a new house and the one she wants won't be covered by selling our present one.'

'Done. Adrian will see to it. Get the information to him at once. And don't call me again. I'll have to destroy this sim now. You do the same. No, on second thoughts, give it to Adrian in exchange for a new one.' The line went dead. Bitch! Who did she think she was? She was sitting pretty because of the information he gave her. Whereas he sat out here day after day, night after fucking night. He'd had enough! She needed a full Private Eye unit. Well, he wanted to head it up, not do the ground work. The price of this information would be just that, plus what he'd already negotiated, and a good budget to run his operation. And that's what that fucking lackey of hers will hear when he contacts.

*

Layla paced up and down. 'Every fucking man and his dog wants a bigger slice of the cake!!'
'Look, this is something I have been mulling over anyway. I hoped that you would come up with it. You need good people around you and you need to reward them well to keep them loyal. None of them are in this because they love you. Only I hold that medal. Any one of them, would turn on you if they thought you were making it at their expense, or they could get a thicker lining to their pocket by betraying you. You're dealing with money orientated people. People who would kill for a better life. They take risks. Risks that could put them behind bars for life, or worse, see them dead! You need to be on the ball with these things. Reward for good work, keep giving out treats.'
'Why haven't you told me all of this before, Adrian?'
'You're the boss, you should know it. Feel it. Come down from your Ivory Tower, Layla. See what your people are doing for you. Look how I had to fight and

to beg to be let in on everything and to become a partner. You can't treat people how you do.'

After a few moments, what Adrian was saying sank in. Hadn't Nina said the same to her, and then reiterated it about her grandfather?

'Right. Call a meeting. Bring Graven in on it. He will need a title. Head of Security. Yes, that will do it. We need more anyway. Guards on the doors here, at my home, and more than one keeping an eye on me at all times, they will need choosing with care and managing.'

'Now you're talking. Keep ahead of the game, Layla. You have to. You can't afford this unrest among the ranks. Everyone has to feel important, valued and rewarded for what they bring to you.'

'I get it. Now, what the hell are we going to do about this new twist? Gosling has found a way back in with Joe. Joe on his own is dangerous beyond words, but with Gosling as his henchman once more, we're in trouble.'

'I have to think about it all. Let's get all security tightened.'

'One step ahead you said. Well I was fifty steps ahead of you in the beginning. Didn't I say we needed Gosling on our side? Well, now's the time. Though we should have done this a long time ago. Do it, Adrian. Get Gosling to play ball with us, not Joe. I have something much bigger to plan. The demise of Joe – Count, fucking Rolleski!

37

Gosling rubbed his hands together. It worked! He knew the phones in Joe's house were tapped. Knew all the info he gave would be relayed back to Layla, and had hoped for this very result – a communication for a meet up with Layla and the Fat Cat. And now he had it. Sitting in Crawley Motorway Services, reading his paper, he'd already clocked the heavy a few tables away. Armed, no doubt, and trained in techniques that if there was one false move from himself, he'd be frogged marched out of here and put to his rest without a single person of the hundreds milling around, being any the wiser.

Well this meet wasn't going to go that way. He'd be up front from the beginning. He wasn't supposed to know that they knew he'd contacted Joe, so he'd come clean about that, and make out that he'd be more useful in both camps.

He sipped his less than hot, too strong, vending machine coffee and wanted to spit the sour taste it gave from his mouth, but instead concentrated on what he'd achieved while he'd waited for this contact.

Red Cap had been a stroke of genius. He'd responded well to being told his ex-adversary, was looking to build a team, especially after he reminded him that what he had on him could send him away for two life sentences.

Yes, Gosling told himself, the dossiers were the best thing he'd ever done with his life so far.

Telling Red Cap that I'd be joining two big operations, but needed my own men and the deal would entail a special price on some smack, reeled him in like a fish caught on a hook.

The usefulness of Red Cap, would be to supply low-lifes to do any dirty jobs for the price of a hit, and to keep his nose to the ground, informing on anything that was relevant.

Gosling knew he had to build his own hard-man reputation as well as to surround himself with the right people. His name in the underworld had to carry a fear-tag. Though it wouldn't be his own name and very few would know who he really was.

His mind began to ponder on what that name should be. He'd thought of a few so far. The usual, Big Wig, or Boss, didn't appeal, they were too much like the films and made a mockery of what he intended to create.

'The Cop' appealed but might lead to discovery. He thought about using a Shakespearean name, no one knew about his love of the Bard's works. Sara had known, but he doubted she'd told Mike. A bitterness entered him. *Adulterers don't talk about their husbands. . . Christ! Why did she do it?* The tears threatened, but he wiped them away. She didn't deserve them.

Forcing his mind back to how he would be known, he went through the plays he'd seen performed, but then it hit him. He'd call himself 'The Bard'. Ha, yes, no one would think of him as a poet!

Gosling saw Layla out of the corner of his eyes. He hadn't expected her to come in person. He'd thought that maybe the Fat Cat would come and they'd chat before being taken to her. As usual she attracted attention. Her inbuilt elegance assured that, without her immaculate, designer appearance.

Whether she'd clocked him or not, Gosling pulled the rim of his trilby down further, and raised his newspaper. He needed to shield his face. He had no other means of disguise as his alopecia didn't allow him to grow a beard or moustache, and any one of the crowd could know him from having had a run-in with him during his police work. All those who had would know he was a missing person. No one had bothered to look at him so far, but now . . . *The stupid Bitch! What was her game?*

As Layla approached the table, sweat beads ran down his neck. But she walked straight past The Heavy walking behind her dropped a mobile in front of him, without him seeing him do so, so he doubted anyone else had noticed. Within minutes, it rang.

'Don't look around for me.'

'What's the point of this? You could have rung me from anywhere and me be anywhere, instead you've put me in danger of recognition.'

'I needed to see you for myself and to see if you have the balls to follow instructions that would put you in the kind of environment you would normally avoid.'

'That's shit. You wanted to show power over me. Well, it won't work. I'm nobody's henchman. I'm in, or I'm out.'

'There's a Cabrio parked opposite the doors, three rows back. Walk out of here and get into the back seat. I'll join you later.'

'And if I don't?'

'You've clocked my man. He'll ensure that you do.'

Christ, I'm dealing with a fucking game-player.

'You've watched too many gangster films, lady.'

'This is no TV show. Get used to my ways if you want in. Caution at all times.'

'Ha. Some caution. It's a wonder you don't have some press or other on your tail with what you've been involved in.'

'I do. She's sitting a table away from you to your left. No, don't look. Just do as I told you to do. I didn't come in that vehicle and we will leave in different directions. The Daily Star will follow me. That's all I'm telling you as I have too many ears around me.'

The phone went dead.

Something about the planning of this caused fear to clutch at Gosling's stomach muscles. He was getting rusty. He should never have agreed to meet in such a public place. His eagerness had stopped him from thinking straight. She held all the cards. Not just by having the Heavy on standby, but by ensuring the press were around too.

Sitting a moment, Gosling made an effort to calm himself. A glance at the reporter told him she hadn't any interest in him. He followed her gaze. Layla was still on the phone. Clever. Not putting the phone down at the same time as he had, was a good move. Maybe she wasn't as stupid as he'd painted her.

Still holding the mobile, he'd spoken to Layla on, he put his hand in his pocket and felt for his police mobile, that he kept charged up. He could only hope that it was still live. Taking a gamble, he enabled his locator. He'd done this manoeuvre many times without anyone detecting what he was doing.

His next glance was towards the Heavy who'd been eyeing him the whole time. His stare was unnerving. Gosling realised, he had no choice but to follow instructions. Cursing himself, he behaved like any other well-trained nerd and took his paper cup to the bin provided, before walking towards the doors.

*

'This is fucking kidnap!'

'You can't kidnap a missing person. You're abroad with your wife and proof of that is about to be texted to her family and friends, so shut your mouth, unless it's to tell us the truth. 'Why did you contact, Joe Parrondski, before contacting Layla? What's your game, eh?'

Gosling felt acutely aware of Droile sitting in the corner of this vast warehouse – empty, but for three chairs. *Shit! I walked straight into their trap. Idiot!'* And a text from Sara's phone would further implicate him as the Fat Cat knew. It all looked hopeless. He hadn't actually got anything on Layla fucking Parrondski. Yes, he knew she was up to something, and that was confirmed now, but what? He only had proof of the gold deal, but he couldn't use that without his own part coming to light. He knew better than to underestimate her and her Fat Cat. Doing so had landed him in the hole he found himself now. The phone call had back-fired on him. His story of knowing about the tap on the phone and using that method of making them contact him hadn't washed. *Why? Christ! I'm up shit alley!*

He looked into the steely eyes of Adrian Prindell. There was no mercy there. He should have done his homework on this one. He must come from criminal, or bent stock.

'Right, if you have no plausible answer as to why you contacted Parrondski and planted the idea of Layla being his adversary, tell me, what use can you be to us? We know you want a route back to being a cop. We want to know your game. And we want access to all of your dossiers.'

That's it! I've been that scared, I hadn't thought straight. The beautiful dossiers. They daren't kill me,

315

while they're still out there with my instruction to send them all to the cops. Bingo!'

'What I've told you is the truth. I've suspected for a long time that you and Layla Parrondski are up to something. You know my previous involvement with her husband. I've weighed up the two of them, and to me, Layla has the edge. I want to be a part of something big. Yes, I've been a henchman for Joe Parrondski, but I know his ultimate aim is to kill me if he could find a way of destroying my dossiers. His method would be torture, no doubt. I've seen the remains of others that he's had done over. I know a lot about him, and how to get him. I don't know what Layla's got set up, but I know it has Joe on edge, though he thinks it's Jade who is his enemy. No doubt she is, but I think Layla is the one, and all of this proves it to me. I'd work for her, but seem as though I'm working for Joe. The perfect scenario for you. But, the one thing I would never reveal to anyone is the whereabouts of my dossiers. I can't, as I don't know where they are. I've entrusted them to someone, who has sworn, that even if I ask for them, he won't give them up. The only chance we have of him doing that is if I die. I check in with him every week. And the time for that check-in is fast approaching. If I'm not let free within the next few hours, the release of the dossiers will take place.'

Power pumped around Gosling's body at the sight of Prindell's face. He had them. He had the whole fucking lot of them in the palm of his hand. He'd be top-dog and they'd all dance to his tune.

Prindell didn't speak for a few moments. Gosling could almost see the cogs of his brain computing the facts. The man was in deep shit. And he knew it. Gosling almost smiled.

316

'You Bastard, Gosling! I'd rather die than let you in. I'm going to the police myself. I'm going to tell them all I know about the killing of your wife. I'm not taking any rap for you, or for Mike Bealver. This mess belongs to you both, not to me.'

'Ha, they'll never believe anything you say. A Fat Cat lawyer going to a murder scene? It'll stink and anything you come up with won't be believed.'

'Oh, I have a plausible story, alright. I'll tell them that Mike Bealver called me to the scene. That he told me what had happened and that he didn't know what to do as he couldn't risk his affair with your wife coming out. I'll say that as I was counselling him not to try for a cover-up you came back to the scene of your crime. That you took a photo of me and Bealver with the body, after which, I left the scene and have no idea what happened after that. I'll say it was the fear of what the photo implicated that held me back from going to them earlier, but that you have contacted me wanting money. I'll take the charge of withholding information and being an accessory to the fact. It won't carry much of a sentence under the circumstances. A suspended, perhaps, and yes, I'll be debarred, but that won't be any big deal with what I've got lined up for my future. You and your dossiers can live happily together in your prison cell. Because with this much on you, they'll dig out the rest, and you won't be going anywhere but those four cell walls for the rest of your natural.'

'You bastard!'

'That's right, I am, because here's the twist. I'll tell the police that you told me you have a whole lot more information on the players in the Parrondski mystery and that if they keep your arrest secret for a couple of weeks so that you can't check in with whoever holds your dossiers, then they will have the whole lot given to

317

them on a plate. Layla has nothing to fear from that happening as you have nothing on her. Nothing!'

The knowledge that he was done for hit Gosling's gut. His bowels churned. He'd seen many a lag shit himself and thought this was about to happen to him. He couldn't let it. He clenched his buttocks. Pain creased his stomach. A tear trickled down his face. It was over. Over . . .

The Fat Cat laughed out loud as he left.

*

Mike Bealver watched Prindell's car pull away from the warehouse. He waited. Gosling didn't follow.

What to do next? What was going on?

When he'd gone back into work this morning after taking a few days off, he'd been given the news of Sara's family reporting that she'd text them telling them that she'd gone away to join her husband abroad. The location had been checked with the provider, known through paperwork taken from her home during the investigation into Gosling's disappearance.

As Prindell had said it would, the message had been sent from The Philippines. Who Prindell knew out there that would carry out such a request, Bealver couldn't imagine, but Prindell had promised to send the phone out by express parcel delivery, and he had accomplished that.

Now the mystery was, why Gosling had switched his police phone to showing 'in use' and activated his location?

Thank Goodness it had been George Fromer, who'd picked up on the activation.

George wasn't getting on too well with Riley of Scotland Yard, and didn't always co-operate with him. That was Riley's loss, he should respect the old-timer more, George was better on side than working against you.

George didn't question him when he told him that they would continue to keep this quiet. Together they'd watched the route mapped, then set off as soon as the location was stable.

Bealver began to wonder about this. What was George's game? It was strange he didn't even raise a small objection and agreed too, to switch the monitoring of Gosling's phone off.

Brushing these thoughts away, Bealver looked out of his mirror. George was parked a few cars away on the opposite side of the road.

Getting out of his car, Bealver signalled to George to follow him.

The door to the warehouse stood open. Bealver and George, flattened their backs to the wall each side of the opening. 'Police!'

A sniffle was heard. Bealver tried again. 'Police! Come out now.'

'It's me, Mike. I'm tied up. There's no one else here.' Not trusting this statement, Bealver signalled. George reacted at once and kicked the open door. It swung on its hinges. Nothing happened.

'I tell you, I'm on my own, and if I'm not untied soon, and allowed to make a phone call certain dossiers and pictures will be released!'

Again, Bealver signalled to George. This time, to stand his ground, while he took a stealth step himself into the darkened interior. Using his torch, he shone it around the room.

'There's a light switch on your left, why not use it?' Goslings sarcastic tone, grated. Flicking the switch illuminated him sitting on a chair in the centre of the empty room. The haggard look on Gosling's face told that something terrifying had gone on. What was Prindell up to? Yes, he knew he dabbled on the wrong side of the law, and that was the reason he'd known who to turn to when he'd needed help, but what had he got on Gosling, and why leave him unable to make the vital call they both relied on him making? *God, is Prindell about to betray me? No. He wouldn't! The photo is as damning on him as it is on me.*

'I can see your brain working, Mike, well let me fill you in. Prindell's on his way to clear any blame from himself. He could have had me killed. Droile was here, ready and waiting for the order . . .'

Listening to Gosling telling what Prindell intended, made Mike's blood run cold, but at the same time, sweat poured from him, dampening his shirt.

'Don't just stand there, man! Untie me. Let me make the call to stop the release of my dossiers. And while I do that, you make a call to Prindell. Tell him we've foiled him. He should know better than to mess with us cops.'

'You're no cop. Never was and never will be.' Untying Gosling, Bealver stepped towards the door, pulling his own mobile from his pocket. As he did so, Gosling mocked him. 'Me, no cop? You, you slimy bastard, got where you are through arsehole creeping. If you were good at your job, you'd have left me tied up, let me make the call, then taken my mobile and found who I'd contacted. You'll never be a cop if you live to be a fucking hundred years old! You should have stood outside and let George come in, he'd have my mobile the moment the call was over!'

Bealver knew he was right. Humiliation mixed with the fear of what would happen if he didn't stop Prindell. He pressed the speed dial on his own mobile. The phone rang out. No answer. The sweat increased. Bealver mopped his brow and tried again.

George appeared in the doorway. 'What's going on, Chief?'

'It's under control. Gosling was kidnapped. I've untied him. We'll fill you in soon. Get back to your car and be ready to follow me.'

Again, Bealver pressed his speed button to Prindell. Three rings and the smarmy voice came down the phone. 'I'm on my way to visit you.'

'Save yourself the bother, you Bastard! I've just released Gosling, he's checked in. Your skin is saved, you fucking traitor.'

There was a silence. Bealver's patience ran out. He shut the call down.

38

Layla's fury mixed with despair. 'You've fucked up big time, Adrian. Gosling should have been in, or dead. What were you thinking? Now, he has allies in Mike Bealver, and that other cop. And, he knows that I'm up to something. Yes, he had his suspicions, but that was all.'

'He doesn't know what you're up to, yet.'

'He'll soon find out. He holds all the cards. His dossiers, for one, which, don't forget, contain damning evidence on you. Now, he has Bealver back on his side, because you've pissed him off big time. You're an accessory to a murder, for Christ's sake! You helped to dispose of the body, and arranged for the house to be cleaned. You sent a mobile phone to The Philippines for a text to be sent to cover that murder up! The shit has hit the fan. You're a fucking liability!'

'Bealver won't move against me. He's caught in a trap. I know too much about him.'

'What do you know? Think about it. You know he was having an affair with Gosling's wife. You know he visited prostitutes. You know he called you when he was scared. Having an affair isn't against the law. Visiting prostitutes in the circumstances he did, doesn't carry much of a sentence. Yes, he'll lose his job, but right now he has a lot more on you. He called you to help him when he found himself in a compromising situation with a dead body at his feet. You did the rest, Adrian.'

'Him agreeing to it, makes him an accessory too. And that does carry a sentence. I'm not panicking here. I still think I should go to Scotland Yard's Inspector Riley and shop the lot of them. We'd be rid of them then.'

'But what if that blows our organisation wide open? Gosling could disappear again. He has the perfect cover as he's meant to be in The Philippines, remember?'

Layla pressed the intercom on her desk and spoke into it, 'Get in touch with Nina Farrow, tell her to come to my office, immediately.'

'What are you bringing her into this for?'

'She is grooming Detective Sergeant George Fromer, and has already made a good contact in Sergeant Helen Tring

'Who?'

'That bitch who hit me when I was in the cells.'

'I can understand Sergeant Fromer, he'd be a good asset, but what use is a custody sergeant to anyone?'

'She has her ear to the ground, and in the right place. She's bitter over what happened to her lover-boy, Cleaston. She thinks he should have been believed and then he wouldn't have had to go it alone. She likes money. She's been taking bribes for information. I needed to know what the buzz is at the station. Nina's already found out that I'm on the incident board. There's a possible link through me to the murdered children. It's a tenuous one, but after all, the bodies were found in my front garden. Then there's a link to Joe, and another to my father and the missing gold. None of them are significant, but I need to have inside information on what moves on that board. The Rottweiler gets the latest run down for me through that bitch Tring. Through the information she gathered, I know that the text message from Gosling's wife was received and that it upped Gosling's profile in the case. Tring could keep us informed on a lot of what is happening. After all, your cock-up has got to result in some activity at the station.'

'I wish to God I'd let Droile take Gosling out, and had gone to the police station, I made a big fucking mistake there, but I fancied having him behind bars. A sort of revenge for him beating my father in his defence of yours. But it's not too late. Order it done, Layla, and let me go to the police and limit the damage of what could happen to me. Think about it. In one fell swoop, you'll bring Joe to his knees too. And while you're at it, give Droile twenty-four hours to rid us of the contract on you. He hasn't done that yet.'

'That's one thing I can't understand and will be chasing Frankie on. However, he's done good as he does know where Gosling is. He hung around the warehouse, even though you told him to leave. He thought I might contact and countermand your orders. When I didn't he saw Bealver and another detective arrive and drive off with Gosling.'

'You didn't say! Where? Where have they taken him to?'

'To a flat in Gowers Walk, wherever that is.'

Adrian pulled up his google map. 'It's in the East End, off Commercial Road. Not an area you would expect him to choose, but then, Gosling is clever. Very clever, we should never underestimate him.'

'Clever enough to get the police to trail him to the warehouse. I want you to off load that property. I don't want it on my portfolio.'

'It was done before taking Gosling there. It's been transferred to Volcan Holdings, our German portfolio and is impossible to trace to us.'

'Good. I like it when you think like that. Pity you didn't do so over this business.'

'I can make amends.'

The door opened. As it did, Adrian's phone pinged. He looked at the message, not bothering to acknowledge

The Rottweiler as she entered. What he read on his screen made his blood run cold. 'Prindell, You're dead.'

He tapped out a reply to Bealver. 'I've taken a leaf out of your new bestie's book. I have lodged dossiers, with a lot more than either of you would want exposing. Remember my CCTV CD's, eh? And tell Gosling not to forget the phone has been tapped for a long time. He'll know where. I have enough to hang you both. . . My insurance policy. Take care, Bye.'

Adrian knew this would probably shut down the phone tapping on Parrondski, but he wasn't having his neck on the line. Graven had a new snoop in place and information was still trickling through of Joe Parrondski's future intentions through the insider.

When he brought his attention back to the two women in the room, Layla was saying: 'Nina, I need you to be extra careful over this cop you're grooming, he was on the operation that freed Gosling. I can't imagine that it was a kosher police job as they didn't arrest Gosling. Instead, they both went to his aid. How they knew he was there we don't know. We know why Mike Bealver would go to Gosling's aid, but not why George Fromer would.'

'Unless he thinks the Golden Goose has another chance of laying the egg for him, maybe?'

'That could be a reason, and if so, then that means he's planning to work with Gosling. Keeping himself one step ahead of the game. Maybe pull back from grooming him. Or at least play it steady till you're sure of him. And there's only one way to be that – we need to think about Gosling's demise.'

'Consider it done.' The Rottweiler looked over at Adrian, her face held a triumph as she told him, 'I heard.'

'I didn't expect anything different. Your grandfather needs to do his job and to stop snooping on mine.'

'I have it that he saved the day. Knows where all the players are. I think you need a babysitter, whether it's him or someone else. You think too much of yourself.'

'Don't start, you two. But, Nina has a point, Adrian. If Droile hadn't followed Gosling, we would have lost him again. I want him on my radar at all times. The thing is, do we go ahead with taking him out, or try to work with him again?'

'Christ, you can't work with him. He's totally untrustworthy. He wants it all. He'll play you off against, Joe. But most importantly, he doesn't know what your operation is. He knows nothing of what you own, or what trades you're going into. Let him in and you will become one of his dossiers. And that isn't a comfortable place to be in, believe me.'

'For once, I agree with Adrian, Layla. Gosling's the single most dangerous fly in our ointment. More so than the guy who has a contract on you.'

'Talking of that, I gave your grandfather all he wanted, why hasn't the job been done yet?'

'He told me that Jed-the-knife is being watched. He's difficult to get at. He hardly leaves Joe's house in Essex. Ronnie Flinch is the main man on the outside. Granddad thinks the threat has been lifted.'

'Why?'

'Because, Joe would hardly want it carrying out sometime-never, and nothing has happened, apart from that one day when you went to the Tête à Tête. With you changing your mind and driving away, Joe probably realises you're on to him. He still thinks you are low risk, as the taped conversation between him and Gosling indicated. '

'I can't take any chances.' Once more Layla pressed her intercom. 'Ask Mr Graven to come in please.'

'We'll soon have enough for a party.'

'This isn't funny, Adrian. You've pressed my panic button. I need all the I's dotting and all the T's crossing again. I feel vulnerable, and I don't like it.'

Graven walked in. In his hand he held a wad of paper. 'Latest information. Part of it is what you've been waiting for, but it cost me most of this month's budget.'

'We'll look at that in a moment. I want you to step up your surveillance on so-called, Jed-the-knife. I don't want him to even go to the toilet without me knowing about it. And if you can find a way of getting him out of that house, do so.'

'That's one of the items I have a report on. He left the Essex mansion about two hours ago. He caught a train for London.'

'Christ. Did you have a tail on him?'

'Yes.'

'But why didn't you let me know sooner?'

'I was told you weren't to be disturbed.'

Adrian cringed as Graven's glance fell on him, followed by a furious one from Layla. *Christ, I'm in it whichever way I turn.* 'I put up the 'Do Not Disturb' tag to everyone because I needed to inform you of what had gone on. I had to have your full attention.' Layla's look told him his position all round was not looking good. It was as if the forces were working against him. 'Look, we know now, and Graven has a tail on the hit-man, so there is no harm done. What was the other news we should know, Graven?'

Layla cut him off, 'I'm running this meeting. The other news can wait. I want this hit-man dealt with. Nina, get on to your grandfather. Tell him he has to act fast. Graven, let Droile know every move this fucking Jed makes. Give your tail a direct line to Droile, and instruct the doormen that nobody, no matter who it is, gets into this building until further notice.'

Ripping a sheet from a note pad on her desk, she scribbled on it. 'Here, get a watch on this address. It's where Gosling is. I want to know everything that happens there, every coming and going. I even want to know if the curtain blows in the breeze. Make that top priority. We believe Gosling is there at this moment with two of his ex-colleagues. Keep tabs on them. Once you've done that come back here and we'll hear your other news. Now, Nina, get on to the Bitch and make sure she lets you know if there is any reaction to this morning's happenings at the warehouse. I want to know the moment anything is reported to the station That's *if* it is. Something tells me that none of what went on will be logged.'

Adrian began to feel as if he'd lost control. What happened earlier had really blotted his copy book. Until then he'd felt that he was pulling Layla's strings. He was far from doing that at the moment. Everything seemed to be slipping away from him. He needed to get back in control. There were those that would kill him if he was downgraded in this operation.

The door closed on Nina and Graven. Adrian waited.

'Today has been a terrible mistake, Adrian.'

'I know. I've received a death threat. Listen to me, Layla. Let me get this threat off you. I came here before going to the police after I received Bealver's message because at that point with them all in on it, I thought I should let you know. I should have carried on and talked to Riley. Gosling holds all the cards this way.'

'Yes. You're right, he does, and that's your doing. I know that we have to limit the damage on you. And I agree with you that we can't let Gosling in now. He needs to be taken care of but that means his dossiers will be released. My worry is, what will happen if you go to Riley? He's going to want to know why you were called to Gosling's house by Bealver. Through your involvement, he will make another connection to me on that damned incident board as you will go on it for sure, and as my lawyer, provide another link to me. I want off it, not more suspicion placed on me. If only we could get hold of the dossiers.'

A relief entered Adrian. At last, Layla was thinking along the lines of trying to save his skin. And her last statement began an idea forming in his head. Graven came back into the room before he could formulate it. 'Right, everything is in place, we should hear of Jeffrey Cumming's – Jed-the-knife's demise shortly. The doormen have to contact me for clearance on anyone visiting the building, and Frankie Droile has a direct line to my man trailing Jed-the-knife. When I contacted Jed's tail to set this up, he told me that Jed is heading towards Tête à Tête, which indicates that his information isn't good, or that he's gunning for Jade. That seems unlikely though as we know from the phone tapping that Gosling has that remit. We can only assume that Jed doesn't know about these offices and is starting his search for you there. This could mean that Gosling doesn't know of these offices either.'

Adrian stepped in, his idea now fully formed and giving him hope. 'That's good. Now, contact Frankie Droile again. Do it now. Tell him that both me and Layla are ordering that Gosling is taken out today as well as Jeffrey Cummings. Before he disposes of Gosling's body, he must get Gosling's mobile phone and anything else he has on his person. Tell him to contact the tail you have on Gosling, the moment the job is done. They must meet, and Droile must hand over all Gosling's possessions. Instruct your tail that as soon as that has happened, he must act fast. He needs to break into Goslings place and bring every scrap of paper he can find in the place, including the loo rolls, then arrange a meet with him and bring the whole lot back here.'

'What's your thinking, Adrian?'

Adrian turned to Layla. I'm thinking that we might, just might, find a clue as to who has Gosling's dossiers.'

'That would solve a hell of a lot. Yes, put all that into action, Graven. Then you can tell us your other news.'

As she said this, Layla sat on her desk, treating Adrian to a nice show of her long legs. He began to wonder if she'd forgiven him. He hoped so, he fancied her like mad at the best of times, but when she was in this dominant mood, his imagination went into overdrive. They waited while Graven put in the necessary calls. When he'd finished, he glanced at Adrian, as if unsure who was now in charge. Layla left him in no doubt.

'Right. Tell me, this other news that is so important?'

'It's big. I have the contact for The Brazilian. My insider got hold of a file that contained a lot of information and was able to take photos of it all. Joe, or rather, The Count, is rather behind in his sophistication regarding his security since he broke ties with Gosling.'

'Don't even think about updating him!'

'I won't, Layla. I'm your man. I know I had that blip, but I'm more than happy now that I have a standing in the firm. It was no joke being a one-man band. I now have the best Private Detectives and bodyguards in the business on my books. We've everything covered.'

'Good. Right, Adrian, make contact with The Brazilian, as soon as.'

'It's not that easy, Layla.'

Adrian smiled at the surprised look on Layla's face, as this was said by Graven. Her, 'Why?' showed her naivety.

Graven outlined how getting a word in the ear of one of the biggest drug barons in the world wasn't done by picking up the telephone. 'We need the word dropping in the right quarters that we took the delivery of the last dispatch from under the Count's nose. That will give us street cred with the right people. We need to outline our operation to them and how we plan to dispatch the drugs. Convince them that we're watertight, have the right connections and are a professional operation. I know just the man for the job. I've had contact.'

'Who? And how much will it take?'

'He's not coming cheap. He's someone very close to you, but he's pissed off with you. You've given him grief. He's had death threats on himself and been told there is a contract on you too.'

'My father?'

'Yes. But his price is going to be high. He wants half of your business.'

'Christ!' Adrian felt as if someone had punched him in the gut. This news was dangerous. Keeping his head, he asked, 'Loyson is the go-between?'

Layla had stood up. Now she sunk back into the armchair on the left of her desk. Her face registered shock.

'You know what this means, Layla? Your father has been working with Joe! How else did Joe get this information?'

Adrian watched Layla's face turn deathly pale as he said this. After a moment she spoke as if trying to make herself believe what she was saying, he desperately wanted her to: 'Not necessarily, he may have supplied the contact when Joe was still with me, not knowing

332

that he planned to leave me and make me penniless, let alone implicate me in a stolen gold deal. Yes, that's what happened. I trust my father.'

'I think you're going to have to if you want to set a deal up with The Brazilian, and you're going to have to appease him too.'

This from Graven annoyed Adrian. He and he alone was Layla's adviser. He hoped elevating Graven didn't give the Private D thoughts above his station. 'Not necessarily so. We can make a deal with Loyson. And that deal won't entail half of Layla's business. Get a message to him. Tell him that we have another method of contacting The Brazilian. Tell him your snoop came across it. Tell him we prefer to use him, but won't unless he drops his price. A quarter share is all we're offering.'

Graven looked at Layla. She nodded. Graven left the room.

'Christ. What a day.'

'Don't worry, darling, it could turn out to be the best one we've had.'

'How do you make that out?'

'We could end up with Gosling out of the way. And all of his dossiers in our possession. We'll have something on everyone then. I'll be in the clear, and we'll have your father back in line.'

'You're putting a lot of store on finding the dossiers.'

'Graven will do that. With the mobile phone that Gosling made the calls on, and anything else we find, he'll have the location in no time. Besides, we have a week. Don't forget, Gosling checked in earlier today, and he said he has to do so once a week at a specific time. If not, I go to the police. It's the only other way open to me. I'll think of a way of limiting the damage

on you. Just think, with the dossiers in our possession, all of our problems will be solved in one fell swoop.'
'Not all. I'm shocked to learn about my father's involvement. I need it clarifying just when Joe made contact with The Brazilian.'
'We'll get Graven on to that too, darling.'
'Stop calling me that. I'm still mad at you!'
'Good. I like you like that. Keep simmering about my misdemeanour until later, then I'll calm you down.'
A small smile curled her lips. Adrian wanted to grab her there and then. He moved towards her. She didn't protest. The kiss he meant to keep light, deepened on her insistence.
Her body moulded into his. Still not sure of himself he whispered, 'Shall we break the rules?'
Her hand reached out and pressed a button that would lock the door and engage a 'Do Not Disturb' sign. If he needed any other answer than that, what she did next with her hand gave it to him, as she slid it down his thigh and kneaded the hardness her kiss had given him. Now he knew he was forgiven. He was back where he wanted to be, her man, her lover. But most of all, back holding all the Aces.
With gentle caresses he turned her and bent her over her desk.

39

'Right. I need some answers.'

Gosling raised his eyebrows as Mike shouted this at him the moment he returned to his living room from his bathroom, having at last relieved himself. 'Well, ask away.'

'What the hell's going on? You know and I know, Gosling, that I have a lot on you. Besides which, I've always known you were up to your neck and on the wrong side of the law, but you, George? Why did you come direct to me with the information that Gosling's phone had logged in, eh? And, how come you were in agreement on keeping it quiet? Don't tell me that you're in cahoots with him?'

'Not yet. But I've thought about it. I've been at the same game as him, keeping a check on everything he does and logging it in a secret place. I knew – well, I thought, he'd make it good one day, but whilst I wasn't up to acting how he did, I wanted a slice of the cake he was baking for himself. I'm no bent cop, but I didn't fancy a retirement in a semi in the suburbs, trying to make ends meet out of my meagre pension.'

'So? What is all this with Prindell? Who's behind him? And, more importantly, have any of you wise boys any idea how we get out of this? We're all in the shit if Prindell goes to Riley. And, it seems, everyman and his dog has dossiers on everyone else! We need out of this situation. And fast.'

'Appeasement is the only way. And a little double crossing.' Gosling saw the relief on Bealver's face as he looked at George. Some small hope must have entered him as it did himself. If anyone had any sense of how to control this situation, George would.

'What's your thinking, George?'

'I've been approached by a newspaper free-lance, Sir. Her name's Nina Farrow. She says there are people she knows who will pay good money for information. How she knew about what I was up to where Gosling is concerned, I don't know, but she said she'd heard the goose I'd relied on was no longer going to lay the golden egg for me, and it was time I got my hands dirty to earn my own retirement. I have no idea who she is working for as I told her to do one, but she gave me her card. It could be the same people who did this to you, Gosling.'

'Layla Fucking Parrondski, that's who we should be gunning for.'

'Have you proof of that? You've tried this one before, Matt, and it didn't stick then.'

'I do, Chief.' It felt good to call Mike that again. *Christ, how did everything go so wrong?* But then a picture of this man in bed with Sara came to him and all buddy-buddy feelings left him as hate curled his insides once more. 'Look, we can't pretend to be friends any longer, Mike, you broke my heart, but we have to work together on this or we all go down. It seems that everyone but you, has something on everyone else in the game, and that's our insurance. But what's yours? What's *your* plan?'

'I'm not going bent, if that's what you mean, and I hope you don't George, either. A wealthy retirement isn't worth the risk. You'll end up spending most of it behind bars, or dead. What I'm going to do is put you undercover, George. You engage with this Nina, but as a cop. Any payment you take is handed in, right?'

'Yes, Chief.'

'Good. Now, you, Matt, well, I just don't know what to do about you. As much as I've been a straight cop, I've had my weaknesses, and you capitalised on those. You, George, may know some of it, but not all, and I can't entrust you with it. Just so you know though, if Matt so wanted to, he could put me behind bars. Most of what he can provide proof of is lies and was contrived by him, but it would be damning evidence against me. No one would believe me if I fought it. Therefore, I have to dance to his tune. But, let me tell you, Matt, I can't do that forever. You either do your worst now, or get out of my life. Really out of it.'

'I can't do that until I have reward for all that I've done. There's a hell of a lot that I'm due payment for that you know nothing of. I've put my neck on the line for a certain bloke, and I'm near to getting my big pay-day. Once I've done that, I'll disappear, and that will be that'

'And your dossiers?'

'My man knows a certain code. When I give him that he destroys the dossiers as that will mean I'm home and dry and away from here and no longer fear for my future.'

'That day can't come soon enough for me. As a cop I want to see you face justice, but as a man I can't face the consequences of that on myself. But, will our paths cross again? What more do you plan to do?'

'I don't think we will need to deal with each other again. I hope not, because I never hated a man's guts like I do yours, Mike. The big pay-off day I just mentioned, just needs a little more wrangling on my part, then that will be it. I've too many after me now, and I don't have dossiers on them all. Layla Parrondski for instance. She is after me, she has nothing to lose by killing me, yet some people she hates, or doesn't care a jot about, do, and that is motivating her, as my death would be payback for them. You included, Mike, as she hates all cops. My only hope is that she fears what I have on you and Prindell. If he's told her, then maybe, just maybe, that might sway her to keep me alive. But I'm not relying on that as she's ruthless. Therefore, you should concentrate on getting her, Mike. That will be your insurance policy against the dossiers on you coming out. Get her, before she gets me.'

Gosling noticed George's facial expression getting more and more puzzled, but he didn't ask any questions.

Mike made as if to go towards the door. 'I'll do my utmost to keep you alive, whilst wanting to see you rot in hell. See you back at the station, George. Make contact with that Nina as soon as you can.'

'Yes, Sir.'

Gosling waited until the door was closed and he saw through his window that Bealver had crossed the pavement to his car. As it pulled away from the kerb, he said, 'Don't go, George. I've an earner for you that will see to that retirement for you.'

'You heard what the Chief said, Matt, he wants me undercover. I'd rather do things legit.'

'Will legit net you £500k? No. Thought not.'

'Run it by me.'

'Look, you're not going to like it, but it's to do with the case you're working on. Not the Parrondski Mystery.'

'You're well informed. We didn't name the case that until after you disappeared, which made you part of the case and put you on the incident board. And how do you know what case I'm working on now?'

'I have my sources. I have to stay ahead of the game. I even know that my profile has been raised on the incident board this morning, after a certain text was received and reported by Sara's family. I took a phone call while I was in the bathroom. But, the good thing about that is that if I'm meant to be in the Philippines, I am free to do as I please as the law won't be looking for me here.'

'That's if the text is believed. There are some dissenters. Those who think it's a hoax.'

'I can guess who they are, but I can tell you, it's in Mike's interest to make everyone believe it is kosher.'

'What is this that you have on him? I know about the visits to the walk-up, but that's not enough for him to go this far for you.'

'You knew that? There's a lot more to you than meets the eye, George. I like that. But I'm not telling what I have on Mike bleeding Bealver, only that it's big, very big.'

'Then, I for one believe him when he says you've contrived it. The Chief hasn't got it in him to take part in anything that big on the other side of the law. Illicit sex, yes. Who wouldn't, married to that cold fish of a wife of his, but nothing more.'

'Whether it's the truth or not, I have it. And need it. Bealver will be dancing to my tune until I'm ready to flit. Now, hear me through. For a start, the person you will be dealing with when you contact that Nina, is Layla Parrondski . . . don't sigh like that. Listen to me, George. I know. One thing I want you to do for me is to let me know everything you find out about her. The other concerns the case of the people-smuggling you're working on.'

'Now, hold on a mo. That's huge, and will elevate me if I crack it. Besides, how did you know about it?'

'That's for me to know. How far have you got with finding out who's behind it? I know you have a lot of information, and have rescued a couple of the girls when you raided that cheap brothel.'

'Christ! Who is your bloody informer, the Chief?'

'Ha! No. But I could make him be so. The prick's that scared of me revealing all.'

'How did you come to hate him so much? You were good buddies. So close, none of the rest of us could get a look in. You had the best jobs, the most budget allocation, What the bloody hell happened?'

'I told you, you can gnaw away at that one and never find out.'

'Don't underestimate me. If any one of the underground mob know, then I will, I only have to ask the right questions.'

Gosling knew this to be true. This wasn't going well. He doubted he'd crack George and he needed his help. He had to supply the Count with kids. It was the single thing that would put him back in the good books with him. Yes, he had Jade to deal with, and the acquiring of Tête à Tête, which wasn't going to be easy, as he was sure Jade wasn't in that on her own, but Joe would pay well for a supply of kids, maybe enough for him to get the hell out of it all.

'Look, George. If you're not remotely interested in the £500k then leave now. And you know what? That Nina, whoever she is, is right. This goose isn't going to lay you a golden egg, because whatever you have on me counts for nothing now. You couldn't make me more wanted than I am, and my route back to the force is completely cut off anyway. So do your damnedest. Add more to your poxy incident board. Elevate me higher in your Parrondski Mystery, because I'm up to my neck in it as it is, and you fucking lot are nowhere near to the truth of it. But while you're doing all that, remember, that you're merely a cop undercover where your connection with this Nina is concerned and whatever

340

she has to offer ain't going to be yours. Ready to say goodbye to the retirement you dreamed of are we?'

George had paled. Whether he had felt that he still held some cards or not, Gosling didn't know, but if he did, he had just been trumped, well and truly, trumped.

'Look, George. Give it some thought. That's all I ask.'

'Tell me what it is you're after, then I'll give it some thought.'

'A name. Who's behind the people-smuggling. The big wig, no side-kick. No one need ever know the source was you. Nothing much will change in the operation that's already in progress. Only where some of the girls and boys land up.'

'£500k for a name? Is that all you want?'

'It is. But remember, I do have a very reliable source of information, and I can get the name anyway once you document it. But I know you, nothing is reported until you have a rock solid case. That's never been a practice that I admired, and I fought against it. If anything happened to you, your knowledge dies with you. You used to annoy the hell out of me.'

'Didn't mind when I dropped the right information your way though, did you?' George turned towards the door. As he did so he lowered his voice to a whisper. 'I've clocked the camera, you snidey bastard. Meet me in the Cock and Bull in an hour, and don't wire up, because I'll take you to the gents and frisk you before I give you anything.'

As George reached the door, Gosling saw him glance back and look up to where Gosling's camera beamed down into the room, and said, 'Go stuff yourself! Everything that's happened in this room today will be logged back at the station, whether that suits the Chief or not!'

Gosling knew he'd met his match. A smile creased his face. *Good old George. It would have suited me to have something on him, but fair play to him. It seems I've underestimated him for years!*

*

The Cock and Bull was crowded with workers having a drink before travelling home. The talk was loud and irritating, but suited Gosling's purpose.

George sat in a corner, an untouched pint in front of him. He shuffled along the bench when Gosling approached. 'Right, I'm here, and I'm clean.' Gosling opened his jacket to show he wasn't wired. 'Now, you know what I want. I'm not hanging around here. I've a tail on me. I managed to duck him, but if he's any good, he'll soon relocate me,'

'I'll do it, but I don't want to end up as one of your fucking dossiers. Everything will be done my way. You'll deposit the money in an account I give you. And, don't bother clocking it, as it will be closed within an hour. I've had it open and ready for the day, I thought I would make you pay me a chunk to stop me blowing your antics wide open. That's not going to happen now, so I'm going for this. I receive text messages from the bank as to any activity generated, even though there hasn't been that much going on in the account. It can't be traced back to me and when I'm ready to take advantage of the money, to all intent and purposes, it will emerge as a legacy, but that's all you are going to know. I've had my cover in place for a long time as to why I should suddenly come into money. Once I have the money where I want it, I will give you the name. I won't meet with you. This is the last time we see each other. But think on. I'm getting closer to solving the people-smuggling case, and I'll not hang back.'

Full of admiration for this old-time copper, who'd always been the butt of his jokes, Gosling didn't protest or doubt George, though he did add a threat in his answer, 'Give me the account. The money will be in there tomorrow. But double cross me and you're a dead man, George.'

George passed him a piece of paper. 'I believe you. But put this in your pipe and smoke it. Me; far from the truth of the Parrondski case? Ha, don't you believe it. I know exactly what's going on, so take that to your precious Count Rolleski, and tell him that if anything happens to me, this is one case I've made provisions for. It definitely won't go to the grave with me.'

As George left, Gosling sat back. The air had left his lungs and he felt as though he'd never be able to draw it back in again. *Fucking George. Fucking policeman plodder . . . how the hell did he know about Parrondski now being the Count?* For the second time that day, Gosling felt his bowels loosening. As he rushed to the gents his thought was, *Christ, George could wipe the floor with the lot of us!*

40

The Count's irritation level was high. 'Fuck off out of here, Doc. You're getting on my nerves. You told me we have the best in the business onto finding the hiding place of the dossiers, that pissing Gosling holds so dear. I need my hands on them. And when I have, I'll personally torture the bastard to a very slow death.'

'We have. It's only a matter of time, duckie, I promise you. Now what have I told you about your blood pressure, eh?'

'How much time? I need that smarmy git off my back.'

'Days. I have this new boyfriend. Well, he's not to my taste, but I do make sacrifices for you, darling, always have done. Anyway, Dom knows everything about everyone. And, he was a friend of Gosling's wife. Gosling trusts him. Even to the point of keeping him in the know about his whereabouts. They drink together.'

'I'm not liking this. Since when did Gosling keep company with queers?'

'Ooh, that's not PC. These days you have to call us Gay men.'

'Shut the fuck up. You're a fucking queer to me and will always, be. How kosher is this contact of yours? And don't cock around with me!'

'I'd love to, darling. You don't know what you're missing. Anyway, getting in a temper with me won't help. Dom's in love with me, but he's more in love with money. He's ready to arrange a meet-up with Gosling.'

'And what good will that do? Do you think he's going to ask Gosling where the dossiers are kept and being so buddy-buddy with him, Gosling's going to tell him? You're living on cloud cuckoo.'

'Dom is a pick-pocket – the best in the business. Oh, not a criminal one, a magical one. He works on the stage. He takes things from an audience member sitting three rows back from him. As soon as you make him a rich man, he'll get Gosling's mobile. He'll replace it with an identical one . . . don't ask, I have no idea how he knows the make, colour and size, duckie. Anyway, doing that, the theft won't be known to Gosling until he tries to make his next call.'

A smile creased Joe's face. *Got him! With that phone I'll have the contact in no time.*

As he was about to do a rare thing – praise The Doc, his mobile rang. Mouthing 'Piss Off.' To The Doc, he almost smiled as The Doc minced out of the room with a hurt expression on his face. Looking at the screen of his mobile, a surge of pleasure hit Joe as he saw who the caller was. The very man. 'What can I do for you, Prick?'

'Mr Gosling to you if you want to do business. I need respect from my partner.'

'Partner, Ha, You've got aspirations above your station. Not going to happen.'

'I have everything in place. It just needs funding. Give me access to a million and you can have the kids you want, and Jade, and the operation run by Layla. The lot, only besides the million, which will go on expenses, I will need an agreement that makes me a full partner. Not an, in-your-face, one, but one on the other side of the world, who personally sees to the drug deals, and handpicks the kids for the operation. You can keep the sleaze business here. But I'll know everything you do. I'll have contacts who will be keeping an eye on you, and if I don't receive my half of everything into my account, you're a dead man and I take the lot over.'

The Count smiled, *poor little Gosling, wanting to be the daddy swan, when he has no idea just who he is dealing with. Still, I have no one else who has access to kids, so I'll let him be useful for the time being.* 'Right. You've got your million. Deliver on the kids and we'll take it from there.'

'Not good enough. I told you what I want.'

'You're beginning to bore me. One million for setting up delivery of the kids, then five million for the name of the contact who will keep me supplied, and delivery of everything you say my ex has, but there's a clause, you have to disappear out of my life, and that's my final offer.'

'I'll take it. When can we meet? And, I want it to be in a public place, with the first million, all in cash, in a holdall. I will want to check every last penny. You have to bring it personally and on your own. Once the jobs are complete, I want the same arrangement for the big money when I will give you the contact's name. Then, when I'm away from here, I'll activate a code I have with the holder, which will mean that all my dossiers will be destroyed and you can live happily ever after.'

'And fucking good riddance to you. Ring me in two days, I'll have everything fixed up.'

As he put the phone down the Count smiled. *Playing right into my hands. With that mobile in my possession, you, mister wannabe swan, will be dead meat once I have that name. Ha, and when I've had Ronnie let loose on you, you'll know what it feels like to be butchered alive.*

*

Gosling also smiled as he replaced the receiver. Joe's cocky attitude showed that he'd fallen for The Doc's

347

story. He liked that. He and The Doc had Count Bollocks good and proper. They were working him. Giving him false security. Five Million would see them both right for a good while to come, but it would only be the beginning.

His smile lasted as he looked into the melting eyes of Helen Tring. 'You're a naughty girl squeezing in here with me. Telephone boxes weren't made for two.'

Helen giggled. 'You're going to have to punish me, big boy.'

'Pleasure. Let's go to yours.'

'Promise you'll keep that wig on? I like you with ginger hair. I'll use the nipple pincers on you if you don't.'

Gosling caught his breath as his desire pumped around him. Why hadn't he realised what a beauty Cleaston had in Tring, or *The Bitch* as most called her? Or even that Cleaston was into the same kind of sex as himself, he'd always looked a weedy, puny, bugger.

Helen had it all. She liked her sex rough, the more pain the better, but then, when satisfied, she was all loving and giving. He couldn't get enough of her.

I had a stroke of golden luck the day I clocked her talking to that woman and guessed a wad of notes had changed hands.

He'd been waiting for George to emerge from the station and had sat in his car in the road opposite, a high street lined with shops. Keeping his head down and his trilby pulled forward to shield his face, he hadn't worried about the car, no one would have recognised it. He'd idly looked around and caught sight of Helen through a shop window. He'd only glanced at first, but then something had caught his eye. The dresses that she wasn't looking at, moved on the rail where they hung. Helen had quickly put herself in front of the gap. Then a few minutes later the young woman reporter, who always got on everybody's nerves, emerged from the shop. Glancing back at Helen he saw her closing her bag and making for the door. All his detective instincts went on red alert.

As Helen had stepped out of the shop, he'd got out of his car, opened his passenger door, and told her that if she valued her job she'd get in quietly. She did, albeit her mouth gaped at the sight of him.

Enjoying her caressing of him now, he couldn't help but wonder at how smoothly they'd gone from that encounter to being involved. And it had all happened because he'd cut up rough with her. He'd driven her out towards Brighton, but then taken a road that led into the countryside. On the way, he'd told her he wanted an insider. He couldn't pay much but eventually he would be able to. She'd played him, coming over all smug, saying she'd turn him in. He'd pulled into a lay by and hit her. She'd loved it. She'd grabbed him and kissed him. The shock had taken him aback. Then she'd told him she'd always fancied him. Had heard he was well hung, and now she knew he liked to dominate his women, she fancied him like hell.

They'd driven to a hotel and he'd had some of the best sex he'd ever had. She didn't care that he came too soon. Her answer was to get him ready again, and the second time had been much more controlled, vicious and amazing. He'd met his sexual match.

'I promise, the wig stays . . . But, I might be naughty and break my promise. Now let go of me before I cum in my pants.'

'Now, now, none of that. That's the old you. The new you, can last and last, remember?'

Nodding, he felt like a little boy. He liked the feeling. Loved it when Helen played the mummy figure. She'd taught him a lot. The best thing she'd given him was an end to his premature ejaculation – a long-time source of embarrassment to him. A picture of Gina came to him. He could see her laughing at him. His temper rose and with it, his eagerness to teach Gina a lesson once more. He'd imagine it was her he was fucking. Helen was in for a treat. Taking her hand, they left the phone box. He had things he had to do, but it all could wait.

*

By the time he left Helen's apartment, Gosling felt exhausted, and his body ached with the bruising she'd given him. The little minx had gone a bit too far for him, he'd tame her next time, good and proper, he felt almost angry with her. Not in the way he used to with Gina. Gina took something his Sara couldn't have, but the fact he'd felt a lot for Gina used to make him wild with her. No, Helen had dominated him too much today, and he didn't like the feeling. He'd wanted her more submissive. Scared. He'd pay her back.

He had plenty of time. Him and the *The Doc* had everything planned to the last detail. Gosling's smile returned as he thought of how The Doc had everything in place for him to have the same makeover that had transformed Joe Parondski. Only his was to take place in Rio. Joe wasn't the only one who could become someone different, and Gina wasn't the only one who could have filled the role of his personal Moll. The Bitch would do very nicely. He'd persuade her to go with him. He wasn't sure of his new life. If he could set things up in Rio or not. But he'd be back. Or rather, the new him would be.

His smile widened as his phone rang and he saw the name, 'The Count' flash up on his screen. Taking the call, he asked, 'Are we good to go?'

'Ring me from a call box. I want this over and done with'

350

Getting in his car, Gosling drove back to the phone box. When he came out after the call, he had what he wanted. The meet was to take place much sooner than he'd anticipated – just one hour from now, in a café in the West 12 shopping centre. Not a million miles from Parondski's old home in Holland Park. Funny choice. But the layout was perfect. There were toilets just around the corner from the café. He and Joe would go there, take a cubicle each while he checked the money was all there and none of it was fake. He wasn't about to be caught out by that trick a second time.

Life was looking up in many ways. Yes, his dreams were finally coming true.

He put in a call to George. 'The money will be in your account in two hours. Meet me as soon as you get confirmation. Same pub.'

'I'll meet you as soon as I have the money transferred. And that account closed. So give me at least an hour after you pay the money in.'

'Right.'

Once again, Gosling had the feeling that George was dangerous. *Why didn't I take more notice of what he was capable of? I'm a fucking idiot!*

*

In response to a text message two hours later, George set up his lap top and accessed his accounts. There it was. £500k, sitting in an account in the name of his dead Uncle Ernest Wright. Opening the transfer money tag, he transferred the lot to a Mrs Emily Wright, and closed his Uncle's account.

Dear, doddery, Aunty Emily. In the name of your dead husband, your power of attorney, the beneficiary of your will, and your only relative, has just made you a rich woman. Which reminds me, I must tell you he died

last week. His mistress in India came into all he had, though she'll never know about this little lot!
A recluse, living in a huge country pile, George's Aunty Emily was on the last leg of life's path. Now, he wouldn't have to sell the beautiful house she lived in, when she died. When the time was right for her to do so, a little shove would help her on her journey. *Well, it was a doting nephew's duty wasn't it? Especially for a miserable old cow like her.*

41

'Darlings, mummy promises. I will be down to the cottage in the next couple of weeks. And then we can really start your school holiday.'

The usual groans came back down the receiver to her as the boys talked about being bored, and there being no Internet. 'I'll get that fixed. I forgot to have it switched back on. I'll make a phone call. But don't spend all of your time playing computer games. Get out and about a bit. Don't forget you're going on an adventure holiday very soon, you don't want the rest of the kids to think you're couch potatoes and can't keep up.'

This brought about more protests, but as she listened patiently, Layla became aware of a noise somewhere in the house. 'I've got to go. Oh, Richard, do me a favour and ring Adrian Prindell as soon as you put the receiver down. Tell him to come to mummy's in Holland Park, ASAP.'

'Why can't you ring him?'

'Just do it, darling. I have to go. Love you both.'

By the time she replaced the phone on its hook, Layla could feel herself shaking. She was certain that someone had entered the house. She buzzed her emergency button and listened for her bodyguard to respond over the intercom. Nothing. *Christ, why hadn't Droile contacted? Had he done the two jobs, Jed-the-Knife and Gosling? Surely he'd have called in if he had?*

Thinking quickly, she pulled the drawer open next to her bed. Her hand found her gun. She knew it was ready-loaded. Pointing it towards the door, she waited, desperately trying to stop her hands from shaking.

As the knob slowly turned, she could hardly breathe. Her mouth dried.

A face appeared. One she didn't recognise. A knife held aloft, glinted as it caught the light from the bedside lamp. The face looked boyish and yet evil, before an expression of shock and fear spread over it.

'Don't shoot. I – I'm not going to hurt you. I want to talk to you. Look, I know stuff. Your husband isn't dead, he –'

'Tell me something I don't know.'

'You know! How . . .?

'That's none of your business. I'm guessing you're the so-called, Jed-the-Knife? The unfortunate bugger chosen to do his dirty work, but who, sadly, is going to land up in an unmarked grave, somewhere no one will find you.'

The man's face paled. He took a deep breath. 'Don't shoot! I have more information for you. I could have killed you long ago, but I wanted to get close enough to you to make a deal. I want out. I've tried to get in with the big names for a long time, but now I have, I don't like it. I know there is only one ending, it's happening all the time. I want to get away, go abroad and forget the whole thing. If I had the right money I could do that.'

'And what do you have for me that I might want to buy?'

'Information. Think about it, haven't you wondered why Droile hasn't killed me? Yes, you needn't looked surprised, I know you gave him a contract to do so.

'I don't know what you're talking about. Who's Droile, anyway?'

'I know that you know who I'm talking about. He's Gerry Loyson's man. And Gerry Loyson is your father. Droile does everything your father tells him. Droile hasn't killed me, yet, because he's under instructions to wait until I've killed you. He's also been told not to kill

354

Gosling yet, as it doesn't suit a certain person to have all the beans spilt on everyone at this moment in time.'
'What! What are you saying? Christ, you mean . . .?' Layla fought to keep control as everything this vile creature said fell into place. Her own father! 'How do you know this? You're making it up to save your own skin.'
'I know because my brother, and a cousin of a friend of mine are serving time with your old man. They are very close to him, but like all lags, they see a chance to better themselves. They figured that with me on the outside and having connections, they could step in before Gerry Loyson can. After all, they're both due for release three years before he is. They know about you and your operation through your dad. They know of his plans to take everything you have, and all what your husband has. Though at the moment your husband thinks he has your father in with him. Loyson is playing a double game. And he's been getting me brother and me mate's cousin ready for specific jobs when they're released. But as they see it, you could give them a big payday, if they rid you of your old man. Something worth coming out to. None of them want to be involved in the underworld dealings again. They want to join me and live life out in the sun, free from all the fear and the agro of having to be one step ahead.'
As he spoke sweat dripped from him. Layla, feeling sick and repulsed, stared at him. She willed Adrian to turn up. As if reading her mind, the man spoke again.
'I heard you ring for Prindell. If I were you, I'd be long gone before he gets here, he's in with Gerry Loyson up to his neck. He's the one on the outside doing all the planning and pulling the strings. His job is to make sure you die tonight. Your dad's getting impatient.'

Layla's legs almost gave way with the shock of this. She stared at the man that she'd never label *a hit-man*. Weedy she'd call him. Keeping the gun pointed at him she played for time allowing him to speak.

'I've got it all planned. Your phoney bodyguard is out cold, so we'll have no trouble. Get your driver to collect us as soon as. He's straight up, I've checked. Then ring Prindell and make some excuse. Put him off coming here. We need to be out of here.'

Recovering, Layla told him to shut up. She had to think. It all sounded so plausible, but what if this man was trying to lure her into a trap? But then, why would he risk coming here, and how did he escape being killed by Droile, unless what he said was true? *God, how many more are into this? I've been a bloody fool.*

Not dropping her guard, she reached for her mobile and pressed a quick dial number. Adrian's voice came to her. Normal sounding. 'I'm on my way. Why the cloak and dagger way of getting me there, are you in trouble. Your son didn't have a clue, he just said I was to come to your house ASAP?'

Confusion settled in her, but the doubts won. Steadying her voice, Layla answered with a laugh. 'Panic over. Next door's cat knocked over an ornament in the garden and I couldn't contact my bodyguard. I've spoken to him now and he's sorted everything. I'm just leaving. I'll meet you in Claridge's as we arranged. It's not hearing from Droile. It's made me nervous.'

'Are you sure there's nothing wrong? I can call in, I'm only a couple of streets away.'

'Quite sure, you sound surprised. Should there be something wrong then?'

'No, No, no, of course not. Look, don't worry, you're very protected, that bodyguard is a good man. I made sure Graven let me hand pick him. I'll try to contact

Droile before we meet. I'm sure there's a reason for him not getting in touch. He's probably done the jobs and is waiting for the right moment to let us know. After all, he'll have two bodies to dispose of, it's not just the killing. Leave it with me.'

Leave it with him, Oh, My God! The Bastard! He's probably already called Droile off killing Gosling.

Nick answered her next call. 'I thought you'd never be ready. I'm outside waiting, you told me seven-thirty, remember?'

'I told you that?'

'Well, Prindell did, he said the instruction was being passed on through him to save you time. He told me to ring the bell if you didn't appear. and I was just about to do that. You did know, I presume?'

'No. Look, Nick, can you see my bodyguard?'

'No. No one's about. I thought that was funny. Is everything okay?'

'Use your key and get up here, Nick, and bring your gun. I have an unwanted visitor. I don't want him killed, but I need him guarding while I make some calls out of his earshot.'

Nick came through the door in seconds as if he'd been standing on the other side of it. This gave Layla confidence that he was one who still had her interest at heart, for at this moment she didn't know who to trust. 'Let's get him downstairs, Nick. He's the hit-man, only he's enlightened me on a few things that I need to take care of. We'll tie him up and you can keep guard while I get some business seen to. There's some stockings and tights in that top drawer under the window, we'll use them to secure him.'

'You don't have to –'

'Shut up! You don't get a say in what we do to you.'

357

'Nick grabbed Jed-the-Knife's arm and turned him around. His gun poked into the terrified man's temple. 'Keep your mouth shut.'

Once the hit-man was secured, Layla held her own gun to his temple. 'Right. Tell me who else is in on this takeover. I want all names, and quick!'

'Droile and Prindell on the outside, and the Count thinks he is. And they think they have me an' all. Then there's me brother, and me mate's cousin and your dad on the inside, that's it. But like I say, me brother and me mate's cousin are ready to double-cross if the money's right. And, if they get a good bung for the separate job of seeing to yer dad, he'll be a gonner inside a week. It'll look like suicide, it always does.'

Nick's face showed his shock, then as quickly registered concern. 'Don't ask, Nick. I've no time. I've a lot to activate and at speed. Just keep your eye on him, but I want him alive. I need him at this moment in time. Oh, and if Prindell rings, tell him we're stuck in traffic.'

Layla's first call was to Jade. 'Everything okay, Jade?'

'Yes, fine, are you still coming in later? I have some very good figures for you. We had over six hundred in the main club last night, just here for the ambiance, the great music and oblivious to what we really sell. But in the *real* hub of our business, we clocked a record. Fifty Arabs were entertained, and boy did they enjoy our finest Champagne, and our 'extras'.

'Jade, shut up and listen. We have a crisis. Make sure you don't go anywhere in the building without an armed bodyguard. And instruct your doormen to be extra vigilant on making sure no one that enters is carrying. I can't tell you everything I haven't got time, but Joe thinks you are leading an operation that's designed to take all that he has. He thinks you're seeking revenge, besides which, Tête à Tête is cleaning up all the business and fuelling his anger. But worse than that we have traitors in our midst and they are involved with Joe. If Prindell contacts, trust nothing that he tells you. He is no longer authorised to speak for me, only be careful that he doesn't know that.'

Giving Jade no time to react, Layla closed down the call and pressed another speed dial. Graven's voice came to her. She cut off what he was about to say, 'Graven, the shit's about to hit the fan. There's a conspiracy. My bodyguard is out cold, somewhere in my grounds. I have Nick with a gun trained on Jed-the-Knife. We have traitors in our midst. Where's the tail you had on Jed the knife?'

'I can't reach him. Nor the one on Gosling. Droile hasn't contacted either, but I know where he is. Is he the traitor?'

'One of them. Christ, even Prindell, the bastard. And, I'm worried to death, can I trust you, even?'

'You can. My tails were compromised, and if Prindell is part of the conspiracy, then that's how everyone knew they had a tail, even Jed-the-Knife must have known as he slipped his. Gosling has given his tail the slip, too but that won't be down to Prindell. Gosling's a cop who knows it all. This isn't the first time he's slipped my net.'

'How do you know where Droile is?'

'I have a tail on him. I did that off my own back, so Prindell doesn't know about that one. I just thought it funny that Droile was taking his time getting rid of the hit-man with a contract on you. My man's last report was that Droile was circling Gosling's house, but Gosling isn't there. We're trying to pick up his trail again. But it looks like Droile is still intent on carrying out the killing of Gosling.'

'More likely making sure no one else kills him. I have been told that one of the main men in the conspiracy doesn't want Gosling dead. But we do, then his damn dossiers can do their worst. They'll finish Prindell. Though he mustn't know that it was us that took Gosling out, because he knows too much about us. For the moment we have to appear to be working with him to try to get him out of the shit he'll be in, whilst all the time dropping him in deeper. I'll play the broken hearted girlfriend part. But I want him screwed.'

'Right, our first job is Droile. What about his granddaughter?'

'I don't know. She hasn't been mentioned, and she did warn me when the hit-man tried to get me the first time. We'll leave her for the moment. Concentrate on making Frankie Droile disappear forever. And send Gosling on his way to his maker, too.'

'Is Gosling part of this conspiracy against you?'

'No. He hasn't been mentioned. I think he's still working away on his own trying to get in with Joe, as he did us. I want his dossiers to go to the right people, and that can't happen while he's alive. Oh, and check all those you have around Jade.'

'Done. The moment I heard of Joe's interest in her, I doubled up on guards around her. She has some she doesn't even know about. I'll get Prindell covered now. We want to know his every movement. How did you find all of this out about him, and who are the others?'

'No time to tell you all of that now, but those that matter have been mentioned. I have to go to dinner. I don't want Prindell suspecting a thing. I'll leave Nick here, but get someone over to take care of Jed-the-Knife. Not to kill him. But to take him somewhere and keep him safe I need to talk to him. I'll have to take a taxi, but I will need Nick to pick me up, or Prindell will suspect something. And take care of the bodyguard and have him back on duty, and keyed up on the story I had to tell Prindell.' She outlined the story of the vase and the cat. 'To make my story believable, break the vase on the small wall. The blue one. I don't like it anyway. I might even bring Prindell back here so that everything appears normal, so make sure there's no sign of anything unusual.'

'You've got it.'

'Good.' Remembering what Adrian had told her about rewards, Layla added, 'And Graven if this all goes to plan, that house your wife wants, consider it yours and all paid for. I'm relying on you, and won't forget your loyalty when I reorganise the company.'

Layla didn't wait to hear his reply. Cutting the call, she dialled their trusted cabbie. 'I needed to be in Claridge's five minutes ago.'

'I'm just around the corner, be there in two minutes, love.'

Grabbing her jacket from where it lay on the bed, Layla ran downstairs, told Nick what was happening and left.

*

'Darling, you look beautiful, worth waiting for.'

'Thank you.'

The waiter had showed Layla to a central table in Claridges restaurant. Adrian, looking stunning in his tux, had stood to greet her. A Gin Sling stood in her place, glass iced, mint and lemon beautifully arranged, and just the right shade of pink. As her chair was pulled out for her, she felt herself relax. The beautiful aubergine and gold décor; always pleasing to the eye, gave her a sense of being in familiar surroundings where nothing horrible could happen.

361

As Adrian took his seat once more he looked quizzically at her. 'Why only one earring, darling?'

'Oh, I hadn't realised, I was putting them on when I got the fright. Ha, I must have forgotten to put the second one on.'

Cursing to herself, Layla removed the diamond drop and placed it in her purse.

'Yes, funny that, didn't know anyone had cats in your street, they must be posh moggies.'

'Of course, and not let out often unless it is to go somewhere in mummy's Rolls. Anyway, I'm starving, and presume you have ordered for us, you always do.'

'The only little concession you allow me. Yes, we're having sautééd foie gras and roasted veal sweetbreads, braised confit and roasted Herdwick lamb followed by elderflower panna cotta with strawberries and vanilla ice cream.'

As Layla listened to him she sipped her drink through the glass straw and studied his face. He was beautiful, and had an effect on her no one else had ever had, how could he have betrayed her? An anger welled up inside her, but she controlled it. He must never suspect that she knew. When it all blew wide open, she would have to stand by his side. She could have him killed tonight, but she wanted him to suffer. To know the humiliation of being arrested. And, she would accidentally say things in her distress that would further damn him, while all the time he would think she was supporting him. She'd let him believe that he had a high position in her operation, and riches waiting for him once he'd served whatever sentence an accessory after the fact of murder would have to serve.

But then, when he'd been taken to the lowest place he could ever imagine, she would drop him. Yes, he could still try to shop her, but as a criminal with a record, he'd

362

face going down with her, but for a lot longer than she did, because she could prove that he'd been with her every step of the way, been instrumental in murders, while she would play the innocent, who relied so much on him after her husband left her. No, she didn't think anything he came up with would hold water after what he'd be found guilty of through the evidence of the dossiers. For old time's sake she'd give him a small allowance. All sweet revenge. And how good it would be to have Joe discovered as being alive, and all his dealings exposed, ha, she would love to see his face, but then, he now had a face she wouldn't recognise. Brushing away the small hurt this thought gave her, she allowed the pleasure of the revenge she sought, to dominate and to cheer her. She could kiss Gosling. Only he wouldn't live long enough for her to do so. An excitement filled her. She couldn't wait for the call that would tell her he was dead.

What to do about her father, was another matter. She would think more about that one. Did she want him dead? A picture of him playing with her, and holding her on his knee, calling her, his little princess came to her. For a moment she thought she would cry.

'Layla? Layla, are you all right?'

'Y – yes, sorry. I'm tired, that's all.' Taking another sip of her gin, she let the soothing taste calm her. Waited for the alcohol hit, to steady her.

'For one moment I thought you didn't like my choice of dinner.'

'No. It's perfect. She forced herself to smile.'

His smile back was dazzling. Her stomach lurched. She didn't want to lose him.

'Would you like to go back home, darling?'

'No. And stop calling me that. I told you once about it.'

363

'Oh, oh, we're not going to fight are we. Look, something's troubling you. You know what they say about a trouble shared.'

'No. there's nothing.' But as she said this she jumped when her mobile rang.

'Don't answer it, it can wait.'

'No, it's Jade. We're meant to be going there after, I'll tell her we won't. I'd like to just go back to mine and snuggle up to you.'

His expression as she said this lit a fire inside her. *Oh God, how am I going to exist without him?*

'Jade, hi. I was going to ring you. I think I'll go straight home with Adrian, I'm very tired. I'll fix a meeting up with you for tomorrow, is that okay?'

Graven's whisper came back to her. 'It's done. Droile is in a watery grave. The other target is in our radar.'

A shivery thrill zinged through Layla. 'That's fine, well done. Fantastic. You're going to make us richer than we dreamed . . .Yes, till tomorrow then. Oh, what was that?'

'I said, we have to keep this secret from Prindell, or he'll have time to sort out a plan before the dossiers are released.'

'Oh, yes, I agree. Good thinking. Must go, my first course has arrived. Bye.'

Adrian seemed unsuspecting as he asked, 'Good news? Apart from we're going straight to your house of course.'

'Yes, Jade had six hundred punters last night, and that's just in the kosher dance rooms and bars. There were over fifty Arabs taking advantage of our other offerings and all swigging the best champagne as if it was going out of fashion. You know, we should have a restaurant there. Something like this, so we can give them the whole experience, what do you think?'

'I think that we shouldn't discuss business tonight. I heard you say we'll fix up a meeting tomorrow. Well, that brilliant suggestion should be on top of the agenda, but tonight, I just want to enjoy you.'

And you will.

Layla was on fire. Her revenge on this man was in place, and knowing that, fuelled her hunger for him. *I'll think of it as giving him his last supper.* The thought both elated and saddened her, but there was no room for sentiment. It was him or her, and it was damned well not going to be her.

42

'I can't understand it!' Adrian paced the office, his face looked drawn. Sweat stood out on his brow. His eyes showed lack of sleep. 'Where the hell, is Frankie Droile?'

The Rottweiler sat fidgeting in the armchair next to Layla's desk. Adrian turned on her, 'Well?'

'I don't know. Me and gran are frantic with worry. He's just disappeared. It's been four days now since we heard from him, and he has never, ever, not contacted before.'

'How can you be so cool, Layla? There's a hit man out there after you and we have no one taking care of him.'

'I trust Graven, Adrian. He has all the security I need in place. Besides, how do we know that Droile hasn't taken him out? We have no source of information. Unless you've heard something, Nina?'

'N – no, nothing. The cop I had in mind contacted me, but I didn't like it. Why did he go from not wanting to work with me, to wanting in at all costs? I just don't know who to trust anymore.'

'What about The Bitch?'

'She's avoiding me. Look, that's not true. I'm avoiding her. I found out that she's having an affair with Gosling.'

'Gosling! But he's . . .'

'He's what, Adrian? Do you know something, Adrian?'

'No. Well, not really, just that he's gone to ground too. Bealver told me. He's worried. He hasn't got Gosling on his radar at all, and neither has the detective sergeant you're talking of.' Adrian wiped his brow.

Layla leaned back in her chair. She wanted to tell him exactly where Gosling was. She also wanted to smile at

Adrian's distress, but didn't. She maintained her worried look. 'There must be some word out there? Speak to everyone we have on our books, no matter what they do or how far removed it is from what Droile's profession is. Even if we know that they didn't know Droile. Someone must have heard something on the grapevine.'

Adrian answered, 'I've tried that. Have you thought of going to the police, Nina, after all he is a missing person, surly his family want him found?'

Layla again felt a smile playing around her lips. Poor Adrian, he was trapped between being a person of law and a gangster, and didn't fit into either category properly.

'My granddad would kill me with his bare hands if I did that. No one of the Droile clan goes to the cops about anything. We deal with it ourselves.'

'Something has to be done. Layla, put Graven and all his resources onto finding him and tracking Gosling, too!'

'Why should we pay to find Gosling? He's nothing to us.'

'He is to me. Or are you forgetting what he has on me? And, to Jade. Christ, we know there's a threat to Jade from Gosling.'

'Graven has that covered. Jade has 24-hour protection that no one could get through. I really think you're worrying too much. Surely if anything had happened to Gosling we would know. Of course, I'm concerned about your position, but we just don't have the proof that anything has happened to either of them.' As she said this, Layla had a moment when she felt sorry for Adrian. He obviously knew more than he could tell and was frantic with worry. Good. She liked that.

'What if Gosling is dead? I'm going to the police. No, you can't stop me. I should have done so in the beginning. My story would have been really plausible then, but might still hold water if I get to Detective Riley before the dossiers do.'

'Do that and you put our whole operation in jeopardy. I'll call a board meeting and take a vote as to whether you're a fit person to be on the board, or if the liability of what you've done by going to the police is too much for us to risk.'

Adrian almost staggered. He steadied himself by leaning in a sitting position on the windowsill. 'You'd do that? Why?'

'Because you *would* be a liability. You're panicking. Look, I'll do as you say and get Graven on to finding out what he can. We'll carry out our original plan and raid Gosling's house. He hasn't been near there, so that won't be a problem. Obviously we won't have his mobile and that would have been a vital source of information on who holds the dossiers, but we still have two days before Gosling is due to check in. Let's do this the sensible way. If the holder of Gosling's dossiers can be found, then Graven will find him.'

Layla buzzed for Graven.

Graven's voice came over the intercom. 'I was just going to come to see you. Somethings just come in.'

As soon as Graven entered the office, Adrian pounced, 'What's happened, is it to do with Gosling?'

'Adrian, calm down. Give Graven time to speak.'

'Yes, it is to do with Gosling, and our troubles may be over. Four days ago Joe Parrondski paid Gosling a lot of money. A huge amount. He's flitted, apparently.'

Layla looked at Adrian. Saw him turn a deathly colour. Graven continued, 'I'm a bit sceptical because the information was passed on through the bloke they call

The Doc in a conversation with Ronnie Flinch, Joe's henchman. It seems it was meant for our ears as the Doc made play of having it in front of our man telling Ronnie it was fine as our man doesn't speak English. If I'm right, that in itself is worrying as it means our man's cover is blown. At least to Gosling and his co-conspirator, but why make sure we know?'

'That is strange. Right, get on to finding those dossiers. We have to save Adrian, whatever it costs.'

'But, I could do that for myself, at least, limit the damage. Please, Layla. Please let me go to the police.'

'We've been over that, Adrian. Give me this one last chance to save the day. Perhaps if you could work with Bealver, Graven? Pool information. I know he hasn't been very forthcoming, but he must be shitting bricks at this moment. I'd think he'd welcome help to find the dossiers.'

'Will do. Will you clear that for me, Adrian? He seems to only want to meet with you.'

'That's because he can do so under the guise of me working with a client on a case he's involved in. Everything might have to come through me, but that's not a bad thing, I want to keep my finger on the pulse of this one, seeing as though I have a vested interest.'

'Right. All of you. Out. I need some peace. And Nina, tell your gran that I'm sorry about Frankie. Frankie Droile is like an uncle to me. If he can be found, I will find him. Graven knows he has to work on that at the same time as on finding Gosling. And take a couple of weeks off. There's nothing you can do here at the moment.'

Nina didn't protest.

Adrian was the last to walk through the door as he did, he looked back at her. He looked almost defeated.

Layla wanted to go to him and to hold him, but she

fought against it. She thought of how she had everything in place.

In a few hours from now, the balloon would go up. She wouldn't let Adrian have these two days of hope. Joe had hope as he thought the dossiers had been destroyed with his pay out. *Ha, little did he know!*

The shock to them both would make the revenge even sweeter.

Then she remembered that Adrian must know that Jed-the-Knife was missing too, but he couldn't say so. His mind must be jumping from one conclusion to the next. The stress was running him ragged. He was vulnerable and he knew it. Something in Layla, liked him like this. Loved him even. But she had to stay strong to save her own skin and to emerge the winner.

And she would. Graven's men were making sure that Gosling and his Bitch, who was thought by her police colleagues to be in bed with the flu, got on the aeroplane to Rio tonight.

Gosling's lackey, The Doc, was preparing to join him. And five million of her money as well as Joe's, was going with them. She didn't think she would ever see Gosling again. But she didn't rue what it had cost her to get rid of him. It was a small price to pay for the beautiful dossiers. And they were explosive.

Graven had scrutinised them. Everything about Joe, was there. He was going down for life. Adrian's and Bealver's file wasn't so big, but an upstanding figure in the community like Bealver, would be made an example of. And Adrian? Well, the dossiers told it all. There wasn't just the photo as he believed. Everything was there. Even how, and where he'd disposed of the body. She had to admire Gosling.

Not that she would ever trust Gosling. But he could never come back to Britain so it didn't matter. It would come out that he'd murdered a man and set up the DNA on the body to match Joe's, and that was enough to send him down for life even if nothing else he'd done ever surfaced. And she knew he was responsible for a lot.

No. She'd be rid of him. Rid of Joe. And still have a further sweet revenge moment to come with Adrian; when he found out she'd lived a lie and there was nothing for him to come out of prison to.

The Parrondksi Mystery would be solved. Gone. The dossiers would dot the I's and cross the T's. Gosling had every bit of it covered.

At first she'd been annoyed that Gosling had slipped their net. But Graven, who she now thought of as a Diamond Geezer, had caught up with him and had turned everything in their favour.

Her mind went over the future. She'd take everything Joe had. She'd have to build it all up again, as the police would seize all his assets. But, those he worked with would be looking for a new boss, and she would be ready and waiting. She had all the right contacts now and operations in place that were set to soar with the vacancy Joe would leave. Only the child porn ring would no longer operate.

There was still the question of Joe being proven to be alive. She didn't know how she would stand legally over what had passed to her on his *death*. She presumed that everything he ever owned as Joe Parrondski, as well as Count Rolleski would be taken. If so, she'd just have to start again. It would be a wrench, as not just her beloved home but the Mayfair jewellery shop would revert to being part of Joe's estate. She had to prepare herself. She was in a strong financial position and had assets that were growing and growing, but in some ways it felt as though she stood to lose everything too. A lot of which she held dear.

A pain tugged at her heart. Three men she'd loved the most in her life had betrayed her. Joe, Adrian and her own father.

*

The two hours passed. Her nerves were on edge. She willed the new special mobile she'd gained, to ring. It did.

'He's a gonner. It happened during the night. But, it's breaking news right now.'

Layla's heart dropped as if it was made of concrete. Keeping her voice steady, she gave instructions as to where the promised money could be found once she heard what he'd told her was official. 'There's plane tickets with it. Contact your brother and his mate on this same phone. Let them know that once they step outside those prison gates, they will be whisked away with their share, and will be on a plane to join you. Tell them too, that I have established other contacts inside the prison. They're watching your mates' every move. And are in a position to kill if they detect one false move between now and their release. If you're still in this country by tonight you are a dead man. Go away and live the life you dreamed of, but remember, you will never be out of my radar. Never. Have you got that?' Hearing the affirmative, she said, 'right, leave the phone you're using in place of the money.'

Ending the call, Layla bent forward holding her stomach. Every part of her shook. But then she stood tall. This was her moment.

She crossed over to the other side of the office and switched on the television. On the ticker tape running along the bottom of the current news, she read: 'Gerry

Loyson, the gang-leader of the gold heist from Heathrow Airport has been found dead in his cell. Early reports suggest he had taken his own life.'

Layla strode back to her desk. Picked up her phone.

'Put the money in place for Jed-the- Knife, and release the dossiers. Have them in Riley's hands within the hour. Where's Adrian?'

'Ha, he's where he's going to be for a long time, at the police station with his mate Bealver. They're probably plotting how to find the dossiers from the stuff we gave them. Poor sods, they don't know that what they seek is on its way to the same building.'

Layla didn't smile. Her insides churned.

Swinging her chair to face the window, she looked out across London. Her domain. Hers, Jade's, Marcelle's and yes, Nina's. She trusted Nina. She just hoped she never found out what happened to her grandfather, and the part she herself had played in his demise.

The only men they would ever let be a part of their set up would be Graven and Nick. Both were Diamond Geezers.

But she'd never give her heart to a man again. The three that she had given it to had used her and betrayed her. She would grieve for her dad and all she'd dreamed of for him in the future and what he had been to her in the past. But, Adrian and Joe? No.

Joe would rot in jail. And Adrian? He would have a dream for the next few years, until she shattered it once the danger to herself had passed.

Now she did smile. Because although all three had caused her victory to have a bitter taste, the sweet taste of revenge overrode that.

THE END

About Mary Wood

Molly Kent is a pseudonym of the Sunday Times Best Seller, Mary Wood.

Mary first became known as a ebook writer publishing her work on Amazon Kindle. She was so successful that an editor at Pan Macmillan publishers spotted her and offered her a seven book contract. This was the realisation of a dream Mary had nurtured since the 1980's when she first began to pen full-length novels. She is the thirteenth child of fifteen children. Born to poverty, but had a childhood she describes as rich in love and support.

Her mother came from an upper-middle class family and her father was an East End Barrow Boy. An unlikely match, but one that worked.

Mary's paternal Great Grandmother, Dora Langlois was also an author in the late 1800's and early 1900's writing novels and educational literature which was ahead of her time – advising on the upbringing of girls. Dora also wrote short stories for magazines and theatre plays, many of which she and her husband starred in. Mary is very proud to follow in her footsteps.

Mary's family have a wealth of talent, her sister, Felicity Dwyer and three of her nephews, John Skillen and Peter Skillen, and Steven Watts are authors, and many of the family have successful careers in the arts. They number singers, musicians, painters and photographers in their midst. Mary is proud of them all.

Mary has written ten books, nine of them are sagas, which she writes for Pan Macmillan. Of these, four are Northern sagas and five are set during the World Wars, with two of these yet to be released. The tenth novel, The Sweet Taste of Revenge, written under the pen name of Molly Kent, is her first thriller, however, more are planned.

Her Northern Sagas are stories of women and their struggles during the 1800's and early 1900's when the belief was that there was no such thing as rape and domestic violence was the right of a man to keep his missus in check. Rich or poor, women and children had no voice, and it is against this background that strong women emerged. These women and their conquering of adversity form the basis of Mary's gritty Northern sagas.

Her War Sagas also feature strong women, and women who find strength they never knew they possessed as they go to war to carry out tasks that involve working as secret agents behind enemy lines with the Resistance, battling to reach and to nurse the sick and wounded, or carried on regardless, keeping the nation fed and the home fires burning. These novels too, are gritty and rich in historical fact.

It has been said of Mary that her readers become the characters, feel their pain, fight their fights and rejoice over their triumphs. Reading her books is a journey that takes, not just your imagination, but your whole being through experiences that make you feel you were there.

For this novel, written under the name of Molly Kent, Mary drew on her experiences gained whilst working for the Probation Service. In her ten-year career with the service, Mary rose from admin to Community Service Officer, which involved holding and administering a caseload of offenders who had been sentenced to do work in the community. For the last three years of her service, Mary moved sideways and became a Probation Service Officer. This meant holding a caseload of a variety of low to medium risk offenders, Court duties, and being involved with drug rehabilitation programmes. This work gave her a knowledge of police and Court procedures, and an insight into the criminal mind. It was a profession she loved, though admits the pressure of work and what is entailed with dealing with some of the more gruesome cases and seeing what the victims went through did affect her greatly.

In her writing her need to show the victims' side, is what leads her to give such depth to scenes that involve rape, child abduction and murder.

"Being involved with the victims of these heinous crimes, gave me a perspective that others outside the Criminal Justice system don't see. To Joe Public these crimes are a one-day headline in the newspaper, then a small column. Something to glance at and turn to the sports page.

I want everyone to know how real the suffering is. What actually happens when a girl or boy is raped, how a person feels when they look down the barrel of a gun, or are faced with a gang about to beat them to death for their wallet.

I admit, my books are not for the feint-hearted."

Mary can be contacted on Facebook: www.Facebook.com/HistoricalNovels
Or through her website: www.authormarywood.com
Follow her on twitter: @Authormary
Mary is available to give talks to groups, libraries, and is an after dinner speaker.

Lightning Source UK Ltd.
Milton Keynes UK
UKOW01f0718011116
286592UK00001B/7/P